QUARRY'S CONTRACT

BY THE SAME AUTHOR

THE FOURTH ANGEL

QUARRY'S

ROBIN
HUNTER

CONTRACT

WILLIAM MORROW
AND COMPANY, INC.
NEW YORK

Library of Congress Cataloging-in-Publication Data

Hunter, Robin, 1935–
Quarry's contract / Robin Hunter.
p. cm.
ISBN 1-55710-021-7
I. Title.
PR6058.U54Q3 1989
823'.914—dc 19 88-29106
CIP

Printed in the United States of America

First Edition

1 2 3 4 5 6 7 8 9 10

BOOK DESIGN BY RICHARD ORIOLO

THIS ONE IS FOR
LEONARD AND JANET GORE

AUTHOR'S NOTE

This is a work of fiction. This being so, anyone who identifies with the characters depicted in the following pages is guilty of wishful thinking.

Acknowledgments are due to some real people who helped me with the background, so my thanks go to Don Philpott of The Press Association in London; Peter Lonsdale of the Layton Arms Company in Doncaster; Patricia Hitchcock, Franca Guggenheim, and Joe and Gabriella Colombo in Italy; Air Vice-Marshal Geoff Eveleigh and his wife, Anthea, who let me think dark thoughts on their otherwise sunlit terrace in Mallorca; Estelle Huxley, who gamely typed the drafts and, while it is said to be tacky to thank one's agent, I thank John Pawsey for doing so much with Simon Quarry in the first book, and waiting so patiently while I finished this one.

Listen! First, we'll start unrest. Don't you know that, even now, we are terribly strong? We have people with us other than those who cut throats, set fires or go in for assassinations . . . I have them all in hand already. We have the teacher who makes the children entrusted to his care laugh at their God and their parents; we have the lawyer defending the educated murderer, because he has reached a higher stage of development than his victims. Schoolboys who, to experience a strong sensation, kill an old peasant, are also with us. Juries who acquit criminals are working for us . . . the anguished judge who fears he is not liberal enough does us a service. Ah, we have so many people with us, and many do not ever know it themselves.

—DOSTOEVSKI, *The Possessed*

PROLOGUE

The kidnappers waited two weeks before they contacted the family. That was just to wind them up and get them anxious. Then they came in with the demand for four million dollars, no arguments, just the money and quick about it, otherwise . . . They didn't expect to get four mil, of course, but it was a good place to start. The old bastard had the money, or could get the money, and he knew the rules, none better. Meantime, they had his daughter.

They kept the girl chained up all the time, fed her sometimes, let her wash once. At other times, when one of them was drunk, or they needed her to scream a little for the tape going to the old bastard to let him know how his little girl was getting on, they would play with her a little. It wasn't nice.

After three weeks Philip Wintle and Lucia got them down to

two million five, and they stuck there for a while. That's when the first tape arrived. It shook the old bastard up quite a bit; maybe he didn't think they would do it, not to her, not to him. Well, people are like that. They see it in the papers or on television every day, but they aren't touched by it. They think, that's terrible but it can't happen to me. Not to *me*. They go on thinking that, even after it *has* happened to them. Some people, especially hard people like the old bastard, take a lot of convincing.

After another week, and a lot of talk, Wintle got them down to two million. They said they would think about that, and rang off. They didn't ring the next day, or the day after that, and Wintle became worried. When they still hadn't rung, and five weeks were up, he went on the offensive. He talked to Captain Cirillo, and called in the cops. Quietly, of course, no Press, no leaks. Klaus Kleiner saw to that. But even so, it was a mistake, and Wintle didn't usually make mistakes.

The big rule is this: While they have your girl, you don't do anything. You can argue about how much, or when you pay, although you had better have a good reason to argue because begging won't get you anywhere. The only thing you can't do is . . . you can't *do* anything. Most of all, you don't go to the police. Not if you want your little girl back.

After five and some weeks, they rang again. Wintle's people were sitting where they had sat at eight o'clock every evening ever since this business began, gathered around the desk in Fiori's study, waiting. Mostly, nothing happened, but when they rang it was on time. At eight o'clock, right on the dot, the telephone shrilled three times, making them jump, then it went silent. This rule they knew, or had learned, so they waited. Three minutes later it rang again, and Lucia picked it up on the first note. Lucia always did the talking.

"*Pronto,*" she said, and listened. That was another rule. They spoke and you listened. When they had finished she replaced the receiver with slow deliberation and looked around at the others carefully, her eyes hidden in the darkness above the spill of light created by the desk lamp.

"Well," said Wintle at last. "What now?"

"The deal is this," said Lucia flatly. "They want one and a half. We must have the money inside three days, not later than Wednesday evening. They will contact us at the usual time with instructions on handing it over. No arguments." Her voice was calm and, as always, she spoke tersely. "They want cash, small used notes, nothing over fifty dollars' value, but marks, Swiss francs, sterling, will be OK. They say you should not have gone to the police. Because you . . . we . . . did that, and to convince us that the dealing is over, they've sent us a present. They said it's already outside on the doorstep. He laughed, then he hung up."

No one said anything for a moment or two, wondering how they had found out about the contact with the police; who had talked? Then Fiori stirred heavily in his chair and turned his head to speak to the man sitting quietly in an upright chair just beside the door. "Fredo?" It was more a command than a suggestion.

Fredo Donati rose and left the room. Nobody said anything, just waited, listening. After a minute or two Donati returned carrying a small cigar box, which he placed carefully right in the middle of the desk, at the edge of the lamplight.

"It was where they said," he told them, keeping his eyes fixed on the box. "On the middle step."

"Don't touch it," said Lucia. All their eyes were on the cigar box, lying there in the light. "We should get Aldo here to open it carefully."

"I don't think so," said Wintle. "They won't do anything now until they have the money."

"Anyway, we don't need Cirillo, or any other police," said the old bastard, glaring at Wintle. "I told you that before."

Wintle nodded. "I know you did," he said, getting slowly to his feet. "Move well back just in case and I'll open it."

It wasn't a bomb—not exactly. Wintle flicked the little brass hooks out of the latches, snapped up the lid sharply, looked in briefly, and slammed the lid shut again, coming down hard with the flat of his hand, his face suddenly hollow.

"What is it?" asked Lucia, moving back into the room from the corner. Wintle said nothing. He waited silently until they had all seen the contents and figured things out.

"We have to pay," said Lucia, looking at her father. "Now we have to pay."

"This is your fault," Fiori said to Wintle.

"Oh . . . please . . . shut up!" snapped Lucia. "It's *their* fault and nobody else's—or *your* fault, for not paying sooner. Don't start on Philip."

Fiori didn't like that. He ignored her and made no reply, his hard eyes still on Wintle, shoulders hunched, his shadow black against the wall behind. "What do we do now?" he asked, biting off the words.

"Two things, maybe three," said Wintle calmly. "First, we do exactly as they say. You raise one million five, inside three days. Meanwhile, I'm going to call in a friend of mine. This game is getting rough. I think we need a little help, and I know someone—"

"Another cop?" interrupted Fiori sarcastically. "Like you?"

"No, not a cop," said Wintle slowly, his eyes still fixed on the box. "Just a friend of mine."

"And what does he do, this friend of yours?" asked Fiori, glancing across at Fredo Donati.

"He kills people," said Philip Wintle.

ONE

Simon Quarry only became a killer by accident. He was not by nature a violent or even an aggressive man. When his wine arrived hot and his food cold he would simply send for the headwaiter and quietly request that this be changed. The careful observer might notice that the headwaiter usually seemed eager to comply. Should an unpleasant brawl break out at a nearby table Quarry would rise quietly from his seat in the corner and walk slowly from the restaurant. Only the most observant bystander was likely to notice that Quarry left by walking round the edge of the room, keeping his back always close to the wall. On another occasion, when two drunken, aggressive Scotsmen descended upon him in a bar down in Puerto, spewing insults and obscenities into his face, for no other reason, it seemed, than they resented him speaking Spanish to the barman, he sat calmly on his stool until they were spent and finished, then left the bar quietly, as usual, and with a smile. The same onlooker—keeping his head down, not wishing to get involved in an unpleasant scene—might have failed to notice that during this encounter, Quarry's right hand rested very close to the half-empty wine bottle that stood beside his glass on the counter.

Having noted all this, he—or more likely she, for women tended to observe Quarry more closely—would have concluded only that Quarry was a careful man who sensibly avoided trouble whenever he could, but could probably look after himself if he had to. Women agreed Quarry was likable enough, a quiet, pleasant man, invariably polite, perhaps a little sad; well, after all, that's not so surprising, is it? Not after what happened to his wife and family. What would you do in his place? Men were less sure, less comfortable with Quarry, less willing to make friends or invite him over for a drink; not that he ever came. He just smiled politely, as usual, and claimed to be busy—but doing what? He didn't work, had no known interests, never gave parties, refused to mix with the other expatriates on the cocktail circuit, and was a good deal too friendly with the natives. And besides, there were these rumors—nothing to put a finger on, nothing specific, just that somebody who knew somebody had heard something, that's all.

Anyway, the men told their wives, if he doesn't want to be friendly and mix in, then to hell with him. So, for one reason or another, people left Quarry alone. After he had been a year on the island they had almost forgotten he existed.

From his chair on the terrace that morning Simon Quarry could see a long way down the valley. The view ran away before him, across the dusty green tops of the olive trees, to where a thin haze hung above the yellow-tiled rooftops of Pollensa. Down there, smoke was drifting up on the first breeze of the morning to meet the white clouds shredding down from the bare, rounded top of Puig Tomir, the high brown mountain that made the perfect backdrop for the view. That view had persuaded Simon to buy this place and after two years of looking at it he still found it satisfying. As the cloud and mist parted, the valley opened up as if theater curtains were slowly being pulled aside. It was going to be a beautiful day. Simon Quarry scratched his bristly chin reflectively and wondered how he was going to fill it.

He was a tall, spare, middle-aged man, his skin deeply tanned by constant exposure to the Mediterranean sun. Above his tattered shorts the skin lay taut across his stomach, and when he shifted in his chair, muscles rippled over his arms and shoulders. He looked fit and lean and much younger than his years, although there were gray streaks in the thick hair about his temples and a fine network of lines around his eyes and mouth; but all in all he looked a picture of athletic contentment, relaxed in his chair, his expression pleasant, brooding thoughtfully on the view. Only his left hand spoiled the picture, the one holding the half-empty glass. Something had flayed that hand, chewing the flesh, breaking bones, no little accident. Shiny scar tissue glistened, from the knuckles of his fingers to as far back as the wrist, shining among the black hair, resistant to the sun, livid against his tan.

Quarry shifted in his chair, listening to the gentle tinkle from the fountain just beyond the terrace wall as it splashed down pleasantly into the waters of a small ornamental pond. In the cool shade down there, little green and blue frogs sat about alertly on the lily pads. Simon had hacked that pond out of the rock himself, days of effort with pickax and spade. He was proud of it. He liked water, and so the sight and sound of water was everywhere around his house. The fountain tinkled, the pond splashed, the water of the swimming pool threw ripples of shadow onto the ceiling of the veranda at his back and up the ocher-red walls of the house, a long, low bungalow, set deep in the dark green of the pine trees. Pines could be gloomy, but there was plenty of color to relieve them. Purple bougainvillaea, scarlet hibiscus, and bright jasmine cascaded over the trellised walls or trailed from hanging baskets. Their scents already filled the air as the sun crept higher over the hill and the heat struck down across the house.

So Simon Quarry sat on his terrace in the sunshine, drinking his first gin of the day. He looked at his wristwatch pensively, thought for a moment, then leaned forward to pour another measure into his glass. According to the wristwatch, it was nine o'clock in the morning. He was to remember that time later, when Lucia asked him how it all began. It began with Lito.

Lito came flip-flopping round the corner of the house, bare chested, his rolled-up trouser bottoms still wet from the morning task of clearing pine needles out of the swimming pool. He stopped at the side of the house and gestured with his thumb across the garden, down toward the gate. Lito was a short, barrel-chested man, the sweat on his arms and forehead shining slightly in the sunlight, teeth white against the dark brown of his suntanned face. His voice came softly across the terrace.

"Señor Simon, there is a car in the lane, a big car. It has been there . . . *yo no sé* . . . *que* . . . dos o tres minutos."

"So?" said Simon. "What about it? It's a free country. The people next door have probably come back for the summer." He leaned forward to put the glass back on the table and then sat back, propping his chin up on his injured hand.

"No, señor." Lito's tone was decisive. "It's not the neighbors. It's not anyone we know—it's not a local car. It has Palma plates, a big black limousine. One man got out and came up to the gate, close enough to set off the sensors . . . *escucha*! You said, you told me . . . I was always to tell you if anyone strange ever came here, always—or if anyone looked interested in us, in you, or Señorita Clio. So what you want me to do now . . . go finish the *pîscina*?"

Simon sat for a moment, considering, then nodded abruptly and sat up. "No, you're right, Lito," he said, "and I'm sorry. Let's get the glasses and see who it is. I just doubt if anyone hostile would drive right up to the gates, but you never know."

Simon swung his feet off the wall and jerked up out of his chair, moving quickly through the open glass doors behind, into the cool darkness of the living room, bare feet slapping on the cold tiles. It took only a second to sweep the big binoculars from the top of a stack of field guides, and then he was out in the bright light of the terrace again, following Lito's retreating back, around the corner of the house, past the pool, up onto the smaller terrace that overlooked the road. He stopped by the wall, slinging the strap of the field glasses over his neck, Lito at his shoulder. Then, resting his elbows on top of the wall, he focused the glasses on the thick steel rails of the gates below and began to scan the road.

"Where is he?" he asked, adjusting the focus on the glasses slightly. "There's no one down there now." He could hear the faint, sharp sound of the bleeper coming from the repeater behind them, but the dusty road below was empty.

"Maybe the man's gone," said Lito in Spanish, "but the car is still there. Look, there it is. It's been reversed into the shade. Perhaps the man has gone back to it. It may be nothing, Señor Simon—maybe they're just lost, but you said always to watch out for strangers, so I thought I should tell you—all right?" Lito's Spanish came thick and fast and his Mallorquín accent was strong, but Simon followed it easily enough, nodding his head as he studied the fenders and radiator of a big black car, half hidden in the shadow of the pines beside the road.

"You did right to fetch me, Lito. It's better to be sure than sorry," he said, the glasses still clamped to his eyes. He lifted his gaze from the road and began to scour the bare countryside beyond his walls, looking around at the slopes of the hills, across the thin strands of razor-sharp wire on top of the walls, checking on the small video cameras carefully concealed here and there among the trees, watching them turning slowly on their relentless, vigilant axes. The hills were empty and starting to shimmer in the rising heat of the morning.

"Whoever it was, everything looks quiet enough now," he said at last. "Let's go back inside and take a quick look at the monitors."

Simon led the way down the steps, across the terrace, and back into the living room. It seemed even darker now after the bright sunshine on the terrace. Once inside the room, Simon took out his keys and unlocked the doors of a wooden cabinet set flat against the wall. The double doors opened to reveal the main camera monitor, a battery of instruments, dials, and switches, glowing greenly in the gloom, clustered around a central screen. The sound of the warning bleeper was much louder now, and Simon flicked a switch up and down, off and on, first to silence it, then to set it again. His eyes were fixed on the screen, where the picture shifted slowly, giving an ever-changing view of the garden and the surrounding hills. A glimpse of the outer wall touched the bottom of the screen as Simon began operating the remote control to the gateside camera, turning up the brightness, focusing on the road, then zooming in on a figure coming out of the trees, walking back up the road toward the gates.

"*Sí*, that's the one! That's the one who was there," said Lito excitedly, pointing over Simon's shoulder. "Here he comes again." Through the loudspeakers they could even hear the crunch of his feet on the gravel as the man came closer. Simon focused on the road, the gravel chips showing sharply, then swung the camera up the man's body, from the well-polished sheen of his shoes to the thin, watchful face. The man stopped and looked up and about alertly, then directly into the lens of Simon's nearest camera. Then he nodded a greeting, knowing they were there.

"Good God!" said Simon suddenly. "I don't believe it." He snapped up the control switch, stepped back, and swept the doors of the cupboard shut, then turned to Lito, grinning. "Let me get down there, then open the gates—OK? Get out a bottle of Scotch, the Glenfiddich. Put it out on the terrace, with fresh ice and glasses and a jug of water—and some beer—*claro*?"

"*Sí*, Señor Simon, *pero* . . ." Lito was startled. "Then you know that man, Señor Simon? He is a friend of yours? No problem?"

"No problem at all." Simon was on his toes now, delighted, practically dancing. "He's a very old, very good friend of mine. Now, quickly, where's my shirt? Come on! Find the Scotch. Get a move on.'

Minutes later Simon Quarry and Philip Wintle were smiling at each other through the thin steel bars of the front gates. Simon could remember the last time he'd seen Philip, his anxious face fading away as the anesthetic took effect, before the doctor went to work on his shattered hand. Since then, for two years, nothing.

"Where the hell have you been this last couple of years? Not even a postcard. What on earth are you doing turning up out of the blue like this?—not that you're not welcome. It's good to see you. It's been far too long."

Philip Wintle smiled back, his eyes narrowed against the sun. "I've always wondered what you would look like behind bars, Simon, and now I know. You look just right." He gestured to the gate, at the camera and the high walls. "What have you got here, Fort Knox? There's no latch on these gates, no bell on the wall, and you're not in the phone book. I've spotted that scanner up there, and what about that very-hard-to-come-by Israeli barbed wire you've got on the wall? Going a bit over the top, aren't you? Or are you a little worried about your dark and doubtful past?"

Simon's broad smile became a little thinner. "You should know all about that," he said shortly. "I've just taken a few simple precautions, that's all. The bell is around here, just out of sight. I simply press it, like this, and from inside the house my backup man, Lito, opens the gate—*Voila*!"

The power-driven steel gates swung open slowly, silently. Simon stepped back to let them pass, then came forward to shake Philip warmly by the hand, eyes alight with pleasure.

"Come along and have a drink, then I'll show you my defenses. They're very state-of-the-art and cost a fortune, but with them I sleep better at night. You are going to stay, I hope? There's plenty of room and, apart from Lito, I'm on my own here. You'll meet Lito up at the house. You'll like him . . . he helps keep me sane. Where's your suitcase?"

Simon's voice was hurried, hopeful, as he urged Philip inside, but Philip hesitated and hung back, turning toward the gates, pulling Simon to a stop. "I can't stay, Simon. I'm afraid this isn't a social call. It's business, and I need your help. . . . And where's Clio?"

A watchful look returned to Simon's face and set the lines

deepening around his mouth. He threw a glance over Wintle's shoulder, down the road to where the big black car stood waiting in the shade, and his eyes were thoughtful as they came back to rest on Philip's face. "I see," he said slowly. "Business, you say? My kind of business or your kind of business?"

"It's got beyond my kind," said Philip, "and it's getting to be your kind. That's if you're willing to do a favor for an old friend. I need your help and I need it badly."

"I see," said Simon again. "Like that, is it? What have you been up to, and at your age? I thought you'd retired to grow roses?"

"I did. It was very, very boring, so I got another job," said Philip. "Look, I'll tell you all about it later but I don't have a lot of time. So may I come in? And . . . er . . . I hate to pry, but where is Clio? I was anticipating a kiss."

"Clio? She's not here," replied Simon briefly. "She left me, if you must know . . . months ago. If we're swapping tales, I'll tell you about it later. Come in, man, come in, for God's sake . . . you're a friend of mine, aren't you? *Mi casa es su casa,* as they say hereabouts . . . so don't hover on the doorstep. Go on up to the terrace and help yourself to a drink. Lito will close the gates and I'll take a quick shower and put on some trousers. I won't be long.

When Simon returned to the terrace ten minutes later, Philip Wintle was sitting well back in the shade, his briefcase open by the side of his chair, looking out at the mountains.

"What do you think of my view?" asked Simon, moving over to the low table where the half-empty bottle of gin had been joined by an ice bucket and a bottle of whiskey. "And what will you have to drink?"

"It's a bit early for me, but I love your view," said Philip. "I've asked your fellow . . . what's his name? . . . Lito, if I could have some coffee—is that all right?"

"Have whatever you like," said Simon, dropping some fresh ice into his glass and adding more gin from the uncapped bottle, "But you don't mind if I do?"

"Of course not."

"Well then—cheers!" said Simon, sliding into a chair. "I'm sorry to have kept you." He had changed into a casual shirt, cotton slacks, and a loose linen jacket. His hair, still wet from the shower, lay close to his head. He had also taken time to shave and his jawline was now smooth, shining in the sunshine.

Philip Wintle had removed his jacket and slung it over the back of his chair, but he still looked formal and correct, the red stripes of his Artillery tie standing out sharply against the crisp white of his shirt. Philip was as tall as Simon, but a thinner, older man. His hair was all snow-white now, not the pepper-and-salt that Simon remembered from two years ago, but nothing else had changed. His blue eyes were alert, his expression pleasant, but the hint of authority and severity was still there. With his slightly Prussian air Philip Wintle did not look like the sort of person wise men trifled with too often.

"Well," said Simon easily, "if matters are as pressing as you say, someone has to set the ball rolling. I'm always willing to help an old friend and in your case that can mean a quart of my blood or the number of my Swiss bank account, but perhaps you can tell me what this sudden descent on Schloss Quarry is all about. How did you find me and what exactly are you after?" Simon's voice had sharpened and quickened during this short speech.

About to speak, Philip waited as Lito appeared from the house, bearing a tray with cups and a coffeepot, and nothing more was said until he had disappeared again. Then Philip poured himself a cup, lifting the pot inquiringly toward Simon, who shook his head.

"Finding you was easy . . . I rang my old office at Scotland Yard and they punched you up on the computer—they have long memories, computers. As to what I want," Philip went on, "that's a bit hard to say, so let me bring you up to date. I retired from the Police Service two years ago. I practically had to after that last little business of ours. Then I tried retirement for a couple of months or so, but it was bloody dull—fortunately I was offered a post as senior consultant with Kleiner Security Insurers. Many police officers go into security work after retirement, and KSI was very keen to recruit someone at my level, a former head of Special Branch who had been involved with terrorism and organized crime, and so on. The pay is excellent and the work is interesting. I enjoy it . . . more than that, it's a very worthwhile job."

"Who are Kleiner Security Insurers?" put in Simon. "I live a very quiet life here and I've never heard of them."

"KSI exists to provide security for the senior personnel and families of international companies trading in places where terrorism or organized crime is common. The executives of international or multinational companies are often targets for kidnapping or other forms of extortion, so they have to be protected. KSI provides advice on security routines, especially on how to avoid kidnapping, be it at home or at the office, or anywhere in between. We also provide and train bodyguards. But even so, people do get lifted in certain parts of Europe or in Latin America or the Middle East. You must have read about such cases. Here in Spain, ETA is active and often kidnap or kill people in the Basque country. Terrorism is a fact of life in many countries and terrorists find kidnapping a good way to raise funds or gain publicity for the cause. You know how such people operate—none better. Anyway, when a senior executive is sent to a tricky location, he or she is always heavily insured and we—KSI, that is—try to eliminate the more obvious security risks and, as far as possible, guarantee protection. The better the security, the smaller the insurance premium can be, though with ransom demands often running into millions of dollars kidnap insurance isn't cheap. Still it's a growth market nowadays, and a very necessary one, believe me."

"I can imagine," said Simon dryly. "This is all fascinating stuff, but I don't see where I fit in. Why don't you get to the point?"

"I'm getting to the point. I'm just putting you in the picture."

"I'm glad to hear it," said Simon, grinning.

"I am currently retained by a small group of Swiss, German, and Italian businessmen who have a severe kidnapping problem. Someone you will certainly have heard of, the industrialist Klaus Kleiner, formed them into a consortium to guard against that sort of problem, especially in Italy, where they all have extensive business interests. By banding together they get cheaper group insurance, better security cover, a degree of support if things go wrong, and so on. There are enough problems—covering their homes and offices, protecting their families, their children, their senior staff, and so on—to make it worthwhile to retain their own full-time security chief—me."

"I'm sorry to butt in," said Simon, "but what exactly is it that you want?" Simon leaned forward to pour another stiff measure of gin into his glass, added some ice, and sat back, waiting. Philip Wintle gathered his thoughts and began again.

"The youngest daughter of a consortium member, Signor Luigi Fiori, was kidnapped in Milan six weeks ago. Her name is Gina, she's just fourteen. The original ransom demand was for four million dollars—they always demand much more than they expect to get. We have since negotiated this sum down to one million, five hundred thou. Now we have to pay. That's not a serious problem because Signor Fiori carries insurance to about that level and Klaus Kleiner is making up the difference. I already have the money and I'll have to hand it over sometime soon, somewhere outside Milan, and get the girl. If I'm going to meet a gang of thugs, with a million-dollars-plus in my pocket and a girl's life to protect, I need some protection, so I want you to come with me in case things go wrong. There may be no trouble at all, but I'd be happier with some backup. *That's* where you come in."

"Why me?" asked Simon. "Why not simply go to the police?"

"We wouldn't normally go to the police," said Philip. "The kidnappers usually kill their victims if you do. The Italian police don't like people funding gangs or terrorist groups with ransom money. There are even moves afoot to make ransom payments illegal. The police feel that if people stopped paying ransoms there would be no point in kidnapping, but of course the families can't take the long view. They just want their people back. However, in this case we did go to the police. Signor Fiori didn't like it but the terms of the insurance cover and my own training insisted on it. Besides, the police have resources I don't have. We were very discreet about it and fortunately I still have my old Special Branch contacts. I got a friend of mine, Aldo Cirillo, who is a SISMI captain with the Squadra Antiterrorismo in Milan and a very good man, to help us out on the quiet. Somehow the kidnappers found out." Philip's face was troubled. "I still don't know how that happened but it did. Now we follow the kidnappers' instructions to the letter."

The silence that fell across the table stretched on, as if no one were willing to break it and carry the matter forward. The door creaked and Lito came back onto the terrace, looking across to check Wintle's coffee cup, then stepping back into the shade to lean against the wall, watching them both impassively. Simon switched his glance back to Philip, then put his glass down, and leaned across to tap Philip lightly on the arm.

"Well, go on," he said gently. "What brought it all to a head? Why have you decided to settle and settle so quickly and for so much? What made you come looking for me . . . what happened next?"

Philip leaned down, reaching into his briefcase to take out a flat Havana cigar box, which he pushed across the table toward Simon.

"This happened next," he said, tapping the lid with his forefinger. "This arrived two nights ago. That's why we settled, that's why I collected the money, and that's why I'm here now. Look inside and you'll see why I need you."

Simon shot a glance at Philip's face, picked up the box, and flipped up the lid, jerking his head back sharply from the strong odor that suddenly hit his nostrils. Then he pulled the cotton wool out and looked inside.

"Ugh . . . Jesus Christ!" he said thickly, disgusted, throwing the box back onto the glass top of the table. The two severed fingers shot out, rolled gently across the table, and came to a stop against his glass.

TWO

Five minutes later, Simon and Philip were walking in the garden. The scars of reconstruction were fading, the plants and ground cover creeping forward again to cover the raw rock. Under the trees it was much cooler than in the open where the sun hit down, hard as a hammer. It was a big garden, half wild, half cultivated; beds of flowers, each with a central sprinkler, alternating with thin soil or bare rock, littered with pine needles.

"When I first came here," said Simon, gesturing around the flowerbeds with his half-empty glass, "this hillside was all just rock and pine and cactus. I had all that grubbed up and then we graded the ground. I had to take out most of the pine trees, as nothing will grow under them, but we've kept enough to provide some shade. Are you sure those are the girl's fingers?"

Strolling along at Simon's side, head down, hands in pockets, Philip nodded. "Oh yes, quite sure, I'm afraid. The police are officially off the case but Cirillo ran a fingerprint check against those in her bedroom and they matched. When an Italian group took the young Getty boy some years ago—do you remember?—they cut off his ear, but there were doubts at the time that it actually was his ear and not somebody else's. It might have been sliced off a corpse in some mortuary. Of course we can always check on fingers and they know that, but God alone knows why they had to chop off two—just bloody viciousness, I suppose. She's just a kid, Simon, and . . ." Philip paused for a moment, then continued. "There was a tape in the box, recording what they are doing to her—then, and at other times. They're giving her a very bad time and we simply have to get her back fast. Do you want to hear it? I have it in my case."

"No, thank you," said Simon firmly. "You've made your point. I'm still not quite clear what you expect me to do. I'd have thought a local man would be more use. Why me?"

"Simon, if I had more time I wouldn't bother you," said Philip soberly. "But there isn't the time to fill you in on all the details now. A fourteen-year-old child is being abused and beaten and scared witless and I want to get her back. The kidnappers call the tune and they've fixed the time span, not me. They gave us just enough time to get the cash but no time to arrange anything elaborate by way of cover."

Simon looked doubtful. "I know I owe you a favor, and you're a good friend of mine, and so on, but why not use your friend Cirillo? If he's a SISMI operator—isn't that part of the Italian Secret Service?—he must be a useful man."

"He's a good man but I want someone I know personally, someone I know won't go off at half-cock. If possible, I don't want any shooting at all. This handover is the most delicate part in a very delicate operation, and the big thing is to get the girl back in one piece. Having you at my back will help me to stay calm. You know how it is—it's a question of confidence."

Simon shook his head again, doubtfully, lips pursed. "Well, I can see that, up to a point, but it's not my turf. I don't know Italy. I've hardly even been there, I don't speak a word of the language, I know nothing of this business. I can't even see why you're involved. Why are you, an Englishman, handling all this?

"It wasn't the original plan," admitted Philip, "but it worked out that way. It's happened before. An American negotiated with the kidnappers over the Getty boy. Anyway, Lucia Fiori, Gina's sister, does the actual talking with the present bunch. Also, don't forget we, or rather the insurers I represent, will have to pay out in the end. Just think of it as a business. The snag with this business is that the people who handle the money tend to get killed."

"I hope you're exaggerating," said Simon. "Why should it be so dangerous? Can't you just pay over the money and get the girl back? Why should there be any shooting? You told me once where killing can lead and you were quite right." He stopped walking and waved a hand toward the walls around the house. "I don't want to do it again, certainly not for a total stranger."

"I'll tell you why you. First of all, you owe me. But for me you'd be dead now. I went out on a limb, personal and professional, to help you, because I thought you'd been wronged and needed help. Now I need help. It's your turn."

"But why *me*?"

"First, because you're you, and I know you. All the others, Kleiner, Fiori, Cirillo, even Lucia, they're foreigners; I don't even know what they're thinking half the time. I'm used to working with a team, at the Yard. It's bloody lonely on your own."

"Don't I know it," said Simon ruefully.

"I'm not sure—not one hundred percent sure—they'll back me up and do what they are told when the time comes. Then there's this girl, Gina. They've cut her fingers off. They've raped her. Surely you'd want to help me mop up scum like that?"

"Yes . . ." said Simon slowly, "but . . ."

"Finally," Philip went on, "this isn't a simple kidnapping.

There's something wrong with the entire setup. I need someone I can trust, someone I know who is one hundred percent reliable and, last but not least, someone who can look after himself. I have enough to worry about. Have I convinced you yet?"

"I'm overwhelmed," said Simon, smiling. "How can I refuse? And now I come to think of it, you might be doing me a favor."

"Really? Well, that wasn't the idea, but if so, why not? But in what way?"

"Well, how can I put it?" Simon pondered. "Let's see. A lot has happened since you and I first met. I lost my wife and family. I got chased by a gang of murderers. My country tried to get me killed and ran me off here to a self-built prison—and even Clio left me. Things like that tend to change a chap. I'm not the bundle of laughs I used to be and I drink too much."

"I've noticed," said Philip.

"So your coming here with the offer of worthwhile employment might be a godsend."

"I might even be doing you a favor," said Philip gravely.

"You could say that . . . we could say that," agreed Simon.

"I'm glad to hear it. I was afraid I might have to get down on my knees."

"Well, hardly that. I just wanted to feel needed . . . and, besides, it's a bad time to leave the garden . . . but for you, old heart, anything."

"I'm glad that's settled," said Philip, sitting down on the wall beside the path. "Why do you live in Mallorca anyway? It's pretty enough but it must be deadly dull in the winter."

Simon shook his head. "Not at all. I like the winter best," he said. "Living here was Clio's idea. Under the circumstances, with the Jihad on my tracks, she thought an island might be safer. Communications are good here, there's a good airport, and, as a bonus, there was no extradition treaty between Spain and Britain . . . So, if your successor, young Mr. Catton, had wanted to pull me in—tough luck!"

"They don't want you," said Philip. "There's not enough evidence to convict; there never was. If you keep your nose clean and don't do it again, they'll let it lie. So, what's the snag? You don't seem too happy."

Simon gestured about him again, and then scratched his head thoughtfully. "The snag here is," he went on slowly, "that I have nothing to do, nothing to think about. I don't like to smoke grass, party all night, or get laid. I don't want to recycle gossip with the local expats, let alone cause it. The most popular theories are that I'm either infected with AIDS or a retired drug king. I don't feel that the truth would sound much better, so I let them talk. I don't want to start a new business, and I can't go back to Britain. So I'll come and help you if I can. Why didn't you just pay over the cash weeks ago and save the girl's fingers?"

Philip looked at him, eyebrows raised. "Don't you think I wanted to? You don't know much about Italy, and you don't know much about this business, so don't judge us too harshly. If we'd given in to the first demand the kidnappers would simply have doubled it. It's not a simple business . . . but you will come?"

"Yes, I'll come, since you ask me," said Simon slowly, "but, since we're being frank, you're much too old to be messing about with this sort of thing. Leave the dirty work to the young tigers. You've done your share."

"You may be right," said Philip amiably, "but it beats sitting around in the sun, growing roses or pushing gin through your teeth. I may have to see some grisly sights now and then, but at least I'm doing something worthwhile."

"Well, that must be nice," said Simon ironically. "Other people who feel that way go in for charity work. You could try that next."

"Maybe, but first things first. How's your hand?" asked Philip, glancing over at Simon's fingers. "It looks pretty good—well, usable anyway. There was a time I thought the whole hand might have to go. You really shouldn't have waited so long before we went to the hospital."

"It's all right," said Simon. "Sometimes it aches, and the

bits that aren't there feel as if they still are, but I've gotten used to it. Most of the time it gives me no trouble. It used to give Clio the shudders, though; after a while she'd jump a yard when I touched her."

"What happened to Clio?" asked Philip. "I thought she'd be here. I even thought you might have gotten married—that was certainly her intention . . . she told me so just before I left you in Limoges. She said she would keep you out of mischief."

Simon laughed a little harshly. "Well, she soon got over that idea when she saw what living here with me would be like. Anyway, she left. She's been gone—what?—eight or nine months. She's back in New York, wheeling and dealing, making a lot of money. Our little affair just petered out."

Philip said nothing. There didn't seem to be much he could say. He let his eyes stray around the walls, taking in the barbed wire and cameras, noting the layout of the ground, the dark windows of the house behind. "I think you'll find that the Arabs will leave you alone if you leave them alone," he said, changing the subject. "After all, it's been two years. The Green Jihad are a spent force these days, thanks to you. But if they did come after you, do you think your defenses would keep them out?"

"Oh no," said Simon, shaking his head. "They could get in if they wanted to. Given sufficient numbers and surprise, I would expect them to get in." He smiled grimly. "They might find getting out a different matter."

"I see," said Philip, nodding. "At least, I suppose I do. Anyway, I doubt if they'll try. If you want to get involved in what I'm up to, you'd be welcome. I think you'd enjoy it . . . on a full-time basis, I mean."

Simon suddenly laughed out loud. It sounded as if he hadn't laughed like that for a long time. "You've changed your tune in the last two years. When we first met, your sole aim and ambition was to lock me away for the rest of my natural life. Now you're offering me a job."

"You were shooting people on my patch and I had my job to do," said Philip mildly. "Besides, it worked out all right.

You weren't the only gunman I'd ever met, Simon. In my forty years in the force I must have met—what?—I don't know . . . dozens. But you were different. I sensed that from the start, long before we found out who you were."

"Really?" Simon's voice was tinged with irony. "In what way was I different?"

"Well," Philip pondered again for a moment. "You didn't shoot anyone who wasn't absolutely begging for it. That's probably what gave you away. After that, well, I just took to you. . . . We got along. There's no mystery in it."

"Yes, we did, didn't we?" said Simon. "It was almost fun for a while back then, stitching up those swine." Simon got up from the wall and turned to go, dusting the seat of his trousers with rapid slaps of his injured hand, reaching out for his glass with the other one. "But the fun didn't last."

"Fun isn't the word I would have chosen," said Philip, getting up. "Interesting might suit the situation better. But fun? Hardly that."

"No, I suppose not," said Simon slowly. "I don't really think it was fun either, yet here we go again. Well, what the hell! Why not? I don't have anything else to do, do I? Come on, let's go and get rid of your car, then I'll look for a few tools—we'll have some lunch and Lito can drive us to Palma. It's time to get the show on the road."

Philip stood back in the shade while the big black car reversed down the road and turned away. When he went back through the steel gate and up the winding path toward the house, the gates swung shut once more, silently, as if powered by some unseen hand. The effect was eerie.

Simon was back in his chair on the terrace, his feet up on the wall, facing down the valley, with another full glass in his hand. The only new element was the heavy, black automatic pistol that lay on the table beside the bottles, amid the litter of cups and glasses.

"We have Klaus Kleiner's second-best jet on a private field near Palma," said Philip, sitting down in front of him on the wall. "Flight time back to Milan is something over two hours, so, to take everything into account, I'd like to take off by, say, three." He nodded toward the pistol. "And where did that come from?"

"From under my jacket," said Simon. "It's been digging into my flesh for the last hour or more. I always prefer to take precautions, so I carry this, or something very like it, all the time. When a group of Arabs may be after my balls with their long, sharp knives, that seems only sensible. Better to have it and not need it than need it and not have it. It's become a habit; no offense meant."

"What is it?" asked Philip, leaning over to inspect the weapon. "Is this the one you had before? The Browning?"

"No, not quite," said Simon, swinging his feet off the wall and leaning across to pick up the pistol. "It's a Browning, but a much later model than the other one. This is the High Power, nine-mil caliber, carries fourteen rounds in the magazine . . . packs a great wallop."

"Very impressive, but can you use it?" asked Philip. "I'm a bit wary of your drinking. After the amount you've put away this morning, I doubt you could hit the ground with your hat."

"Don't worry about the booze," said Simon. "I can still handle it or I wouldn't touch it. This is the last one until this business is over—I promise."

"But can you really cope with it?" asked Philip. "Every drunk I've ever met said he could handle it, and you've put away most of that bottle. Do you always drink such a lot, or is this a demonstration for my benefit?"

"Don't flatter yourself," said Simon shortly. "I either don't touch it or I see off the bottle. I had nothing else to do today, so why not? I like the taste, though, I have to admit that." He swirled the ice around in his glass, drained the contents, and put the glass back on the table. "There . . . finished. No more . . . until I get back here anyway."

"Look, if you have a serious drinking problem," said Philip harshly, "maybe it's better if you don't come along. I've got enough on my hands without having to worry about you falling flat on your face at the crucial moment."

Suddenly there was tension in the air between them. Simon looked at Philip levelly for a moment, then levered himself out of the chair and picked up the pistol, tucking it away under his loose jacket, a slight smile playing over his face. "Don't you remember?" he said. "You invited yourself here. However, I happen to care about what you think of me, so let's see if I can't put your mind at rest. Come this way. Lito! *Ven acá . . . conmigo.*"

Simon led the way off the terrace without another word, closely followed by Wintle and Lito. They went around the back of the house, out through a gate in the wall, and along a narrow path up the steep rocky hillside, over ground where the pine trees grew closely together, shedding a thick, soft carpet of needles over the thin soil. This soon petered out into a naked rock face that rose steeply up the hillside ahead. In a shallow reentrant at the top of the rise, the flat surface of the ground was littered with spent cartridge cases, the torn tops of cardboard ammunition cartons, a few well-riddled beer cans, and the bullet-chewed trunks of several small trees. The three men stood together in the blazing sunshine, Simon and Lito waiting for Philip to comment.

"I see," Philip said at last, slowly. "It looks as if you have a new hobby or have been keeping your hand in. Which?"

"Let me explain something," said Simon. "You've been thinking that I just lie about and booze, but you're wrong. I still stay fit and I try to stay sharp. Besides, a man does need a hobby and practice makes perfect. I've been up here every morning for the past two years. Do you see that far ridge, below the mountain? That's three miles away but I can get there and back in forty minutes flat. I do that every day. Look over there." He took Philip's arm and turned him around, pointing down the valley to the far mountain, now half hidden in the heat haze. "That's Puig Tomir—it's about four thousand feet high. Lito drops me on the far side and the game is to get up one side, across the top and down the other side, and then to the sea at Pollensa—thats about twenty miles in a day—without him seeing me or cutting me off. "We call it 'The Run.' "

Lately he's been doing The Run and I try to spot him. It keeps us busy and you get very, very fit at it."

"May I know why?" asked Philip. "It may be just good fun, but I expect there's another reason."

"No, not really. It just keeps us fit," said Simon briefly. "You tend to stagnate here, and drink too much . . . as you've noticed. Everyone jogs, but jogging is so bloody boring."

"But *why* keep fit? You haven't really told me *why* you run and hide and shoot every day."

"Well, let's say I like to keep fit in case the right thing comes along, or the wrong thing comes along . . . like the Jihad. Let's see if we can't show you something else."

While they had been talking, Lito had been busy. They both turned back to watch as he placed an empty gin bottle on a low tree stump far to the left and an empty wine bottle on another bullet-chewed stump, farther down the hill to the right. That done, Lito turned and looked back at them, shading his eyes against the glare.

"Lito and I spend hours at this," said Simon. "How far away would you say those bottles are? They look quite small at this distance."

"Oh, I don't know—thirty yards?" said Philip impatiently. "Isn't all this a little childish? Don't we have other things to do? I apologize; you can hold your liquor. I'm not impressed with childish tricks."

Simon shook his head, his face concentrating, frowning. "It's not childish at all. Wait and see. The distance is a little less than thirty yards, but that's long pistol range, all the same. The real problem is that the targets are small, at different ranges, and set one on either side—that's what makes it tricky. However, let's see . . . *esta claro, Lito*?"

"Sí, Señor Simon, no hay nadie." Lito moved rapidly out of the way, scrambling over the rocks to one side.

"He's just making sure that no one is about," said Simon, smiling at Philip. "We don't want to hit an innocent bystander, do we? Right?"

It was fast, *very* fast. The pistol came into Simon's hand from under his jacket, blurring into his fist. He stepped back and around, and fired, moving . . . still moving. There was a sudden crash of sound and the gin bottle disintegrated. Simon was still moving, still firing . . . another crash and the wine bottle lost its top, another and the bottle disappeared in a blast of splinters. Before the echo had rattled off the hill behind, the pistol had disappeared under his jacket and Simon had turned and was smiling at Philip once again.

"Well, how was that?" he asked hopefully. "Are you feeling better about me now? How was that for a falling-down drunk?"

"That's not too bad at all for a falling-down drunk," replied Philip slowly, nodding. "Not too bad at all."

"You should see me when I'm sober," said Simon. "Note the fast draw from under the jacket, rather fancy. That's not one of your average shooting skills, believe me. That's what takes practice."

Philip put a finger in one ear and waggled it. His ears were still ringing from the firing. "Bloody hell!" he exclaimed suddenly, shaking his head. "How did you learn to shoot like that? I thought you used to carry a shotgun because you were a rotten shot."

"I've had nothing else to do," said Simon simply. "Now, since I'm off the sauce, how about some lunch?" Simon led Philip back down the hill and left him on the terrace while he disappeared into the house. Presently he reappeared, bearing a tray with a large pot of coffee and a couple of mugs.

"Lunch will be ready in about half an hour," he said, handing over a full mug to Philip. "Sugar is in the bowl, milk in the jug. Now, tell me everything."

"I've explained the basic setup," replied Philip, looking down at his watch, "and full explanations must wait until we have a bit more time.

"We have plenty of time," said Simon calmly. "Don't con me—if this kidnapping was a one-shot you'd handle it yourself, or get this Cirillo person to supply some reliable local talent. You wouldn't come rushing over here to get me . . . not after two years. I know you better than that. What's the real problem?"

Philip spooned a little sugar into his mug and stirred it slowly, his eyes fixed on Simon's face, then nodded agreement. "Well, you're right about that," he said. "This isn't just a one-shot hit. We've had several kidnappings in the Kleiner consortium in the last year, but this one is different . . ." He hesitated, still stirring his coffee, looking thoughtfully into space.

"Yes, well, don't stop there," said Simon impatiently. "How is this one different?"

Philip scratched his chin with the back of his fingers and looked blankly down the valley for a moment. Then he turned his gaze back to Simon.

"Firstly, because it happened to a member of the group I am hired to protect—in spite of everything I could do. Why go for such a hard target?"

Simon nodded. "All right," he said, "your professional pride is engaged. I can see that. And what's the other difference?"

"The other difference is Klaus Kleiner. He's heavy metal, Simon, very rich, very dedicated to catching the gang who are extorting money from his consortium. He's another person no wise man would mess with. Anyway, you've heard of him."

"Who hasn't?" said Simon.

"Coming here to get you was his idea, and not just because we need to get Fiori's daughter back. Kleiner wants to meet you. He asked me to arrange that as a personal favor.

"Why should Klaus Kleiner want to meet me?" asked Simon softly. "How did he even come to hear about me?"

"I don't know how he heard about you," said Philip. "He just asked me about you last week. He got nothing out of me. I know why he wants to meet you, though, or at least I think I do."

"And why is that?" asked Simon.

"Well . . ." Philip paused for a moment. "I think he wants to offer you a contract."

THREE

During the silence that followed, Simon refilled his mug from the coffeepot and sipped from it slowly, his eyes brooding thoughtfully on the valley. It was blazing hot now with the sun producing a shimmer of haze over the distant hills as it crawled ever higher in the sky. Simon still said nothing and eventually the silence between them began to drag. Philip shot a glance at him, reaching his hand back to loosen the shirt from his back. Then he took a look at his watch and gently put his coffee mug back on the table.

"I don't like the sound of that," Simon said abruptly, turning to face Philip, "and what does he mean by 'contract'?"

"What do you know about Kleiner?" asked Philip, looking across at Simon, shading his eyes with one hand against the glare.

"About Kleiner? Very little. I've never met him. I know only what I've read in the papers. He's Mr. Big, the archetypal international business tycoon, into everything: oil, high-tech, banking, newspapers, and so on. Owns a yacht, islands, houses here and there. Always attending charity dos, seen with lots of women. Frankly,he sounds the sort of person I don't much care for. I suppose the contract he has in mind is of the Mafia variety—he wants someone whacked and hasn't got the guts to do it himself. You should tell him to stop reading so many thrillers; life's not like that."

"And you ought to know better than to believe all you read in the papers," said Philip. "Klaus is tough, maybe a touch unscrupulous at times, but he offered me a contract and I'm not too proud to accept it. Anyway," Philip concluded, "somehow he's heard of you and now he wants to meet you."

"How did he hear of me, if you haven't been talking?"

"I suspect he heard about you in much the same way he heard about me. It was common knowledge that I was looking for a job after I retired. The man has contacts in high places, and a couple of years ago your activities caused a lot of talk in those same high places. About two weeks ago he asked me if, during my time at the Yard, I'd heard of a gunman called Simon Quarry; I was quite taken aback. Anyway, I said that I had, though I gave no details, except that I'd met you. He asked if I thought you and he would get on. I thought that was a curious question, but I said you probably would, and he said he was thinking of offering you a contract. He didn't say any more and I didn't ask. How he heard about you in the first place I've no idea. Then this business with the Fiori girl came to a head and here I am. But whatever Kleiner wants is secondary. I'm the one who needs you at the moment. If you don't like his offer you can always turn it down."

"Do you like him?" asked Simon curiously. "I wouldn't have thought businessmen of that caliber were your type."

"I like him well enough, and anyway I work for him," said Philip simply. "He owns KSI, of course. Kleiner is putting up the hard cash to pay Fiori girl's kidnappers, since Fiori can't raise it in the time. I collected the money in Zürich, then flew over here in his second-best jet. Kleiner is very much involved in all this—and lots of other things as well. I'll tell you more about it later."

"You'd better," said Simon. "There seems to be a lot going on you haven't told me about."

"Kleiner will tell you what he wants himself. We can have a meeting with him in Milan and it can't hurt to meet the man. The full consortium meets every month or so to review matters, and we can see Kleiner after that . . . but until we get Gina back you'll stay under cover. Let me just say that Kleiner's involvement is deep and, if I'm any judge, personal—and that's all I can say at the moment."

Simon held up his hand to cut off Philip's talk in midflow. "Just wait a minute," he said. "This isn't good enough. It's time you told me about the people involved in this business before I get in any deeper. I'm coming to look after you, not to shoot people for Klaus Kleiner."

Philip looked anxiously at his watch again and began to get up, but Simon stayed where he was, dark against the sky, looking down at Philip, his face set. "I want an answer," he said firmly, "and I'd like it now."

Philip sighed and shrugged, then dropped back into his chair, and leaned forward to refill his coffee mug. "Kleiner created the consortium. A couple of years back Kleiner's own child was kidnapped. She was only seventeen. She was ill-treated, beaten, raped. God knows why, because Kleiner agreed to pay, to do anything, but the kidnappers just kept putting up the ransom. It was a terrorist group, a splinter of the Red Brigades, and they wanted to make him sweat. That's how he met Cirillo—Aldo heads up the Squadra Antiterrorismo in Milan. When she was eventually released she was in a very bad way and she went on drugs. About two months ago she died. They found her in London—in the Piccadilly Circus lavatories, overdosed, with the needle still stuck in her arm. Kleiner went to London and simply wasn't the same man when he came back. He had already taken me into this kidnap security business full time. My brief is not just to stop the kidnappings, it's to find the kidnappers. He's very determined about that. It's something he feels he owes his daughter. You'll understand that better than most."

"Are these the same kidnappers who took Kleiner's child? Is that the setup?"

Philip shook his head emphatically. "Oh no, no . . . it's nothing like that. They were caught and dealt with and are either dead or doing a very inadequate amount of time. We even got most of the money back. It's simply a matter of principle with Kleiner. He bought into KSI and then set up the private consortium, after he got his girl back—his wife is dead, incidentally. But now his girl is dead too; he's certainly prepared to play rough. That's when he started looking for someone like you. As you can see, you have a lot in common."

"Only up to a point," said Simon, sitting down on the wall. "When I lost my family I used my own contacts and dealt with the bastards myself. I didn't hire a private cop to track them down and a hit man to do my dirty work thereafter. Anyway, if that's what Kleiner has in mind he can forget it. I'm not for rent and I don't want his contract."

"Look," said Philip patiently, "this Fiori business is different. I am asking you to help me, not Kleiner. After that, all he wants to do is talk to you. Why don't we talk while we gather up your stuff? It's not enough to sit back and hope nothing happens to you or yours. The world—especially Kleiner's world—is under attack from terrorists, organized crime—you name it. We have to go after these people and root them out . . . the police won't do it. With them the crime has to come first and for us that's too late. Content yourself for now that Lucia likes Kleiner, and if she likes someone then they're all right. She's a very level-headed girl and nobody's fool, believe me."

"Who is this Lucia?" Simon demanded.

"She's Fiori's eldest daughter," said Philip patiently. "She's not a rough diamond like her father. Lucia's a lady. She's a doctor, a pediatrician at a children's cancer clinic in Milan. And don't knock Kleiner to Lucia—he founded the clinic, and he didn't have his name put above the door either. It wasn't for the personal publicity. I don't much care for Fiori, but he has done all right by his children, seen them properly educated and so on. To be exact, Lucia and Gina are half-sisters: Fiori's first wife died or ran off, so Lucia brought Gina up, at least when she was at home in Italy. Lucia went to school in England, first to somewhere near Ascot, then to Cambridge, then to Guy's Hospital. She speaks better English than you do—a very intelligent girl . . . you'll like her."

Simon grimaced. "I'm sure I will, if you say so," he said. He shook his head as if trying to untangle his thoughts. "But where does she come into all this, apart from being Gina's sister?"

"Half sister. She's been helping me out. When we have to deal with the kidnappers, she's the one who does the talking and the general wheeling and dealing, though I tell her what to say. Usually the family is kept out of it as they tend to get too emotional, but Lucia's very level-headed. Anyway, I don't speak Italian, so we really have no choice."

"I don't speak Italian either," Simon pointed out. "I hope you know what you're doing here. We always used to plan things carefully, but this is all too quick. Apart from anything else, what's my standing in Italy? Legally, I mean. You'd have gone insane if anyone'd imported their own armed bodyguard into England."

"Don't worry about it," said Philip firmly, getting out of his chair. "Italy is different. Kleiner and Cirillo can fix your cover, firearms license and so on, and anyone you are likely to talk to speaks good English. As for Milan, it's just another big industrial city with a mass of office blocks and too much traffic. It has a cathedral, a castle, and the La Scala opera house. Take away La Scala and you could be anywhere. The setting will be no problem."

"All right, I'm convinced," said Simon. "For the moment, anyway." He got up from the wall and started across the terrace toward the house. "Come on," he said over his shoulder. "I'll get Lito to pack some clothes while I look for some hardware." He led Philip back into the house and across the living room, pointing him toward the cabinets that lined the far wall of the room.

"Just wait over there a second," he said, opening the door to the kitchen. *"Lito, ven aća momentito."*

Waiting there, standing before the cabinets, Simon took out his keys again, unlocked the doors and folded them back, turning back into the room as Lito came in, wiping his hands on a towel.

"Lunch for us in ten minutes, Lito," he said. "Also, I want you to put a few things in a bag for me. Trainers, an anorak, pants, night stuff . . . you know the sort of thing. Put in a couple of suits and shirts as well. I'm going off with Señor Wintle, just for a few days."

"Are you going hunting, Señor Simon?" asked Lito, looking past him to the cabinets.

"No, not really, just a little business trip. Probably not longer than a week, but I don't know exactly when I'll be back. Don't worry, I'll phone you."

"Can I come with you?" Lito's voice was anxious.

"Not this time, Lito. You stay here and look after the house. Don't forget to feed the cat, and keep that bloody heron away from the goldfish. Do you have enough money? If not you'll find plenty in the cash box; just take what you need."

"Sí, señor."

"And will you drive us down to Palma in about half an hour? Get out the Mercedes."

"Sí, señor."

"Good . . . go now and pack my stuff; be quick. We're in a hurry."

As Lito hurried out Simon made his way over to Philip, feeling in his pockets for the cabinet keys. "I have this rule," he explained, opening the doors, "weapons should be kept locked up but fully loaded."

"Really?" said Philip. "I can understand the first point, but why the second?"

"Think, man. Every time you hear of an accidental shooting, or read about it in the papers, someone always says, 'I didn't know it was loaded.' Right?"

"Right."

"Well, around here they are always loaded, so you know you have to be careful. Besides, if the Jihad were to come I don't have time to load them, so . . . I take them out at night, incidentally, and Lito keeps a twelve-gauge Winchester pump in the kitchen."

"What have you got in there?" asked Philip, leaning past Simon to peer into the cabinet.

"Not much. A shotgun, a hunting rifle—I hunt feral goats on the mountain, they ravage the valley crops and my garden—and another pistol. One or two pieces that's all." He reached into the cabinets and took out a short, black repeating shotgun and placed it behind them on the table.

"You still have Old Betsy, I see." said Philip.

"Not quite . . . this is New Betsy. Old Betsy went over the side of the ferry with the other Browning the night Clio and I came here. If your pals at the Yard want to find my weapons now, they'll have to dredge the Mediterranean. I thought it best to destroy every single piece of evidence linking me to the Jihad shootings. Incidentally, what did you tell that doctor in Limoges—about my hand?"

"I told him you'd caught it in a lawnmower."

"And he believed you?"

"Not for a second. But I also gave him two thousand dollars and he believed that."

Simon shook his head. "You shouldn't have done that."

"Well, it was *your* money. It didn't cost me a thing."

"I don't mean that. When I came round I also gave him two thousand dollars—the crafty bastard."

"The man's a crook," said Wintle, amused. "We've been robbed. What's this?"

"Something for you. If you need a bodyguard, you need a personal weapon. It's too light for me . . . Colt Cobra, .38 Special, nice and flat. With this alloy frame it weighs less than a pound. Take some cartridges as well, but remember, it's loaded."

"Well . . ." Philip was reluctant. "If you say so."

"I do say so. Look, it would be easier if I knew what we were going to do. I'll take the Browning and New Betsy, of course, but what else?

"What else have you got?"

"I've got my rifle, a Weatherby Magnum. It's really a big-game rifle, and packs one hell of a punch—and then I've got this."

Simon knelt to reach down into the bottom of the cabinet and came back up with a short bundle of oily rags, which he flipped open to show the contents to Philip.

"Good God!" exclaimed Philip. "That's the Heckler-something, the MP5, anyway. The SAS uses those, and they're *very* hard to come by."

Simon laughed. "Don't you believe it! Clio bought this in a gun store in Edison, New Jersey, and brought it back from the States last Christmas. She smuggled it through the Palma Customs, hidden under her knickers. She said she couldn't think of anything else to give me as a present. Our relationship was not prospering at the time."

Philip shook his head. "I want to get a girl back, not start a war. Leave that bloody thing here and take something more discriminating."

"Well, that leaves the rifle. That should do the trick . . . I'm quite good with that as well."

"I just bet you are," said Philip sourly. "And now here's Lito with our lunch."

"There is one other thought," said Philip, putting down his fork. "I think Kleiner sees settling the Fiori business as some sort of audition. You ought to know that."

"An audition?" asked Simon, frowning. "Who for? What for?"

"All of us," said Philip. "Him, me, you, maybe one or two more . . . Cirillo, I think . . . his team. To see if we can work together. He has plans for KSI, personal plans. You haven't met Kleiner yet but he's not the same as the man I met a couple of years ago. He's cut himself off, disappears for weeks on end, doing I know not what. He was in London recently, talking to the government, to our mutual friend Yates, the Prince of Darkness. John Catton told me. Then he spends a lot of time just sitting in the dark, thinking. I don't like it. You used to do that, as I remember."

Simon pushed his plate aside and got up, stepping over the zipped-up gun case at his feet. "So what? Let's wait and see what he has to say. I can always say no. One more snag occurs to me—how are we to transport this little lot into Italy? Airport security police don't usually care for people carrying firearms on the premises."

"The jet is on the club airfield, just outside Palma. We have already filed a flight plan to Seville. That's an internal flight, so there'll be no Customs or Immigration checks, and we'll turn north once we're clear of the main air routes. At the other end we're flying into a private airfield near Milan. No commercial traffic uses it, so it has very low security cover. Anyway, Aldo Cirillo has already fixed all that. In Milan, Lucia will meet us and keep you somewhere quiet until the kidnappers fix a rendezvous. The only people who know about you are Cirillo, Kleiner, and Lucia, and Fiori, of course. Since his daughter is involved I couldn't keep him in the dark. He's not keen on having you, but he's going along with it. I don't want anyone else to know you're with me—you're my backup, my ace in the hole. They don't object to armed bodyguards in Italy and if anyone official should ask, you're on the team as a bodyguard. It's all been arranged through Cirillo—the head of the Squad Antiterrorismo has a pretty free hand."

"He sounds a useful man to know."

"He is," said Philip. "Aldo's main job is counterterrorism, but he's not averse to helping an old friend out on a kidnap case and the two often overlap. Kidnapping is a useful method for terrorists to raise money. I've worked with him before, when I was at the Yard, and he was chasing Red Brigade people all over Europe."

Simon shook his head wonderingly. "I never really stood a chance, did I? It's all wheels within wheels. The old-boy network is alive and well and living in Italy. I bet you knew I would come along all the time. Why didn't you just send me a cable? I could have hopped on the first flight."

"Well, let's say I thought you might agree to help," said Philip blandly. "After all, I'd do the same for you. It seemed a reasonable enough request."

"Yes," said Simon heavily, slinging the gun case over his shoulder. "I expect it did. Come on . . . Lito is already in the car."

Simon turned to look out of the back window of the car as Lito walked back to close the gates, wondering when he would see the house again.

"Do you like my home?" Simon asked Philip. "I do . . . I hate leaving it these days. I hardly ever go out."

"I like it very much," said Philip. "It's quite beautiful. After that rather spartan flat you had in London it's a surprise to discover you living somewhere so spacious . . . and gardening . . . all that. It's hard to see you as a horticulturist."

"I still have the London flat. This house is really Clio's doing," said Simon. "I was responsible only for choosing the site and digging the garden. I liked the view, and I never tire of it. It's the one thing that gets me out of bed every morning—that and The Run across the mountains."

"It's a very beautiful island," agreed Philip, leaning forward to peer out of the windows. "I had no idea that Mallorca was mountainous. I'd rather imagined you living in one of those multistory seaside villas, surrounded by pop stars and television personalities, grinding your teeth at the noise of their parties."

"That's the Costa del Sol scene," said Simon, smiling thinly. "It's not like that here. And Mallorca isn't all tea-like-Mother-made, English Pale Ale and resorts like Palma Nova—is it, Lito? *El señor aquí cree que Mallorca es linda.*"

"Sí, Mallorca es muy linda, señor," agreed Lito, smiling over his shoulder at Philip as he climbed back into the car, slammed the door, and started the engine. They began to move slowly down the narrow lane, stopped briefly before turning out onto the main road, then accelerated away down a wide highway

toward the buildings of Pollensa, away from the distant glinting of the sea.

"What made you choose Pollensa?" asked Philip. "Apart from the mountains."

Simon shrugged. "It was an accident. We just stumbled upon it. I chose Spain because, as I said before, Spain did not have an extradition treaty with the UK. If our caper in the Pyrenees leaked out, or your people found they had enough evidence to bust me for the London shootings, I was safe here. Did you know they found the bodies, up in the mountains?"

"Yes, John Catton came all the way down to Dorset to tell me—accompanied by your friend Alec Yates, wearing his Foreign Office hat. They wanted to ask me if I had any idea how you'd got away with it. Yates doesn't like you *at all*—or me, come to that. He suspects we stitched him up. Some climbers found the bodies in the spring, and it might have looked like just another mountain accident except the weapons gave the game away. There was an autopsy and the news eventually filtered back to the Yard. We should have taken their weapons with us."

"How could we?" asked Simon. "You had me to look after and I was bleeding like a stuck pig. It's a wonder we got back over the mountains before the snows came. Not that I remember much about it. That's another one I owe you, old friend."

"I'm collecting," said Philip shortly. "The snag is that your file is still open. That's why they keep tabs on you, and know where you are. I'd be a bit careful if I went to England if I were you, but if nothing else happens, people will forget about you."

"So they know where I am?" asked Simon, looking over his shoulder.

"Oh yes, of course. You're well enough known. Someone will have seen you here, or heard that you're living here. Don't worry about it, though. John Catton is almost a fan of yours but Alec Yates could turn nasty if you worry him again. He's not the most forgiving man in the world, and you made him look bad."

"Do you see that place up there? asked Simon suddenly,

changing the subject. "You can see the roof over the trees. There! Up on the hill. That's the home of one of Colombia's most active drug dealers, though now supposedly retired. He has the most amazing defenses: dogs, patrols of South Americans armed with submachine guns, American claymore mines, electrified fences, the lot. Much more than I do. A very secretive fellow. The guards are flown home every six months in case they go over the wall, but meanwhile they're kept well supplied with whores from Barcelona. Our hero flies a dozen in every week to keep his lads contented."

"Really!" exclaimed Philip cheerfully, peering out of the window. "And how do you know all this?"

"Lito and I went over his wall one party night and had a look at the goings-on. Quite disgraceful! We had to clamp out a section of live wire to get in and clout a guard on the way out, but it was good training. I think he knows it was me. He keeps giving me nasty looks when we happen to meet at the Yacht Club. I don't go there much, but I keep my boat on one of the moorings. Anyway, a couple of his *pistoleros* came sniffing around my house one night but Lito and I had a chat with them and they went away."

"You're mad," said Philip, shaking his head. "Provoking people like that is crazy. Why do you do it?"

"Well, you know how it is when you're bored," said Simon. "And it seemed like a good idea at the time. I only hope we can say as much about our present trip, in a few months from now."

FOUR

The small jet swept off the runway with a rumbling from below as the wheels thumped up into the wings. The aircraft climbed steeply, gaining height across Palma Bay, before turning back to head northeast across the mountains. Far below, the ground was a patchwork of brown and green fields, dotted frequently with white windmills, their sails turning lazily in the afternoon heat. Pressing his cheek hard against the window, Simon could look down on the bald peak of Puig Tomir, then on the great bay beyond Puerto de Pollensa which, with the long, rocky finger of the Formentor peninsula, came opening up below. Just before the first fleecy clouds whipped across the view, he picked out his own house, white and brown among the trees, the blue of the swimming pool standing out vividly against the drab olive-green of the pines. Then it was gone. They were out over the sea again and soaring into cloud.

Well, that's that, Simon thought, looking across at Philip. *Here we go again.* He unclipped the seat belt, settled back in his seat, and took a long look around the cabin, trying consciously to relax. Simon glanced at his watch, then leaned across to tap Philip on the knee.

"Do you know," he said, "that in spite of all your worrying, it's only just over six hours since you turned up at my gate? We've really hustled to get away in that time. I hope all this haste is really necessary."

Philip shifted in his seat, putting his mouth close to Simon's ear. "We still have to get to Milan, hide you, get to Fiori's house, and be ready for their eight o'clock call. When it comes, we then decide how to react. I've made outline arrangements to cover every contingency I can think of but there's still a lot to do. There's also a lot we can't do until the last minute. They said they'd phone tonight and give us the delivery instructions, but who knows? They like us to sweat. However, I expect they'll want to get their hands on the cash as soon as possible."

"The sooner the better," agreed Simon. "Where is the money, anyway?"

Philip jerked his head slightly. "It's in a suitcase under that seat. It's too heavy to lug about, so I left it with the pilot. It was quite a relief to find the aircraft still sitting on the tarmac when we got back."

"I've never seen a million dollars," said Simon thoughtfully, dropping his head a little to peer at the bag under the seat. "Not in hard cash, that is. I wonder what it looks like?"

"We have a million and a half in there and it's surprisingly unimpressive," said Philip wryly. "Just a lot of dirty paper that hardly seems worth all the effort that goes into getting it." Philip's shoulders sagged slightly. "They gave us until today to raise the money, but the delivery may not be for days. Meanwhile, you lie low at Lucia's."

"How do you like being a go-between?" asked Simon.

"It's quite common to have an intermediary, and, anyway Lucia does the actual talking." Philip settled back into his seat, hands folded, elbows on armrests. "Let me put you in the picture about the kidnap game in Italy," he continued softly. "First of all, it's big business. It's very much the Italian crime and quite common. The estimates are that forty-six people have been kidnapped so far this year, in northern Italy alone. That's about two a week. It may well be more because a lot of cases don't make the papers. The family are contacted, hire a lawyer, he settles as quickly as possible, and they get their relative back. End of story. At least as far as the police and press are concerned. For the families and the victims the trauma can last a good deal longer. It's not a gentle business."

"What about the police?" put in Simon. "Don't they care at all? Don't they want to get involved? Surely kidnapping is a major crime, even in Italy?"

They often aren't told. The only kidnapping to make the papers this year was that of a young woman who was released after being held for nearly a year. That was very unusual. Her ransom was two thousand million lire, about a hundred and fifty million dollars, and she wasn't from a super-rich family. Her father's a fashion designer and it nearly ruined him. He's lost control of his business and is in debt up to his ears. Of the forty-six I mentioned, ten are still being held and the total take for the gangs so far is estimated at about *twenty thousand million* lire—say, ten million sterling. Not bad, eh? Three of the victims were killed by their kidnappers and two of the handovers have involved a shoot-out. I'm not imagining the danger, the risk is real. One poor soul hanged himself within hours of being grabbed, because he knew his family couldn't afford the money to get him back. The strain on the families is terrible; we get suicides, nervous breakdowns, divorce, bankruptcies. Most of the victims never really get over it—remember Kleiner's daughter? It's a dirty business—that's why Kleiner's so hot on kidnappers, and on drugs. He's almost insane on the subject of drugs. If he could, he'd ban aspirin."

"So far, then, the Fiori kidnap has been kept quiet?" asked

Simon. "No news in the papers, no official help from the police, things like that?"

"So far, yes—just," said Philip. "It's difficult, because Kleiner is newsworthy, and the consortium was his creation. However, he owns papers and radio stations, and spends a lot on advertising, so he has clout with the editors and publishers. People in the consortium know about it, but they also know to keep quiet. When it leaks out that they cut off the girl's fingers, that will cause a storm, but by that time we'll have her back. Another advantage of keeping the blasted newsmen and *paparazzi* out of the way is that we can move you in discreetly. Kleiner is a useful man to know."

"As I recall from the papers," said Simon, "Kleiner is just a super-rich kraut."

"Ninety-nine percent of what you read in the newspapers is rubbish," snapped Philip. "Journalists today seem to spend more time inventing news than they do reporting it. He's not German, he's Swiss. He's certainly horribly, stinking rich, but he's no playboy, and the daughter was the apple of his eye. Kleiner seems straight. He's a solitary type, keeps himself to himself, very ambitious, competitive, hates losing or even being jerked around. It's not just his money, he's an interesting man. Don't start getting your hackles up, Simon, give the man a chance. Besides, he's powerful, well connected, very shrewd, the sort of man who could be a good friend or a very bad enemy. You might remember that," concluded Philip with a smile.

"Well, let's leave him for a moment," said Simon. "Tell me about Fiori."

"Luigi Fiori is nowhere near Kleiner's league, but he does all right. He owns a lot of businesses, small and large, mainly in Milan and Turin. He has a flat in Rome, a house in the suburbs of Milan, another by Lake Como, a ski lodge at Bormio, servants, cars, chauffeurs, all the usual stuff. Apart from that, I don't know much except that Lucia doesn't like him."

Simon shrugged off this last comment. "Why did Kleiner get involved with the Fiori business?" he asked. "What's in it for him?"

"You have to go back a bit," said Philip. "He posted a reward of five million dollars for information leading to the arrest or capture of the gang who took his child. That's *twice* what he paid out to get her back. He said he intended to teach the Italians the meaning of the word vendetta. Kleiner's not the forgiving type and he can be pretty lethal if provoked. It was a good idea, but it didn't work."

"What happened?" asked Simon.

"The Italian crooks started killing each other just to collect the reward. They were waist-deep in bodies for a while. In the end it was Cirillo's troops who rounded up the gang anyway. Kleiner's action was much too indiscriminate and it left a bad taste. The consortium is a better solution, or it would be if it worked. But people are still getting taken, and clearly prevention isn't effective. It really is necessary to go after these people, find out who they are, and then either get them jailed or, not to put too fine a point on it, eliminated. That's a terrible admission for a cop of my caliber, wouldn't you say?"

"Not really. Not if you can do it. You also said something was screwy about Kleiner's little group, his consortium. What do you mean?"

Philip looked down out of the window, gathering his thoughts. Seeing him like that, with his face in profile, Simon realized for the first time how tired Philip looked. There were heavy pouches under his eyes now, and deep, new lines around his mouth, lines that had not been there two years ago. It was clear that Philip had been under a lot of strain for a long time. The effect was beginning to show.

"It's different things, really," said Philip at last. "A general feeling—nothing more. The kidnappers have it just a trifle too pat. I've set up good security arrangements for all the members, but they still jerk us around. This is the fourth kidnapping among this one small group of people in the last ten months. I'll willingly accept that once is just happenstance and twice, or even thrice, it could be coincidental, but the fourth time it simply has to be an inside job. I was a policeman far too long not to know a setup when I meet one. The snag is that

I'm not experienced in kidnap crimes. They're not very common in Britain: We had one or two in Northern Ireland, but that was about it. Another problem is that I don't speak Italian. Even though ninety percent of the people I work with speak very adequate English, I miss a lot of the subtleties. On the other hand, routine police work will solve this business in the end, and, thank God, I know all about that. It's also an advantage to have a free hand. I can work on this case full time, and from the inside. Last but not least, I have good contacts. Through Aldo, the police are now quietly screening all the consortium employees. So far they've come up with nothing. Even so, we can trust nobody, and by we, I mean only Kleiner, Aldo, and myself—and Lucia and Fiori, of course.

Philip's voice dropped lower as he continued. "You see our problem? Meanwhile, if you are to protect me we have to protect you, so when we land at Milan you stay on the plane. Only a few people know you're coming, and that few is already far too many. After I've left the airfield Lucia will collect you and tuck you away in her apartment, but I don't know how we'll handle things after that. We'll just have to play it by ear after they call . . . if they call. You're used to playing it by ear, and you may have to. Have you any ideas?"

Simon shook his head. "As Sherlock Holmes was prone to remark, 'You know my methods, Watson.' We'll just go along with what they want, see what happens, and hope we can come home with the girl. The ball's in their court. Now why don't you try and get some sleep? If it all goes as you expect, we'll be in for a few sleepless nights."

Slumped sideways in his seat, Philip slept as the jet cruised on, across the Mediterranean and the Pyrenees to the golden-red coastline of southern France. They flew on, across the wide blue slash of the river Rhône, and over the high, snow-tipped peaks of the Alps, rose-red in the early evening sunshine. He woke as the little jet tilted up suddenly onto one wing and began a rapid descent onto a club airfield outside Milan, landing with a great thud and rumbling down the concrete runway between parked ranks of small aircraft. Simon stayed belted in his seat while Philip reached about to gather up his bags, and said nothing until the aircraft had swung round in front of the hangars and lurched to a halt.

"Oh my God, there's Fiori!" said Philip suddenly, leaning forward to peer out of the window.

"Where?"

"Over there . . . that's his car, the big black one. Giving me a lift into town is just an excuse to get his hands on the money and have a close look at you. He really is the most . . . Well, never mind. You stay here and sit tight."

The pilot came into the cabin to open the door, but stepped back quickly as Signor Fiori came heavily up the steps and into the cabin, stopping inside the door to look around.

"You are late," he said to Philip. "I have been waiting for almost an hour."

"I had no idea you were picking me up," said Philip mildly. "But since you are here, I'm sure you will want to meet Simon Quarry . . . Simon . . . Luigi Fiori."

"How do you do," said Simon.

Fiori said nothing, acknowledging Simon's greeting with the briefest nod. He looked hot and uncomfortable, a big man, long since run to fat, his belly sagging over his belt, half-shaven jowls resting on a limp collar. Fiori was in his mid-fifties, a few years younger than Philip, but he looked much older. He also looked worried.

"Have you got the money?" he asked Philip.

"You're standing by it. It's in that suitcase."

Fiori bent down and lifted the case by the handle. "Ah . . . heavy," he said. "I'll take this."

"As you please," said Philip.

With the ransom money actually in his hands, Fiori relaxed a little and turned his heavy, pouched eyes toward Simon. "So . . . you are the friend, eh? You are going to help Signor Wintle?

"If I can," replied Simon.

"We don't want any trouble. We got enough trouble." Fiori's voice had sunk to a growl.

"So I hear," said Simon. "I'm not looking for trouble."

Fiori let his eyes flick about the cabin, then stood aside to let the pilot out. "All right," he said, turning to Philip. "So we go now, and your friend stays here—right?"

"After you," said Philip.

"Ciao," said Fiori sullenly, lifting his hand briefly to Quarry before turning back down the aircraft steps to the ground, the heavy suitcase dragging at his arm. Philip lifted his eyebrows briefly at Simon, then followed Fiori down the steps. Simon peered carefully out of the small window and watched them walk toward the long black limousine waiting by the hangar, grinning to himself as he saw Fiori resist an offer of help from the chauffeur, pushing him roughly away. Without a backward glance, the two men followed the driver back to the car, where Fiori slung the suitcase onto the backseat and climbed in after it, ushering Philip into the seat beside the chauffeur. Simon could barely hear the engine as the big car slid away. Once they had gone he sat back in his seat and settled down to wait. For the moment there was nothing else to do.

FIVE

Half an hour later a white ambulance came round the corner of the hangar. It braked for a moment, losing speed on the concrete apron, then sped over toward the little jet and swung round to come to a stop by the door. Puzzled, Simon slid even lower in his seat, unable to see the driver behind the opaque side windows of the cab. After a few seconds the rear doors opened and a tall, dark girl wearing a white medical coat got out, looked briefly about her, and then came hurrying across the concrete toward the jet, running up the steps to poke her head into the cabin, resting her hands lightly on either side of the door.

"Simon Quarry?" she called softly, looking about her in the gloom. "Mr. Quarry? Are you there?

"I'm over here," said Simon, getting stiffly out of his seat and moving down the aisle toward her. "You must be Signorina Fiori—Lucia?"

Lucia looked at him for a moment, her face hidden in the gathering evening shadows inside the cabin. Then she came on up the steps into the cabin, holding out her hand.

"*Buona sera,* Mr. Quarry, and welcome to Milan." Her voice was a surprise, even after everything Philip Wintle had told him. It was a clear, well-educated English voice, without a trace of any accent except that of the educated southern English. She had a nice firm handshake. Simon held on to her hand for a moment in his surprise. He had been told that Lucia was intelligent, capable and reliable. Philip had not mentioned she was beautiful.

"Well, if you're ready, I think we should go," she said, breaking the short silence and taking her hand out of his. "If you would bring your things and come with me, I'll take you to my flat. You will wait there until we know what to do."

She was giving him instructions. They stood looking at each other for a second, then she nodded and turned to go, running lightly down the steps onto the ground, turning there to wait for him. Simon picked up his suitcase and pulled the long gun case from under his seat, then followed her down the springy aircraft steps. Out in the open, walking together, she did not seem so tall; the top of her head came to just a little above his shoulder. He tried to lengthen his stride a little in order to edge ahead and glance back, but she kept pace, her dark, glossy hair swinging, the ends just brushing the stiffly starched collar of her coat. He got a glimpse of tanned olive skin, a flash of green eyes, a curve of lip, then he stopped as she moved ahead of him up into the ambulance, her coat tightening across her hips, then turned to let him pass. He tried not to brush against her, putting his guns and the bag on one of the stretchers. Before he could offer her a hand she had swung the rear doors shut and sat down, rapping her knuckles on the side of the ambulance as a signal to the driver. As the vehicle moved smoothly away, Simon Quarry sat down opposite her and treated himself to a searching stare. There was no doubt about it; Dottoressa Lucia Fiori was a dish.

"This was a very good idea," he said, glancing around. "How on earth did you manage to get a hold of an ambulance.?"

"I'm a doctor," she said. "I spend most of my time at a children's clinic, but I also have a post at the Ospedale Cà Grande. I just ordered one and signed it out. Offically, we're picking up a patient of mine at the airport. That could be you. The driver doesn't know anything and doesn't care. Just be sure to speak English while we're within earshot.

"That won't be hard," said Simon, smiling. "I don't speak a word of Italian. What's an ambulance in Italian?"

"Ambulanza," she said briefly.

She fell silent, her eyes studying him closely, moving over him, taking him in, stopping for a moment at the sight of his injured hand, switching across to the gun case, then back to settle on his face. Simon didn't mind. It gave him a chance to look back at her. She had green eyes, a clear, light green, startling in her lightly tanned face. Simon could not recall meeting a woman with green eyes before.

"Your English is excellent," he said at last, for the sake of something to say. "I'm a bit worried about my lack of Italian." She said nothing, but continued to look at him. "And another thing," he continued. "Don't worry about tonight, or about your sister. Philip Wintle knows what he's doing."

"I don't worry," she said simply. "It does no good to worry." She got up suddenly and walked forward, swaying as the vehicle rocked, to look over the top of the compartment into the cab and to speak a few words in swift, liquid Italian to the driver. Simon edged along on the stretcher until his shoulder was against the partition, then rose to stand by her side, peering through the front window.

"I've never been to Milan before. Is your flat far from the airfield?"

"I live on the northern side of the city, just off the road leading to Como. My father's home is out there and so is the new Ospedale Generale. We should be there in about half an hour, but we've hit the evening traffic. The traffic in Milan is terrible: Everywhere in the city is as bad as Hyde Park Corner in the rush hour . . . you see?"

They were driving down a wide, congested, two-lane avenue, between tall office buildings and department stores. On either side of the central barrier several lines of traffic were stopping and starting, while crowds of people were rushing along the pavements or dodging across the road between the cars. It looked very close to chaos.

"This is the commercial center of the city," explained Lucia. "Milan is not a pretty place, not a capital city like Paris or London, but, on the other hand, it isn't dull. There's the cathedral—terrible, isn't it?—so ornate, like a wedding cake. And there's La Scala, the opera house. Do you like opera?"

"Not a lot," confessed Simon frankly. "Well, not at all, really. I can't understand a word and I'm not very musical."

"Neither am I," said Lucia. She let go of the partition and slid down onto the stretcher opposite him, lighting a cigarette with a gold lighter and resuming her study of his face. Half an hour later, breaking free of the evening traffic, they arrived at her apartment block and, under Lucia's guidance, the driver went round to the rear of the building, driving through the gardens and down a ramp to the underground garage. They got out and stood together in the gloom until the driver had reversed the ambulance back up the ramp and driven away.

"We can go up now," Lucia said, walking toward the elevator. "My flat is on the seventh floor, Philip says it is very important that no one sees us together or knows that you are here."

Nothing more was said until they arrived on the top floor. Then Lucia led the way out of the elevator and across the carpeted hall, putting on a ceiling light and fumbling in her purse for her keys.

"Do you have the entire floor?" asked Simon, waiting at her elbow.

"No. Only half of it. There are two apartments on every floor, but it's all right. The occupant of the other one is away at the moment on holiday. There!" The key turned and she pushed the door open wide, stepping aside to let Simon into the room before her.

"After you," he said, holding back.

"Please . . ." she gestured him inside.

"You know the way and can show me where to go," he pointed out quietly. "It's easier; I'm not just being polite."

She looked at him for a moment, then went ahead of him into the room. "You can put your bags in the guest room, over there," she said. "Now, would you like some coffee or a cup of tea?" There was something in her voice that caught his attention. He stood there in the doorway for a moment, the bags swinging in his hands, looking at her, then smiled slightly and took a slow look around.

It was an airy, spacious room, wide, with a high ceiling. A large floor-to-ceiling picture window led out onto the balcony, giving a view toward the distant mountains, rising now above the evening haze. The main colors in the room were soft yellows and browns, colors Simon liked and used himself. One wall was completely covered with paintings and prints, while another was lined with well-filled bookshelves. Flowers stood in Tuscan pots along the window ledges, a framed photograph or two stood on a side table. The effect was feminine but not fussy, comfortable; a room to live in. Simon put his head to one side to look briefly along her book shelves, noting the English titles, then turned back toward her.

"What would you say if I asked you for a very large vodka and tonic, and said you could leave the bottle?"

Lucia flushed. "I should give you a small vodka and lots of tonic," she said, "and remind you that in a few hours you might be busy."

Simon nodded. "Don't believe everything you hear about me," he said. "I've already promised I won't touch a drop until all this is over, so don't worry. I'm not really a drunk. I suppose Philip phoned you from the airport?"

Lucia sighed heavily. "That's right," she said. "I'm sorry . . . but don't blame Philip . . . he worries about you, that's all."

"He needn't—and coffee will be fine," said Simon, dumping his bags on the carpet. "Do you have a newspaper I could use?"

"A newspaper?" Her voice rose a little in surprise. "Yes, I

suppose so. What do you want a newspaper for?"

"I have some weapons in there," said Simon, pointing to the gun case. "I need to clean and reload them, and they're a bit oily. I don't want to make a mess of your table, but I can do it in the kitchen, or anywhere you like."

"I see." For the first time Lucia's voice sounded a little uncertain. "I'll see what I can find." She drifted away to the kitchen and returned presently carrying a tray with a pot of coffee and with a copy of the *Corriere della Sera* held under her arm. She put the tray on a low table, stripped off her white hospital coat and sat down in the center of the sofa, handing him the paper and a cup of coffee. Her eyes were still watching him thoughtfully as he put the paper down on a small table beside him and gazed around the room, the coffee cup in one hand.

"I hope you'll forgive my looking around like this," he said, settling into an armchair opposite her, "but it's always interesting to see how someone else lives. I like the room, very much. I see you have a couple of those Francis Kyle posters. I have that one there, the one with the green shoes. I have it in my bedroom in Mallorca."

"Are you Simon Quarry the publisher, the one who owns the Quarry Press in London?" she asked him abruptly.

Simon hesitated, surprised. "I used to be," he said at last. "I mean, I did own it; I gave up most of my shares a couple of years go, before I moved to Spain."

"But what are you doing here?" she asked. "Philip said he had a friend who kills people . . . but . . . I don't understand. He told me your name, but I didn't make the connection with the publisher. How did you start killing people?"

"It was an accident," said Simon, his eyes frosty. "They started it by killing some people I was fond of."

Her eyes had still not moved from his face. "I remember now," she said slowly. "Your wife and children were killed in that terrorist attack at Athens, three, no, four years ago. Your picture was often in the newspapers. Ever since I saw you on the plane I've been wondering where I had seen you before. I remembered while you were looking at my books."

"You must have a good memory," said Simon bitterly. "Most people forgot all about that the day after it happened."

"Not all of us," she said. "I was doing some postgraduate work at the Marsden and one of our finest consultants was on the plane. He'd been to a congress in Jerusalem and we talked about it a lot. I have some Quarry Press books on the shelf over there."

"I noticed," said Simon, smiling. "Our spine colophon is quite distinctive—it stands out even from here."

"You wrote letters to the papers when they let the captured terrorists go free, didn't you? You wanted them tried and imprisoned . . . it's coming back to me now."

"Yes, I did," said Simon simply, "but it didn't do me any good."

"What happened?"

"About the letters? Nothing." Simon shrugged and leaned forward to avoid her gaze, putting his cup back on the table. "I got fobbed off . . . ignored."

"About the terrorists." Her gaze was even more intense, her eyes studying his expression closely. Simon noticed the green of her eyes again, that beautiful, clear green.

"They got what they were asking for—eventually. That little bunch won't trouble anyone else—but what's the use, there are plenty more where they came from."

"So you found them? Is that what Philip meant? You killed them?"

Simon closed his eyes briefly, then opened them to look back at her. "Yes, that's right," he said heavily. "I found them, and I killed them."

"Is that how you met Philip Wintle?" she asked curiously. "When he was with Scotland Yard?"

Simon smiled, his face relaxing. "Yes, that's when we met; the only good thing that came out of it. He was head of Special Branch and after I shot up the Jihad office his job was to hunt me down. It didn't take him long—he's very good at his job. Anyway, we met, and one thing led to another, and here we are. Now it's my turn to do him a favor. Maybe you can tell me what happens now."

Lucia sat back, crossing her ankles. Without her white coat she looked slimmer, less official. Her long, square-tipped fingers were linked together, resting gently in her lap, her shoulders relaxed.

"Philip told you about the other night? Now that the money is here we think they'll call and tell us how and where to hand it over. I'll drive over to my father's house in an hour or so and take the call—it always comes at eight, on the dot. On our way to the handover we'll come by here and pick you up. That's not much to go on, I'm afraid, but it's all I can tell you at the moment." She looked across at him anxiously. "Is it enough?"

"If it's all we have, it'll have to do. With any luck," he continued, looking at his watch, "by this time tomorrow it will all be over. The waiting is always the worst part. Once you start to move it's not so bad." His voice was thoughtful, brooding.

Lucia leaned forward toward him across the table, their heads coming close together as she reached over to refill his coffee cup. When Simon lifted his eyes a little he could see the outline of her breasts under the scooped-out neckline of her blouse, and he had to try quite hard not to stare. Her clothes were good and stylish, but still practical and neat, a green blouse to reflect her eyes, and a soft brown skirt to set it off. Simon felt the pistol digging hard into his side, thought about it, then took it out and placed it on the table beside his cup. She looked at it for a moment, the coffeepot still in her hand, then refilled her own cup before putting it back on the table.

"You are not at all what I expected," she said, her eyes moving back to his face after another glance at the pistol. "Philip told me your name, and what you did, but I didn't connect it with that other Simon Quarry, not until I saw you." Lucia nodded toward the gun, glinting dully on the table between them. "Do you always carry that?"

"Usually."

"Is this what you do?" she asked. "Kill people?" She seemed to like short phrases.

"No," said Simon firmly. "I can shoot and Philip needs protection. Who says I go about killing people?"

"Philip says so. He said he was going to Mallorca to get a friend who could kill people and who was good at it. It sounded as if you were a little crazy."

Simon looked at her steadily for a moment, saying nothing. Then he moved the coffee cups aside and spread the newspaper out on the table. He leaned out of his chair and picked up the gun case, laying it across his lap and unzipping it; he took out the rifle and the shotgun and laid them out beside the pistol before opening a pocket on the gun case and taking out some rags, a small oil can, and a stiffly coiled ramrod. This done, he looked back at her.

"I want you to understand what I'm about," he said. "Some people in the world need killing. It's a pity, but there just isn't any other way to deal with them. What can you *do* with people like those terrorists who murdered a planeload of people and went scot-free to do it again? They have to be stopped. No one is prepared to face the fact that they can only be stopped with a bullet. They murdered my family, they asked for all they got, and I don't feel remotely guilty about it. If that's wrong, I'm sorry." He gestured toward the weapons spread between them on the table. "Forget what these actually are for the moment," he said. "Regard them just as tools. Give them different names." He pointed to the rifle, the pistol, the shotgun. "Scalpel, forceps, bone saw."

She shook her head. "It's not the same," she said. "That's not a fair analogy."

"It is exactly the same," said Simon, "and I don't think fairness enters into it. To misquote Shakespeare, 'There is a sickness in the body politic and I intend to root it out.' " He tapped the pistol. "With this, if need be."

"I can see that," she said. "But are you here because you owe Philip Wintle a favor or because you like shooting people?"

Simon ran his fingers through his hair and looked at her carefully. "Lucia, the reason I'm here is because Philip asked me for help, and besides . . . Have you ever read Montaigne, Michel de Montaigne, the essayist?"

"Montaigne? The French writer? No."

"Well, he had a great friend, a man called La Boétie. When La Boétie died, Montaigne was quite desolate—in fact he never got over it. He grieved over La Boétie for the rest of his life, and when someone asked him why, Montaigne said simply, 'Because it was him, because it was I.' And that's the way it is with me and Philip. I liked him from the moment we met and I'd do anything in the world for him—even this."

"I can understand that," she said, looking at him directly. "I can even envy people who have a friendship like that."

"But frankly, there's another reason," Simon added suddenly. "I didn't find it until I was on my way here, but maybe it's more important than anything else."

"What is it?" she asked.

"Philip was telling me about the kidnappers, about their methods. They make me sick. They take your children, they take your money, and they don't even let you go to the police. You have to sit here and take it, or they beat and kill your people. I . . ." his voice thickened. "I have an inbuilt dislike for people like that. Who the hell do they think they are?"

"They are people who do what they want," said Lucia sadly.

"Are they?" said Simon. "We'll just have to see about that."

The young man pulled the stocking mask down over his face. Then, taking the key from the hook on the barn wall, he began to unlock the door, pausing for a second, smiling, as he heard the swift, nervous rattle of the chain inside.

"Ciao, cara," he said, pushing the door wide and letting the light stream in. *"Va bene?"*

The room had been a pigsty before they had made it a prison. There was hardly room for the narrow bed with its thin flock mattress, the can of water, the stinking bucket. He liked that. It meant that even without the chain linking her to the bedrail she had nowhere to run. The chain rattled again frantically as he moved in, crawling after her across the mattress, locking his fingers into her hair, kneeling on her, one knee on her stomach, panting, clawing at her dress, one hand holding her thin wrists, twisting, hurting, the other loosening his shirt and belt.

"Easy, *cara* . . . gently," he said. "I have good news. The old bastard has the money, so soon you go home. Don't miss me too much, eh? So . . . one kiss . . . maybe, a little present for me?"

One hand came free, the unbandaged one. She clawed at him, laddering the stocking mask, raking her dirty, ragged fingernails down his neck and across his chest. He jerked back and slapped her hard. Then he folded his fists and beat her, on and on, long after she had ceased to scream.

At the airport, Antonio Puccio had felt the money, had hefted the weight of the notes; he had come that close to it. He flexed his fingers, smiling to himself, remembering how the old bastard had snatched the case away and pushed him back, not daring to do more with the Englishman there. Antonio grinned at that. Then, catching his reflection in the polished hood of the limousine, he paused to turn his head and admire his profile, smoothing the hair away from his forehead.

Hey, you're a good-looking boy, you know that? he said to himself, *and with money the girls will eat you up.* They did now, but with looks and money too? Antonio tossed the polishing cloth onto the roof of the car, opened the rear door, and climbed inside, sitting squarely on the backseat, smelling the rich scent of the leather upholstery, running his eyes over the fittings, the cocktail cabinet, looking out through the windshield, contemplating his future.

Money! Not just wages, a pay packet, just enough money to get by on with enough over for a few drinks on a Saturday night, but *real* money, thousands millions of lire, to spend or save; *his* money, and money taken from the old bastard, which was even better. When he had his share, he would spread it on a bed, note by note, inches thick, then get a girl, strip her naked and lay her on the top . . . that was a dream. Antonio wondered what Signorina Lucia would look like, naked on top of the money. If he had money she would look at him, not just at men like Signor Kleiner. Kleiner could have all the women he wanted with that jet, the big cars, that suite he kept at the Principe . . . just because he had money, women wanted him. Well, soon, maybe tonight, Antonio would have money—and more than the rest of them, right? After all, he, Antonio, was taking the biggest risk, staying here in the old bastard's house, watching points, reporting back, tipping them off to the Englishman's moves. The other night, when he slipped the box onto the step, he had seen death in the old bastard's eyes, and he still saw it, every time he looked up and caught those eyes in the car mirror. The old bastard had deadly eyes. The others had the girl, but if anything went wrong, or if the old bastard snapped . . . Antonio suddenly found that his palms were wet. Looking down, he saw damp patches on the upholstery of the seat, where his hands had rested, and wiped them hurriedly on his pants leg. It was better not to think about things going wrong; it was better to think about the money. He shook his head and looked up, into the eyes of Fredo Donati. Like the old bastard, Fredo had reptile eyes, black as night. He was using them on Antonio now, standing by the open door, so slight a figure that he had no need to bend his head to look inside, neat and dark in that immaculate suit, raking Antonio with those eyes.

"What are you doing in there?" he asked softly.

"Thinking," said Antonio. "Just thinking. It's nice in here, eh?" Antonio patted the seat. "I was thinking that when I am rich I will ride in the back of a car, like this, with a beautiful woman beside me. How about that, Fredo? Will you ever do that?"

Donati's expression didn't change. "Right now you are paid to drive it, not sit in it. How much gas have you got?"

"Plenty."

"I asked you how much."

Antonio raised his eyebrows thoughtfully, then shrugged. "I don't know, she drinks gas . . . maybe half a tank."

Donati took a fat wad from his pocket and peeled off some notes. "Fill it up," he said shortly. "Check the oil and tires . . . check everything. Then come back here. No joyriding for you today, you get that? I want you here, where I can keep my eye on you, inside half an hour."

Antonio grinned, boldly leaning across to take the money. "I won't be long," he said, climbing out of the back and stepping over to the driver's door. "I wouldn't miss being here for worlds."

Halfway down the drive he looked back in the mirror. Fredo Donati was still standing there, looking after him, a black figure in a shaft of sunlight. Turning the wheel to go through the gate, Antonio found that his palms were sweating again.

SIX

The kidnappers did not ring that night. Wintle and the others gathered round the desk in Fiori's study as they had gathered just before eight o'clock every night for the last six weeks, and waited, silent, their eyes on the clock as the hands clicked past the hour. At five past eight, Wintle pushed his chair back from the desk and stood up.

"They're not going to ring," he said. "They're going to make us sweat again. Maybe they're going to try and screw us for a bit more money."

"This is the amount they wanted," Kleiner pointed out. "This is the deadline they set for us to collect it. I can't think why they haven't called, if only to make sure that we have it."

The others said nothing, their eyes on Wintle's thoughtful face.

"Well," Wintle said at last, "there could be two explanations for that. The first is that they already know we have the money, so why risk a phone call?"

"How could they know that?" asked Fiori.

"Why not?" said Lucia "They know everything else."

Everyone thought that over for a moment or two, each avoiding the others' eyes.

"This is just speculation," said Kleiner at last, getting to his feet. "Nothing has changed. We have the money, they still have Gina. We are in their hands and we can do nothing until they make contact. One thing we can be sure of—they want that money. Shall we meet here at the same time tomorrow?"

As the group broke up, Philip led Lucia over to the corner, turned her so that their backs were to the room, and spoke softly.

"How is Simon?" he asked.

"He's fine. He's rather nice, very helpful. In fact, he's cooking dinner."

"He's what! You're joking . . . surely."

"Not at all. He's not what I expected."

"Really? And what did you expect?"

"I don't know; someone like James Bond, or a great big thug with muscles. You should have told me who he was, and about his family."

Philip shook his head. "I don't see how I could. That's Simon's business. Are you working tonight?"

"No, I took the evening off because I thought they would telephone. I'll go in tomorrow though. I still have patients to look after."

"You are not on duty?" Fiori had arrived at her elbow.

"No, I was telling Philip . . . not tonight."

"How is your guest?" asked Fiori. "Behaving himself?"

Lucia hesitated. "I think he knows how to behave." She turned her head toward Philip. "I ought to go in to work tomorrow, but maybe you and Simon could have dinner sometime? I don't think he likes being cooped up too much."

"I might do that." Philip nodded.

When Philip and Lucia left the room, hard on Kleiner's heels, Fiori was already deep in conversation with Fredo.

"Nothing?" asked Simon from the kitchen door.

"Nothing," said Lucia. She stood in the center of the room, stripping off her raincoat and placing it neatly over the back of a chair. "We waited but they didn't ring. Not even to see if we had the money . . . the bastards!"

Simon was watching her carefully, wiping his hands on a dishcloth, tossing it aside as he came out into the room, and walked past her toward the tray of drinks by the bookcases.

"You ought to relax," he said, "or at least try to. This could go on for days."

"Christ!" said Lucia explosively. "I don't need to relax. I just want to get on with it."

"I know," said Simon, "but the ball's in their court. Relaxing, staying calm are all part of the game. Do you want a drink . . . and why don't you sit down?"

"Don't tell me what to do in my own home," snapped Lucia, "and I'm not a child you have to humor."

"I'm giving you advice, that's all," said Simon. "Do you want that drink?"

"Yes, of course. A large gin. What about you?"

"I found some Perrier in the fridge. That'll do me."

Lucia sat down suddenly on the sofa, reaching across for the table lighter. Then she sat back, lighting a cigarette, blowing a long cloud of smoke into the air as Simon came back from the kitchen to hand her the glass, ice clinking lightly as it passed from hand to hand.

"You are a strange man," she said, smiling. "You cook me dinner, you fetch me drinks. You've already made yourself quite at home here. I feel that you've been here for years . . . it's funny."

"I've also watered your plants," said Simon. "I hope you don't mind. I don't mean to be pushy, but they were wilting more than a little."

Lucia let her eyes rest on him for a moment, then shook her

head, smiling again suddenly. "I don't mind," she said. "I rather like it—and whatever you're cooking out there smells good."

"A poor thing, but mine own, madame," said Simon lightly. "Besides, a girl has to eat."

"This could be a new career for you," said Lucia. "Cooking must be a better pastime than shooting people."

"It probably pays better," agreed Simon, "but the hours are terrible. How do you feel now . . . a little, well, calmer?"

"I feel better," admitted Lucia. "And I'm sorry I snapped at you. I'll try to relax, promise."

"You should," said Simon. "It will be better for you. And now, shall we eat?"

Lucia stubbed out her cigarette and stood up, looking closely again at Simon. "You're quite nice really, aren't you?" she said at last. "Quite kind. Do you think they'll ring tomorrow?"

Simon's shoulders lifted slightly. "I think they'll ring when they're ready," he said at last. "Not before."

They didn't ring the next night, or the one after that. Each evening Simon helped Lucia into her coat and stood in the window to watch her drive away, sitting on the sofa to wait out the time until she returned, waiting for the call that would tell him to get ready.

Each evening the little group gathered round the desk in Fiori's study, falling silent as the hands of the clock in the corner ticked slowly up to the hour, groaning out loud as the hands ticked past it. By the third evening nerves were beginning to shred.

"Maybe she's dead," said Lucia suddenly, jumping up from her chair. "Maybe that's why they don't ring us. Maybe they have nothing to exchange. Why else are they making us wait like this? I think she's dead."

"Steady," said Philip. "We don't know that . . . and they won't hurt her, kill her. They want the money."

"You are very sure of everything," said Fiori sourly, "but you still know nothing. You, who are supposed to be the expert, you know damn all about these people."

"Come now," said Kleiner quietly, "let us not quarrel among

ourselves. We have to stay calm and wait. They will phone when they are ready. We should know that by now."

"That's what Simon said," put in Lucia. She was tapping a cigarette hard on the desktop, lighting it with trembling fingers. "But he's used to the waiting."

"How is he?" asked Philip, anxious to change the subject. "He sounded all right when I spoke to him on the phone."

"He *is* all right," said Lucia. "A bit bored. You should take him out for dinner. I . . . I think I must go to work . . . for something to do. This waiting is getting too much for me. I can't go on like this much longer."

"Then why don't you go to work?" said Philip. "It will take your mind off things. Or you could get Simon and we could all have dinner together, maybe in that little place we went to the other week?"

Lucia shook her head, reaching for her coat. "No, you two go on your own. I'm not good company. I'll go and get him now and explain—whatever there is to explain—and drop him off. Can you bring him back afterward in your car?"

"That's fine. Give me half an hour to tidy up here, OK?"

"Half an hour," said Lucia. "Until the same time tomorrow, then."

"Until tomorrow," said Wintle. "And let's hope something happens soon." Wintle glanced around at the others, chatting together softly round the desk, nodding as Fiori rose from his chair and went across the room to talk to Fredo.

Hidden in a doorway across the road, Ettore waited until Simon entered the restaurant, until the rear lights of Signorina Lucia's car had vanished into the night, before he approached the car. Those were his orders, direct from the *capo*. The two Englishmen were to be together and there must be no risk to the signorina. In the old days, when Ettore had made bombs for the *Autonomia,* bombs they would plant in factory parking lots, they had not been so fussy, for one dead capitalist was as good as any other but, still, orders were orders. The Press gave you even more space if you gave them lots of innocent blood.

There was no one about. It was raining and, like cats, the

Italians dislike getting wet. When the rain falls on the city, that thin, dirty city rain, smearing the sidewalks with slime, the streets of Milan empty, or people huddle in doorways, moving along only if they have to, slipping from shelter to shelter, shoulders hunched beneath umbrellas. Tonight even at this early hour, Ettore had the street to himself.

First, he circled the car, trying all the doors. You never knew, people could be careless, but no, they were all locked. That delayed him for only a second. He produced a screwdriver, forced it into the driver's door lock with several hard slaps from his hand, then wrenched it round to spring the catch. The door clicked open and he was inside, reaching for the hood catch.

Once out in the rain again, he eased up the hood and latched it before feeling around for the wires. It was dark under there, but Ettore had done this before and at least the hood sheltered the electrical connections from the rain. He found the spot he wanted, hard against the driver's partition, where the transmission cable ran out from the engine block. After one more swift look around, one fleeting glance at the lighted windows of the restaurant across the road, he took the explosive from his raincoat pocket and began to ram it into the space, packing it in tight, molding the plastic into position. It worked more easily as it warmed up under his hands—but then came the tricky bit.

That detonater was simple enough, a small cylinder with a battery attached to wires running between the tremblers. That went in easily, deep into the plastic, and he molded it firmly into place. Then Ettore licked his lips and, wiping his hands on the inside of his pockets, took out the small screwdriver. Teeth set gently over his lower lip, working by touch alone, a turn here, a turn there, he began to unscrew the tremblers, letting them rise up gently, evenly—above all, evenly—until they rested firmly against the engine block. When that was finally done, sweat was sticking his shirt to his back. He stayed there, half under the hood, as a couple passed by, the woman's heels clicking loudly on the pavement. Then he stood up, wiped his sweating hands, and, releasing the catch, eased the hood down slowly and gently. There, it was done. The old Englishman would climb in, start the engine, and as it fired the first tremor would tilt the trembler, close the circuit, and *pouf*! Maybe even slamming the door shut would do it. Ettore would have liked to wait and watch, but it was raining; so instead he would go and find a little bar, somewhere close. Even on a night like this a kilo of plastic going off would make quite a bang. That would be something.

Philip was studying the menu, a glass of wine at his elbow, when Simon slipped into the opposite side of the booth.

"Buona sera," he said. "Do you want a glass of wine?"

Simon shook his head. *"Buona sera* to you, but I'll have a glass of mineral water. San Pellegrino, *per favore*."

"The Italian is coming on apace, I see." said Philip. "And what is all this about cooking dinner? Things like that can play havoc with your image."

"Simon grinned. "Well, I don't pay rent, so a few chores can justify my bed and board. Besides, it was needed—some food and wine, a little conversation—that girl is wound up as tight as a watch spring. If something doesn't happen soon she'll go off in a thousand pieces."

"I know. It's amazing it hasn't happened before now. Has she gone to work?"

"Yes. She dropped me off on the corner."

"I'll run you back later. My car is just across the street."

At half past nine, midweek, the restaurant was half empty. Just a few people were dotted about the room, a family at the far end, several couples in the booths along one wall, one or two solitary diners at the tables in the center. Simon sniffed the atmosphere, heavy with sauces and cheese, and realized that he was hungry. They ordered, chatting about this and that until their minestrone arrived, and then got down to business.

"So, once again they didn't call?" Simon began. "They're being very cagy."

"They certainly are," replied Philip, "and it's beginning to worry me."

"It shouldn't," said Simon. "Handing over the money is the

trickiest part of the whole deal. You said so yourself."

"It is," agreed Philip. "The kidnappers usually hold on to the victim until they have the cash, partly to check that the cash is all right, partly to stop any hanky-panky from the police. In this case I insisted, right from the word go, that no girl meant no money. We swap cash for Gina at the same time. It's not a good idea to let them have it all their own way."

"I quite agree," said Simon, "but it complicates matters from their point of view. I would bet that right now—even tonight—they are checking out the arrangements for the handover."

"I think they would have had that all worked out weeks ago," said Philip.

"Maybe, but even so they'll check it again. Murphy's Law operates even for the bad guys. It would be a shame if the city council chose today to dig up their getaway route, or the locals spend this week having a *festa* or their car finally blows a gasket. They have to check it and check it again. They can't take any chances. They'll ring when they're ready, so relax."

"You're probably right" said Philip. "And how are you getting on with Lucia?"

"You didn't tell me she was beautiful. She's also charming, intelligent . . . I'm overwhelmed."

"I'm glad to see she has made no impression on you at all," said Philip, smiling. "I always thought that beneath your flinty exterior there beat a heart of stone."

"How true. No, she's very nice. I like her. We've become very domesticated. I cook, she eats, I clear away, she washes up. She likes four-minute eggs."

"Really?"

"Really. She prefers cold white wine to red, and Barolo to Chianti."

"Wise girl."

"I agree. She is teaching me Italian and in between times we play records. It all helps pass the time."

"Good. Stay with her. One other reason I'm glad you're here, and staying at Lucia's, is to keep an eye on her. I've already lost one of Fiori's daughters; I don't want to lose another one."

"You won't lose this one," said Simon. "That I promise. and now . . . here comes my *costoletta*."

The street was empty when they came out of the restaurant a little after eleven, just the occasional car swishing past pavements empty of people.

"I can get a taxi," suggested Simon.

"No, my car's over there. I'll drop you off."

When they reached the car, Simon went round to the passenger door and waited while Philip fumbled with his keys at the driver's side.

"Oh, blast! Not again!" exclaimed Philip suddenly.

"What is it?" asked Simon, looking across at him over the car roof.

"The car's been broken into. That's the third or fourth time. What a city!"

Simon bent down to peer through the windows, shading his eyes against the reflection from the glass.

"Is anything gone? I don't see any damage. What have they taken?"

"Nothing," said Philip shortly. "There's nothing to take. I'm not daft enough to leave anything in the car in this thieves' kitchen of a city. But the lock's been forced—I can't get the door open."

Simon tried his door and it swung open wide.

"Mine's all right," he said, bending to climb inside, reaching across the seats for the driver's door.

"Get out! Get out now . . . *move*! Don't touch that door."

"What . . .?"

"Get out! Get out!"

Seconds later they were both standing several yards down the road, looking back at Philip's car. Simon could feel Philip's hand trembling slightly as it gripped his arm firmly just above the elbow.

"What on earth is going on?"

"The hood is unlatched," said Philip. "I just noticed it."

"So . . . so what?"

Philip sighed, and let his grip relax. "You weren't heading up the Special Branch when the IRA were putting car bombs around London. Remember Harrods? We had another one, right outside the Yard. The beat bobby noticed the hood was unlatched and when we looked, there were four pounds of jelly under the engine. You get to notice little details after a few events like that."

"So what now?"

"You stay here and don't let anyone touch the car. I'll be back in a minute."

Simon waited while Philip went across the road, back into the restaurant, and reappeared a few minutes later with a large flashlight in his hand, flicking the beam on and off experimentally as he crossed to the car.

"Borrowed from the owner," he said. "Now, if I can stop my hands shaking, I'll take a look under the hood."

It took a long time. Simon watched from a distant doorway as Philip felt gently under the hood for the latch. Then Philip walked round to crouch by the open door, examining the tangle of wires under the dashboard by flashlight. Finally he came back to the front of the car, put the flashlight on the ground, and slowly eased the hood up. When it was latched he picked up the flashlight again and shone the beam inside. He stayed there, dark behind the beam, for several minutes before easing the hood down again and returning to Simon.

"It's a bomb," he said quietly. "A bloody great lump of plastic explosive packed behind the engine block, enough to blow us both to smithereens."

Lucia was sitting curled up on the sofa when Simon let himself into the flat. He looked at her briefly as he walked across the room into the kitchen, returning in a couple of minutes with a cup of coffee. He stood in the center of the room, holding the cup in both hands, sipping from it slowly.

"You're late,' she said. "I've been back for over an hour. I was beginning to worry."

"I'm sorry," he said.

"Are you all right? Has anything happened? How is Philip?"

"He's fine . . . just. Someone put a pound of plastic explosives in his car while we were in the restaurant."

"Good God!" Lucia sat up, startled, swinging her feet onto the floor. "What happened? Tell me."

He told her. ". . . then Philip phoned Cirillo, who sent the Bomb Squad over. They checked the car and removed the device. Apparently it was on a trembler detonator and would have gone off when the engine started or on any hard vibration. That's why they didn't dare slam the hood down. Thank God Philip has sharp eyes . . . but . . ." He hesitated.

"But what?"

"Philip thought—thinks—that the bomb was meant just for him."

"Well, why not? The bomb was in *his* car."

"I know. But if you want to kill just one person, a bomb is a very messy way to do it."

"So . . ." Lucia's voice fell a tone. "What are you trying to say?"

"Nothing, really. Its just that I think the bomb was meant for both of us. But only a few people know I'm here. Interesting, that, isn't it?"

Everyone jumped when the telephone rang. As usual it rang three times, then stopped. Nobody around the desk attempted to pick it up. Lucia and Philip Wintle sat and looked at it, ignoring both Fiori, who had risen from his chair and was pacing about the room at their backs, and Fredo, who sat in his usual chair by the door.

"Well that's them," said Philip heavily. "At last. Four days late, but right on time." Three minutes later it rang again. Philip nodded to Lucia to answer it. "If it's instructions for the exchange, get very precise details. I'll handle the maps."

Lucia reached for the phone, her hand hesitating slightly before she picked up the receiver. Then she tossed her hair aside, slipped off an earring, and began to listen. Philip and Fiori watched her face in the light of the desk lamp, listening intently, the crease of a frown on her forehead the only sign of tension, nodding sometimes, saying nothing, scribbling a note. She hunted among a pile of maps on the desk to find the right one, hurrying Philip to unfold it, tracing a route across it with her finger. The call lasted barely a couple of minutes, and all the men in the room heard the sharp click as the caller hung up. Lucia replaced the receiver slowly before turning to face them, and when she spoke it was to Philip. She ignored Fredo and her father.

"It's on. They want the money tonight. We are to leave here within the next half hour, in the big limousine. I am to drive. You are to bring the money and sit in the front." She pushed the map round so he could see it. "We're to drive along this road here, into the foothills above Como, up here, to this road, and then drive to and fro along it, between here—this village—and here, this point on the mountain. They'll watch for us between ten-thirty and eleven. If they're satisfied that we are alone, then somewhere along this road another car will flash its lights at us three times. We stop at once and wait and the other car will come close and stop. We put our headlights out and theirs will come on. You get out with the money and put it in front of the car, in the open where they can see it. Then they will hand over Gina, take the money and go. We wait fifteen minutes and then we leave. That's all. He even said, '*Arrivederci, signorina*' before he hung up."

"Is that all?" asked her father, staring down at her across his desk. "So simple? Why did you not ask to speak to Gina, just to be sure she is still all right? Why do you let them push us around like this?"

Lucia ignored him. When she spoke it was to Philip. "He said they will watch us in the hills. If they see another car, or even a helicopter, or anything at all, if they see any sign of the police they will simply dump Gina in a ditch with her throat cut. He said it must just be you and me—no tricks, no changes. They . . . he . . . sounded very sure of himself."

"Did he ask if we had the money?" asked Philip. He was

sitting forward in his chair, one hand sprawled across the map, his face half hidden in the darkness above the spill of lamp-light.

"No, no, he just told me where to take it."

"Curious," said Philip, rubbing a forefinger along his upper lip. "It's the first question I would have asked. He must really be sure of himself." Philip's eyes were fixed on the desktop, his face thoughtful.

"Now that we know what they want us to do," suggested Fiori, "why not trick them a little? First, Lucia should not go—you said yourself it might be dangerous. Let Fredo drive. He speaks English and he can translate if necessary. Once you are there and they see the money they won't mind a little change of plan. Anyway, with him and your friend Quarry you can handle anything."

Philip looked directly across the desk at Lucia. "Your father has a point there, Lucia. It might be dangerous and I'd be happier if you were right out of it now. We can put Fredo in a hat or something, so it isn't too obvious. It would be something less for us to worry about."

"I'm going," said Lucia flatly. "That's what they want, and no one—not even you, not even my father—is going to take any more chances with Gina's life. She's already been hurt enough. If they"—she nodded toward the phone in the center of the desk—"try anything against us, we have Simon. That's why you brought him here, isn't it? And if he can't handle it, why is he here?" She got up and began to gather up the maps. "Come on," she said impatiently. "Let's get the money and go. We still have to pick up Simon."

"It seems too easy," said Fiori. "Much too easy."

Philip had listened to Lucia thoughtfully, but he shook his head, glancing up at Fiori. "Simon once remarked that simple plans are best. These people may know that, but anyway they've been quite clever. We arrive up there after dark so they can see by the car lights if we're being followed. No one can drive along that road without lights. They can approach when they feel like it and that might not be till dawn. Once they have the money they simply drive off. Look at the map; it shows a network of little roads and paths up there. Even if we had half the policemen in Italy at our disposal we couldn't cordon off and search this area in a couple of months, let alone in the next few hours. No, it's quite neat."

"So what are you going to do?" asked Fiori. "Let them get away with it?"

"I'm going to do exactly what I'm told," said Philip simply. "The only difference is that Simon will come along. If we do as they say, and *they* do as they say, I'll just hand over the money and bring the girl back. That's the best way. Simon is simply our insurance in case they turn nasty. I'm not looking for trouble. We can go after them, and the money, when we have your daughter back. Until then we play it their way."

Wintle waited until Lucia had turned the big car out of the gates and was accelerating down the road toward the city before he spoke, shifting sideways in the front seat to look across at her.

"It's probably none of my business," he said quietly, "but exactly what is it that you have against your father?"

"It is none of your business," said Lucia, staring ahead, "but since it is you who asks me, I'll tell you. He's a pig. He always has been. A selfish, ignorant pig. Don't tell me you can't see that?"

"Well, he's a businessman. A little aggressive, highly competitive, even a touch crude perhaps," said Philip mildly, "but then he had to make his way in the world without any of your advantages, my dear; money, education, a secure home. A hard life makes men hard. But you shouldn't make your dislike so obvious. It really does you no credit. After all, you are his daughter and he has done all right by you. You've lacked for nothing, had every possible opportunity. At the very least you owe him common politeness."

Lucia laughed softly. "I should have agreed it was none of your business and left it like that," she said. "Philip, I grew up with my father. I know him better than you. I'm not a child—there is twenty years' difference between Gina and me. It's too late to change my mind about him. It's a long story and I don't want to tell it. Now, let me concentrate on the driving."

Philip was content to do so. Lucia was a good driver, forcing the big car hard through traffic, easing down the main highway between the cabs and speeding trucks, then swinging off onto her own quiet road, round to the apartment blocks, then down the ramp into the darkness of the underground garage, reversing the car round to point the hood back toward the entrance. Then she switched off the lights and they listened for a moment to the ticking of the cooling engine.

"Where is he?" asked Philip. "Do we wait for him here?"

"No. He's upstairs. I'll go and get him. Just wait here. I won't be long." Then she was gone, the sudden blaze from the interior light going out again as she slammed the door, her heels clicking on the garage floor as she headed for the elevator.

Antonio Puccio ran for his life. With a little more time, or a little more luck, he might have made it. He waited until the car left, watching from the side of the house as Wintle manhandled the loaded suitcase into the car and the signorina drove off. Then he ran, fast.

He ran full tilt to the back of the house and vaulted into the saddle of his motorcycle. One kick—thank God, it fired—then away across the garden, bumping down the short flight of steps to the orchard, keeping low across the fuel tank, beneath the branches of the trees, turning right at the wall along the path, one foot down, gravel spraying as he turned out through the gates he had carefully opened wide that afternoon, down the bank and over the single plank across the ditch and away down the road, accelerating fast.

He stopped outside a café a mile away, heaved the bike up onto its stand, and walked inside, feeling in his trouser pocket for a few *gettoni*. He was out again two minutes later, kicking the bike into life, then puttering more slowly down the road out into the country, thinking of the big payday, of all the things he could do with his share of the money. He should have paid more attention.

The big car stayed back until he was out in the country, clear of the houses. Then it came up fast from behind and simply ran him off the road. There was a screeching of metal, a line of sparks in the dusk as the footstand raked the surface of the road, the shocking impact as he hit the wall and rolled clear of the cycle. For a brief moment he even thought it was an accident, cursing that it would happen now, of all times. That was before he realized his legs were broken.

Then he saw the men getting out of the car. He screamed then, in sudden pain and fright. He screamed more, later, when he had no more left to tell them and they kept kicking at his broken legs.

SEVEN

As they pulled out of the garage Simon lay flat on the floor of the car, the rifle and shotgun resting across the rear seat beside his head. When they were clear of the side road he eased himself up into the seat, keeping his head below the window level and leaned forward, putting a hand between the front seats to tap Philip on the arm.

"Tell me what's happened, and what we have to do," he said. He listened carefully while Philip told him the details, with Lucia putting in the occasional word, her eyes on the road ahead as she weaved the car through the traffic.

When they had finished Simon was silent for a moment. "Well . . ." he said at last. "That sounds simple enough. Lucia, try cutting up and down a couple of side roads, but nothing too obvious. Make it look as if you are trying to dodge the worst of the traffic, but see if any lights keep coming after us."

There was silence for a few minutes while Lucia swung the car on and off the main road. "No, I don't think we're being followed," she said, her eyes still on the mirror. "At least, there's nothing staying behind us all the time. Most of the traffic is going into Milan at this hour."

"I don't think so either," said Philip. "I don't think they ever intended to follow us, whatever they said on the phone. Why should they? I think they'll wait up in the hills and let us come to them. What else can we do?"

"Where's the money?" asked Simon.

"Down here, under my feet," replied Philip. "In the suitcase it arrived in—all ready to hand over."

"Fine. Now listen carefully. We won't be able to rehearse this," said Simon, still lying across the backseat. "Philip, can you find the inside light and remove the bulb, or make certain the light's switched off?"

"Why?" asked Lucia, glancing over her shoulder.

"Because," said Simon, "I don't want the light coming on when I open the door at the rendezvous and slip out of the car. When they flash their lights at us I'm bailing out and finding a position where I can cover you. I'm no good to anyone stuck here in the car, so when we get there I get out."

Thinking about this. Lucia shifted slightly in her seat. "But what if they tell us to follow them to somewhere else? You are left out of the car and we have no protection."

"God knows," said Simon frankly. "You'll just have to use your initiative. Meanwhile, keep your eyes on the road."

They drove on, through the residential suburbs of Milan, through streets full of the evening crowds, past the outlying factories and warehouses that surrounded the city, leaving the wide flatlands behind them as the road narrowed on toward the mountains around Lake Como. Simon reclined on the back seat, the rifle resting in the crook of his arm, while Wintle did the navigating, shining a flashlight down on the map now and then, murmuring an occasional instruction to Lucia. After an hour they left the main road and began to enter the foothills of the Alps, the road rising steeply, winding up into the hills above the lake.

"We must slow down," said Philip warningly, his face green in the light from the dashboard. "Either the traffic has been much lighter, or you have driven too fast, Lucia. How do you feel in the back, Simon? Getting a bit stiff?"

"No, I'm fine," said Simon calmly. "Two more points before we get there: Lucia, whatever happens, stay in the car. If shooting starts, get down on the floor, right under the steering wheel. A big engine like this should stop a rocket, let alone a bullet. I'm going to put the shotgun here, near you, between the front seats. It's loaded and cocked. If anyone but Philip or me opens the door, give them a barrel, full in the chest, and keep on firing. Philip, don't come back to the car without letting Lucia know who it is. If they intend to whack you I expect they'll wait until you're well clear of the car and they've seen the money. That will be the tricky moment. If they make the slightest twitch, get down. Fling yourself onto the road and lie still, or, if you can, roll out of the light. A lot of dead people would be alive today if they had simply got down flat when the shit started flying. Move very slowly, do as they say, don't make any sudden gestures. Try to stay calm. They'll be as nervous as you are, so try not to alarm them."

"That's easy to say," said Philip, looking out into the night, "But it's not so easy to do."

"Just follow their instructions and think about getting your hands on young Gina," said Simon. "Once you're moving it will be better. Forget I'm there, but leave the rest to me if it turns tricky."

The moon was still out of sight below the hills, although plenty of reflected light came down from the clouds, sending deep pools of shadow drifting across the land. The road was narrow and stony, little more than a bumpy track. It climbed steeply, forcing Lucia to work hard at the wheel, swinging the big car slowly round the bends, out of the darkening valleys and onto the moon-scattered shadow landscape up on the crest of the hills.

They drove slowly on, to and fro, the headlight beams swinging out in a wide arc into the darkness at every curve. Then suddenly, startingly, headlamps blazed out at them from somewhere up ahead. Lucia gasped and braked hard, making the car swerve. The lights blazed again, once, twice, three times in all.

"That's them," cried Lucia, reaching a hand across to clutch Philip's arm fiercely. "God! Is that really them?"

"I imagine it must be," said Philip, his voice calm. "Steady, Lucia, just take it easy and remember the routine. Stop now."

"No, don't stop," snapped Simon from behind, reaching across for the door handle. "Not yet. Slow right down but don't stop. Get ready to put your headlights on, full beam—now!"

As Lucia leaned on the switch they felt a swift rush of air, heard a louder engine noise as the rear door gaped open, and then the swift, hard click of it closing; Simon had gone. Lucia let the car roll on for a few more yards, then braked hard as instructed, and switched off the headlights. The lamps of the other car swept down the hillside ahead and disappeared into the valley, the beams flickering off the rocky hillsides in the darkness, up into the sky, coming toward them.

"What shall we do now?" she asked Philip again, her voice suddenly shaky, her mouth dry.

"We do exactly what they told us to do," replied Philip. "When I get out of the car, get down as low as you can, but where you can quickly get back behind the wheel. If there's any trouble, any trouble at all, shove the car into reverse and drive off as hard and as fast as you can. God knows how you'll turn it round up here, but go—you'll manage somehow."

"I won't leave without Gina," said Lucia flatly, "and I won't leave you."

"You'll do as you're told," snapped Philip. "Let Simon and me worry about your sister. Here they are! Stay calm, take a deep breath, and wind down the window. They must be feeling pretty nervous and we don't want to alarm them."

The other car came slowly over the crest and coasted toward them, headlights undipped, stopping some twenty yards away.

Through the open windows, Philip and Lucia could hear the steady rumble of the engine, but the people inside the other car were invisible behind the blaze of the headlamps.

"Just remember what we were told to do," said Philip softly. His voice was steady, his hand on her arm firm. He even gave her a slight smile as he reached for the door handle.

"Be careful," she said, and began to slide gently down, lower and lower into her seat until she could just see out of the window, the cold barrel of Simon's shotgun brushing against her arm. Pushing the door wide open, Philip got slowly out of the car. With one hand shading his eyes from the glare, he heaved the suitcase of money out onto the road. There was no sign of movement from the other car, but he could feel their eyes upon him. He picked up the case and walked, as directed, round to the front of the car, out into the full glare of their headlights. From up ahead a voice called out to him in Italian, and Lucia passed on the instruction from behind.

"He says you are to stop there and put the case down. Don't go any closer to their car."

Philip did so. The voice ahead spoke again, and again Lucia relayed the instruction through the side window. "Open it up," she called. "They want to see the money. Turn the case toward them."

Philip laid down the case, and snapped the locks and threw back the lid, then tilted the case up toward the lights. A small, sudden breeze came sweeping across the road, sending a swirl of dust up into the lights and ruffling the notes, so that he had to bend down quickly and put his hand on them to stop some blowing away. There was another shouted command from up ahead.

"He says to close the lid and step back here," said Lucia. "He says be quick."

"No," said Philip, speaking over his shoulder, eyes still fixed on the other car. "That's not the deal. First, they show us Gina. Tell them we want to see your sister. Then he can come here and count the money, or do what he likes, but we must see the girl first. Tell him that."

Lucia had no time to speak. A rear door opened in the car ahead and a man got out, square and dark behind the headlights. Then he leaned back into the car and dragged out a slighter shape, a frail, slumped figure in a short, tattered dress, pushing her before him into the lights.

Standing beside the suitcase, Philip looked on carefully, one hand raised against the glare, eyes squinting. His gaze took in the girl's lank hair, her pale face, and dropped to the dirty bandage around her left hand, the frayed, unraveled ends tugging sharply in the sudden breeze.

"Is that her? " He threw the question over his shoulder to Lucia. "It must be. Just look at her and tell me."

"Yes . . . my God!" exclaimed Lucia. "What's happened to her?" As the man caught Gina's arm and pushed her forward into the light, Philip heard the door behind him open.

"Get back in the car!" he cried, over his shoulder. "Stay put! Lucia . . .!"

He was just a little too late; she was out and running forward. "Oh yes, dear God! It's Gina. What have . . ."

Everything fell apart.

Thinking back, later, Philip remembered hearing the door behind him open. He remembered hearing Lucia call out to her sister. He saw the girl before him raise her head at the sound of Lucia's voice, then jerk away, trying to snatch her arm from the man's grip. He saw the man place the muzzle against the young girl's head and fire, saw her face burst open and fly away into the night, saw red rain falling into the glare of the headlights, heard the booming thunder of the shot. After that it all became a blur.

He had no time to move. There was only time to grab Lucia's arm as she ran toward the falling body of her sister, and time to swing her round and fall with her into the road. Rolling over in the whirls of dust, Philip saw the pistol glinting blackly at them in the light and waited for it to fire, flinching from the expected impact.

Then the man went down, cartwheeling back, crashing into the front of the car, the pistol spinning from his hand, dead.

Philip didn't hear the shot that killed the man, but he heard the next one as it slapped past overhead, one headlight exploding, then another, the crash of glass plunging the scene into sudden darkness. Somewhere behind them Simon Quarry was firing. Philip gathered the struggling Lucia into his arms and held her down, flat on the road. Behind them the heavy rifle boomed again.

Up on the hillside, a hundred yards away, Simon cursed, snapped up the open sight on the rifle, and fired again, twice, spacing his shots carefully across the windshield of the kidnappers' car. Engine roaring, the car began to reverse down the road, swerving wildly to and fro, crunching into a wall, once, and then again, coming to a halt against the rough stone. Simon got up on one knee, jerked open the bolt, and thumbed four more rounds into the magazine. He slammed the bolt home, looped the rifle sling tightly about his upper arm, and put another round into the windshield, just over the steering wheel. When a dark shape came bursting from the wreckage, he fired again, twice, and saw the body spin away into the darkness and fall. Suddenly there was silence. The echo of the shots was still reverberating in Simon's head as he ejected the last hot cartridge case into his hand, slipped it into his pocket, reloaded the rifle, and began to pick his way carefully through the rocks down to the road. Simon found Philip in the car, sitting in the front passenger seat, his feet on the road, his head in his hands, slumped sideways against the doorjamb.

"Are you all right?" Simon asked him sharply. "Are you hurt? Where's Lucia? What a bloody balls up!" He reached out and shook Philip savagely by the shoulder. "Philip!"

"I'm all right—not a scratch. My legs have just gone a bit weak, that's all. Did you see what they did to that girl? The bastards! They never intended to let her go. It was a setup all along. They wanted, her, me, Lucia, the money, the lot. Christ! They must really have it in for Fiori."

"Yes, I saw it," said Simon bleakly, looking about him in the darkness. "I was ready to fire when I saw him raise the pistol, but Lucia ran right across my sights. I *told* her . . . I told her to stay in the car. Where is she now? Is she all right?"

"Of course she's not all right," said Philip sharply. "She's there in the road with her sister—wait!" He leaned across to the dashboard and put the headlamps full on. Twenty yards ahead, Lucia was kneeling in the road, in the center of a spreading pool of blood, hugging her sister's body.

"Jesus!" whispered Simon. "What a mess."

Further on, at the very edge of the headlamps' glare, the first man he had shot lay on his back in the road, the dusty white soles of his shoes reflecting in the light.

"Come on," said Philip. "This won't do." He got up unsteadily, heaving himself out of the car, and they went toward Lucia together, moving slowly. Wintle reached down to ease her arms away, taking Gina's body. Lucia pulled back, holding on briefly, as Simon took her hands, and then she rose with a rush, letting him hold her as Philip laid Gina down again gently in the road.

"Why did they do that?" Lucia asked dully. "They could have had the money—you showed them the money." Her voice rose and fell as waves of shock swept through her body, making her tremble uncontrollably.

"I don't know why they did it," said Philip gently. "Come away now, Lucia . . . please, come back to the car. There's nothing you can do for her now. Come back and wait while we see about these gentry."

Lucia shook her head and broke free from Simon, sitting down again in the road beside her sister.

"Look at her hand—see?" said Lucia pathetically, staring down. "Look at it, look at it.! See what they did to her. They . . ." She looked up into Simon's face. "I'm glad you killed them. I'm glad they are dead. I'm glad, I'm glad, I'm . . ." She began to cry then, with great deep, racking, choking sobs, her cries the only sound in the silence that had rushed in on them after the shooting stopped.

Avoiding Philip's eyes, Simon stepped round the pool of blood and put his rifle down across the suitcase. Then he went forward, toward the crashed car ahead, taking the pistol from his belt. Wintle had got Lucia back into their car when he heard the crash of slamming doors and the whirr of an engine up ahead. Presently, Simon returned, carrying the rifle and the suitcase loosely in his hands.

"They're both dead," he said. "Two men up there, both young, tough-looking types. The car's a write-off, full of holes. They probably stole it. I've had a look inside, but there's nothing to help us and nothing on them either—no papers, nothing. They came well prepared."

"It's very professional," said Philip, "and it means there are more of them; we haven't nailed the gang. No identification means there's less for us to go on if something went wrong for them up here. It's a pity we don't have one alive."

"I'm sincerely sorry about that," said Simon harshly, "but that's their doing. I did the best I could in the circumstances."

"All I'm saying is that if we had a live one he just might have told us who organized all this, that's all."

"Anyway, this is a total fuck-up," said Simon. "Let's get out of here and back to Milan. There's nothing more we can do here."

"We're not leaving without my sister," cried Lucia, pushing out of the car against Philip, trying to get to her feet. "I . . . we . . . can't just leave here here, lying in the road like that. We just can't."

"We can't take her with us either," Philip said gently, taking her hands in his. "How can we explain all this? Simon has shot three people. We'll telephone the police from the first village and they'll come here and look after her. It wasn't supposed to turn out like this, Lucia. Now it's a mess and we need time to sort it out. Please, Lucia . . . it has to be done. We have to go. We have to get Simon back to your flat before the police get involved . . . we need time to think."

Lucia began to weep again, harsh sobs coming from somewhere inside her as she clung to Philip. He disengaged her hands slowly and gently, then moved her into the backseat, opened the front door, and slid in behind the steering wheel.

"Look after her, Simon," he said. "I'll drive."

Simon slid into the backseat alongside Lucia. "I've got the money," he said quietly.

"Damn the money," said Lucia gulping, wiping her eyes with the back of her hand. "But for that money my sister would still be alive."

The engine sounded unnaturally loud as Philip started up, groped for the gears, and reversed the car down the road, turning it round in a narrow gateway. As he swung out against the headlight beams swept one last time over the wrecked car ahead and the litter of wind-tugged bodies lying in the white dust of the road.

EIGHT

Fiori was on to them even before they got out of the car. He came running out of the house as they turned up the drive, plunging down the steps to snatch the driver's door open, shouting questions, tugging urgently at Philip's arm, the dark form of Fredo Donati trotting from the side of the house to arrive at his back.

"Where is she? Where is Gina? What happened up there?" He shook Philip fiercely, his voice frantic, his stocky body quivering with anxiety. Whatever it took to make Fiori lose control had clearly happened. Philip had to push him back against Fredo in order to get out of the car, and by the time Simon and Lucia had joined him he was again shrieking questions at Philip.

The five made a tight little group in the darkness, standing outside Fiori's house, before the small knot of curious servants who stood in the light spilling out from the doorway, listening in shock to Fiori's mounting anger. Finally Simon lost patience and came forward to grab Fiori by the shoulders and shake him hard.

"Shut up!" he snapped. "And get rid of all these people. Let's all go inside and we'll tell you what happened. This is no place for a scene." He waved one hand at the crowd of servants and pushed Fiori toward the steps. "Tell everyone else to go away."

"But where is Gina? Where did you leave her? Where is the money?" yelled Fiori. "What have you done, you bastard?" Simon started toward him again until he was blocked by Fredo, who stepped in front of Fiori, his arms spread, and stared calmly into Simon's face.

"No, signore," he said. "*Prego* . . . you must not."

"Look . . . I'm sorry, but she's dead," Simon said flatly. "They never intended to give her back, Fiori . . . and they would have shot Philip and Lucia as well. The money is in the car." He looked directly at Fredo. "Why don't you make yourself useful and carry it up to the house?"

Though he had expected an outburst and was too tired to care, Simon was startled by what followed. Fiori pushed Fredo aside, put his head back, and screamed out loud, choking back sobs, tears suddenly flooding down his face.

As Wintle moved toward the house, leading Lucia forward by one arm, Fiori exploded into rage again and leaped after him across the gravel, tearing at his back, dragging him round again, away from Lucia.

"You killed my daughter!" Fiori yelled at him. "All of you. You . . . you told me you would get her back, and now she is dead. All this is your fault. Everything, everything."

"Shut up!" said Simon again, moving in to stand beside Philip. "And get a hold on yourself. No one here is to blame for what happened. None of this helps. Let's all go inside," he added to Fredo, "and send everyone else to bed."

Fiori fell silent, slumped against the side of the car, his twisted face sagging. The servants, voices subdued, began to move back into the house ahead of Fredo, leaving Simon, Philip, Fiori, and Lucia standing in the darkness by the car.

"Come on," said Lucia quietly, breaking the silence. "Simon's right, let's go inside."

Her voice was shaky, her face pale in the darkness, but they finally did as she suggested. They went up the steps together, passing Fredo in the doorway. No one spoke until they were all seated around the big desk in Fiori's gloomy study. A few minutes later Fredo came in carrying the heavy suitcase and, having placed it beside the desk, sat down in his usual position by the door.

"There's the money," said Simon, nodding at the bag. "One million five in small notes. Much good it did us."

"Is it all there?" asked Fiori harshly. "Every dollar?"

"Yes," said Simon wearily. "If you don't believe me, count it."

"No, no . . ." replied Fiori, his eyes avoiding Philip's sudden glance.

"Why don't you count it, it you think we've helped ourselves?" said Philip gently. "You'll find it's all there, every dollar."

"Who cares about the money?" asked Lucia, angry. "Gina is dead . . . that's all that matters now. She's lying in the road, back there in the dark. They killed her. They always intended to kill her, Philip . . . me . . . all of us. Who are these people?"

There was a long silence. All eyes except Simon's looked down blankly at the floor; Simon switched his gaze slowly between Fredo and Fiori but said nothing. There was too much to tell, but no place to start an explanation of what went wrong.

"So," said Fiori at last, his voice quiet. "Tell me what happened out there, and tell me what you have done about Gina. From the beginning, every detail."

They told him. They went over it step by step, second by ghastly second. Taking turns, they described the scene and the shooting, how the man had murdered Gina in the road, how they had driven back as fast as they could, stopping only to pass on the news to Philip's police contact, Aldo Cirillo. The local police would be on the scene by now, trying to work out what had happened, bringing down the dead. Wintle told the tale bluntly, as if making a formal report. Lucia covered some points with little bursts of Italian, with Simon interrupting now and again when a point seemed too vague. When they had finished, Fiori got up from his chair and took a turn or two across the rug in front of the empty fireplace, hands thrust deep in his pockets, head bowed, thinking.

"I am sorry," he said at last, grudgingly, turning to look directly at Philip. "You did your best. I was wrong to accuse you outside. As for you, Signor Quarry," he turned to Simon, "I am grateful for what you did. I am glad you shot those men. I only wish I had done so myself."

Simon said nothing. He gazed back at Fiori and nodded, his face expressionless. Fiori's voice was reasonable, but the look in his eyes and on his face was anything but forgiving. After a moment Fiori looked away and went back to staring into the fireplace, his back to the room.

"What about Gina?" cut in Lucia. "What will happen to her?"

"Cirillo will take care of all that and bring her to Milan," said Philip, still speaking to Fiori's back. "He will be there by now with the *carabinieri.* It's a killing and not just a kidnapping, so the police will be everywhere. We'd better decide what we're going to say when they turn up here."

Simon broke in to answer Fiori's other question, the unspoken one. "Signor Fiori, it's like this," he said flatly. "Had Gina been injured, we would have brought her away with us, of course, but . . . well . . . she was dead. We can't change that. It's a fact, and we all have to face it. There will be other problems, involving the police, maybe bigger ones. The kidnap is over, now we have murder. Four people are dead. There was no real time to think it through, but Philip and I considered it best to leave the scene up there exactly as it was. The police will want to know what happened and who shot those men, and we still need to know who organized the kidnapping. Could three men do it?" Simon asked Philip. "It seems a bit unlikely to me—but if not, what happens now? Where do we go from here?"

"What Simon means," put in Philip, "is that he would rather not be publicly identified as the gunman. He went there to protect us and he fired in our defense, but if some person or persons unknown were held to be responsible for shooting the kidnappers, that would be better than having his name in the papers. Better for him, and probably better for us. It might even be better if he left Italy at once, but we really have nothing to hide. They fired first, they murdered Gina, they would have killed Lucia and me and taken the money. I'm sure that was their intention. That's our story anyway, and it happens to be true."

Fiori's gaze rested broodily on Simon for a moment, then he shook his head. "I don't think you should go . . . I don't know . . ." He shrugged. "Signor Cirillo or Klaus Kleiner can arrange this matter for you. Cirillo can do anything. He is the head of the Squadra and he does what Kleiner wants. He can keep you out of it. Maybe he can let the police claim the credit for shooting the kidnappers. They don't have many successes, so that will please them. They won't care that my daughter is dead. You will want to clean up before they arrive and I would like a private word with Fredo. Lucia will show you the way. Then in the dining room you will find food and wine." A bitter smile twisted his mouth again. "Ready for a little party I arranged to welcome Gina home."

The men dragged Antonio Puccio from the trunk of the car, careless of his shattered legs, unmoved by the terrible sounds coming from behind the gag, dumping him onto the muddy ground. Antonio lay on his back in a deep, rutted puddle, his bulging eyes filled with pain and fear, while the rain pattered down on his face.

There was construction work going on in this area. The rain was slanting through the beams of the arc lights and running in streams down the raw concrete of the half-finished overpass. Whimpering now, Antonio wriggled round, working with his elbows in the mud, until he could see the legs of his captors under the car, standing close to those of a man in slick rubber boots. As they turned and came toward him, Antonio lay still, closing his eyes, fearful of another kicking, feeling the pain wash over him again. There was talk among the men standing over him, agreement, the passing of money, the clink of a bottle, a heavy boot in his ribs . . . laughter. They were laughing about him.

The hands gripped Antonio hard, twisting into his hair, knotting the shoulders of his jacket. They dragged him like that across the churned-up mud of the work site, face down, his broken legs trailing, cursing as their shoes sank into the muck, down a slope into a square hole where steel reinforcing rods jutted crazily from a concrete base. Two of the men tied him there, lashing his ankles and wrists to the rods, while the others stood on the edge of the hole, dark against the arc-lights, and watched. Antonio knew then what they intended to do . . . what they were going to do. He would have begged them to stop, done anything, but his mouth was dry, and so he wept, the tears washing over his face with the rain, as the men, still laughing, clambered back out of the pit.

The men were gone now, all but the last one. He stood on the edge looking down as the mixer truck appeared, waving it along slowly to the rim of the hole, then stepped aside as it tilted, letting the concrete flow down into the pit. The last thing Antonio saw before the heavy tide reached his face were those dark and pitiless eyes.

By midnight they knew there had been a hitch, that something had gone wrong. No phone call came, no delighted cries, no handshakes or back slapping, no talk of money anymore. By one o'clock they were worried, huddled round the table in the sitting room, drinking a little too much, one eye fixed on the telephone. Still it didn't ring. By two they were more than worried. They were frightened.

Old Man Puccio knew what to do. After all, he'd had a good teacher, he had plenty of experience, so he took charge. They went through the farmhouse one room at a time, finding and removing all their possessions, piling them into the cars. They cleaned out the girl's cell, burned the stinking mattress, everything, anything, wiping off the bedstead, doing all they could think of to remove anything that might link her to them. They listened continuously to the radio, spinning the dial between the all-night stations, and brief news of the shooting came on the three A.M. broadcast. They listened, shocked. Then they ran, back to the city, to the safety of the crowds, their car bumping down the farm track, accelerating away down the main road.

Sometime on that journey, hammering down the autostrada, someone asked the Old Man a question. "We do it again, of course," he replied. "What else can we do? And keep your speed down, we don't want to interest the *polizia stradale.* Slow down, and let me think."

Simon, Philip, and Lucia sat around the dining room table, tired, silent, ignoring the food spread out before them, the frost-beaded ice buckets crammed with bottles of champagne, the sheen of the silver, and the glinting glasses on the sideboard. A small, dark maid came into the room, bringing them coffee and a bottle of whiskey, then went out without a word.

"Do you want a drink, Simon?" asked Philip, getting to his feet and reaching across for the Scotch. "You look as if you need it. I certainly do."

Simon shook his head. "No, thanks," he said heavily. "Maybe Lucia would like something?"

Lucia went on filling her coffee cup, the spout of the coffee-pot rattling briefly against the rim, before she answered. "No, not for me," she said. "Just this. If I have anything else I'll be sick. I may be sick anyway."

"Don't you want to change your dress?" asked Simon softly, "or maybe go upstairs and take a shower? You'll feel better if you get out of those clothes."

"No, I won't," said Lucia flatly. "I'll never feel better again. I'd just like to go home. What are we waiting here for?"

"We're waiting here for Aldo," said Philip, putting his glass back on the table. "He'll come here, whatever time it is. He'll need to see Simon about the shooting and we need to get things straight before the press arrive. But Simon's right, you must be exhausted. Why not go home? We can handle the rest of this."

"No, if you are staying, I'm staying too," said Lucia steadily. "At least until I hear what has happened to my sister's body." No one spoke after that. They sat on around the table, silent, gazing into space. Eventually, Simon put his head down onto his folded arms and slept. All of them were waiting for Cirillo.

Two hours later, as the first gray light of dawn began to steal around the edge of the curtains, they heard the police car come sweeping up the drive. Tires crunched on the gravel, doors slammed, voices were heard outside, then a doorbell rang. A few moments later the maid ushered a man in civilian clothes into the room. With a nod to Philip and a curious glance at Simon, he went directly to Lucia and took her hands in his.

"Lucia," he said softly, bending down to look into her face. "I am sorry, so sorry about all this. We've brought her in, very carefully, I promise, to the Ospedale Cà Grande. They know what to do there. But what can I say?"

"Nothing, Aldo. There is nothing you or anyone can say. But thank you. I'll go over to the hospital later."

Simon and Philip watched them, listening to Cirillo's liquid Italian, grateful for Lucia's slight, warm smile. Then they straightened up in their chairs and tried to shake off their weariness as Cirillo turned his attention to them.

Aldo Cirillo was a powerfully built man, medium height, with a frame like a wedge, broad shoulders tapering sharply to a narrow waist. Watchful eyes were set in a tanned face; a swift flash of white teeth showed briefly below the wide moustache that covered his upper lip. He was a sharp dresser, his shoulders filling out the jacket of his suit, a good inch of cuff at the end of each sleeve, light blue shirt and dark blue tie, shoes polished until they shone. He squeezed Lucia's hands once more, replaced them gently in her lap. Then he turned to Simon and Philip. Like everyone else Simon had met in Milan, Cirillo spoke excellent English and his tone seemed friendly.

"Well, Philip," he said, looking from one to the other, "are you all right? You look tired. This must be the formidable Simon Quarry. Good evening, Mr. Quarry, or, rather, good morning. Do you mind if I call you Simon? I hope, like Philip, you will call me Aldo." That sounded hopeful. Cirillo was like a breath of fresh air, sweeping briskly into the room, bringing everyone to life again. He jumped up to fling open the curtains, letting the light into the room, heaving open a window to create a draft of cold air. Outside the window they could hear the first hesitant birdsong of the morning.

"We're damned glad you're here, Aldo," said Philip, getting to his feet and stretching slowly. "Can you tell us what's been happening, and what happens now?"

Speaking easily in English, with occasional asides in Italian to Lucia, Aldo gave them the news. He had followed up Philip's phone call, visited the scene with the local *carabinieri* and removed all the bodies. These had been brought by ambulance to Milan for identification and autopsy. Aldo had personally arranged for Gina's body to travel separately. He had spoken to Kleiner. A statement was being prepared and some announcement had already been made on the radio. The press could therefore be expected shortly.

"I had a look at the three men," said Aldo. "Apart from the pistol we found in the road, in the car they also had a sawed-off shotgun and an American submachine gun. Those are sophisticated weapons for small-time crooks. The car was stolen from a supermarket parking lot here in Milan, about seven o'clock last night. That could mean they came from the city. I hope they have police records or they may be hard to identify. They had no papers on them. Which sort of gun did you use, Mr. Quarry . . . Simon?"

"Hunting rifle, a Magnum," replied Simon briefly.

"Hmmm," said Aldo. "Well, that's a lot of gun and it made a mess of them." His eyes came to rest thoughtfully on Simon, and he rubbed his chin with his forefinger. "We have a small problem," he said. "We have three dead men and one dead girl. The men managed to fire one shot, from the pistol. It is a pity you used such a powerful rifle, Simon. It looks bad . . . it will look worse if it comes out that an Englishman can come here to shoot three Italian citizens and get away with it."

"I'm in your hands," said Simon, "but I was brought here to guard Philip and I understood I had clearance."

"You have," said Aldo, "up to a point . . . but it still takes some explaining away. If we can identify the bodies it should be easier to find the rest of this gang," he continued. "Meanwhile, to keep the press off your back, I am putting it out that these people were killed in a police ambush during the handover of the money. I will let them assume it was a shoot-out between a terrorist group and an undercover unit of my Squadra. I will still need a statement to satisfy the investigating *magistrato*. I suggest that you leave Italy before the press get on to you. It's almost impossible to keep matters quiet for long here and after this gets out I cannot be responsible for the newspapers."

"Simon can't leave just yet," said Philip firmly. "There's a meeting of the Kleiner consortium tomorrow—I mean today—at the Hotel Principe. I was hoping to go there with Gina. Now I need Simon to come and help me to explain the situation. Klaus Kleiner is anxious to meet him, and Simon is willing, so I hope you won't object."

"Well," said Aldo, smiling, "if Klaus Kleiner is on your side, Simon, you don't have a lot to worry about." He glanced briefly at his watch. "We can do more tonight, so why don't you all get some sleep? Can I give anyone a lift? I suggest everyone stays away from here while the press are sniffing about. Shootouts between the police and the gangs are all too common here, but one involving the beautiful Dottoressa Lucia Fiori, and the rich Klaus Kleiner, and a man from Scotland Yard, *and* a mysterious English rifleman—well, that would be front-page news anywhere."

"I have to stay for the moment," said Philip. "Signor Fiori has placed a room at my disposal, and I am responsible for Kleiner's money. There's a spare bed in my room, Simon, and you're welcome to it."

"Simon will come back to my flat," said Lucia firmly, looking at him directly. "My car is outside; we'll go in that, and I'll get him to the Principe by eleven. Is that all right?"

"That's fine," said Simon mildly.

"You certainly shouldn't be alone," said Philip to Lucia, hurriedly. "Not after last night. Don't you agree, Aldo? Someone should stay with Lucia."

"Yes, of course." Aldo sounded surprised. "But I can send a car for you later on, Simon, if that would help."

"I told you, I have my car," said Lucia quietly, looking only at Simon, "and I'll drive Simon to the Principe before I go on to the Ospedale to see about Gina."

"Then I'll just get my stuff . . . the rifle . . . from the big car," said Simon, looking across at Philip, "and I'll see you at eleven. The Hotel Principe, you said? And I'll see you after that, Aldo? There are one or two things we should talk about."

It was daylight when they got outside, stepping into a gray, drizzling dawn. The air was damp but fresh, cooling to their hot skin, soothing to tired, gritty eyes. They said good-bye to Aldo and watched him drive away, the red brake-lights of his car still bright in the murky morning. Simon brought his rifle and the shotgun from the limousine to Lucia's car, waved a hand at Philip, who stood alone in the doorway, and slid into the car beside Lucia. They said nothing until they were once again in her apartment.

He placed his weapons on the kitchen table, slipped off his anorak, and then went back into the living room, opening the curtains to let in the light. He paused by the window for a moment to watch the big red ball of the sun hoist itself up above the peaks of the eastern hills, climbing quickly into the sky above the city. Later on, it was going to be hot.

Lucia had slumped down onto the sofa behind him, her head bowed, her face hidden in the shadow cast by the light from a single lamp. Simon went over to sit beside her, switched off the light, and reached across to take her hand.

"I know. It's a bastard," he said, "and I'm sorry for my part in it. But . . . well, talking won't change anything. Lucia, there's blood on your dress," he said softly. "Why don't you take it off and have a shower? It'll make you feel better."

"I'm all right," she said. "And I won't cry any more. But nothing will make me feel better. I will never feel better again. And, please, don't be nice to me. If you're nice to me I think I'll fall apart."

"I want to be nice to you," he said. "For both our sakes."

He reached out and pulled her close to him, gently, slowly. Then he began to unzip her dress. He slid it down over her smooth, tanned shoulders, then got up and lifted her to her feet, letting the dress rustle down softly onto the floor. Gina's blood had soaked through the dress and dried on her shoulders. She had dried and crusted blood between her breasts, and more of it was caked thickly in the ends of her hair, on her neck and along the line of her jaw. Her face was pale, her green eyes unnaturally bright.

"Come on," he said, placing an arm round her waist, leading her slowly, one step at a time, toward the bathroom. "I won't be nice to you, I promise, but we must get you cleaned up a little. Trust me."

"I was so frightened," she said suddenly. "I was so *frightened* up there. I'm used to blood, but not like that! It was all so quick, so sudden. There was so much noise."

"I was frightened, too," said Simon soothingly. "I always am, at least until it starts. I nearly killed you when you ran across the road toward your sister. You ran right into my sights. Don't think about it now, or at least try not to. It doesn't help. And, whatever you say now, you *will* feel better after some sleep . . ."

Still holding her close, he walked her into the bathroom, one arm supporting her around the waist while he turned on the shower taps and adjusted the temperature of the water. She leaned against him heavily, eyes closed, body trembling, while he removed the rest of her clothes and pushed her gently under the shower, letting the hot water loosen the blood from her hair and skin, sending it flowing down her body and legs in long red and brown streaks, spattering onto the glass walls, splashing onto the tiles. Finally, seeing her standing there, wretched and shaking in the hot flow of water, her arms folded pitifully over her breasts, he ducked under the shower with her, taking the soap to wash Gina's blood out of her hair and off her body. When it was all gone, and she was out again, wrapped in a towel, dry but still shaking, Simon took off his own wet clothing, toweled himself dry, and put her to bed. He sat beside her, holding her hand until she slept. Then he went back into his own room and stretched out on the bed. It was a long time until his eyelids finally closed.

NINE

Lucia drove Simon to the meeting at the Hotel Principe, forcing her bright yellow Fiat through the traffic, controlling it well on the greasy cobblestones. It was still dull, a thin rain drizzling down from fat clouds that seemed to rest on the rooftops of the city. Simon sat slumped in his seat, looking out through the rain-flecked windows, feeling Lucia's knuckles brush against his knee from time to time as she changed gear. He felt drained and very weary.

"I feel shattered," he said, looking over at Lucia, "and you look absolutely exhausted. Mind you, it's always like that. While it's going on you keep moving, but when it stops—well, you feel whacked."

"You'd never make a doctor," said Lucia. "We are tired all the time. After a while you get used to it."

"I don't want to get used to it," said Simon. "If I don't get a solid eight hours' sleep every week or so I'm a total wreck."

She glanced at him sideways. "Is that supposed to be a joke?"

"Only a small one, and the best I can manage, just to lighten the atmosphere."

"I'm sorry," she said. "But I'm more than just tired this morning. I'm not looking forward to the things I have to do today. This is not what I had planned. What about you?"

Simon shrugged. "I don't know. It really depends on Philip, and what happens with Kleiner and the others. Everything has changed now and I may have to leave. Who knows? And you?"

"First, I'm going to the hospital, and then to the undertakers, to make the arrangements about Gina. Then I must look in at the clinic to see my patients. Then I must go and see my father about the funeral. I expect he'll leave all that to me or Fredo, like everything else. You're not going home, are you—or at least not yet? Philip and Aldo want me to look at the people you . . . met last night and see if I know them."

"When did they ask that?" asked Simon, surprised.

"They phoned this morning, while you were in the shower. Are you going home . . . back to Mallorca?"

"I don't know. Do you know something? I never think of it as home. I don't intend to go back there, at least not yet, and when I do go, you're coming with me—aren't you?"

"Am I?"

"I think you are . . . or I shall have to stay here. Either way, I don't want to lose you when I have just found you."

"I have work here—patients. I can't just *leave*."

"You can find work there. There are plenty of sick children in Mallorca. Anyway, you're coming, aren't you?"

"I can't think about that right now. But shall I see you this evening? We could go out to dinner and talk. I'd like to do something . . . normal . . . after last night."

"I'd like that, too," he said, "but it rather depends on what happens at the meeting. May I ring you when it's over?"

"Philip knows how to find me," she said, "and I have a beeper on the hospital phone. I'll see you at my flat, later. Now, here's the Hotel Principe, and there's Philip, waiting in the rain. Kiss me now and run . . . *ciao.*"

Philip and Simon stood in the shelter of the doorman's umbrella, watching the yellow car cut its way back into the traffic before turning to go through the swinging doors into the warmth of the foyer.

"Did you get much sleep?" asked Simon, looking around him at the throng. "You look pretty tired."

"Not a lot," replied Philip. "You know how it is when the brain won't stop churning. I just couldn't drop off. I've already had a chat with Kleiner, who's not too happy about last night. On the other hand, he's glad you're here. You were wise to get away from Fiori's house. The press arrived half an hour after you left and still have the house under siege. I'm moving in here today, and leaving all the clearing up to Aldo. The official story is that last night's events were purely an Italian affair, involving the terrorist Red Brigades—all right with you?"

"All right with me," said Simon. "Where's this meeting?"

"Before we go up," said Philip, leading him over to a long, leather-covered bench at the side of the foyer. "I'd like you to read this."

"What is it?"

"Some extracts from my file on Kleiner, a bit of background for you, just to let you know who we're in league with. I'm not asking you to like him. He's hard, difficult, and he can be tricky. I have no illusions about him, but you've taken a dislike to him for some reason and I don't like that. It could make my life difficult."

"I don't know him," said Simon.

"Then read this and you'll know him a little better. Can you still read as fast as before?"

"Like lightning . . . it's a publishing skill. It's also a big snag if you live in a cultural desert like Mallorca . . . I can't keep myself in books. Only last week I read Manchester's *Death of a President,*—that's one thousand, three hundred pages—in eight hours."

"I'm impressed," said Philip ironically. "Just see what you can do with this in a couple of minutes."

The file he handed to Simon consisted of press cuttings, all featuring Kleiner or concerning his companies. A *Time* Magazine "Man of the Year" cover, and *Economist* special report, clippings from *Fortune, Newsweek, Le Point;* Klaus Kleiner, industrialist, philanthropist, yachtsman, at the races, attending an auction at Sotheby's, pictures of him as a young man with a beautiful woman on his arm, or older now, hand in hand with a young girl. Then there was a haggard Kleiner, standing outside Claridge's, with two policemen keeping back a crowd of photographers.

"I've got it," said Simon, nodding and handing back the file. "Even rich men get kneed in the groin now and then. I apologize. "I'll try to keep an open mind."

"It would help," said Philip. "Just go along with him, as far as you can, if only for my sake. All right? Just do what he wants and keep your thoughts until later—right?"

They got up from the bench and headed toward the elevator. The hallway was crammed with people talking in loud voices, stripping off wet raincoats, getting in the way. Passing the news kiosk, Simon noticed the name Fiori and Gina's photograph on nearly every front page.

"The meeting is in the conference room, on one of the upper floors," said Philip, taking Simon's arm. "If we get through quickly I'll take you to lunch here. The decor may be a bit overpowering but the food is very good. I've often dined here with Klaus."

"Does he own this place as well?" asked Simon ironically. "He seems to own everything else."

"No. At least I don't think so," replied Philip casually, "but he lives here whenever he's in Milan. He has an apartment on the top floor, overlooking the garden. It's rather nice—I wouldn't mind it myself."

"I might have known it," said Simon, shaking his head. "Last week I'd hardly heard of him. Now we can't move for him. The man's ubiquitous."

The conference room of the Hotel Principe was already full when Simon and Philip entered, and the people inside were clearly awaiting their arrival. They were on their feet, standing in little groups around the table. Silence fell, all eyes turning toward the door as Philip ushered Simon in, but Philip, unruffled, smiled quietly at everyone and made simple introductions as he led Simon down the room toward the head of the table.

"Morning . . . good morning. Monsieur Tronson . . . Monsieur Paulet . . . Signor Colombo . . . Signor Veccio . . . Signor Cavanti . . . Mr. Quarry. Herr Strassen . . . Herr Franck . . . Signora Fratelli." Simon knew some of the names, recognized one or two of the faces. They appeared often, usually in the financial pages of the papers or in the flash photographs of the gossip columns. This consortium of Kleiner's was a formidable assembly of Italy's money—the people here were bankers, entrepreneurs, industrialists, business chiefs. Even today, though their eyes were worried and their expressions concerned, they gave off an air of confidence, power, and influence. Simon found himself impressed, not least by the man who stood beside the head chair, watching their approach down the room, a slight smile on his face.

". . . and finally, the chairman of our consortium, Herr Klaus Kleiner," said Philip, waving Simon forward and stepping aside. "Klaus, this is my associate, Simon Quarry."

Kleiner's handshake was firm and pleasant, his look direct, his smile welcoming. In spite of himself, Simon found his slight sense of antagonism slipping away. Kleiner said nothing more than "Good morning," but this manner interested Simon. He had the look of a man who could have anything he wanted, of a man used to getting his own way, but there was something else besides that. All the people in this room were obviously successful, but Kleiner stood out. The others stood flat on their feet, foursquare, solid, while Kleiner seemed to be on his toes, lean, fit, more alert than the rest, a man who would be at home in a fast car or happy plummeting down the steepest ski slope. Simon found himself ready to like Kleiner, especially when, after the briefest welcome, his manner became strictly businesslike.

"There is a lot to discuss this morning, and we are all busy people," Kleiner said in English, calling the meeting to order, pulling out his chair and sitting down, while waving Simon and Philip into the chairs on either side. "So let's get started. I have spoken to Signor Fiori and conveyed our regrets on the death of his daughter. He tells me that in his opinion last night was a disaster, which is understandable. This group exists to prevent kidnaps if possible, and to get our children back safely if or when they occur. Well, last night a child was killed, so we all want to know what went wrong." Kleiner's voice had cut into the shuffle and murmur of those who were still arranging themselves around the table. Silence fell and in the stillness that followed Kleiner's short speech all eyes turned on Philip and Simon at the head of the table. They exchanged brief smiles, then Simon sat back, leaving the floor to Philip, who rose, towering above the others, resting one hand on the polished tabletop, looking round the room for a moment before speaking.

"Signor Fiori is entitled to his opinions," he said mildly, "but, with all due respect, he wasn't there. The kidnappers killed his daughter, yes, and that was a terrible thing, but I now believe that was their original intention anyway. They killed the girl during the handover, and without reason. There was the money, right in front of them, lying in the road. All they had to do was let the girl go and take it, nothing more. But let me begin at the beginning. The telephone call came through as usual, at about eight . . ."

The room was silent, all eyes except Kleiner's fixed on Philip's face as he told his tale, rather as he had told it to Fiori the previous night. He told it plainly, without elaboration, and Kleiner listened, nodding sometimes, his eyes fixed on the blotter before him, playing with a pencil, and he kept his eyes down when Philip finally stopped. Everyone waited, digesting the story. It was Kleiner who broke the silence.

"I see," he said slowly, nodding. "We must thank Commander Wintle for his efforts and patience over these last weeks, and for this explanation. Last night must have been a terrible experience. However, the fact remains that our arrangements failed, the handover went wrong, and a girl is dead. How are we to react to that? What happens now and where do we go from here?"

At this, a babble of discontent and disagreement came from around the table. Frightened people need someone to blame and Wintle was the obvious target. Could he not have foreseen this? Why hadn't he told the police? Why hadn't he listened to their advice? Maybe he wasn't up to the job, or out of touch, or English?

After a minute or two Simon had heard enough. He was tired of hearing Philip tell the same story to people who always seemed to think they could have done better.

"Look," he interrupted, his voice cutting sharply into the talk. "Let's just stop all this high-toned, critical crap, shall we? Philip Wintle here has not been trading with a group of Oxford-educated gentlemen, but with a bunch of dangerous scum. The sort of people who kidnapped Gina Fiori are the sort of people you haven't even met and couldn't begin to imagine. They *despise* people like you. They want all you've got, and last night that meant the girl, the money, and the man who is after them. They got very little. No . . . wait." He held up his hand, thinking Kleiner was about to interrupt. "You still want to know what happened? It's still not clear? Right, then I'll tell you. The man came for the money and shot the girl in the head, so I shot him. Then the driver drove off, and I shot him. Then one ran for it, and I shot him. Then we took the money and went back to Fiori. The money is here, the girl is dead. That's all. Any questions? What more would any of you have been able to do? No questions? Good! Then maybe we can go now. Philip and I didn't get much sleep last night." He glared, inviting anyone to take up the challenge. It was their turn to look down at the tabletop, shrugging, murmuring brief excuses. Finally Simon's gaze came to rest on Kleiner, a flat challenge in his eyes. Kleiner kept his face straight, but there was a hint of amusement in his eyes, a slight smile tugging at the corners of his mouth.

"Well," said Kleiner at last, "I think we are now all fully

aware of the events of last night. But is this the end of the gang? Are these the same people who kidnapped the other children? Will they strike again? There is a lot we still don't know, and with our thanks for the risk you took last night, Commander, goes the hope that you will continue to act for us. I am sure I speak for us all when I say that." There was a sudden, surprising murmur of agreement from the others around the table.

Kleiner looked at Simon, inquiringly. In spite of his still simmering anger, Simon smiled back, then shrugged his shoulders, turned to look around the table, and forced himself to look pleasant.

"Well, Mr. Quarry?" asked Kleiner. "Will you join us?"

"If Philips thinks I can be helpful, I'm happy to stay," said Simon. "But there remains the possibility of trouble with the police. I expect to see them today and they may not appreciate your hiring a bodyguard. But if that point can be arranged, then I'm at your service. I have my own reasons for wishing to stay in Milan at present."

Satisfied for the moment, Kleiner nodded before turning to address the room. "Well," he said, looking at his colleagues round the table, "where do we all go from here? In the last three years we have experienced eight kidnappings and paid over the astonishing sum of around fourteen million dollars. Now one of our children has been killed, and none of those taken has been returned unharmed. Well . . ." He sighed, and looked away for a moment. "I won't go into that, but we all know that the cost in misery far exceeds the value of the cash. All we have to show against these people is the death of three of them last night."

"I think I shall send my children to America," said Herr Franck, from the end of the table. "I do not see how we can keep them here while this situation continues. It is no longer just the money—now they are killing the children."

"This situation has been going on for generations," said Signora Fratelli, a quietly elegant lady sitting across the table. "If you send your children to America you lose them anyway, and maybe you have other worries. I want mine here, in Italy, with their family, where I can look after them. How can we take them into our businesses if they are educated abroad? We simply have to stick together, find out who these people are and stop them. Signor Wintle, tell us exactly what you think will happen now."

Philip got to his feet again, his face grave, and thought for a moment or two, choosing his words carefully. "Without being alarmist," he said slowly, "I think they will try to kidnap someone else, and soon. I have already put all your homes, every chauffeur, every bodyguard, every system, on full alert. You must remember that the dice game goes on. I will continue to change routes and routines daily, or as I see fit. Meanwhile, Aldo Cirillo is doing all he can to help us get a lead on the gang. They are a big, well-organized group, and not one to be easily discouraged. There is too much money in it to stop now. They must expect reversals from time to time, and I don't think last night will discourage them for long."

"But why so soon?" asked Kleiner, puzzled. "Won't they need time to think it over and work out another plan? Accepting your theory that all this is the work of one organization, last night must have been a shock—three of their people are dead."

"That gives them every reason to strike again," continued Philip firmly. "They have lost three people and a lot of money has slipped through their fingers. Once they had you people on the run. If they said, 'Jump!' you ladies and gentlemen simply asked, 'How high?' Or, rather, 'How much?'—and paid the money. They will want to keep it that way. They have been picking up your children at the rate of one every three or four months, in spite of everything we could do to stop them. One or, at the most, two kidnappings in a year would be a lot among a dozen or so families, but four—five? It must mean inside information and advance planning. The kidnap rate is also speeding up—four in ten months. I suspect they're already setting up one grab while negotiating the ransom for the previous one. It's their business. They're very good at it, and their take is currently averaging one hundred thousand dollars a week.

That's a clear, no-tax profit. Even you, ladies and gentlemen, would not sniff at that. There is no business to touch it."

"In view of the Commander's forecast," said Kleiner, addressing the room, "I think we will all want to return to our families as soon as possible. We must all be very careful, particularly over the next few days. This business took a nasty turn last night. It may get worse before it gets better, so just be extra careful, all of you."

As the meeting broke up and people rose from their places round the table, Kleiner leaned across to place a hand on Philip's arm. "I have arranged coffee in my suite upstairs," he said, "and I would appreciate a few moments alone with you and Mr. Quarry. My secretary is waiting outside and he will show you the way. I'll come and join you in a few minutes."

Pushing their way gently through the throng toward the door, nodding brief good-byes, Simon and Philip found their guide waiting outside the conference room. They followed him into the elevator, then up a floor to Kleiner's apartment. They were shown in and invited to sit down before the secretary left them without another word.

"He's a chatty type," said Simon, looking around the room. "I thought Italians talked so much that the country was full of three-legged donkeys."

"He's not Italian, he's Swiss," said Philip. "Kleiner doesn't care for idle chit-chat, and if he were given to gossip, Klaus would probably fire him."

Simon got up and wandered across the room to look out of the window, down through the dripping treetops, to the rain-drenched garden far below. Then he perched on the window-sill and looked back into the room. On the whole he liked it. It was clearly a working room but not a fusty or gloomy one like Fiori's cigar-reeking study. The carpet was thick and the curtains silk; the furniture and fittings light in color and design, and chosen with quiet good taste. Apart from that, the room gave no clues to the occupant. There were no books, no records on the shelves, no papers on the desk. Like its owner, this room gave very little away. They only discordant object was the battered suitcase that had carried the money last night. Still covered with dust from the road, it lay on the carpet at the side of Kleiner's desk.

"Well, Simon, what do you think of our clients?" asked Philip, looking across from his place on the sofa, his pipe in his hand. "A pretty mixed bunch, wouldn't you say? Not the easiest group of people to work for, but Klaus can keep them in order, thank God."

Simon waved his hand carelessly, indicating the room. "He's the big wheel, after all. I was just thinking that we came a long way for a few rounds of rifle fire and a ten-minute chat," he said. "Still, there you are. I'm just very glad I don't have to wear a three-piece suit anymore, and spend my time in meetings. I wonder what their collective worth can be? It must run into billions."

"At the very least," agreed Philip. "And yet it's interesting. They can run industries and have investments all over the world, but be quite impotent against this particular threat."

"Most people would be," Simon pointed out. "You and I were just as baffled a couple of years ago, if you remember. You wonder why all this is happening to *you,* what you have done to deserve it, and, most of all, why doesn't someone—or, rather, someone *else*—do something about it. The snag is that the mind recoils from the fact that in this situation you are on you own—everyone else is just damned glad it's you and not *them.* I half-apologize for speaking so bluntly down there, but they have to understand what's going on. The game got rough when they shot Gina Fiori—and that's the way we have to play it."

"I know," said Philip. "And I think they do as well, deep down. They don't like it, though, and . . . ah, here's Kleiner. He's not looking too happy."

TEN

Kleiner came in briskly, his secretary close on his heels. He offered them drinks, speaking to them in English, but spoke to the secretary in German, sending him in search of coffee. He made a few phone calls in French and Italian, putting down the receiver as the man returned bearing a tray. Then Kleiner came over to join them, sitting beside Philip on the sofa, waiting until his secretary had poured the coffee and left the room. As the door clicked shut, Kleiner picked up his cup, drained the contents in one swallow, sat back, and looked directly across the table at Simon.

"Well," he said, locking his fingers together and repeating Philip's earlier question, "what do you think of my colleagues in the consortium?"

"That's what Philip asked me," said Simon. "Last night's

shootings seem to have worried your colleagues more than the death of the girl, maybe more than the thought of threats to their own families. Maybe they've learned to live with that, but it's a different game now. They don't really want to get involved. They'd rather pay the money and have done with it. If it was only that easy I think I'd agree with them."

Kleiner nodded. "They certainly don't like it," he agreed. "It's one thing to be a victim, quite another to be a vigilante. There is the publicity, wild stories in the press, the effect on their shares in the stock market. I don't want that either—bad publicity costs millions. They also wonder what their wives will say, what the media would make of them hiring a gunman. Having Commander Wintle as our protector was simply good sense. Some one like you, who comes to our monthly meeting and calmly says, 'I shot *him*, then I shot *him*' . . . well, that is something else. So they are worried. Several of them, Herr Franck in particular, now want to opt out of the group. That's what delayed me downstairs. I don't want the consortium to break up."

"Herr Kleiner, I simply don't see myself like that," Simon said wearily. "All right, I can use a rifle, but I am not a gunman. I came into this affair only because Philip asked me to. I didn't start the shooting last night, they did. Why, I don't know. The money was right there—and I see you have it back."

"So I do," said Kleiner, smiling. "I can't think how we'll account for it. It represents the weekly cash float for a small chain of supermarkets I own around Berne. Philip and I went to collect it. It was quite exciting, watching people put wads of notes into that case, just like in a movie. Normally, I simply sign drafts—I hardly ever see actual cash."

"You'll want to get it back to Switzerland," said Philip. "It's risky, leaving it lying about like that."

"I can't return it to Switzerland," said Kleiner calmly. "The comptroller said he had lost it over the last few days. According to his books it no longer exists. We can't return it in one go or our computers will go crazy. We seem to have it on our hands for the moment."

"How did your comptroller manage to lose it?" asked Simon curiously. "That amount of money must be hard to overlook."

"I've no idea," said Kleiner carelessly. "Juggling about with the cash returns, or destroying wholesale receipts and cash register accounts fed into the central computer, I expect. Such things are hard to stop at the top. Our systems are mainly designed to stop pilfering lower down. It's all chicken-feed to a computer thief."

"Not week after week, for years," put in Philip, "and that's how they get caught. They get greedy and go on bleeding the system, but we latch on to them eventually."

"I'm surprised to hear you own supermarkets," said Simon. "I thought you were in heavy industry and high-tech . . . from what little I've read about your activities."

"I am," said Kleiner blandly. "That's how the group began, but I own lots of supermarkets, and hotels and drugstores, in Europe, in America, even in Australia and Africa, and I hope to own many more. They produce cash, and cash flow or liquidity, call it what you will, is the oil of business. Sometimes it's useful to have ready money, and that brings me to the reason I wanted to meet you."

"I'm glad we're getting to that," said Simon, glancing at Philip. "When Philip said that you had heard about me, I became . . . well . . . a trifle concerned."

Kleiner looked down at the floor between his feet for a moment, thinking, then rose suddenly and walked across to the window, speaking over his shoulder into the room. "Mr. Quarry, I know many people like those you met this morning. Not all of them are upright citizens by any means, but this is the first time I have had coffee with someone who has killed so many people. According to my sources, you have killed eleven men in the last three years, not including the three you shot last night."

Simon and Philip exchanged glances, then looked together toward Kleiner's back. He continued to look out across the rooftops, his voice drifting back to them from the window.

"Don't be surprised," Kleiner continued, quietly. "I know a

lot of strange people. Big business leads to many contacts. You *are* that Simon Quarry whose wife died in a terrorist attack at Athens some years ago? All sorts of stories are going around on what happened after that. No one actually says so, in as many words, but the sum of it suggests that you wiped out that group of terrorists. Then I discover that you and Commander Wintle are good friends, and I find that very curious indeed. I asked the Commander to introduce us, and here you are."

"I'm glad you're getting to the point," said Simon ironically. "Yes, I'm that Quarry. Yes, I came here because Philip is a friend of mine. That apart, I don't see the need to give any details. I'm sure Philip won't either."

"He doesn't have to," said Kleiner calmly. "I have talked to many people about you. In recent years I have seen a need for someone with your talents and your discretion. Those qualities are hard to find, Mr. Quarry." Kleiner turned to look at them, a dark silhouette against the window. Then he came back to sit on the sofa and reached across the table to pour himself another cup of coffee.

"Mr. Quarry, how would you like to earn a great deal of money?" he asked, looking directly at Simon.

"No, thanks," said Simon. "I already have a great deal of money, more than I'll ever need. Anyway, I don't kill for money and I won't kill for you, not at any price. No amount of money is worth one death. You'd better come up with a better reason than money, but if you you want someone killed who really needs killing you ought to do it yourself. That'll concentrate your mind on whether the killing is necessary, or whether you're just crazy."

"I will . . . I mean I have," said Kleiner softly, looking at Simon across his cup. "I'll find you the best reason for killing that a man ever had. However, don't turn down the money. Your particular skills deserve a high fee, and I need you to know that I'm serious, very serious, and not a bit crazy. I want to offer you a contract, to assist us to eliminate this gang which has preyed on us for the last four years. I will pay you the sum of one million dollars, or as much more as you like, once we know this particular threat is out of our lives forever. I am paying a smaller, but still substantial, sum to Commander Wintle. In his case the deal is that anyone apprehended and turned over to the law receives a minimum sentence, before remission, of twenty years."

"If it costs you a million dollars every time you want to show someone you're serious, you either have more money than sense or you need a psychiatrist," Simon said bluntly.

The silence that followed was so deep you could have heard a pin drop on the thick-piled carpet. As a rule people did not talk like that to Klaus Kleiner.

"Then let me put it another way," said Kleiner heavily. "Have you ever heard the story of the rich man who wanted to sleep with the beautiful, unattainable woman?"

"Tell me," said Simon, sitting back.

"Well, he finally took her out to dinner, and plied her for hours with champagne and caviar. Then he said to her, 'Tell me, honestly, would you sleep with me for a million dollars? Be honest now.' She thought about it, and she was an honest woman, so she said, 'Well, yes, for a million dollars I probably would.' Then he said, 'Fine. Now, would you sleep with me for ten dollars?' And she said, 'Certainly not—what do you think I am?' And he said, 'We've established what you are; now we're haggling about the price.' "

Simon permitted himself a small smile, a raised eyebrow. "And the moral is?" he asked.

"Mr. Quarry, you keep saying you are not a killer, not a gunman, but what would *you* call a man who has killed fourteen people in the last couple of years? You are what you are, Mr. Quarry. Why not face it?"

"They needed killing," said Simon.

"So I understand. I'm not sitting in judgment, far from it, but let's not play with words. You have a certain talent, and I value it at one million dollars—per contract."

"You don't seem to have heard me," said Simon. "I don't want money. I want something worthwhile to do. I can hit what I aim at, but *I* choose my target, Mr. Kleiner, not you, not at any price."

Philip placed his coffee cup on the table, and put his hand on Simon's arm, interrupting. "Look, Simon," he said, "Klaus isn't trying to insult you. He's quite serious and he'll play his part. He's offering to pay a fee for your help; to cover our backs, to help us work this out. It's dangerous, and if you are going to help us you might as well get paid for it. You can give it away to charity, or buy Lucia an expensive present. It's only an offer. I can tell you that I'm being well paid and it doesn't bother me one bit."

"Herr Kleiner didn't hire you to shoot people," Simon pointed out. "And I have other things to do with my time than go about shooting perfect strangers. Besides, I don't want more trouble with the law. If you think the money matters, why don't *you* take it? I don't want it."

Kleiner leaned forward in his seat and turned toward Simon. "Mr. Quarry, let me try to deal with a few of your doubts. I'm a businessman and I always like to work within the law. I can assure you that everything I do—we do—has the support and approval of Captain Cirillo and the Squadra. Nothing we have done or propose to do is illegal. It may be extra-legal, but it's not actually wrong."

"But who elected you to do it in the first place?"

"Well . . . you have a point there. Let us say I volunteered my services because these kidnaps have to stop. The police can't stop them on their own, or they haven't managed to up to now. I can give you three good reasons for my involvement if you wish."

"It would help," said Simon.

Kleiner paused for a moment, gathering his thoughts, his eyes resting for a second on the tabletop. Then he turned again toward Simon. "Firstly," he began, "there was the matter of my daughter. I won't elaborate on that and I think with you especially I don't have to. You lost your own children to such people . . ."

"Yes, I know," said Simon shortly. "And secondly?"

"Secondly, the business community in this country is being bled white by these people, and I don't just mean the money. Any senior manager is liable to be kidnapped, abused, shot, maimed, even killed, either by terrorist groups or professional kidnap gangs. It costs millions to protect them and their families, and it still doesn't work. There is trouble all the time. It is hard to get any highflier to come and work here now. Would you accept a job if you knew you ran the risk—the higher the job the higher the risk—that you or your wife or child could be kidnapped? I doubt it. Two of my own directors have been kneecapped . . . all right, they are insured and received heavy compensation, but how do you compensate a man for a life on crutches?

"The final reason is that I intend to do something about it. I am dealing myself in. I have extensive interests here in Milan. I own radio stations and newspapers, I have influence here. I didn't put the consortium together out of the goodness of my heart. I did it to extend that influence. Together we employ over a quarter of a million people in this city. Those employees have families—and Italians have big families—so we can affect millions of voters. That's clout, Mr. Quarry. If we are going to make a stand against these people, we'll make it here, on our own ground, and the authorities must support us. If not, we pull out . . . and this city will see economic devastation on a scale you can't imagine."

There was a long pause after that. Simon thought it all over carefully, his eyes resting thoughtfully on Kleiner's face.

"Well, what do you think?" he asked at last, looking around at Philip. "It sounds exactly like the sort of setup you're totally against. However nicely Herr Kleiner wraps it up, he's forming a private army."

"It's up to you," replied Philip quietly. "It's useless to say that we must leave everything to the police—it isn't that simple. We have to find solutions that work. I need you here, and if you stay on you might as well get paid for it."

"But why me?" asked Simon bluntly.

"You can handle firearms," said Philip. "That's more than I

can do. If push ever comes to shove, we need to be able to push harder. What would have happened last night if you hadn't been there? Besides, what else do you have to do? You say you want to do something worthwhile, and this might be it."

"You can see what the Commander means," urged Kleiner. "The three of us would make a good team, so why not give it a try? I don't want employees, I want partners. Together we can do something to clear up this kidnap business."

Simon stopped him. "All right, all right. I'll help you with this because I'm in it already, and it's not over yet. Has Philip told you his theory? That you're being set up from within . . . that this series of kidnappings isn't just coincidental."

Kleiner nodded and put out his hand toward Simon. "I know that. Look, we have to get to know each other, so I will give you a contract for this job, a written contract, and the fee as agreed." Kleiner indicated the well-traveled suitcase by his desk. "That's found money, as the Americans say. You can have a million out of that, or I can give you a certified check in any currency you like, but it will take a few days to clear. You will have to trust me."

Simon laughed and glanced wryly at Philip. "I never believed that situations like this existed," he said to Kleiner. "Are you seriously suggesting I just walk out of here with a million bucks of your money?"

"Well, why not?" asked Kleiner, grinning back at Simon's surprise. "The whole thing is mad, anyway. You can have it if you want it. We might as well start trusting each other straightaway."

Simon shook his head. "No, thanks . . . and you don't buy trust with money. It's not a commodity, Mr. Kleiner, it's a quality. If you're keen to get rid of the money, give it to Philip. He can be your stakeholder. But if it will make you feel any better, draw up your contract. If the terms look reasonable I'll sign it, but on a one-time basis. I think we need to take this one step at a time."

Kleiner got up from the sofa, moved over to his desk, and unlocked a drawer to pull out a blue folder. He opened it, took out a document, and studied it closely for a moment, nodding to himself, before returning to the sofa and handing the paper over to Simon.

"I have the contract right here. Philip has already seen it," he said. "I drew it up on the basis of what he told me about you."

Simon glanced at the pair of them, then read the paper through once, and then again. Finally he put it down on the table and looked across at Kleiner. "You don't mess about, do you?" he asked. "You're taking one hell of a risk drawing up a document like this and giving it to a total stranger. Look at this clause here . . . *'That the principal'*, that's you, *'will fund any operation by the partners'*, no names, *'leading to the elimination by any means, leading to the arrest, imprisonment or death of named criminals.'* If that leaked out, you'd be on every front page in the western world."

"I doubt it," said Kleiner blandly. "I own quite a few of those papers. Even so, I don't have to worry, since I intend to stand by the terms. I'll do my best to keep the police off your back and you will keep the wasps from stinging us when we poke into their nests. I can't name the criminals in this case, so I suggest we add ". . . *the Fiori kidnappers*." That should be clear enough. I would be much happier if you took the money, if only for expenses."

"No, thanks," said Simon. "If I spend more than I can afford, I'll bill you."

"It's not a legal contract," put in Philip, "in the sense that any of us could go to court and sue for breach, because it is an agreement to act illegally—and that's not binding. What it does do is to put us in each other's pockets. We will have to stick together because we are all in it together. It's also called conspiracy."

"It's also called good business practice," said Kleiner. "You know what they say? A verbal agreement is not worth the paper it's written on."

"So I've heard tell," said Simon. "However, having had some experience of contracts myself, most of the experience tells me that all contracts are one-sided. Someone is always trying to screw someone else, Mr. Kleiner. A written contract is simply damage limitation, nothing more, if the parties—or one of them—wants to wriggle out of it."

"Well, that may be," said Kleiner, "but . . ."

"No, let me finish," said Simon. "I am not a tycoon or an international wheeler-dealer, but I did all right in my business days, and had no trouble with my authors, provided the people I dealt with remembered my one simple rule."

"Yes? And that is?" Kleiner's eyes were watchful.

"If I make a deal, I stick to it. If anyone has any other ideas, I will give one gentle warning and then hit them like a train. If you attempt to mess me about, our deal is off, contract or no contract. I hope you remember that."

"And who will decide what constitutes 'messing you about,' as you put it?" asked Kleiner.

"I will," said Simon, smiling. "Let me be frank. I don't know exactly what's going on here, but you're up to some cat-and-mouse game and for some reason you want me in on it. Well, that's fair enough. Maybe you'll tell me the whole story in your own good time, but you have to remember that in a cat-and-mouse game, the outcome is usually more dangerous for the mouse. Do I make myself quite clear?"

"I'm afraid not," said Kleiner, "but I get your general drift."

"All right, let me put it like this. Do you intend to take an active part in all this or just put up the fighting fund?" asked Simon, looking directly at Kleiner.

"That depends," he replied. "You might not find my physical assistance as helpful as my financial help, but if things get critical I'll help if I can. I hope it won't come to that. I was thinking of staying in the background and dealing with other matters—contacts, information, finances. You have been very frank about your motivations, Mr. Quarry, so let me be equally blunt about mine. I don't believe in fairy godmothers, or do-gooders, or golden-hearted whores. I like to know why people are doing what they do, and I like to pay my way. I don't want your help on a grace-and-favor basis . . . I want to know I can rely on it as and when I need it, and I want you to take that money."

"No chance," said Simon. "Nobody owns me but me—and that's it."

Kleiner looked at Wintle and spread his hands. "Impasse," he said.

"I warned you," said Wintle. "Some people aren't for sale."

"So, let's find some compromise." Kleiner's eyes switched to Simon. "Can we discuss this, Mr. Quarry? I'd be much happier if our arrangement was, well, businesslike."

Simon shrugged, smiling slightly. "All the cards are on the table," he said. "It's just that I'm not playing this game by your rules. I have to say that making you happy does not feature as a major priority in my life."

"But you see my point?"

"Only just. I thought Lincoln put an end to the slave trade—but maybe I was wrong."

"Simon . . . please." Wintle leaned forward, coming between them. "Will you listen a moment? Knowing you, and knowing what Klaus had in mind, can I propose that if you don't want the money I can keep it for you? And you can . . . what? . . . give it to a charity, if you like."

"Why me? Why don't *you* give it to charity?"

"Wait a moment. Money is a tool to Klaus, just like that rifle is to you. And we may need money, lots of it, in cash—for all sorts of things, before this business is over."

"Like what?"

"I don't know . . . for hush-money, bribes, to buy whatever we need, expenses—who knows? I'm saying, for the moment, let's keep it. Don't spit in Klaus's eye—his cash may come in handy."

"You keep it, then," said Simon. "Be my guest."

"Fine—if you are agreeable, Klaus?"

"I don't care what Mr. Quarry does with it. If he wants you to have it . . . if he is too proud to touch it, that's his affair."

"Simon?"

"Oh, for God's sake . . ." said Simon. "You can paper the

bloody walls with it for all I care. Stick it in you car, and if we need it we'll use it. Is that all right?"

"Klaus?"

"Whatever you both want. I have said all I have to say."

"Good." Wintle sat back in his chair, relieved. "Then maybe we can get back to business, and I'm sure Simon will find that you can give us a lot more than just money."

"Can you handle a pistol or a rifle?" asked Simon, turning toward Kleiner.

"Not like you can. I can hit what I aim at with a rifle," replied Kleiner slowly. "With a pistol I can hit anything, even something quite small, at up to thirty meters."

"What if the 'anything' you are shooting at is someone quite large and shooting back?" asked Simon. "What happens then?"

"Then we shall have to see," said Kleiner, shrugging. "I can only do my best."

Simon got up and took a turn or two about the room for a moment before turning back toward Kleiner. "All right," he said, "I'll accept your contract, at least for this current problem. After that, we'll see how we get on. Aldo Cirillo must keep the Italian police off my back, both during the present hunt and after it is over. The man who pulls the trigger is the one who gets into trouble, not the paymaster, so I'm relying on you to keep me clean—agreed? And it's protection work—I'm not your personal hitman."

"Agreed."

"Can you do it? Can you perform what you promise in the contract, with the police and so on?"

"I can do it," replied Kleiner, nodding, his tone quietly confident. "Money talks, in any country, Mr. Quarry, and I can talk bigger than most . . ."

"That's good," said Simon, edging toward the door. "Let's leave it there for now. I'll go and get some rest. If you need me I'm at Lucia's. Are you coming, Philip? We can share a cab."

Philip shook his head. "No, I'll see you out but I'm staying here for a while. Fiori is not my only problem. I run the security for Klaus's group and I'd like to know how one of our people can 'lose' over a million dollars in cash. I'm supposed to prevent things like that."

"Just one other thing," said Simon. "Have you got Lucia's number at the Ospedale?"

Philip took out his diary, found the number and wrote it out for Simon on a strip of newspaper. "There you are," he said, handing it over. "It's the city code—just dial."

"Thanks," said Simon, putting the paper in his pocket and turning to go. "Well, Mr. Kleiner. I'm glad we know where we stand, and I expect we'll get to know each other better in the next few days."

"I expect we shall," replied Kleiner gravely. "Why not begin by calling me Klaus?"

Simon hesitated a moment, his hand on the doorknob. "Well, why not? Right, Klaus . . . good-bye for now."

Nothing was said as Philip and Simon walked together to the bank elevator, Simon waiting while Philip pressed the button, his eyes on the flashing numbers above the door.

"Well," he said at last, "your friend Kleiner is a pushy bastard. He doesn't like to take no for an answer, does he?"

"Maybe not," grunted Wintle, "but then he doesn't have to. I did ask you to go along with him, if only for my sake. Why did you have to flare up at him like that? Most people would jump at a million dollars."

"More fool they. I know what you asked and I went as far as I could. But while I'm being helpful to you I have to be fair to myself. Do you think he's happier now that he's got some sort of commitment? That's all the commitment he's going to get. I hope he understands that."

"He's happy enough, I suppose."

"Well, then . . . don't worry about it." Simon put his hand out to hold back the door of the elevator. "He has to know who he's dealing with."

"Don't we all?" said Philip.

ELEVEN

A million dollars is a great deal of money. Thinking about it, Simon Quarry wandered through the lobby of the Hotel Principe, then out into the gardens, shrugging on his coat, pacing along slowly in the rain. He had no use for such a sum and no need of it. Simon Quarry wasn't very interested in money. He had enough to keep him adequately and his wants were few. Money was Kleiner's weapon, his language, his way of keeping score, and he valued Simon's work in the Fiori affair at one million dollars. Even to Kleiner that wasn't small change, so what Kleiner was really saying was, this is serious. Simon stood watching the rain dapple the gray surface of the pond and decided that he had been right to go along with them and see what happened. He was still coming to terms with this decision when the rain from his hair began to trickle down his neck.

He went back to the hotel, found the bar, and ordered a tonic and Angostura. Three of the consortium people were already there, seated round a table in the corner, but, although they looked at him and fell to talking quietly among themselves, there was no invitation to come across and join them. *Maybe they don't like to drink with the help,* thought Simon sourly.

Seated on a barstool, he saw his face reflected in the mirrors behind the bar, half hidden between rows of bottles. *You're looking tired,* he thought to himself, *and there's more gray in your hair than there used to be.* Looking down at his watch he realized that this time five days before he was just getting into all this. Since then, a flight to Italy, a shooting, Kleiner's contract . . . and Lucia. It was nice to think about Lucia. And it was interesting to work again with Philip. Life was never dull when Philip was around, unlike life in Mallorca. That had been dull, bloody dull. Maybe that was why he had drunk so much. Now, he didn't even want it. He drained his glass, crunched a nut from the bowl before him on the counter, ordered an espresso from the barman, and began to think again about Lucia.

When Simon had gone Philip went into Kleiner's study. The New York and Toronto stock markets had opened, and Kleiner was punching facts into his computer, relaying instructions to his brokers via the satellite dish, for even at a time like this business was business. Philip watched the green numbers fluttering across the computer screens for a while, passed a few memos and requests for information through to Kleiner's secretary, then went to phone Lucia. Half an hour later she joined him in the restaurant of the Principe, slipping into the chair at his side and stripping off her gloves.

"You look tired," he said, "and I think you need a drink . . . waiter!"

"I am tired, very tired. Aren't we all?" she said bitterly. "But don't worry about me. I'm used to it. I told Simon so this morning. But I'll have a gin and tonic—make it a large one, with lots of ice."

Philip ordered the drinks and collected menus from the waiter, passing one to her. "Well . . . how are you getting along with my friend Simon?" he asked, raising his eyes from the wine list.

Lucia gave him one of her long, level stares. Philip didn't look away and she didn't speak.

"Well?" he asked again.

"I haven't been to bed with him, you know," she said. "Not yet. Don't look so shocked, Philip. My father told me once—in one of his typical helpful moments—that I had a weakness for unsuitable men. I am beginning to think he might be right."

"Is Simon unsuitable? He's pleasant, rich, amusing when he wants to be, certainly never dull. And I'm not shocked—surprised perhaps. But on balance I approve. He's very suitable."

"But dangerous," she put in. "Look at last night."

"Simon isn't dangerous. Not to you, not to me. Unless severely provoked he wouldn't harm a fly. He wouldn't let the wind blow on either of us if he could help it."

Lucia put down her menu and leaned across the table toward him. "But he kills people. You said so yourself and I've seen him do it. It doesn't seem to affect him. This morning he was absolutely normal. He woke me with coffee and toast and went off to water the houseplants . . . and he makes jokes."

"And that frightens you?" he asked. "What he can do, or the fact that he makes jokes?"

"What he did last night doesn't bother me. He had to do it, I know that. It's that he doesn't seem to care."

"He cares," said Philip. "But talking won't change things, will it? Listen, I want you to be extra careful over the next day or so. The gang are still about, three men and a million or so dollars short. They have it in for your family and if they were to take *you* then we'd all be in a jam. So don't use your car if you can help it; use public transport or taxis and never take the first taxi that comes along. Make your movements irregular and stay as close to Simon as possible."

She smiled then, suddenly. "Well, I intend to do that," she said, "but I'm glad to have your approval, especially if it stops you worrying about me."

"Well . . ." Philip considered the remark carefully. "Let's say that anyone who tried to lift you while Simon was about might find that he'd bit off more than he could chew. He can be quite remarkable if he's provoked."

"You really like him, don't you?" she asked. "I mean, *really*."

"Yes, I do. He's very likable when you get to know him, and I know him very well."

"Yes? Tell me . . ." She paused. "Does he have anyone else? I mean . . . it's been some time . . . I just wondered . . ."

"There was a girl . . . a woman. A very attractive, very tough lady. I gather she left. He lives on his own now."

"He's asked me to go with him, to Mallorca."

"Has he now? Well, why not? There is one point I'm worried about, Lucia. Simon is . . . elemental. He really doesn't care if he lives or dies, and it gives him a tremendous edge. Most people, even killers, want to live and get away with it. Simon simply doesn't care, either way. All that went when his family died."

"Ah." Lucia nodded sadly. "Yes, he talks about that. Not about his family, he never mentions them, but he says you must always have an edge, and backup. He's here as your backup."

"That's right. He is, and I need him. That's why he came, but he's staying on for you."

"What are you trying to tell me?"

"It's obvious to everyone that he cares about you and you care about him. At any other time I would be glad for you both."

"And what's wrong about now?" she asked shortly.

"Nothing. Except that not caring about anything gives him his edge. He said to me once, 'The most powerful man in the world is the man with nothing to lose.' "

"That's a quotation," she said.

"It's a rough translation of Ibsen."

"So?"

"Don't blunt that edge. He may need it. And finally—this isn't easy for me to say, and probably none of my business—try not to get in any deeper."

"It's too late for that," she said. "Much too late for that."

* * *

The next kidnapping was swift and ruthless. The car left the Colombo house, exactly according to plan, at ten minutes to four in the afternoon, heading down the leafy, tree-lined avenue to the main road into town at the bottom of the hill. That road led into the center of Milan from the residential suburbs, and now it was crowded with the early evening traffic.

The chauffeur knew his job. He handled the big car well, easing it out into the traffic stream, cutting in and out among the cars and lorries, moving up through the heavy traffic, and turning into a side road to arrive outside the school exactly on schedule, at precisely four o'clock. He looked at his watch, leaned across to open the lock on the rear door, and shifted into neutral. He kept the engine running, according to the rules, and his eyes flicked regularly between the road ahead, the rearview mirror, and the school gate over to his right.

It happened just as the clock above the school gateway chimed the first stroke of the hour. The chauffeur opened his own door and got out, walking round the back of the car and putting his hand on the handle of the rear door, ready to open it. The school gate opened and a man came out, a teacher, looking down, chatting to the small dark-haired schoolboy in white T-shirt and jeans who walked at his side, books and a tennis racket jutting from the blue sportsbag that swung from his hand. It was a peaceful scene; the only sound other than the clock was that of children's voices from somewhere inside the school. Nobody even heard the other car coming.

It came up fast, very fast, from the main road behind and suddenly swerved across to their side of the street, bouncing heavily up onto the curb, then a long, skidding halt on the wet paving stones, the front wing clipping the rear door of the limousine and smashing it shut. The impact sent the chauffeur sprawling across the courtyard as he leaped, rolling away from the danger. Brakes squealed and two armed men jumped from the car. They fell on the boy and the teacher. The leader clubbed the teacher to the ground with rapid, savage blows to the head from the barrel of his machine pistol, while the other man began dragging the terrified boy away, kicking his feet from under him, bundling him into the back of their car, scrambling in after him, fists swinging, smothering the boy's screams, forcing him to the floor of the car.

There was a yell. A man had appeared at the corner of the piazza, and came running hard toward them, a small dog scampering at his heels. The first kidnapper looked up from the teacher, gave him a final kick in the head, and, jerking the machine pistol into his shoulder, fired a short burst directly into the running man's chest. The sudden, harsh chatter of the gun drowned out the reverberation of the clock's chime. The impact of the bullets stopped the man in his tracks, lifting him from the ground, flinging him back and down, and he rolled in his own blood across the cobbles, the small dog leaping aside, barking wildly.

The kidnap car was already on the move, wheels spinning on the wet cobbles, engine roaring, rear door open, the boy screaming. The gunman smashed his foot again into the teacher's ribs and jumped over him, planting one foot on his back, slipping on the wet stones, bumping heavily into the chauffeur, who was just scrambling to his feet. Then the car came sliding round, slowing to let the gunman scramble inside. The open swinging door clouted the chauffeur hard, sending him reeling back to trip over the teacher and fall, his head hitting the cobbles with a great crack. The car screeched off, bumping down the curb; a hand reached out to pull the door shut. Then the car was gone, accelerating down the road, leaving only a trace of blue exhaust fumes in the wet air. Apart from the three sprawled bodies and a litter of schoolbooks on the pavement, all was exactly as before. The clock above the gateway chimed the last stroke of the hour.

Simon rarely dreamed, but he was dreaming now. He was asleep in Lucia's wide, comfortable bed, his teeth grinding together slightly, his dreams shot through with dark shapes, red flashes, the sound of engines. It seemed that he had hardly closed his eyes before something woke him, and he swam up slowly from the depths of sleep to find that the telephone beside the bed was shrilling loudly. It was dark in the room and he had to fumble for the light switch before reaching across for the phone. Glancing at his watch, he saw that it was just six-o'clock, and he had been asleep for about four hours.

"Yes?" he said thickly. "Er . . . *Pronto*. Who is it?"

"Simon? It's Klaus Kleiner. There has been more trouble, I'm afraid. Another kidnap."

"What's happened?" Simon threw back the blanket and got to his feet, rubbing the sleep from his eyes, passing one hand across his bristly face. He felt heavy, drugged with sleep, only half awake.

"About two hours ago, here in Milan. I've just got the call. There was a killing, too. I don't have all the details, but it was one of our people, one of the consortium. That's why they rang me."

Simon swayed slightly, the telephone at his ear, looking around the room for his clothes. "Well . . . Philip warned us . . . even so, that's very quick. Where are you?"

"I'm at the hotel, and, quick or not, it's happened. They have taken Signor Colombo's boy. You met Colombo this morning at the meeting. Philip Wintle is over at Fiori's, picking up his clothes. Can you meet him there as soon as possible and come up to my suite at the Principe? I've already rung Philip and he's expecting you. Colombo is on his way here now. He's in a bad state."

"I imagine he would be, poor bugger," said Simon. "Right, we'll be along as soon as possible. Give me half an hour."

Simon replaced the receiver and walked heavily across the room to where his clothes were dumped on a chair and felt in his jacket pocket for Philip's piece of paper. When he had it, he returned to the bed, picked up the telephone, and, glancing at the paper, began to dial.

"Pronto. Ospedale Cà Grande," a voice said. Somewhere, in the background Simon could hear a loudspeaker gabbling in Italian.

"Er . . .' Simon thought for a moment. *"Signorina Fiori, la Dottoressa Lucia Fiori, per piacere."*

"Sì, signore—momento."

A minute later Lucia was on the line.

"Pronto!" Lucia's voice—sharp, impatient.

"Lucia, it's Simon."

"Oh . . . Simon . . . where are you?" Her voice grew instantly warm.

"I'm in your bed, or rather sitting on it—I've been asleep all afternoon. I hope that's all right."

"I think it's very all right. Stay there—I'll be back soon."

Simon shook his head, keeping the phone at his ear. "I can't wait, I'm sorry. There's been more trouble and I have to go out."

"What's happened now?" Her voice was becoming tense again. "Not another, not so soon."

"I'm afraid so, a boy this time. I don't know any details, but Kleiner just rang with the news. Philip said this would happen. Lucia?"

There was a muffled noise from the other end of the line, then Lucia's voice came on again, stronger, calmer.

"Right, I've shut the door. Do you know who? I had lunch with Philip. We looked for you at the Principe but you'd gone."

"Kleiner said it was someone called Colombo—something like that, anyway. I was half asleep."

"Colombo? Yes, there is a Colombo in the consortium." Lucia's voice trailed away thoughtfully. "A nice man—he has a son. Poor man. What are you going to do?"

"I'm going to get dressed and pick Philip up from your father's house and get over to Kleiner's. Do you want to join us at the Principe, or what? Dinner tonight is probably off, I'm afraid. I don't know quite what will happen. How was your day?"

"Pretty awful," she said. "Let me think for a moment." There was a short silence. Simon held on to the receiver, rubbing the sleep from his eyes. "No-o," she said at last. "I won't join you. I have some arrangements still to make for the funeral, and Gina's body has already gone home. I have to go there and see that everything is arranged. But I want to see you. Let's make dinner if we can."

"Lucia . . . ?"
"Yes?"
"Never mind. I'll tell you later. *Ciao.*"
"Ciao," replied Lucia, "and be careful."

It was still raining when Simon came into the street. He had to walk down to the corner of the road, shoulders hunched against the rain, and wait there for a while before he found a taxi. Five minutes later he was outside the Fiori house, heaving open the heavy gates and crunching up the gravel toward the front door. The knocker on the door was almost hidden behind a heavy wreath of lilies and ivy, tied there with a long, black weeping ribbon, but as he stood on the step, hunting for the bell, the door opened. Fredo Donati stood inside, his face as impassive as ever.

"Buona sera, Signor Quarry."

"Good evening," replied Simon briefly. "I've come to collect Signor Wintle. More of this kidnap business, I'm afraid," he went on. Then, nodding toward the wreath, "Let's hope it doesn't lead to more of that."

"I know. We had a telephone call from Herr Kleiner. Signor Wintle is upstairs. Please come in. Can I get you a drink? It is very wet outside tonight."

"No, thank you." Simon half-smiled at the suggestion. "I've given it up."

The hall was dark, the house very quiet. The only illumination came from the dim light of a small candelabrum that stood on an oak table set against one wall. The air was full of the odor of Fiori's cigars, mixed now with another, heavier scent, of hothouse flowers, clinging, sweet, overpowering.

"They have brought Signorina Gina home," said Fredo, answering his unspoken question. "She is through there, in the main dining room, with my *capo.* Would you like to see the body?"

"Er . . . well, no. Thank you." Simon was startled. "That's very quick, isn't it? Doesn't there have to be an autopsy or an inquest, something like that? I'm glad the rain has driven the press away, at least for the moment. They're bloody ghouls."

"Oh yes . . . *sì*, of course there are many details, but all that has been arranged by Signorina Lucia. Many people are expected this evening, to pay their respects before the coffin is closed. That is the custom here. I expect the press will be there at the funeral; they have no respect."

Simon dabbed the rain from his hair and face with his handkerchief, and nodded, looking curiously at Fredo's calm face.

"You've known the Fioris a long time, haven't you, Fredo?"

"Many years, Signor Quarry."

"You must have known Gina from when she was a little girl?"

"Oh yes, from when she was born, and Signorina Lucia even before that. But her father . . . since boyhood I have known him, in Naples, when we both lived in the South."

"Perhaps I should have a word with Signor Fiori, but I don't want to bother him right now. Can you tell me where I can find the Commander? And do you think the chauffeur could run us over to the Hotel Principe? It's hard to get a taxi in the rain."

"His room is on the first floor," said Fredo, gesturing to the upper landing. "Turn left at the top of the stairs and it's the one right at the end. The chauffeur is no longer here but I will ring for a taxi if you wish."

When Simon looked back from the head of the stairs, all he could see in the darkness of the hall was the pale, still face of Fredo Donati looking up at him from the gloom below.

Simon entered the bedroom close behind his knock. Philip Wintle was lying back on the bed, hands linked behind his head, staring at the ceiling, a pen and notebook resting beside him on the coverlet. He glanced at Simon without moving his head, then swung his feet down onto the floor and sat up.

"You really ought to wait before bursting in like that," he said mildly. "For all you knew, I might have been entertaining a beautiful woman."

"You should be so lucky," said Simon shortly. "Anyway, I did knock. Have you got any more details on the Colombo kid? Klaus didn't know much when he called me."

"I've talked to the police and to Cirillo. The police are in at the start on this one because the kidnappers shot a civilian while getting away. It happened right outside the boy's school. I've just been looking over the Colombo security routine to see where it went wrong."

Philip began to fill Simon in on the details, looking down now and then at the jottings in his notebook. "So, there you are," he finished. "It's another consortium disaster. I can't help but wonder if setting it all up was worthwhile. They're simply a bunch of targets. Several of them will probably drop out now and go on their own. I can hardly blame them."

Simon took a chair and twirled it round to sit astride it, arms folded on the back. From this position, chin resting on his folded arms, he gazed at Philip thoughtfully.

"You look like hell," he said bluntly. "You're the brains here and you need to conserve your energy and get as much sleep as you can. It's hard to think when you're out on your feet with fatigue. How did it go with Kleiner after I left?"

"All right—he didn't mention you again. I took the money and he didn't say a word. Now it's in the trunk of Lucia's car. I don't fancy leaving it there and I'm already fed up looking after it. Besides, I think this case is beginning to break."

Simon looked doubtful. "I'm glad to hear that, though I don't see how. Anyway, you'll have to put off thinking for a bit. We ought to get over to the hotel. Signor Colombo will be there by now and I expect they'll want you to come up with some bright ideas."

Philip showed no reaction. He lay back on the bed, switched his gaze back to the ceiling, and scratched his chin reflectively, fingernails rasping gently over the slight evening stubble on his thin cheeks.

"I know you're a cool fish," said Simon mildly, "but His Nibs is already champing at the bit. Shall I go over there and hold the fort?"

"Just relax, Simon, and we'll go there presently," said Philip calmly. "Do you remember the story of the two bulls? No? Well, the young bull said, 'Look at that herd of cows in the next field. Let's rush down there and jump a couple of them.' But the old bull said, 'No, let's *stroll* down there, and jump the lot.' Nothing will happen on this Colombo business for at least twenty-four hours. The bastards like to worry you and have you lose sleep before they get in touch. It all helps to wear the victims down. I call this the sweating time. It's my fifth since I started in this business, and just for once I'm going to relax and wait them out. Simply reacting to one event after another just won't do. The whole affair is completely off balance."

"I must say you're taking it all very calmly," said Simon. "I know you were expecting something like this to happen, but surely not quite so fast? It hasn't been twenty-four hours since the last event ended."

"I also told you why I was expecting something like this," admitted Philip, talking over his shoulder as he headed for the bathroom. "This is an inside job and obviously the work of one gang. How else could they react so quickly?"

The telephone on the bedside table rang sharply. Philip turned back in his tracks, picked up the receiver, and listened briefly, looking across at Simon, winking before he spoke. "Simon is already here. Yes. We'll be along in about half an hour. No, I want to brief Simon first." He hung up. "Kleiner," he said, in answer to Simon's raised eyebrows. "I think I could hear Colombo's voice in the background. Kleiner has his hands full."

"I'm sure he can handle it," said Simon, "but what exactly do you think is going on? Getting the facts from you these days is like drawing teeth."

"Come into the bathroom," said Philip, turning toward the door, "and I'll tell you about it while I shave . . . and you're crumpling my last clean shirt."

"First of all," said Philip, wiping steam from the mirror and peering in it at his lathered face, "I never have believed in the theory of the professional kidnap gang, not as far as this particular business is concerned. I don't see this series of kidnappings as the work of organized crime, from the Sicilian Mafia or the Naples Camorra, or the work of starving peasants somewhere up in the hills who snatch a rich kid to help tide them over a poor harvest. Neither is it the work of the Red Brigades, or the First Line, or any one of a hundred other little terrorist groups that keep Italy in a permanent tizzy. The second time they contacted us they said they were the Red Guard Faction—which certainly sounded like a terrorist group, but they didn't make the usual demands for publicity, or use the normal jargon, or refer to that again. I think that was just a blind. Cirillo has first-class contracts in the terrorist world and he tells me he has never heard of a Red Guard Faction."

"Don't all of those groups go in for kidnapping?" asked Simon. "On the flight here you told me that kidnapping is big business in Italy, and that every criminal group dabbled in it."

"It is, and they do, from time to time. Kidnaps happen continually, even in the industrial North. Countries tend to specialize in various types of crime, you know. In Britain the gangs go in for armed robberies, payrolls, banks, but kidnapping is almost unknown. However, both Aldo and Kleiner agree with me that these are different."

"In what way?" asked Simon. He had perched on the edge of the bathtub and was shifting uncomfortably from one hip to the other, watching while Philip sluiced the remains of the shaving soap from his face, scooping up the water from the basin with his hands, then reaching across for a towel.

"In almost every way. Take the money. In the last two years, this particular group has been bled of over *fourteen million American dollars!*" Philip laid stress on every word. "How could *any* Italian peasant community account for that sudden windfall? What would they do with it? They couldn't begin to spend even a fraction of it. On the other hand, fourteen million is almost small change for organized crime. The Mafia or the Camorra can clear that in just one shipment of cocaine. As for the terrorists, left or right wing, they would make a song and dance about it. But apart from one halfhearted claim, we haven't had a hint that terrorists are involved."

"Fourteen million dollars sounds like a fair piece of change to me," said Simon, frowning. "I have an adequate amount of money, but fourteen million dollars is much more than just nickels and dimes. Any crook might find it worthwhile to get his hands on such a sum."

Philip sat down on the bathstool, drying his hands on the towel, then reached for a brush and comb.

"Totally, yes, but in installments over years, no. In the way this sum has been extracted, it's still small change," he said. "Just forget the peasants and the Mafia, and the politically motivated nutcases, Simon. I was a policeman for thirty years, and being a good policeman takes a lot of different skills and qualities; some I had, and some I didn't have, but one skill I *did* have was gut feeling. This whole business simply feels wrong. Then there are other things."

"Like what?" asked Simon curiously.

"Firstly, the snatches have all been very precise jobs. No errors, very little blood, nobody hurt much—at least until last night. That means *either* long surveillance to spot a good moment for the kidnapping, *or* inside information. There's no other explanation. The sums demanded are another pointer. They're very precisely calculated to what the victims can pay, even if it cripples them financially to do so. But for Kleiner's backing many of the consortium would have been ruined. So, what remains is simple. Forget the terrorists. This is no big deal. We're not tackling some vast organization. We're dealing with a criminal, probably one man, and the real crime here is extortion."

Simon listened to this carefully before replying. "In what way are the sums precisely calculated?" he asked. "And if we have a crook, can't we have a gang to back him up?"

Philip shook his head again. "Forget the kidnaps for a moment and consider the ransoms. The ransoms have a pattern. They are always to much for the victims to raise out of their own reserves. They always have to sell substantial fixed assets, subsidiary companies, businesses, large blocks of shares, and usually sell at knockdown prices. I've checked, and that happens every time. Now, if they are selling, who's buying? If one person is behind the purchases, might there be a link with the kidnaps? That's what I'm trying to discover at the moment. What we have here is extortion. Kidnapping their kids is just the lever—the best one there is."

Simon nodded slowly, thoughtfully. "I see," he said. "Well, it's thin but it's certainly an idea. Is there anything else?"

"Life-style," said Philip positively, reaching for his jacket. "Who was it who said, 'The rich are different?' Whoever said it, it's true. The rich move in different ways and go to different places from us less well-heeled folk. Yet this gang, if I accept that there is a gang, can come into their lives like a hot knife into butter, cut out a slice of the action, and get clean away with it, time after time. It's all just too neat to be accidental or just plain luck. There's a brain at work here, on the inside."

"Perhaps . . . but maybe you simply don't believe in luck," said Simon. "I think a little luck—or a little bad luck—can make all the difference."

"I entirely agree," said Philip, pushing Simon ahead of him into the bedroom, "and I think our villain's luck is running out. It's stopped being simple. His victims are not lying down anymore. Criminals despise honest folk, you know. They think honest people are mugs, but I think they're worried about you and me and Kleiner. They want us out of this business one way or another."

"Hence the bomb?" asked Simon.

"Hence the bomb. That might have been a shrewd move, but it didn't work," agreed Philip. "And what's more, it's given me an idea . . . Pass my tie." Philip tied the knot, and bent down to adjust the tie in the mirror.

"Well, go on," said Simon.

Philip stood up, tucked his shirt into his waistband, and reached for his jacket. "What if there's not one kidnap gang but two?"

Simon snorted. "That's pretty unlikely, isn't it? Even Kleiner's consortium couldn't be *that* unlucky."

"But it's a possibility . . . given the facts we now have."

"Anything's possible, I suppose, but what are the facts?"

"The bomb is a fact."

"So? What about it?"

"The bomb didn't make sense unless . . . look, let me lay a few facts out for you. Remember, there has to be a reason for everything. Nothing just happens."

"Go on."

"Well, there was no reason for Gina's kidnappers to send me the bomb. I was their contact and they needed me—and Lucia—to set up the meetings. After weeks of negotiating why throw all that away? The conclusion is inevitable."

"And it is . . .?"

"That Gina's kidnappers did not send the bomb. Therefore someone else did . . . right?"

"C'est logique, mon brave," said Simon, nodding.

"Right. Now, although the kidnappers gave us a deadline for collecting the cash, they waited until four days *after* the deadline to get in touch and—please note—when they did call, they didn't ask if we had the money. In fact they *never* asked. So?"

"So, they already knew you had it."

"Right. Now, let's suppose that the bomb in the car was not meant for me but for both of us. Let us therefore assume that your arrival has got somebody worried—but only a few people were supposed to know you're here. That narrows the field a bit."

"I'd already thought of that. If they, whoever they are, wanted you off their backs, they could have done it before and with a bullet. A bomb is messy and not so sure."

"On the other hand, a bomb is better to hit two people, and there's less risk of the killer being caught."

"Well . . . yes. Anything else?"

"One or two points. You said the gang needed four days to set up the meet. Maybe they needed time to set up the Colombo snatch. Ever thought of that?"

"No . . . not until now. But it's an idea."

"Finally, and I'm assuming that because the facts point that way there are two gangs, why kill Gina Fiori—and Lucia and me? It's pointless, unless . . . well, there is a reason. I just haven't quite worked it out yet. But I'm getting there."

"So I see. Any conclusions so far?"

"Not yet. I need a few more facts. But one thing's clear. Kleiner's collection of big fish includes a shark. The shark certainly knows we're hunting him and he has two choices—to go deep and hide or come up and attack. Hence the bomb. If that's the choice he has made, he'll try again and . . ."

"And then," said Simon, "someone will have to step in and cover you and Kleiner. The pair of you have drawn a killer onto yourselves and you can't even guess who he is. Nice work. No wonder Kleiner's contract is worth a million dollars."

TWELVE

Gina Fiori lay in her coffin, her pale face tilted to one side, a position that concealed the great wound in her forehead. She looked asleep, her eyes closed, her dark hair washed and combed neatly forward, framing her face and spread across the satin pillow. The top half of the lid was hinged back, and the tall, flickering candles that stood about were smoking a little, sending little shadows over her head so that sometimes it seemed as if her face changed or her lips moved. It was just an illusion. The real Gina Fiori simply wasn't there anymore.

"They've gone," said Fredo, coming in and closing the door. "They're on their way to Kleiner's. I got them a taxi."

Fiori sat in a heavy chair at the foot of the coffin, head turned round to look at Fredo. The dining room had been converted into a chapel by the undertakers, who had hung long black and silver drapes over the walls and windows, removed the table, and set out row upon row of chairs for those who would come later on to sit for a while and view the body. That was the custom.

Fredo came across, looked at her for a moment, crossed himself, then sat in a chair beside Fiori.

They sat there together for quite a while, looking down at the dead girl, before Donati finally broke the silence, shifting round in his creaking chair to look directly at Fiori.

"A drink, *capo*?" he suggested. Fiori took his eyes slowly from the coffin, turning to look at Fredo blankly for a moment before nodding.

Prego—una grappa," he said heavily.

Fredo got up, moving across the room to the cabinet against the wall, pouring out the drinks with a clink of glass, returning with the one grappa and one large whiskey, passing the grappa to Fiori, and sitting down again.

"I am sorry about Gina, *capo,*" he said quietly. "I meant to speak before but there has been no time. Thee is nothing I can do, but you must know how much I am sorry for this."

"She was a good girl," said Fiori, nodding. "She loved her father anyway, not like Lucia. That girl disappoints me. I spoiled her, Fredo. I blame the English for that; sending her to school there was a mistake, and look at those two we have here. All this trouble is their fault. Where are they now?"

"They have gone to Signor Kleiner's, because there has been another hit . . . they took the Colombo boy."

Fiori shrugged, sipping his grappa, brooding. He had no interest in Colombo's problems. "That Kleiner, he's another one. Until he came along, we had no trouble at all. Do you see that, Fredo? Kleiner, then Wintle, now this Quarry. . . . If they were not here interfering, maybe Gina would still be alive. We can take care of our own without any help from the English. But Kleiner . . ." Fiori shook his head. "Why is he doing this, bringing in these people? I don't know what he wants, Fredo. What's in it for him?"

"We must wait, *capo*," said Fredo. "Let them do what they can, it might help. With Gina gone, we are almost free again. And the English will go away soon, if we show them they are not wanted or needed."

Fiori's eyes were back on the coffin. "I think I would like that, Fredo," he said at last. "I think that would be good. So I would like to believe that you are right, but I don't think so. Leave me now . . . I need to think."

Fredo finished his drink, placed the glass gently on the floor beside his chair, and got up, crossing himself again before the coffin, and then left the room as silently as ever, closing the door softly behind him. When he had gone, Fiori felt in his pocket for a cigar, lit up, and began to smoke it, his face heavy with thought. Around Gina's head the candle flames still flickered on.

"Well, that's all we know," concluded Kleiner. "The chauffeur has concussion, severe bruising, and superficial cuts to the face, but otherwise he seems to be all right. They've kept him at the hospital overnight. The teacher has a hairline fracture of the skull—these people play rough. The man who tried to help him was dead on arrival at the hospital with multiple gunshot wounds from a small-caliber machine pistol. He had a wife and three children, incidentally. The police found the car within ten minutes, parked in a side street near the school. It had been lifted from a supermarket parking lot in the suburbs off the Monza road an hour before. There was no sign of the boy, of course, not even a note. So, now we wait for them to make contact."

The three of them, Simon, Philip, and Kleiner, were seated around the big table in Kleiner's suite. The rain had stopped at last, and the curtains stood open to show lights sparkling far across the city. Only a single standing lamp in the corner and the light in the center of the table, shining up on their faces, illuminated the room. Simon wondered at this liking for half-lit rooms and shot a look across at Carlo Colombo, who sat slumped on a chair in the corner. He had said nothing while

Kleiner gave them the news; he simply sat in the corner, his head in his hands. Colombo, completely crushed by the sudden kidnapping, was unable to comment or join in the discussion. He was leaving everything to Kleiner, who sat back in his chair and looked inquiringly at Simon and Philip.

"I'm the new boy here, so I think it's your move, Philip," said Simon. "What do you think will happen now? Is there anything we can do?"

Philip had said nothing during Kleiner's summary; he had sat looking at the tabletop, doodling on a pad with a pencil, deep in thought. Now he got up and went over to stand by the window, looking out across the rooftops. He slowly removed his gaze from the darkening scene outside, then wandered back to the table and sat down.

"I shall want to talk to the chauffeur as soon as possible," he began slowly. "He should have followed the dice game. An ambush like that is hardly possible if the dice game is followed, so clearly something went wrong. I shall want to know what."

"What on earth is the dice game?" asked Simon curiously.

"It's a security procedure, based on chance," explained Philip. "I set it up as soon as I was retained here. I have given every family in the consortium a set of twelve security patterns for their day-to-day routines, covering routes to work or schools, shopping, golf trips, whatever they do as a rule. It depends on the options available, but the idea is to avoid a regular pattern of movement, to shops or office or, as in this case, to and from school. Kidnappers or thieves quickly latch on to a regular pattern, but the dice game is a completely random procedure and quite simple to use. Every morning you roll two dice. Let's say you get a nine–fine . . . you look up Pattern Nine and it says you leave home an hour later than usual, with two bodyguards, and get to the office by route B. Had you rolled a six, you would go by taxi, and by route A, perhaps unescorted. With school the pattern is tighter, because of lessons and so on, but even so the choice is still fairly random, and certainly never regular. The pattern is dictated by the dice, so we call it the dice game. It makes planning an ambush to the split second like this practically impossible. If you need more options you add more dice, but two are usually sufficient. But . . ." continued Philip ". . . the car was taken an hour before and abandoned ten minutes later, and the snatch took only a few seconds. That's very tight. So I want to know what number the chauffeur rolled on the dice and if he stuck to that routine. As it is, I don't like it. I don't like it at all."

"I can guess what went wrong," said Kleiner resignedly. "The chauffeur didn't bother with the dice game because Signor Colombo wasn't there, and after the Fiori business he felt the pressure was off for a while. That happens after every snatch. I remember it happened after my own daughter went. It's like the IRA bombings in London—you remember those times, Simon? Philip? For a while the security is as tight as a drum. Everywhere you go they want you to open your bag or briefcase. But then—what the hell?—weeks go by, nothing happens, so people get slack. I know the dice game is designed to be so simple and effective that they will always use it, but you have to allow for human error. I bet the chauffeur just got the car out and drove directly down to the school with no diversions, and I also bet he's been doing that for weeks. On the way back home, with the boy on board, he would have been more careful and chosen a different route each day; that's understood. But on the way there, without the boy, no dice. You expect too much of these people, Philip, but they get careless. It's human nature."

Carlo Colombo took his face from his hands, rose, and came over to sit at the table. "I will dismiss the chauffeur anyway," he said softly, "but, *scusate,* what are we going to do about my boy?"

"We must not have the chauffeur dismissed until Aldo Cirillo and I have had the chance to see him," said Philip. "I hope Cirillo has him under wraps at the hospital. You may well be right," he said, turning to Kleiner, "though it still doesn't explain why the kidnap car was lifted an hour earlier and how they knew the pickup was at four o'clock. The dice game varies the pick up by up to half an hour each way, but the kidnap car drove straight up onto the pavement—wham, bang, thank you, ma'am—and away goes young Carlo. Come on, Klaus, be reasonable. It's much too pat.

"If he used the same route regularly when going to collect young Carlo, the dice game flopped," pointed out Kleiner. "The gang could just zero in on that and follow him. And, as you yourself said, that could be what they have been doing for the last few days."

"Well," said Philip, "I suggest we shake the teeth out of that chauffeur anyway. None of them is any bloody use. Even Fiori's has skipped, or quit, or gone off somewhere. We had to get here in a taxi."

Kleiner glanced across at Colombo in the corner and lowered his voice, leaning forward between Simon and Philip. "Did you talk to Aldo about your main idea?"

"I did," said Philip, his tone equally soft, "and he took to it. The Guardia di Finanza are running a full check into stock exchange dealings here in Milan, in Zürich, and in Rome, covering all sales or transfers of stock and so on for all the companies owned by consortium members. I told him to include you, incidentally," he finished, flashing a grin at Kleiner.

"Thank you," said Kleiner, grinning back. "That's very thorough of you. I only hope he can handle an on-line computer. We need to find a pattern. When unknown people are making stock raids on my companies, and we don't know who is doing it, we look for a pattern. We call them the Dawn Raiders. Businessmen hate using their own money, so if I find someone buying a position in a company, and I learn that someone else is borrowing heavily, then I can put two and two together. Mostly, I am right."

"There is another pattern you might take a look at," Simon put in suddenly, his eyes fixed thoughtfully on the table. "I didn't think of it until you told me about the dice game, and I don't know if there is a pattern, but it's worth a look."

Philip and Kleiner turned their eyes on him attentively, but he avoided their gaze and sat staring, deep in thought, across the shadowed room toward the window, drumming the fingers of his right hand lightly on the table.

"Well, come on, what is it?" asked Philip, after waiting for a moment.

Simon took his eyes from the window and looked at them each in turn. "Don't rush me. I think it goes like this." His voice was quiet, persuasive. "Philip is hired by Klaus to protect these consortium people. I don't know the ins and outs completely, but I expect he looked at their houses, lectured them on security, put in the odd alarm, got Cirillo to put in a little muscle with the city police to cruise past the consortium houses a bit more often—things like that?"

"Ye-e-s," said Philip cautiously. "I did all that, and a bit more. How do you think I recognized that Israeli barbed wire you have strung around your house? Because I bought ten coils of it myself, for the consortium. We've wired up their houses, fitted scanners, got them Fiat Uno kidnap-proof cars, done all sorts of things."

Simon held up his hand, his tanned face turning cheerful. "I'm not sniping, Philip, I'm just clearing the undergrowth. Now, when you'd protected their homes and offices, and made them all streetwise and security-minded, and convinced them that, yes, it *can* happen to them, you then set up the dice game to destabilize the areas you could not control. Am I right so far?"

"I do wish you'd get to the point," said Philip. "The underlying object of security, my dear Simon, is to let the client, the potential victim, live a normal life. The most secure man in the world probably lives, at least for a while, on Death Row. But in the real world, Simon, people have to live, eat, work, shop, go to school, go on holiday. That's what life is all about."

Philip's voice had sharpened a little during this recital, and he stopped only when Simon leaned across and put a hand on his shoulder, patting it.

"I'm not criticizing," said Simon. "I'm simply describing how it looks from the outside. It's logical to cover all you can, and to cover the bits you can't control you organize a totally random system. In other words, the dice game. Am I right?"

"Yes," said Philip, his voice patient. "I've already told you that. I can cover them at home, office, factory, in aircraft, or on ships, but I can't do anything about it when they simply move around. Therefore I beg or plead or demand that they avoid regular patterns and follow the bloody dice game. What are you trying to say?"

"I'm saying it's the chauffeurs," said Simon flatly. "Didn't you tell me that these last kidnappings have been from cars? Is that right? Yet you also say the chauffeurs have to play the dice game. If it is difficult to break the dice game once, twice must be bloody near impossible and three times, with young Colombo—well! You know what they say: That's not coincidence, that's enemy action."

"I don't see the connection," said Kleiner abruptly, "or, rather, I don't see why we should concentrate on chauffeurs. It's obviously easier to snatch people outside their homes or offices. That's why we have the dice game in the first place. It does not follow that the chauffeurs are organizing the kidnappings."

"Maybe not, but what is happening is against the laws of chance. Were there any car kidnappings *before* you introduced the dice game?" asked Simon. "*That*'s what I'm getting at."

Kleiner and Philip exchanged questioning glances, Philip doodling on his pad while thinking hard, waving a hand toward Klaus, bidding him to think back and answer.

"No," said Kleiner slowly. "At least, I don't think there were, as I remember. My daughter was taken from a friend's swimming pool. There may be no connection, as that was before the consortium, but there was no random security then, certainly no dice game. Fritz Langer's boy vanished from a train on his way to a skiing holiday in Bormio with the Fioris. They picked up Maria at a children's party by Lake Como last summer. We think she went off in the caterer's van. But Gina was at the high school and the chauffeur had picked her up, like today, and was driving her to the Fiori home when she went. You're right, the last two have been from cars. And that's in spite of the dice game. We guard the children at home and in school.

Only when they move about are they vulnerable. Yes . . . yes, yes . . . I begin to see what you are getting at."

"I think you should look at the chauffeurs," said Simon. "There is one big weakness in any game of chance. If the dealer is crooked the bettors will lose. When Philip introduced random chance with the dice game, it didn't make any difference to the kidnappings, but don't you see, it *should* have made a difference. And it's the chauffeurs—or some of them. No one else has access to the dice game."

Philip nodded slowly, a warm smile spreading across his face as he turned toward Kleiner and clapped his hands together once or twice enthusiastically. "There you are, you see?" he said, half proudly. "Didn't I tell you he has a way of seeing what other people don't? We couldn't see the wood for the trees. Of course . . . find out who can break the dice game and everything follows. They should have varied their methods. As it is, they gave themselves away."

"Maybe they didn't care. Maybe they planned just two kidnappings, back to back," said Kleiner slowly. "So they can afford to take a chance and break the dice game. Besides, you covered all the other angles, so they had no choice. What do you suggest we do about it now?"

"My chauffeur has been with me for three years," said Colombo from the corner. "He's a good boy. I can't see him harming young Carlo. They are good friends, and he was hurt as well this afternoon."

Simon shook his head. "Maybe your chauffeur is different, I don't know. It's only an idea, we have no proof, but it's still worth looking at. What screwed up the kidnappers was Philip's new security arrangements. When they breached them to stay in business they had to give themselves away. Don't you see that?"

"It's still only a possibility," put in Philip, speaking over Simon's shoulder, "but I think it's worth following up." He turned back to talk directly to Kleiner. "I think we must now trawl through the chauffeurs' backgrounds with a very fine net. Cirillo can pull them in one at a time and give them a hard time.

If Simon's theory holds up, we'll screw the truth out of them eventually."

"We can't do anything yet," pointed out Kleiner. "Even if Simon is right, the kidnappers still hold young Carlo. We can't give them any reason to be . . ." He looked over at Colombo. ". . . Well, difficult. Sooner or later they will contact us. Maybe then we can begin to move. Until then . . ."

Philip put his elbows on the table and rested his head on his hands for a moment, sighing. "Why are our hands always tied?" he asked. "I hate to pour cold water on your theory, Simon, but it's only recently that the dice game has been breached. Why now, after we have the dice game, do they kidnap from cars, which, as you say, gives the game away? It doesn't make sense."

Simon shrugged. "I don't know why. I can only say that the only people who could break the dice game are the chauffeurs or the consortium people themselves."

"That must all wait until we get a lead on where the boy is," said Kleiner. "And, since we have no other new leads, I think we should get Cirillo to lean on Colombo's chauffeur."

"I think not," said Philip firmly. "The last time we involved Cirillo a girl got mutilated. Someone in the consortium is feeding information to the kidnappers, so we follow the rule . . . no cops. I learned that rule the hard way."

"But this man might tell us where the boy is," Kleiner protested, glancing over at Colombo and dropping his voice. "We need to get him back, both for his sake and because—to be frank—the consortium can't stand any more blows."

"I know that," said Philip, "but let's think it through. Let's not rerun old errors. If Simon is right and the chauffeur is involved, we have one great advantage this time that we haven't had before. We know who one of them is and we can put our hands on him. Let's not throw that advantage away. I say we wait and we think. Another twelve hours won't make a lot of difference."

"Then I think that's all for the moment," said Simon, breaking in. "So, may I use your phone?"

He tracked Lucia down at her father's house and told her they could still have dinner. He heard her talking in the background for a moment and then agree. "Fine," he said. "Then I'll wait for you at the flat. You can decide where we go. Ciao!" He hung up and turned back to the others. "You know where I am," he said to Kleiner, "and I'll be back there sometime after ten. Are you coming, Philip? Good night, Signor Colombo. Try not to worry."

They left Kleiner talking softly to Colombo and let themselves out of the suite, walking together silently over the thick carpet, heading toward the elevator.

"Congratulations," said Philip at last. "I think you may be on to something with the chauffeurs. We'll need to get the Colombo boy back first, and think the whole thing through a little more, but it's certainly a possibility. Maybe Aldo can come up with a few more facts on who is behind all this. In the end, it all comes down to information."

"I'm sure you're right," replied Simon. "But at least we know what the rules are now, and we have a lead on the chauffeurs. We know what not to do, and that's a start."

"That's true," said Philip ruefully. "But there's still one major flaw in your theory."

"Only *one* thing wrong? Is that all? And what's that?"

"What would a bunch of chauffeurs do with fourteen million dollars?"

THIRTEEN

The press were out in force, gathered in little knots outside the gates of the Fiori mansion, sitting on the wall before Lucia's apartment, constantly on the telephone to her.

Lucia had been trailed home from the hospital, badgered at the gate and only shook them off in the basement garage. When she and Simon left for dinner, they did so separately, Simon leaving first on foot and waiting a street or two away until Lucia picked him up in her car. Eventually they made it to the restaurant.

"This is nice," said Simon, pulling his chair up to the table and looking round the room. "I'm starving. We don't seem to have eaten much during the last day or so."

"I'm glad you like it," said Lucia quietly. She looked exhausted, elbows resting on the table, shoulders sagging, dark half-circles under her eyes. She was smoking incessantly, nervously, her thoughts elsewhere. They were dining in the center of Milan, in a small, quiet restaurant off the vast, echoing Galleria. The air was full of the warm smell of pasta, the lighting diffused from small lamps on the walls and tables. There was a merciful absence of piped music. A long, copper-topped bar ran down one side of the room, matched by a row of booths along the opposite wall, with a number of well-spaced tables occupying the floor in between. The lower half of the bar was occupied by a long, bubbling fishtank where fish finned and crabs and lobsters crawled about—waiting. Lucia and Simon sat at the far end of the restaurant, Simon with his back to the wall as usual, looking over Lucia's shoulder. From there he could see all the way down the room to the window facing onto the street. People hurried past, shoulders hunched against the rain. Apart from the old couple behind the counter and a single waiter hovering by the door, the restaurant was empty. Simon remarked on this.

"Does everyone else know something we don't know, or are we early?" he asked.

"We're early," said Lucia, beckoning to the waiter. "People tend to dine late here. In an hour or so it'll be crowded. Anyway, let's order and talk. *Il menu, per favore.*"

They ordered, Lucia taking care of the food, Simon poring over the wine list. "Orvieto?" he suggested. "White? Cold? And for me, of course, San Pellegrino—I'm beginning to like the stuff." When the bottles arrived he took them from the waiter and poured out two full glasses before placing them back in the ice bucket. Then he raised his glass toward Lucia.

"Drink up," he said. "It'll do you good. You need a lift."

Lucia drank deeply, her green eyes studying Simon's face over the rim of her glass. She put the glass back on the table, her face troubled, and lit another cigarette. Simon was doing his best to be cheerful.

"I'm sorry," he said. "I'm trying to help. Maybe we should have stayed in. You look tired."

"I am tired," Lucia said. "It's been a bloody day. People are very kind but they can't help. Anyway, it's all arranged . . . the funeral . . . but, well, it's all difficult, isn't it?" She shrugged her shoulders and looked directly at Simon. "You and me—how can it ever work? We can't even have a normal conversation. . . . 'How was it at the office? Did you see the Pinter play? Shall we go to Como for the weekend?' Yet I want that. I want us to be normal, like normal people, but how can we? After last night, after arranging Gina's funeral all day, then having to go out because the Press bastards keep pounding on my door—that's unnatural. And what can I say to you 'Shot anybody lately? Did your rifle shine properly?' It's not normal, is it?"

"No, but you'll get used to it," said Simon, "after a while. At least, I hope you will. You see, I'm restricted—there are lots of things I can't do, not safely. There are countries I have to avoid, situations I mustn't get into, people I have to watch out for. If we continue—no, *as* we continue, I just hope you can stand that. It's not easy, but it's not always like this."

"I think I can stand it," said Lucia. "It's the getting used to it that's difficult. It's like a dream, like a bad film you can't walk out of. There are millions of people in this city who'll never know what this is like."

Simon twirled the stem of his glass in his fingers, and smiled at her briefly over the table. "It's like strata," he said. "We are living on one stratum, where violence is committed, criminals roam, people get killed. Lots of people live there: police, soldiers, people who live on the rim of the law. In some countries that's even the norm. In some Latin American countries, in parts of Northern Ireland, the threat of violence is always there, and people learn to live with it. Those people out there"—he nodded toward the window—"only meet trouble when they cut across the strata."

"But I don't understand how you can do this . . . live like this," said Lucia. "Don't you want to lead a normal life, go to work, have friends, be like other people? Don't you want to be normal?"

Simon smiled again slightly, and continued twirling the glass. "If I catch sight of myself in the mirror, I am sometimes surprised to see how normal I look. No fangs, no razor scars, no marks of Cain. But to answer your question, yes, I would like to get back to the world and be like other people."

"Then why don't you?" Lucia's tone was edged with impatience.

Simon's shoulders lifted slightly. "Because it's not that easy. You can't just walk away from a killing. Even if you could, people won't let you." He leaned toward her, his face close across the table. "I don't know if you will understand this. After my family were killed, I felt . . . numb. Hard as you think it might be, it became harder and went on getting harder the more I tried to put up with it. I didn't just grab a pistol and start gunning Arabs in the street, you know. I tried everything else, every legal way for a little justice, until there was nothing else to do—and only then did I . . . well, start all this."

"Did you enjoy it?" asked Lucia curiously. "Hunting those people?"

Simon shook his head slowly. "No, not really . . . but it was interesting. It kept my mind going, just working it out. Until the first time I didn't really believe, not deep down inside, that I would really go through with it and actually shoot anyone. I had to concentrate on what they had done to go through with it at all . . . and then it was too late." Simon shrugged again. "And it's too late now."

"No, it isn't," said Lucia firmly. "Or it doesn't have to be."

"No? Isn't it? Why not?"

"Well, because . . . because you have me to think about now. I need you to look after me. Isn't that something else, something better than all this?"

"It's a lot," conceded Simon. "But are you sure? It won't be easy. I'm in very deep here. Once you start something like this, you can't just say 'Enough' and walk away, you know."

"I'm very sure," said Lucia. "I've thought about it and I can be sure for both of us, if I have to be. And all you have to do . . . is do something else."

"Like what?"

"Anything. Anything but this. What do you like doing?"

Simon switched his eyes from hers to look down at the checked tablecloth. "Well, don't laugh, but I'd quite like to go back into publishing. I'd like to publish poetry."

"Poetry?" Lucia could not keep a note of startled surprise out of her voice, and Simon looked up at her, smiling.

"There you are—you're laughing at me. . . . But why not? I like poetry. If you run your eyes along my bookshelves at home, they groan under the weight of poetry books. Mallorca is a great place for poets—Robert Graves for one. He lived most of his life at Deyá, up in the hills. There's no money in it, of course, but then I don't really need money. We could use Kleiner's money, to set up a little press. It might be fun. It would at least be something else."

Lucia smiled at him. "You really are a surprising man. If I'd thought of a thousand things for you to do, publishing poetry would not have been among them."

"Well . . ." Simon grinned back at her. "As long as I keep you amused you probably won't want to leave me, will you?"

"No. Now that I've found you," said Lucia smiling, "you are not going to get away. People don't get too many chances to be happy, Simon."

Simon reached across to take her hand, gathering it up in both of his. "It's curious," he said with a smile, "but you have the knack of taking the words right out of my mouth. Look . . . er . . . why don't we eat our dinner quickly and then rush back to your place?"

"Good idea," said Lucia.

Simon looked up as the doorbell clanged briefly at the far end of the room. Two men entered, stripping off their coats, calling out a noisy greeting to the waiter, who came round the counter, a plate in either hand, bringing Lucia and Simon's first course to the table. He put the plates down and went back to welcome the new arrivals.

"You were right," said Simon, poking at the food with his fork. "This place is starting to fill up. This pasta smells very good. What is it?"

"Paglia e fieno alla ghiotta," said Lucia. "I thought you would like it."

There was silence for a few minutes as they tackled the pasta, and when Simon spoke again his tone was conversational. "Lucia," he said calmly, "promise me you won't look round, but I think we may have a problem."

"What?" she said slowly, looking up. "Why . . . why do you think that? Who with?"

"Two men just came in. The proprietor wanted them to sit by the window, like he did us. They always do that. Restaurateurs like to fill up the window tables first because it makes the place look popular. The men wouldn't go there. They've gone into one of the booths, about ten or twelve feet away. They've already looked over here a couple of times. That's very interesting."

Lucia didn't look around. "Well, perhaps, like you, they simply didn't want to sit in the window."

Simon was still looking down casually at his plate. "It's not a question of my not wanting to. It's safer here at the back, away from the street. That's why I took this chair, with my back to the wall. I can cover the room from here and watch the door. They are hard-face bastards and . . . well, I just wonder if they came here looking for trouble."

"What if they did?" asked Lucia.

"Then they've found it," said Simon. "Keep on eating."

They continued with their meal and managed to keep the conversation going, but the mood was wrong. Lucia heard the men's voices behind her, voices too loud for that place and that hour. She heard remarks she was intended to overhear. Simon kept his eyes on hers, smiling, willing her to relax, and not look around. "Stay calm," he said. "It's up to them. Let them make the first move."

The trouble arrived with their next course. As the waiter passed the men's booth, a hand reached out, stopped him, and examined the dishes. As the hand let go, there was a burst of laughter, and two heads looked around out of the booth, one of the men calling out to Lucia: *"Ciao, bellissima . . . Lascia quel vecchio rompiscatole e vieni a prendere qual cosa con noi?"*

Simon saw Lucia blush, noticed the unhappy face of the waiter. "What did he say?" asked Simon, "or can I guess . . . ? Something like 'Leave the old fart and come and have a drink with us?' "

"Something like that," said Lucia.

"Really!" said Simon, smiling broadly at the two men who were standing up now and looking over the top of the booth at him. "I think they're starting to get antsy—just sit still until they settle down again."

The nearest man called out something else to Lucia. Then he tried to trip up the waiter as he hurried past them again, heading back toward the counter. There was another burst of loud, aggressive laughter.

"That was worse?" asked Simon, smiling at her.

"Yes, much worse," she said, tight-lipped. "You're almost enjoying this, aren't you?"

Simon's smile broadened. "Well, it's nice to see two slobs digging their grave with their mouths. Don't let it worry you. However, since the waiting is the worst part, let's get it over with." He looked at the men and half rose from his chair. "Hello," he called cheerfully. "*Buona sera.* Can you speak English?"

"Fuck you," said the farthest man, sliding out of the booth and coming toward him. The other man reached out and jerked him back, saying something. Then they both sat down again, out of sight behind the high wooden back of the booth.

"Well, there you are," said Simon to Lucia. "They do speak English."

"What shall we do?" whispered Lucia. "They are between us and the door. There's no other way out."

"I know that," said Simon calmly, picking up his knife and fork. "And so do they. It's a setup. Why don't you eat your dinner? It's getting cold."

"I can't eat," Lucia hissed at him. "I'm too nervous. I've got this big lump in my throat. What are they going to do? Shall we get the waiter to call the police?"

Simon shrugged. "No . . . no police. I doubt if they're just a couple of jerks who dropped in by chance for a pizza, so it depends very much on what they have been told to do. At the very least, to kick the shit out of me, I imagine. Are you quite sure you want to leave? They'll only follow us, and there may be more of them outside."

"Yes, please, let's go." Her voice was shaky. "Let's get out of here and run for my car."

Simon took her hand. "We're not running anywhere," he said. 'Listen to me carefully. We'll settle this now, but I'll need your help."

"What are we going to do?" she asked, forcing herself to be calm, putting her cigarettes and lighter back into her bag.

Simon thought for a moment, still holding on to her hand. "When I say 'Go!' we'll get up to leave. Move quickly. We must be at their table before they can rise. While I deal with the nearest one you just sit on the other one's lap. Just sit on his lap and hang on. If you can do that, there'll be no problem. Can you do that?"

"Yes," said Lucia, nodding. "I can do that."

"Then let's do it," said Simon. "Ready? Go!"

They rose together and were at the booth in a couple of strides, Simon on the inside, holding Lucia lightly by the arm. At the table he stopped and looked down, smiling. The two men were rising, half on their feet, knees trapped under the table, two young, tough-looking men.

"Evening!" said Simon briefly. "Now, which one of you two bastards wants a swift trip to the hospital?"

The nearest one reached up, cursing, and grabbed Simon by the shoulder. That was a mistake. Simon raised his arm and drove his elbow back hard into the man's face, smashing his nose and teeth. Then he flung Lucia around the table, into the second man's lap, and hurled himself into the booth, pounding the first man's bloody head hard against the far wall, sending blood spattering across the tablecloth. Someone was screaming, someone else was shouting. Simon jerked the man forward, fingers sunk deep in his hair, and dragged him bodily from the booth. Then he tucked the man's head under his arm and ran him full tilt across the restaurant, tables and chairs scattering, smashing the man's head into the glass of the fish tank. Then came the splintering of glass, a great gush of water pouring into the room, a cascade of fish flopping onto the floor. Simon kicked the man's legs away, smashed his heel down into the man's spine, and leaped back across the room, behind the tidal wave of water.

The second man was on his feet, forcing his way out of the booth, pushing Lucia's encircling arms aside with one bunched fist drawn back to pound her face, when Simon arrived, sweeping up a giant peppermill from a table and driving it into the man's face. The brass top smashed through lips and teeth, deep into the yelling mouth, and when Simon jerked it out again, teeth and blood came with it. The man screamed, putting his hands up to his ruined face, but Simon beat them aside and smashed the heavy wooden mill hard against the man's head, once, twice, first one side and then another, following the man as he stumbled down the room, vomiting blood, beating him down with full arm swings, until he, too, sprawled on the floor among the overturned tables, the water, the shards of glass, the floundering fish. Behind the counter, the waiter, his face pale and shocked, came suddenly to life and reached for the phone.

Simon threw down the peppermill, reached under his jacket, and pulled out his pistol. "Just don't!" he said quietly, leveling the weapon. The double click as he thumbed back the hammer sounded loud in the sudden silence. "Just stay away from the phone. Tell him, Lucia." Half hidden behind the waiter, the old woman looked out with horrified eyes across the counter, her apron pressed to her mouth. From the kitchen door, her husband's head peeped out, his face stunned at the ruin of his restaurant.

"Everyone just stand still," said Simon, looking around for Lucia. She had collapsed onto a chair and was looking down at her feet, her shoes deep in the water swirling from the smashed fish tank.

"Are you all right?" he asked. She didn't answer him. She just sat there, her shoulders hunched, trembling, raising her eyes slowly to look at him across the litter of the room.

"I said are you all right?" he asked her again, sharply.

"Yes . . . yes, I think so."

"Now tell these good people to behave."

Lucia looked up and gestured the waiter away from the phone. "*Lascialo,*" she said. "Leave it. *Non toccarlo.*"

The room was a shambles. Pushing a crawling lobster aside with his shoe, Simon stepped across to where the first man lay and turned him over with one foot, kneeling down to go through his pockets. A wallet, an envelope, a knife, and a leather-covered cosh were removed and placed on a table. After a pause for thought, Simon bent down again, picked up the lobster, and, putting his arm carefully through the shattered glass, placed it back in the tank. "I'm sorry about that," he said to the owners. "Er . . . *scusate* . . . *mi dispiace* . . . sorry."

The second man was crawling on his hands and knees toward the door, choking, sobbing, a long gobbet of bloody spittle hanging from his mouth. Simon went after him, reached him in two long strides, and seized him by the collar to haul him up and fling him into a chair. The man kept his hands to his face and made no resistance as Simon flicked open his jacket and emptied his pockets onto the table. Another knife, another cosh, another bulging envelope, and a well-filled wallet came into view.

"Wait there," said Simon to the man, and carried these items back to join the rest on the other table. As he expected, both envelopes were full of money. Simon riffled it into one pile and pushed it down the counter toward the proprietors, who were still looking at him fearfully.

"Take it," he said, nodding at the money. "It will pay for the damage. It ought to cover your losses. Hell, Lucia . . . tell them the money is theirs . . . to pay for the fish tank. Tell them these men came here to attack me."

"*Questo è per voi . . . vogliamo pagarvi il danno . . . non vogliamo picchiarvi,*" said Lucia.

The owner and his wife said nothing. They made no move to pick up the money. Simon shrugged and dropped the pile of cash over the counter, out of sight. Then he walked back to the man in the chair, stepping over the now stirring body of his companion. Simon pulled up a chair and sat down, face to face with his attacker.

"Listen to me," said Simon intently. "I think you understand English. Take your friend and get out of here. And don't come back. I'll keep your knives and your wallets and give them to my friends in the police. When I tell them about this they will come looking for you."

He reached out to seize the man's hair and jerked his head up sharply, revealing a pair of fear-filled eyes above the bloody hands. "You don't want to tell me who put you up to this, do you?" he asked. "I could beat it out of you, but he'll probably kill you if you talk—right? Well, hear this—I don't like you, or your friend here. If I see you again I'll kill you. If you walk in front of my car I'll run you down. If you bother this place again, or the people here, or that lady over there, I'll kill you. Do you understand that?"

The man's eyes gaped, but he said nothing and the pistol appeared again in Simon's hand. He slammed it against the side of the man's head, knocking him off the chair, sending him sprawling across the wet floor. Then Simon reached down and hauled him up again.

"Do you understand?" asked Simon, looking closely into the man's face. "Answer when I speak to you."

"*Sì, sì.*"

"Speak English. I know you speak English."

"Yes . . . yes."

"Good. Now that we understand each other you can go." Simon got up heavily, put the pistol away, and looked across the counter at the waiter and his wife. "We are going now," he said slowly. "This man may need some help to get his friend outside. Let us leave and then throw them out. You don't need the police—and they would take the money anyway—it's evidence. So no police, OK? With luck you can have all this tidy again before the evening rush begins. It's not as bad as it looks. Tell them, Lucia."

Lucia told them, the old people nodding as they took it all in. Then she was at Simon's side, leaning against him so hard that he could feel her trembling. He put one arm about her, holding her there tightly.

"It's all right," he said soothingly. "It's all over. Just for once, they lost."

"Then can we go now?" she asked. "Please . . . please, let's go."

Simon took a last, long look around the restaurant, at the remains of their meal, the overturned chairs and tables, the litter of glass and water, at the two mauled men, and then steered Lucia gently toward the door.

"I'm still hungry," he said slowly. "It looks as if I'm never going to get a quiet meal in this town."

The doorbell tinkled briefly and they were gone.

They said nothing to each other in the car, nothing in the elevator, nothing as Lucia opened the door, nothing until he had gone across to the drinks tray, poured out a generous measure of brandy, and brought it back to where she was sitting on the sofa, still huddled in her coat. There was nothing to say, but something had to be said to break the silence.

"I'm sorry, Lucia—about all this. This isn't much fun for you, is it?" he said, placing the glass on the table. "Not much fun at all."

"Fun!" she said bitterly. "What a word. My God! Fun! Did you have to beat them like that? It was sickening. What kind of a man are you?"

"Now look!" Simon's voice was weary. "They were there to hurt us. They meant to break my bones, and maybe yours as well. It's no good offering to put up your fists and go behind the bike shed with people like that. This is street work and, as we used to say in the Commandos, in a situation like that you don't use your hands until your feet are bleeding. They had to be put down so that they stayed down. Whoever sent them may get the message to leave us alone."

"But it was so violent," said Lucia quietly. "First last night, now this. I was so scared."

"Well, it didn't show. You did well," said Simon, sitting down beside her. "You sat right in his lap and held him. But for you they might have pulled it off. You saved me from a bad beating."

Lucia smiled slightly and stirred in her seat, reaching for her glass. "Did I?" she said dryly. "I think you would have managed." She looked up at him, her eyes steady. "But will it always be like this? Last night you killed three men, tonight you beat up two more half to death. Is this how you want to live?"

Simon shook his head firmly. "No, of course not." He sat down and put an arm around her shoulders. "First of all, it won't continue like this. I don't know what's going on, but I feel, Philip feels, that the whole situation is coming apart. It will all be over in a day or two, one way or another."

"God, I hope so," said Lucia, dropping her head against his shoulder wearily. "I can't stand much more. Tell me what will happen then."

"We'll leave here," said Simon. "We'll borrow Kleiner's second-best plane and fly back to Mallorca. I think you'll like it there, but if you don't like my home we'll sell it and buy another. We won't be bothered. No one bothers me in Mallorca."

"It sounds like paradise," she said, "and I can hardly wait . . . but how many people will you have to kill first?" That put a chill back in the air. Simon stiffened and eased away to sit upright on the sofa.

"I'm sorry," she said. "I shouldn't have said that."

He sighed. "Well, maybe you are sorry but you still said it. What do you expect me to do? Let them blast you, or beat my head in? You're like all the rest, Lucia. You want the dirty work done, but you want to keep your own hands clean. You don't even want to know about it."

"I'm sorry," said Lucia sadly. "I mean it, but I can't get used to all this."

Simon rubbed his eyes wearily with one hand. "You don't have to, Lucia, and you know it. It won't last—it's not forever—but you either understand the problem we have here, or you don't."

"I do understand," said Lucia quietly. "I don't enjoy seeing you solve it, that's all."

"Neither do I," said Simon. "I'd like someone else to do the dirty work, but who else is there? I'm sorry I snapped at you."

Lucia was silent for a moment, her head resting once more against his shoulder. "I'm sorry too," she said at last. "Why don't we start again?"

"Agreed," said Simon, "and let's remember we're both on the same side."

"Before those . . . people . . . came in," said Lucia, "you were talking about what we might do in Mallorca—about starting to publish again. I think you should do that, but what will I do?"

"Well"—Simon thought for a moment, rubbing one ear—"you could try just being happy, for a start. Then I expect you'll want to rearrange the house. You'll have to learn Spanish, although with Italian to start with, that won't be difficult. And you can look after me while I look after you . . . we will be very snug, so why don't we just play house for a while?"

"That's all very domesticated," said Lucia, "but you have people to do all that, and I am a doctor, a working girl, and I like it. So, can I work? Is there something there I can do?"

"I'm sure you can work. As I told you, there are plenty of sick kids in Spain and lots of hospitals. You won't be idle. And we can travel, and see people, and have friends over to stay. We can be *normal*."

"It sounds good," said Lucia, curling her legs up on the sofa. "Tell me more."

"More? Hmmm, well, let's see. In Palma there are theaters and cinemas. It's *years* since I've been to a movie. There is an arts festival in Pollensa. I've never been but we can volunteer to help. We could organize the poetry readings. How about that?"

Lucia looked at him directly. "Are you serious, or just talking? About the poetry?"

"I'm serious. Honestly."

"Then recite some poetry to me—some Spanish poetry."

"Oh Lord!" Simon frowned, thinking.

"There—you see? You can't. It's all talk."

"No, wait . . . I'm just thinking. Can I do it sitting here, or do you want me down on one knee?"

"Here will do." She patted the sofa. "Come on . . . declaim."

"Right . . . how's this?" Simon thought for a moment and began.

Cada diá,
Aumenta mi amor
Hoy,
Más que ayer
y mucho menos que
Mañana.

"How's that?"

"It sounds very nice," said Lucia. "But what does it mean?"

"Well, roughly translated," said Simon, "it means . . .

Every day
I love you more
Today,
More than yesterday,
And much less than,
Tomorrow . . .

"It sounds better in Spanish, of course."

"You made it up," said Lucia, smiling at him. "Didn't you?"

"No, cross my heart. It's by a Spanish poet."

"Who?"

"I can't remember."

"There! You see? You did make it up."

They were laughing now.

"Do you feel better?" asked Simon. "No, so, well . . . better?"

"Yes, much better." She leaned across and kissed him on the cheek. "Much better now, thank you."

Lucia got up from the sofa and began to take off her coat. "I'm still hungry too," she said suddenly. "Tonight I'll cook something. You can set the table out here and open some wine. It's cold in here—shall we light the fire?"

"Why not?" said Simon. "I like firelight. But no wine for me."

"Really? Not even one glass?"

"No, not yet. I find it easier to say no to the first one than to the second one . . . but I'll watch you."

"And we can talk—and make plans—and then go to bed."

"Sounds good," said Simon.

"Maybe we should forget the food, the wine, and the fire and just go straight to bed?"

"No . . . not at my age," said Simon. "First, we'll have a civilized dinner, and I'll pour you a little too much wine. Then we'll go to bed, like civilized people. How about that?"

"I can see you're an Englishman," said Lucia, shaking her head. "I wonder what happened to romance."

"How can you say that?" cried Simon. "I'm terribly romantic."

"For an Englishman."

"Even for an Englishman." He tapped his chest. "Is this not the man who was quoting romantic poetry to you just a moment ago?"

"That's true," said Lucia, nodding. "So it is. I may have to revise my opinions a little."

"You should," agreed Simon, "and—about that poem—I also meant every word of it—even in English."

"I'm glad," said Lucia.

FOURTEEN

The call from Kleiner reached Simon at nine. By ten he and Lucia were at Kleiner's suite in the Principe, where Aldo Cirillo, Colombo, and Philip joined them within a few minutes, Philip fresh and rested, Cirillo and Colombo showing signs of a sleepless night. Somewhat to Simon's surprise, Philip took charge, ushering them around Kleiner's conference table and taking the chair at the head. Before he went any further, Simon told them about the brawl in the restaurant.

"I see," said Philip, when Simon had told his tale. "That's interesting. It shows these people know what we are doing. I think you were lucky, Simon . . . just take good care of Lucia. Has anything else been happening?" he asked, turning to Aldo. "Have there been any other developments since yesterday on the Colombo affair?" He was clearly in charge, and when Aldo replied, he talked to Philip and only indirectly to the others, who just sat quietly by and listened.

"I'm afraid not," he said. "So far there has been no word from the kidnappers, but we do believe the child is still in the city. The getaway car was found within fifteen minutes. By a piece of luck, the police were running a traffic enforcement exercise last night on the roads around the city, so we could quickly switch their patrols to roadblocks and surveillance of all cars leaving. The route out toward Como was even more closely guarded because of the diversions caused by building the new autostrada . . . the traffic jams made national news. The result is that the child is probably still here, somewhere in the city. The police and the *carabinieri* don't have to stay on the sidelines this time, because of the shooting, and we've put taps on Signor Colombo's phones, both at his home and his office. We've put a helicopter on standby, radio-linked into the police monitor, which can be over any point in the city within two minutes. In other words, we're ready."

Kleiner placed an arm around Colombo, who was sitting in the chair at his side, and squeezed his shoulder. "You see, Carlo," he said, "we are not entirely impotent. Captain Cirillo has his eyes and ears open and his men are standing by. Soon we'll have these people in the net and get your boy back safely."

Colombo nodded and tried to smile back, but his face was dark with worry. He was a silent man, sunk deeply in his own thoughts, rather out of place in this brisk atmosphere. Simon looked across at Lucia, but her attention was focused on Cirillo, who, elbows on the table, was leaning forward to attract their attention.

"Signor Colombo may want to go home now and wait by his telephone," he suggested, "but I have information which may have a bearing on the rest of this business. Perhaps we can discuss it here, and then maybe we could have a little coffee?" he suggested to Kleiner. Simon had noticed that Cirillo seemed to live on coffee and cigarettes. They waited round the table, murmuring together quietly, while Kleiner saw Colombo out and his secretary spoke briefly into the telephone. Meanwhile, Simon told them of last night's incident in more detail.

"It means the pace is heating up," he concluded, "and, although I can't see what's going on here, the more these people come into the open the better we'll be able to deal with them."

Kleiner had come back to the table, and stood at Simon's side, looking doubtful. "It sounds a nasty incident to me," he said. "I think that we should all be more careful, but you and Philip especially. Our enemy has decided to eliminate you from the scene—"

"Kleiner is right, Simon," said Aldo, interrupting. "You don't want to—what's the American expression?—push your luck."

"I quite agree," said Simon blandly. "I don't look for trouble, but I make it a rule to defend myself."

"If that's all, I'm glad to hear it," said Aldo soberly. "It took me all yesterday to paper over the previous night's business. Anyway, I have some fresh information you will all want to consider."

Kleiner's secretary gathered up coffee jugs and cups from the tray and brought them over to the table. When all the cups were filled, Aldo picked up his briefcase from the floor and placed it beside him. "What I have here," he continued, looking around at their expectant faces, "comes as a result of Commander Wintle's suggestion last week."

Aldo opened the briefcase and slipped a bundle of papers out onto the table. "Let me explain that Philip advised us to follow two lines of inquiry. Firstly, we were to look for some signs of the considerable sums of money extracted from the victims' families over the past year. Secondly, we were to see if there was some pattern in the ransoms, in the form of share purchases, takeovers, large loans, anything we could find to indicate the directing hand within the consortium. I asked the Guardia di Finanza to check out the consortium members. You may be surprised to learn that one member's enterprises include a flourishing call-girl racket. The Guardia di Finanza have worked very hard, but the results are rather disappointing. In their opinion the kidnap money is by now in some bank vault in Zürich, waiting to be laundered. Maybe it has already been laundered, through Chiasso, which is the normal route out of Italy for gang money. On the asset-stripping side, we have slightly more information, but it may be insignificant. When Signor Otelli's daughter was taken at the end of last year he was forced to sell his business to raise the money. He was already in financial trouble at the time and the worry over the kidnapping did nothing for his judgment. He sold out for just enough money to buy his daughter back. He is now effectively bankrupt."

Aldo looked down at his notes before continuing. "His company was bought by a holding company, based in Chiasso, which is interesting, and called . . ." Aldo riffled through his papers. "Ah yes, here it is, Extramilano S. A. It was a good enough buy, I'm told. In three other cases where all or part of a business had to be sold to pay ransom money, they, too, were snapped up by other companies, all owned by Extramilano, which the Guardia di Finanza describe as a small but active Swiss conglomerate. The Finanza boys tell me this conglomerate has more than doubled its wealth and asset value in the last three years. But it may be nothing. The victims' families needed to raise cash quickly and Extramilano was willing to buy. They drove a hard bargain, but then that's business. You asked me to find a common denominator and this is one, but there is no sign of anything illegal here."

"Who owns this conglomerate?" asked Kleiner.

"That's the other snag," replied Aldo, shrugging. "The Swiss won't tell me. They have very strict laws about financial disclosure and their lips are sealed."

"Really?" said Kleiner, smiling grimly. 'Are they? So they won't tell you? Well, they'll probably tell me. Do you have the name of the Extramilano bank in Chiasso? You'd be surprised what a little direct leverage can do, even to the Swiss."

Aldo searched through his papers again, found the name and telephone number, scribbled them down on a piece of paper and passed it across to Kleiner, glancing around the table at the others, a brief smile passing across his face.

"It's not what you know, it's *who* you know," said Simon ironically. "Isn't that right, Klaus?"

"Very true. This is even better, though," said Kleiner, looking up from the notes. "I know the president of this bank personally. Is this the office number? Let me get him on the telephone. It should take about ten minutes."

"Where is Chiasso?" Simon asked Aldo as Kleiner left the table and went over to his desk. "And why is it so significant?"

"It may be significant, or it may not be. It's a small town, just across the Swiss frontier, in the canton of Ticino," said Aldo. "There are a lot of banks there. Chiasso lies close to the Italian border, so those banks are often used by our criminals to deposit surplus funds. From time to time, if we can produce clear evidence of crime, the Swiss authorities will instruct the banks to open up their depositors' lists, especially if the deposits are in lire or clearly from Italy. They don't like doing it, although we have found kidnap money at Chiasso in the past. It may be nothing, but it is another of Philip's little links. Maybe it all adds up; who knows?"

Kleiner was better than his word. He was back in eight minutes, frowning. "I have the names of the Extramilano board," he said slowly, slipping into his chair, "but it can't help us. There are a number of small shareholders, but the main stockholder and the president of Extramilano is a colleague of ours—Signor Fiori. So where does that get us? Fiori is a victim himself, of the worst kidnap we've had."

There was a long silence, the group staring down into their coffee cups, thinking. Finally, Lucia moved in her chair and spoke directly across the table to Philip. "How can that be relevant to the kidnappings?" she asked. "My father knew all the people and he is always anxious to expand. If he sees a good buy he'll take it. I do not like my father, but his own daughter was kidnapped and murdered. It's impossible to believe that he would hurt his own child!" She shook her head firmly. "It doesn't make sense."

There was a low murmur of agreement around the table, coming from all but Simon and Philip. Philip's eyes were thoughtful and Simon watched him carefully, keeping half an eye on Lucia's face. Finally Philip nodded.

"Well," he said slowly, "in view of what happened to Gina, Signor Fiori is certainly the least likely of all the members of the consortium to be the kidnapper. As you say, Lucia, it doesn't make sense. On the other hand, if we are going to ignore links when we find them, why look for them in the first place?" Turning to Aldo, he said, "We need to know who profits from these events, and the owner of Extramilano has profited immensely. We might ask where the money to buy the Extramilano companies came from. Which companies make up this conglomerate?"

Aldo drew out another file and tapped it with a tobacco-stained forefinger. "It's news to me that Fiori owns Extramilano. It is a new holding group, almost entirely composed of companies once owned by kidnap victims. They are all still operating and doing well, apparently. Extramilano does not operate in Italy—it simply controls companies that do, which, since it is a Swiss company, protects the owners from our investigations. There is a lot in Fiori's file, but nothing there about his holdings in Extramilano. That is curious. Signor Fiori has expanded rapidly since he arrived from the South fifteen years ago, and most of the expansion has been in the last two to three years, since the kidnaps began. But, to look at it another way, that's natural. As Lucia says, Fiori wants to expand, he knows these people, he knows they need money, he helps them out at a price. The point is that he knows them *through* the consortium. There is nothing strange in him getting involved in their affairs, and setting up Extramilano may be a financial hedge, or a tax dodge—or it may not."

Philip nodded. "You're probably right, but let me just play the Devil's advocate for a moment. The Extramilano expansion dates from the start of the kidnappings. Yes or no?"

Aldo consulted the files again, riffling rapidly through the folder. "Well, yes. But there have been kidnappings in Italy, even here in Milan, for generations. There's nothing new about that. It's just this concentration on the consortium members which makes this affair different. And Herr Kleiner's involvement, of course."

"So," said Philip, "let me suggest a possible course of action. Someone kidnaps a child, and receives a ransom of several million dollars. To raise this money the victim has to sell assets. Extramilano buys these assets with kidnap money, recycles it via the kidnappers, launders it again through Chiasso, and it is still acting as a perfectly legitimate Swiss company. I imagine that day-to-day control of the companies owned by Extramilano is exercised by one of the other directors, not Signor Fiori, though we might inquire about that . . . I'm not saying this is what's happening, only that this could account for all the known facts."

Simon watched Philip, enjoying the sight of the old dog following the scent, hearing Philip picking his way from point to point, unraveling a thread of truth from a tangle of facts. Not for the first time it occurred to Simon that being tracked down by Philip Wintle was no laughing matter.

"How did Fiori get started?" asked Philip suddenly, turning to Aldo, ignoring Lucia's anxious face. "Did he always have money?" This question was directed at Lucia, but it was Aldo who answered, after consulting his notes.

"No, no. When he came here from the South, about twenty-five years ago, he had nothing. At first he drove a taxi; we have a note of his license application on file. That's good money if you don't mind the hours. Then he started his own taxi business, with a small fleet of cabs, which has grown until it is now one of the largest in Milan. Fredo Donati was with him back then. Two or three years ago Fiori brought in big American cars, for private hire, and during the worst of the Red Brigade trouble he started to hire out a bullet-proof car fleet to politicians, financiers, film stars, people like that. The cars, the Fiat Unos or the Volkswagen Golfs, were armor-plated, had unbreakable glass, emergency telephones, radios, the lot. He did very well out of that and probably still does. Such cars cost money and not everyone can afford to own one."

"Cars, eh?" murmured Philip thoughtfully. "Anything else?"

Aldo consulted his file again, and looked up to smile at Philip. "It's a good job we've worked together before, Philip. Normally, I would have eliminated Fiori from our inquiries after Gina was kidnapped, but now I cover everyone. Most of his local operations are in service industries, except the Extramilano companies, which are commercial, mostly high-tech. Let's see now . . . Fiori then went into the people business. People are always flooding up here from the south of Italy, looking for jobs, so he started an employment agency. Donati ran it, but Fiori owns it. They train the applicants and hire them out at good rates, usually to rich families who want well-trained private staff—butlers, maids, chauffeurs. It's a good business. Their real specialty is hiring out drivers trained to drive those security limousines. He also has a restaurant or two. He's into all sorts of things . . . Oh! I see what you mean."

A silence fell around the table; their eyes were on Philip, all carefully avoiding Lucia's white face. They concentrated instead on Philip and on what he might say next.

"Chauffeurs!" said Philip heavily. "I thought that would be it." His gaze shifted across to Simon. "You were right about the dice game. That's a pity, isn't it? I'm sorry, Lucia, it's beyond coincidence. I wonder what we ought to do now."

"We ought to watch our step," said Simon shortly. "The man's bloody dangerous."

They sat around Kleiner's table all morning, discussing this and that course of action, wondering what to do next.

"One lesson we've learned," said Philip. "We wait . . . I don't want another child hurt. We'll let Signor Fiori stew for a while until we get a lead on the boy."

"We have no choice," said Cirillo. "You have arranged the facts to fit your theory, Philip, and you are probably right, but it won't hold up in court. There is no firm evidence, no real proof that Extramilano and the kidnappings are linked and both controlled by Fiori. And there remains the question of Gina. I can't see Fiori doing that . . . it's quite impossible."

"I'm afraid that's right." Simon nodded. "Maybe we're only looking at half the facts here, Philip. Remember how Fiori went crazy when he heard about Gina? He wasn't faking . . . he was completely shattered. How does that square with the idea that he's behind the kidnappings?"

"God knows," said Philip stubbornly, "but facts are facts, and they all add up. Fiori owns Extramilano—that's a fact."

"Maybe . . . but look, can I have a quiet word?" Simon got up and led Philip over to a corner of the room, leaving the rest slumped wearily around the table.

"Yes?" asked Philip. "What is it that the others can't share?"

"Keep your voice down," said Simon softly, "and let me lay it out for you. This is an inside job. We agree on that, so let me suggest another possibility for you. We only have Kleiner's word for it that Fiori is behind Extramilano—and the Swiss won't talk to anyone else. We can't disprove it and his word is the only solid bit of evidence against Fiori."

"But. . . !"

"Wait! Look, no one knows better than Kleiner what a good leverage kidnapping kids can be. He paid out millions to get his own daughter back. Next point—you asked what a bunch of chauffeurs would do with fourteen million dollars? Well, maybe it's a fee. Fourteen million is birdseed for Kleiner. He gets the clout, the leverage, and the gang get the money. A sum like that is nothing to him, if he gets what he wants."

"And what might that be? What could Kleiner possibly want?"

"I don't know yet . . . power maybe. Maybe to get all the consortium's business in Italy, as you think Fiori does . . . who knows? The man might be crazy."

"Frankly, I think you're wrong," said Philip firmly. "All the evidence points to Fiori; you said so yourself. Your views now are colored by the fact that you don't like Kleiner."

"And yours are colored by the fact that you do like him, so what's the difference? And, for the record, I neither like nor dislike him. I don't know him, but facts are facts. It depends on how you look at them."

"These ideas aren't facts—they're pure speculation, and I'd rather you kept them to yourself."

"You're the boss," said Simon. "Just let's keep our options open until we get a few more of those famous facts."

With Simon and Philip back at the table, they all went around and around the Fiori information till everyone was exhausted.

"We're not getting anywhere," said Philip at last. "Maybe there are a few more pieces we need to fit in before we can be quite sure." He avoided Simon's eyes.

"I'm glad to hear that," said Simon briefly, glancing at Lucia. "It would be wrong to jump to conclusions, in view of everything involved."

Then they had gone their separate ways, Philip and Kleiner to brood on other problems, Aldo to the Squadra office somewhere in the city, Simon and Lucia back to her flat. Lucia had gone out later, grim-faced and silent, to visit her patients at the hospital, refusing Simon's offer of an escort, returning after dark to pace about the flat, smoking incessantly, saying little. Simon cooked dinner and served it, saying nothing, leaving her alone with her thoughts. Eventually they had gone to bed.

Simon was asleep, dreaming, when the light, persistent shaking slowly worked its way into his head. Suddenly he was awake.

"Simon . . . Simon!" Lucia was kneeling at his side, her face framed by her dark hair, looking down directly into his. "Simon, wake up. I have to talk to you." It was already daylight, with clear, fresh light flooding into the room through the thin curtains.

"Do you know," Simon said to her slowly, "you look incredibly pretty first thing in the morning? I don't know how you do it. What times is it?"

"It's nearly seven," she said shortly. "I haven't slept all night and I have to talk to you. How am I going to face my father today? How can I even speak to him?"

Simon elbowed his way up onto the pillow and gazed at her, trying to think of something comforting to say. Nothing particular came to mind. "It's early days yet," he said finally, "and it may all come to nothing. Philip has a lot of bits, but they don't fit together yet. Why not just wait and see? It might be all coincidental." His tone was not hopeful.

"There is something else I haven't told you,' she said slowly, "and it makes things worse. Papa's chauffeur, Antonio, has disappeared. Antonio was driving Gina when she was kidnapped, but he wasn't hurt. He walked to a café and telephoned to say she had gone. My father was so furious he could have killed him, but instead he kept him on—and now he's gone."

"Gone?" asked Simon sharply. "What do you mean, gone? Where?"

"Papa told me. Do listen! Last night I wanted Antonio to drive me to meet you, but Papa said he had left. I said, "All right, but when will he be back?" And he said, 'Antonio, he won't be back.' He laughed, and even then I wondered why."

Simon thought for a moment. "You're right. When Philip and I went to Kleiner's, Fredo got us a taxi. But so what?"

"Don't you understand? Papa said Antonio wouldn't be back, and he laughed, right out loud, with Gina lying beside him in her coffin. He just sat beside her and laughed and laughed. I thought he was just upset, but . . ."

"Really!" Simon's voice was thoughtful. "I wonder why he did that? Did you by any chance mention the name of the restaurant we were going to?"

"Maybe . . . I think so. Simon, Antonio has worked for my father since he was just a boy. Why would he leave just before Gina's funeral? He wouldn't do that. Antonio and Gina grew up together."

"Did he like Gina?"

"Yes, well . . . not so much as he grew older. He was jealous of her . . . and me. He made cheeky remarks sometimes, but even so . . ."

"Even so," Simon repeated. "Perhaps, well, I don't know. It's another little detail we must give to Philip. We'll pass this snippet on to him and he'll fit it in somewhere and make some sense out of it."

"It still doesn't make sense," she said.

"No, it doesn't," said Simon, "but it's beginning to. Listen, when we heard about Extramilano yesterday, and the link with your father, I thought, for various reasons, it might equally well be Kleiner."

"Klaus?" Lucia's voice rose a note. "But why?"

"Never mind why. I was wrong. Tell me, how long has this Antonio Puccio worked for your father?"

"Years . . . like I told you, since Gina and I were children."

"But before Kleiner came on the scene?"

"Oh yes, years before."

"I remember him at the airport," said Simon thoughtfully. "Antonio, I mean. He grabbed the suitcase with the money from your father's hand, and your father grabbed it back. I wondered why at the time. Your father really tore it away from him."

"So?"

"Well, I think Antonio's disappearance confirms one fact. It can't be Klaus. There is no link. Therefore—I'm sorry, Lucia—it has to be your father . . . and also that your father—this is a guess—your father knows who the kidnappers are. Curious."

"But *why*?" There was desperation in her voice. "Why?"

"I don't know why," said Simon. "As Philip said, we need more facts—but that's enough for now, eh? Now, if you won't come back down here, why don't we do as we decided, and live like normal people—beginning with breakfast."

FIFTEEN

The photograph was in the wastepaper basket. Simon was in the bathroom when he saw it, torn carefully into four pieces, lying crumpled in the bottom of the basket. He hesitated for a moment, then placed his razor on the shelf, picked the pieces out of the basket, and arranged them carefully on the side table, pushing Lucia's lotions and perfumes out of the way as he did so.

The picture was of a man, a pleasant-looking, middle-aged fellow, deeply tanned. The photograph had clearly been taken on a yacht, for the man was leaning against the front of the cockpit—the wire shrouds framing his shoulders, the mast behind—laughing into the camera, brown arms folded. A broad gold wedding band glinted on one hand.

Simon studied this briefly for a moment, sluiced the shaving soap off his face, then picked up the torn photo and walked into the bedroom. Lucia was sitting at the dressing table, her back to the mirror, looking down at her feet, toes poking through the fur of her mules, thinking.

"It's sheer nosiness, and I hate to pry," said Simon, holding up the pieces of photograph. "That's not true, actually . . . I love to pry. But who's this?"

Lucia looked at it and hesitated for only a moment before making one of her usual brief answers. "It's my husband," she said.

Simon staggered. "Your husband! I didn't even know you were married. Why . . . ?"

"I'm not married," said Lucia sharply. "At least, not anymore. He divorced me about two years ago, and we lived apart for five years before that. I don't know why I kept the photo. I don't need it anymore."

"He must be mad," said Simon flatly. "Anyone who could divorce you is crazy . . ." He hesitated. "I'm prying again, but I thought you didn't have divorce in Italy?"

Lucia laughed, a little harshly. "Oh yes, we do. If you have enough money to get an annulment, or have a good enough reason, or are a man, or separate for five years." She looked down at her mules again and went back to twiddling her toes. "But especially if you are a man."

Simon hesitated for a moment, wondering what to say next. Then he took a step back toward the bathroom door, shuffling the pieces of photograph together in his hands. Lucia continued to look at him, smiling at the concern on his face.

"It's none of my business," he said. "I'm sorry I asked. That will teach me to pry."

"If you want to hear about it, you'd better hear all of it," she said, still looking up at him. "He—we—were married nine years ago. He's a doctor, a surgeon, here in Milan. I see him every day, we both work at the hospital. I came back from London to marry him. We lived here in this apartment. After two years he—we—discovered that I can't have children, so . . ." She shrugged slightly. "We separated for the necessary five years and he divorced me. He's already married again and they have two children."

Simon didn't know what to say to that either. "I'm sorry," he said at last. "I, well . . . was it certain?"

"Oh yes." Her voice was suddenly tired. "Quite certain. He gave me every chance. We went to Switzerland, the US, everywhere, saw specialists, but it was no good. He didn't want to adopt, so . . ." She looked up into Simon's face, intently. "You must understand how it is with Italian men. To have children is very important to them, for a lot of reasons, and they make good fathers . . . but for a man not to have children, that's a terrible thing, even if it's the wife's fault, so . . ."

"It's nobody's *fault,*" Simon said sharply, "that's stupid. These things happen." He knew better than to step forward and touch her. She was looking down at her feet again.

"Well, it happened to me," she said, shrugging, "and it mattered to him. Does it matter to you?"

"No," said Simon, shaking his head. "It doesn't matter to me at all."

"You had another woman once," said Lucia. "After your wife died. Philip told me. Did you ever think of having more children with her?"

Simon shook his head. "No. The subject never came up. But if you are worrying about her, don't. That affair is long over."

"Was she nice? Philip said she was beautiful, but was she nice?" She kept her eyes carefully on his face, waiting for his reply.

Simon considered for a moment. "Yes . . . she was nice enough. She was pushy, though. She knew exactly what she wanted and when she realized she wasn't going to get it, she left. I don't really blame her. Living quietly in Mallorca was not Clio's scene. She hated it. If she had stayed, we would have ended up hating each other."

"And what have you done for love since?" asked Lucia.

"If by that you mean, have I gone bed-hopping round the island, the answer is no. I don't need to do that and, anyway, I have my pets."

"You have a dog?"

"No, two cats. Dogs tie you down a bit."

"I have always seen you as a dog person." Lucia was smiling now, her eyes warm again.

"Well, wrong again. I'm definitely a cat person. Mind you, they are very affectionate cats."

Lucia gave him another long look, studying his face closely, then cocked her head to one side, listening. "Then I think you had better go and turn the taps off before your bath runs over," she said. "Cat people hate to get wet."

When Simon came out of the bathroom, knotting his tie, Lucia was sitting on the edge of the bed, wrapped in her robe, a coffee cup held in both hands. She put it down, poured him some coffee from the jug, and passed the cup to him without a word. It was only halfway to his lips when the phone rang. He stood over her while she picked it up, flicking the hair away from one ear as she did so.

"Pronto," she said, and listened briefly. Then she handed the receiver to Simon.

"It's Cirillo, the Supercop," she said shortly.

"Hello," said Simon, putting down the cup and sitting beside her on the bed.

"Simon, it's Aldo. I'm at the Bureau. I'm sorry to disturb you, but I thought I might still find you at Lucia's. Some more information has come in. I don't think Lucia will like it . . . bad news. Maybe you can find some way to tell her."

Simon was suddenly alert. "Go on," he said, pressing the receiver close to his ear. "Let me have it and I'll pass it along as best I can."

"We now have identities for the three people you shot the other night. Their name is Puccio, and they were father, son, and cousin. They came from a little town on the Bay of Naples, near Sorrento. The point is that the son once worked for Fiori and so did another cousin, one Antonio Puccio. Indeed, he still does. He's Fiori's chauffeur."

"I see," said Simon, looking across worriedly at Lucia. "Is there anything else?"

"Yes, there certainly is. It's a big family. Antonio's cousin, one of the old man's other nephews, is named Enrico Guilini, and . . ." Aldo paused temptingly. "Are you ready for this?"

"Come to the point, blast you," said Simon shortly. "Get on with it."

"Enrico Guilini is Carlo Colombo's chauffeur." Aldo's tone was suddenly triumphant. "The whole damned Puccio-Guilini family are embedded in the Kleiner consortium, and Fiori hired them all."

Simon let his breath out in a long, slow blast, staring thoughtfully down into Lucia's inquiring face, nodding quietly, thinking.

"I see," he said carefully at last. "That's very interesting, very interesting, indeed. It's only what we expected, after all. What happens now?"

"Simon?" Aldo's voice sounded sharply in his ear. "Are you still there? Do you see what I see? Can you see what they were doing? Apart from breaking the dice game?"

"Not yet. I'm still thinking about it," said Simon. "Where is he now? The Colombo chauffeur—what's his name?"

"Enrico Guilini. He's still in the hospital. There's nothing much wrong with him but a slight concussion and bruising. We kept him under guard because he's a witness to a murder. I think we should pull him in just in case he tries to slip away, or his friends come to get him out."

"No," said Simon firmly. "Don't touch Guilini. His friends may simply kill the boy and run again. Apart from that, he'll just clam up and tell us that you are imagining things. It's not a crime to have criminals in the family, and so far—unless there's more you haven't told me—the fact that they are related is the only link we have."

"You're right," said Aldo reluctantly. "But it's pushing coincidence too far to say there's no connection. This is more than a kidnapping, it's murder. They killed Gina and that man in the street. I can't keep the lid on that for long, and I don't intend to. But we can't hold him for the murder because the schoolteacher witness knows he didn't do that, and I don't really want to touch him for the kidnapping until we hear from the gang or get a lead on the boy's whereabouts. Why should he tell us? We won't get that from him. It's an admission of involvement."

"No, he won't tell you that," said Simon. "It blows the whole thing. Incidentally, I have more news for you. That Antonio you mentioned—Fiori's chauffeur? Well, he's gone too, vanished. Lucia thinks that's very odd. Maybe you can put out a discreet alert and pick him up. Maybe he panicked when Gina was killed. It's another piece of the jigsaw we have to fit in."

"Wait a minute . . ." There was a long silence before Aldo returned to the phone. "Simon, I've put out a general call, not to pick him up but just find, observe, and report to me. Thanks for the tip. Any other ideas?"

Simon thought for a moment, his eyes resting on Lucia. "Well, you won't like this, but why not leave the Colombo chauffeur to me?" he said. "Or rather to Lucia and me. Don't go near him. I'll talk to him and find out what he knows. That will keep the police out of it."

"What can you do that I can't?" asked Aldo. "If he's guilty I can get him twenty years."

"First you have to prove it," Simon pointed out. "I don't have to prove anything. If he's a crook he's used to cops, but I'm the one who blew away his relatives. That should make his hair stand on end. All you have to do is trust me."

There was a long pause on the phone while Aldo thought this over. "Well . . . it's an idea, but don't mess it up," he said at last, "I beg of you. My superiors won't like this, but if you can find out where the boy is we're in the clear. What are you going to do?"

"I'll think of something," said Simon briskly. "In about half an hour phone the hospital and pull the police guard off Enrico Guilini. Then get your team together and wait for me to call in. If I can't find out where the boy is, no one else can, so what can you lose? I'll be in touch. *Ciao*." Simon put down the phone and glanced at Lucia.

"Well, what's happened?" she asked impatiently. "What was all that about? Do they know who took Colombo's boy?"

"No . . . but at least they have a lead. Aldo strongly suspects that Colombo's chauffeur, Enrico Guilini, set up the kidnapping. He's related to the people I beat up the other night, and most of them were supplied to the consortium by your father. I still don't see where kidnapping and killing Gina fits in. Anyway, we have other fish to fry at the moment."

"You will forgive me if I don't forget Gina so soon. It's her funeral this very afternoon." Lucia's voice was edgy.

Simon paused for a moment and took her hand. "I know—I'm sorry. I mean that priority number one now is to get the Colombo boy back. I didn't mean that what happened to Gina doesn't matter."

"I know that," she said impatiently, "but how are you going to do anything when we still don't know where the boy is being kept?"

"We don't know, but it's a fair bet that Enrico Guilini does. What we have to do now," said Simon, "is to pick him up at the hospital and take him somewhere quiet. Then I'll reason with him and he'll tell us where the boy is being held. Even if he won't squeal, it's a standoff . . . they may have the boy, but we have Enrico. We might do a trade."

"Enrico won't tell you anything," said Lucia decisively, shaking her head. "As long as he keeps quiet he's safe. Even if you or Aldo could prove all of this, he would only go to prison for a year or two at the most. But if he is involved and he talks, he dies. You can take my word for that."

Lucia was standing in the center of the room, dressed all in black, ready for Gina's funeral, her face startlingly pale. She walked over to Simon, turning round to let him pull up the long zipper on the back of her dress.

"He's from the South. They are all from the South," she continued. "You could tear his heart out first and he would say nothing. And what was that about scaring him to death? I can't see you torturing anyone. You're not the type."

Simon looked at her, surprised. "I don't mean to do anything like that," he said mildly. "I wouldn't even know how to begin. I'll reason with him and point out the situation. I have an idea how to do it, and he'll do a deal if we can find a way to convince him that otherwise we mean business. He probably despises the police and he knows his rights to the inch, so he'd just sit and yawn and ask for coffee. With an outsider like me he's on dangerous ground. The choice between life or death is really no contest, believe me, and, as I say, I have an idea that should appeal to him if we put it the right way . . . but I need to think about it."

"Why don't you get Philip?" suggested Lucia. "He'll know what to do, or maybe Aldo can find a way."

"Aldo's agreed to leave it to me, at least for a while. Philip would bring Enrico cups of tea, talk to him for three days, then lock him up for life. We simply don't have time for that. Will you help me or not?"

Lucia seemed to be back to using short sentences. "What do you want me to do?"

Simon rubbed his nose slowly, looking out into space for a moment. "Let me think. . . . You met me in an ambulance when I arrived. Where did it come from?"

"From the Ospedale Cà Grande," said Lucia. "I work there, remember? I just signed it out. No one asks any questions."

"Right. Well, that's where the chauffeur is. I'm just going to play it by ear, but can you go in, get him released, and steer him out to me? I don't want him scared or he might run. Does he know you?"

Lucia thought for a moment. "No, I don't think so. Do you want me to get him in an ambulance? That could be difficult because the drivers are all assigned at the central office."

Simon shook his head. "No, let's keep it simple. We'll use your car. Just go in, bring him out, and leave the rest to me. What time is Gina's funeral?"

"At three. I thought I would go to the house first. I don't particularly want to see my father, especially now, but what else can I do, today of all days?"

"Nothing, I suppose," said Simon gently, looking at his watch. "Could you put on a white coat over that dress first, and help me grab Guilini? Then you can go home. It's only just after nine, so we have five or six hours."

"I can do that, but I'll come with you," said Lucia. "I don't want you doing anything to him we'll both regret."

"You don't need to come with me," said Simon briefly, "and I won't hurt him, I promise. Don't worry about that."

"I'm not worrying about him," said Lucia. "I'm worrying about you."

The Ospedale Cà Grande was a vast, gaunt building, a wall of windows on every side, quite old, sadly in need of a new coat of paint, and with the universal hospital smell, a mixture of stale air and ether. It came drifting across the parking lot, where Simon stood by Lucia's car looking over the roofs of the other vehicles to the wide flight of steps that led up to the main door. It was a busy morning, and a constant stream of people were hurrying in and out. Lucia had been inside for over half an hour and Simon was becoming worried. He pushed himself away from the car, weaving his way through the parked cars toward the steps, then stopped to wait again on the low wall beside the door, ignored by the steady stream of staff, patients, and visitors who came pouring past. He got up once to peer inside, but there was no sign of Lucia. Ten minutes later, when he was just on the point of going in to find her, she finally appeared.

Dressed in her starched white hospital coat, she was pushing a wheelchair in which a dark-haired, stocky young man sat slumped, his head on one side, apparently half asleep. Lucia hesitated briefly at the top of the steps as Simon got up off the wall and hurried to help her.

"Where the hell have you been?" he hissed, taking the weight of the chair as they eased the rear wheels down the ramp. "I've been going crazy out here. Does he speak English? What's the matter with him?"

"I don't know if he speaks English," replied Lucia shortly. "Though he may understand it a little. You think it was easy getting him here? Why don't you try it! When I told him the police had departed and he was free to go, he practically leaped out of bed. I had to calm him down first and then sedate him, or he would have been gone. I told him it was an antitetanus shot."

"And what was it really?"

"Heroin."

"Heroin!" Simon was startled. "What in the name of God are you doing with heroin?"

"Heroin is an excellent pain-killer . . . that's why it's not totally banned and why I have access to it. When we get to wherever we're going, I can give him something else to bring him around. Don't worry," said Lucia, opening the back door of her car, "I know what I'm doing. I'm perfectly competent. Now help me get him in here."

"I'm sure you're competent, but where are we going?" asked Simon as he bundled Enrico Guilini out of the wheelchair, rolling him across the backseat of the car, then throwing a rug over him to hide the body from the casual eye, glancing around hastily for any onlookers. "I haven't thought that far ahead. We need somewhere quiet, but not too far away."

Lucia looked over at him sharply. "You hadn't thought of that? What else have you forgotten to think of ? We have a zonked-out criminal in here and you tell me you don't know what to do with him!"

"Let's take one thing at a time," said Simon mildly. "I'm an improviser. I'm also a stranger in town, so if you have any bright ideas let's have them."

"We can take him to our house in the country. No one will be there. It's only about an hour away, on the road to Como. It's in its own grounds, very secluded, and I have a key. Will that do?"

"It sounds perfect," said Simon. "Let's go."

Enrico was still dreaming when they arrived at the house. His body was a dead weight as Simon dragged him from the car and dumped him on the gravel. It took their united strength to heave him up over Simon's shoulder, who staggered under the weight as he followed Lucia across the gravel toward the steps at the front of the house. The house was a pleasant, vine-draped farmhouse, the windows covered with heavy wooden shutters, the grass in the garden thick and overgrown; a heavy vine, hung with dark grapes, was suspended on a trellis above a cobbled terrace on one side.

"Where now?" asked Lucia from the top of the steps, fumbling in her shoulderbag for keys. "Do you want to bring him into the house, or what?"

"It would be better somewhere bleak," said Simon, panting. "Is there a cellar here, or stables? We need somewhere not too pleasant, to give him a nasty surprise when he comes to."

"The cellar is over here," said Lucia, coming back down the steps from the door and heading off toward the terrace.

"Wait," said Simon, gasping, "don't walk so fast. He's very heavy."

The cellar was dark and cool and full of junk. Old suitcases, garden tools, broken lamps, dusty furniture stood lined along the walls in front of half-empty wine racks. An old iron bedstead stood in one corner of the room, and Simon dumped Guilini onto this, his body bouncing heavily on the springs as it landed. With Lucia's help, he dragged and levered the bed into the center of the room and began to strip off Guilini's clothing.

"What are you doing?" asked Lucia sharply, watching this. "You said you weren't going to hurt him. Don't do this, Simon . . . please! The man's helpless—you promised."

"I said I wasn't going to hurt him," said Simon, "and I won't. I also said I could scare him out of his wits. If you can't take this, then go home or go back upstairs. Look, when this laddie here went to sleep, he was in a nice, comfortable bed, being given some good news by a pretty lady. When he comes around, he's stark naked and tied to a bedstead in a dark cellar. That's not nice, is it? That can give you a distinct feeling of insecurity. Then there is this nasty Englishman who kills people standing over you with a big pistol—that's even worse. I've never actually grilled anyone before, but when I was in the Service I was sent on several interrogation courses. The first thing they do is take all your clothes off. A lot of confidence goes away when you find yourself naked. Hey! Look at this. Is there some light down here?"

Lucia went over the the switch by the door, then came back trailing a table lamp on a long cord. Under the glare of the unshaded bulb, they examined Guilini's hairy chest. Several long, red, angry-looking, just-scabbed scratches had been ripped deeply across the skin, down from the neck. Simon considered them for a moment, then looked up at Lucia.

"What would you say caused those?" he asked her carefully. "In your considered, professional opinion? Would you say, for example, that a cat did that?"

"No . . . I'd say a woman did that," said Lucia, looking at him coldly. "I'd say a woman's fingernails did that, just a few days ago. The scratches are just starting to heal."

"You don't think they might have been caused when he got knocked down during the kidnapping?"

"No. Look at this little bruise on his face here . . . and this graze here on the leg. Those scratches on his chest are older. Besides, well . . . they just look like the work of a woman's nails—deep here, then getting shallow lower down. I've seen such scratches before, in Casualty."

Simon gave her a careful look. "I see," he said slowly. "Have you thought that your sister could have done that? They gave her a very bad time. Did you . . . I'm sorry to ask, but did you hear the tapes? Philip said they sent tapes of what they were doing to her."

"Yes." Lucia looked at him directly, her pale face bright in the light. "There were tapes and I heard them. You don't need to be delicate, Simon. I'm quite capable of working these things out for myself. What do you want to do now?"

"Bring him around," said Simon. "While you're doing that I'll think of what we're going to do next. All I ask is that you don't argue with me in front of him."

When Enrico Guilini's eyes came slowly into focus half an hour later, they widened, then filled with disbelief. As he looked around, the disbelief was followed by fear. He was cold, very cold. He lay in a dark, dank room, lit only by the light of a single, glaring light bulb, which hung over a bedrail just above his head. A woman in a white coat was sitting in a chair beside the bed, looking down at him absently, smoking a cigarette. Enrico seemed to remember this woman in the white coat, but his mouth was too dry to speak to her. When he tried to move, he found he couldn't do so. He raised his head painfully, looked down at his naked body and saw that his wrists and ankles were bound to the frame of the bed. He began to thrash about, then found his voice, cursing at the woman to release him, to tell him who she was and where he was. He kept this up for some minutes. It did him no good. She said nothing and did nothing, just looked at him, drawing quietly on her cigarette. When he fell back exhausted at last, his body bouncing lightly on the bare springs, a dark shadow moved out from the corner of the room and came closer, a tall man, who edged past the woman and sat down on the edge of the bed frame beside Enrico.

"*Ciao,* Enrico," said Simon pleasantly. "Do you speak English? If not, the lady doctor here will translate for me. But I see you can understand. A little, or a lot? A lot? Good . . . Of course, you are a chauffeur, not just a mere driver, and one of those special, Fiori-trained chauffeurs, too. A man with talent and a future."

"*Chi sei?* What is all this?" cried Enrico, his voice thick with fear. "Let me go . . . Please . . ."

"Oh! Good English. Quite grammatical. I'm a friend," said Simon, patting Enrico's cheek with the palm of his hand. "In fact, I'm your only friend. You see this lady here?" He indicated Lucia. "Do you know why this lady is not your friend?"

"Who are you? What do you want?" Something stark and fearful crept into Enrico's voice. "I don't know her, or you. What is all this? Who are you, anyway?"

"I'm the man who killed your cousins the other night. But no more questions, Enrico," said Simon. "We want answers from you, not questions. Do you know who this lady is?" Simon's voice was quiet, soft, barely audible. "Let me have an answer."

"No. *Io non so.* I not know who she is. Or why I am here." Enrico found it difficult to breathe now, jerking his head from side to side, panting, looking from one to the other.

"Then I will tell you who she is, Enrico. She is the sister of the young girl who put those scratches on your chest. The one you and your friends raped and then murdered. Do you remember Gina? It's her funeral today. We are going to her funeral, when we have finished with you here. You shouldn't have hurt little Gina like that, Enrico. It has made you enemies."

"I did not do it. I not know this lady, or . . . any Gina, or . . . is lies, all this is lies."

Enrico tore again at the lashings, his efforts jerking the bed about until Simon had to get up and stand back, letting Enrico exhaust himself once again. When he was finally still and glaring up at him, Simon sat on the edge of the bedstead again and smiled that slow, dreadful smile.

"You did kill Gina," he continued, nodding. "At least this lady here and I think you did, which comes to the same thing. So, it's like this, Enrico. Either you tell us what we want to know, or this lady here will do things to you that you wouldn't believe, even while they are happening. Now, the big question. Where are your friends keeping Carlo Colombo? Answer that. If I am still your friend I may kill you, or I may let this lady do things to you. We shall see. I may even persuade her to let you go. Time is short, Enrico, so let's get on with it. Where is the boy? There is no help for you here, you are on your own. We can do anything we like and there is nothing you can do about it. Look!"

Enrico saw Simon reach under his jacket. Then there was a pistol in his hand, a big black pistol. Simon looked down at Enrico and smiled again. Then he reached out and pressed the muzzle of the pistol against Enrico's left eye. Enrico gasped. He heard the hammer click back, a loud, oiled, slow double click, sharp against the sound of his own desperate panting. He said nothing, his one uncovered eye glaring up at Simon, defiant.

"*Vai al diavolo!* I not tell you," he said. "Shoot!"

There was a long, dragging pause, lasting for a minute or more. "So," said Simon at last, easing the hammer forward gently with his thumb and putting the pistol back under his jacket. "It's like that, is it? You're a tough boy, and you're right, I'm not going to kill you, not yet. But you see the situation? Do you understand those words? You can scream if you like, but it won't do any good. The damage we can do to you will be permanent, and bad for a strong young man like you. Think about that."

Lucia stirred in her chair and reached across the bed to pluck gently at Simon's arm. They walked off into a corner of the room, while the naked body of Enrico Guilini plunged about wildly again on the creaking springs behind them, his arms and legs wrenching at the light cord that tied him to the bed frame, his shouted curses drowning their conversation.

"What are you doing?" she whispered. "I have sat and stared at him like you said for as long as I can, but even though he did rape Gina I cannot go on like this. I am a doctor, not a sadist. If you are sure he did it, call the police and let them deal with him."

Simon smiled, his teeth gleaming briefly in the darkness, but his eyes, now close to her, were steady. He put out his hand and gave her arm a small squeeze. "He's a tough boy, but he's frightened," he said softly. "He's in a trap and scared, whatever he pretends. All we have to do is turn up the gas a bit and make him an alternative offer. He doesn't believe we have the balls to kill him, at least not in cold blood."

"And we don't," she said. "He may be a pig, but enough is enough. Let's call Aldo."

"We haven't done anything to him yet," said Simon shortly. "Think of your sister, and do as I say for a little longer. I've just thought how to make him tell us what we want to know. When I tell him, he'll go practically insane. Well, I would. Have you got your bag of tricks with you, and a hypodermic needle?"

"Yes, of course. You saw me give him that shot. What are you going to do to him?"

Simon's smile broadened and he winked an eye as he leaned forward to whisper in her ear, hushing her, his fingers brushing across her lips.

"Remember what you told me this morning, about your husband?" he said. "About him wanting children? I think we can persuade that young, virile, potent piece of garbage back there to tell us what we want to know without hurting a hair on his head."

"What do you mean?" asked Lucia, frowning, "and why are you smiling? What are you going to do?"

Simon's smile broadened. "Didn't you see the movie?" he said. "I'm going to make him an offer he can't refuse. Now, let me have that needle and the keys to your car."

SIXTEEN

When George Orwell's torturer, O'Brien, told his victim, Smith, that the worst thing in the world varied from individual to individual, he was right. For Smith the worst thing in the world was rats. For Enrico Guilini it was castration.

At his first sight of the needle in Simon's hand, Guilini began to plunge about on the bare springs of the bed, and when Simon bore down across his body, as if to hold him steady for the knife, he began to scream. Finally, at the first prick of the needle, a mere scratch against his scrotum, he fainted. Simon got up from the bed frame, pulling the sweat-soaked shirt away from his body, and looked across at Lucia, a sudden smile spreading across his face.

"You don't like this, do you?" he said.

Lucia was not amused. "This is disgusting," she whispered. Her voice was thick and unsteady, as if she was swallowing bile. "How can you *do* something like this?"

"Because it works," said Simon. "And I'm not stopping now. Why don't you go outside and leave the rest to me? It's better to leave us alone for the next part . . . as if you're waiting in the wings . . . don't close the door."

When Enrico's eyes rolled up and focused again on the man standing over him, the bright needle still held in his hand, he screamed, straining down desperately to see if he was still intact, then fell back exhausted, his body bouncing slightly on the springs. Simon stood over him, one foot propped up on the bed frame, smiling, letting the silence hang heavily in the basement, broken only by the creaking of the rusty bed springs and Enrico's frantic panting. Then Simon nodded, and turned to put the syringe down on a dusty tabletop.

"Well, do you get the picture, Enrico?" he asked, turning back. "I can do anything I like with you. I can let the lady make you into the first male soprano at La Scala, or I can blow your head off, or—and here is the good part, Enrico—you can put your pants on and walk out of here with a lot of money. Look!"

Simon heaved the battered suitcase up onto the bed frame, unsnapped the locks, and threw up the lid, tilting the contents toward Enrico.

"See here, Enrico . . . money. Look!"

Enrico strained his head up enough to peer into the case. What he saw drove out all his fear.

"*Mamma diavolo.* Is that real? *Ecco* . . . is fantastic!"

"Tell us what we want to know and it's all yours—and there's a million dollars in here."

Enrico flopped back onto the springs. "You're joking . . . you not mean it . . . you get me tell all I know an' then you shoot me . . . or she cut me."

Simon took a few wads of notes out of the suitcase, and dropped them one at a time onto Enrico's chest. "Look, Enrico, let me explain it to you. You're in deep shit. You can tell me what I want to know and you have the chance to walk out of here with enough money to run away or hide from your friends—who will soon be in prison anyway—or you can die. Now I'm tired and busy and the lady outside has her sister's funeral to go to, and we are both sick and tired of fucking around with you. So you either start talking or I'll blow your head off. OK? Now *Choose*!"

Enrico looked up at them steadily, switching his eyes from Simon to the money, nodding.

"You give me the money?" he asked.

"Just talk."

"OK. But if I talk, you not kill me, an' you give me the money."

"That's right."

"How can I be sure?"

"You can't. But I'm not interested in killing you—and what choice do you have, anyway? You want a bullet in the head that badly? Just say the word and that's what you'll get."

Enrico shook his head violently, jerking it from side to side, straining to convince him that he was serious. "No . . . no . . . I'll tell you what you want to know."

Simon pulled up an empty wine crate and sat down beside the bed. "That's good," he said heavily. "I'm glad you understand. Now, did you and your friends kidnap the lady's sister a few weeks ago? Answer, yes or no?"

"*Sì*."

"What? Speak English."

"Yes. Yes." Enrico's voice was desperate. "I speak English."

"Right. Well, we'll leave that for a minute. Two days ago, did you help kidnap young Carlo Colombo?"

"*Sì* . . . yes. We need money quick. But they not hurt the boy, honest. The boy, he is safe."

"What happened to you? Why didn't you go with them?"

"They not take me. Always one must stay to watch the family . . . like Antonio, you know. I bleed, so they leave me. They frightened, I think. It's all too quick."

"Why didn't you leave the hospital and get back to your

friends as soon as you could?" asked Simon curiously. "Or go back to the Colombo house?"

"I cannot—I not go back there—but I can't leave hospital, there is a *carabiniere* on guard on the door. Anyway, I am safe there. With the police outside, maybe is good for me to stay there till the money paid. Then I go quick."

"Safe there from whom? Who is after you, if not the police?"

Enrico's eyes flicked rapidly between Simon and the door. "Is better not to say. If I say that, is bad for me. Maybe I get in much trouble. Please!"

Simon chuckled dryly. "You don't seem to realize the trouble you're in already. Is the boy still in the city? We want him back in one piece. Do you know where he is?"

"Yes, I think so . . . sure. Yes . . . I know, honest. We have safe place, here in the city. Sometimes we go back south, or into the mountains, but the city is safer now, with plenty of children about people don't notice."

"So where is he being held?" asked Simon. "Don't stop now, I want all of it—the lot."

Habits of a lifetime are hard to break. The words came out of Enrico reluctantly, like cold treacle from a jar. "In an apartment, on the outskirts of the city," said Enrico slowly. "Out near Malpensa, near the airport."

Given a little more urging he told everything he knew, gave details of the apartment and the kidnappers. Simon untied one arm and let Enrico draw a plan of the apartment, making him mark all the exits and windows. Finally he gave Enrico a drink of water and tied his wrists back to the bed.

"If any of this doesn't stand up," he told him shortly, "if any of this is lies, the lady outside will sport a new line in earrings. If it checks out you get a lot of money and a few hours' start."

Lucia was sitting on the wall outside the door, away from the heat of the sun, smoking a cigarette, her white coat and pale face just patches in the shade. Simon closed the door behind him and went over to her. "Is there a phone in the house?" he asked quietly. "He's spilled the beans and I think we can trust him, but I must get Aldo to check it out. Then we'll see."

"There's a phone in the hall. It will still be connected. We used to come here at least once a week, until . . . until Gina was taken." Her eyes were looking past Simon, toward the house. "Here are the keys."

"Thanks," said Simon softly, taking them from her hand. "I'll go and ring this information through to Aldo. Keep an eye on Angel Face while we sort something out. I'll be back soon, and then you must leave."

"I'll be all right," replied Lucia quietly. "Just leave me your pistol."

Simon reached under his jacket and handed it over. "The safety catch is on, but don't mess about with it."

"I won't. I just want to talk to him." She weighed the pistol in her hand, then pushed Simon aside and went down the steps, closing the cellar door behind her, turning to lean back against it, listening as Simon hesitated for a moment on the other side of the door, hearing his footsteps fade away across the gravel as he made his way to the house. Only then did she lift her gaze and look across the room to where Enrico Guilini lay spread-eagled on the bed, his head raised painfully from the springs, looking toward her.

"Ecco, Enrico. Come vai?" she asked quietly.

"Tutto potrebbe andare meglio, signorina."

Lucia had never held a gun before. It felt strange, heavy in her hand. She walked over to stand above Enrico, turning the pistol over in her hand, examining it closely in the half-light from the lamp.

"What is this?" she asked him in Italian, turning the weapon on one side and showing it to him. "What sort of gun is this? Do you know anything about guns? Is this a revolver?"

"No, it's a pistol. A Browning, I think."

"And this?" Lucia asked. "This little catch here?"

"That's the safety catch," he said, his voice a little breathless now, nervous. "It stops you pulling the trigger, if it's set on. I don't know how, but it does. Be careful . . . it might not be."

Lucia leaned over him, smelling his sweat, and held the pistol closer to his eyes, turning the safety-catch lever toward him, pushing it up. "Is it on or off? Can you see?" she asked. "Can you tell?"

"Yes . . . now it's off. Set like that it's off. Be careful not to touch the trigger or it'll fire . . . it'll go off . . . if it's cocked."

Lucia sat down on the crate, the pistol set firmly in her hand. It felt good, a solid, balanced weight, filling her fist, powerful. She could feel the power all the way up her arm.

"The gun will shoot now?" she asked him. Her tone was conversational, almost friendly, like a chat between a teacher and a willing pupil. "I don't know about guns. Will it work now? Is it ready to fire?"

"Perhaps, if it's cocked. If there's a bullet in the chamber it'll fire. But you might need to pull back the hammer. That thing there, at the back." He jerked his head up at the pistol. "That's called the hammer."

"How do I know if it's loaded?" asked Lucia curiously.

"You pull back the top, there, where it's marked . . . there, those lines there, and it slides back. You see?"

Lucia pulled hard on the top of the pistol, her thumb and finger gripping the milled surface, and to her surprise it slid back easily, allowing a bright brass cartridge to slip into view. She jerked her head back nervously and looked down at Enrico, holding out the pistol, letting him see inside the breech. Enrico was smiling broadly, unafraid now, amused at her ignorance.

"Let it go now . . . there," he said. The mechanism clashed forward noisily. "It's loaded all right. It'll work OK."

"It's ready to shoot now?" Lucia asked.

"No. You still have to pull back the hammer, with your thumb. Yes, like that."

Lucia did so, using both hands to hold the weapon steady. There was a sharp, oiled click from the pistol, a loud sound in the sudden stillness of the room. Their heads were close together like conspirators, Lucia sitting on the crate, holding the pistol close to Enrico's eyes.

"No, not there. All the way back—that's only at half-cock,"

said Enrico Guilini. "It should go further." The pistol clicked again.

"Is that it?"

"That's it."

Then Lucia turned the barrel down toward him. The round black end of the muzzle was like a vast tunnel, yawning open before his eyes.

"Why did you hurt my sister?" she asked softly. "Why did your people kidnap her and kill her, and do other things to her before you killed her?" The barrel drifted away from his eyes. He felt it resting cold against the scabbed scratches on his chest, then the muzzle came up again before his eyes. "Why did you do that?"

Enrico gazed up at her, his stubbled face wet again with sweat, but said nothing. He kept his eyes on the black muzzle of the pistol, close to his face, his mouth set shut. Maybe there was nothing much he could say, maybe he had said too much already.

"She was just fourteen," continued Lucia quietly. "Just a child. I brought her up. I looked after her since she was a baby. I loved her more than anything, anyone. We would have paid you the money. We had it with us the other night, and you could have had it. Your cousin saw it, and we were going to let him have it, and yet he killed her. You always intended to kill her, and the rest of us as well. Why?"

Enrico laughed harshly, high and nervous. He shook his head hard until the whole bed frame vibrated, his body bouncing up and down on the springs.

"You think your father would pay? You really believe he would? Never! Why did he wait so long? He waited nearly two months to pay the money. He hired an investigator, he called in the cops . . . we know this. And you sent a gunman up there who killed my uncle and my cousins. You never wanted to pay, or you would have paid quickly. We have to look after ourselves . . . it's a *business*, signorina, a *business*. We needed the money quickly, but he didn't pay. We killed her to keep him busy while we took young Carlo."

Lucia's calm and steady eyes were looking down at him over

the black muzzle of the pistol. "I still want to know why you hurt her," she said, her voice quiet, reasonable. "Isn't it normal to argue? If we had agreed on your first price, would you not have wanted more? It was hard to agree on a price we could pay and you would accept. You know that."

"Your father would *never* have paid. Not if he could help it," said Enrico. "He didn't intend to pay. He was looking for us all the time, hoping to find the girl before he had to pay. Also, he was afraid the Englishman would find out. He had Fredo looking for us, too, but he couldn't touch us, not even Antonio, in your house, not while we had his girl. We had to move her five, six times, just to stay ahead of the old bastard's people. He only agreed to pay because of the Englishman sniffing around. He tried to kill him, you know? Not us . . . him." He jerked his head toward the door, the springs twanging rustily under him. "And now there's another prying Englishman. This is not how it's done, signorina . . . it's not done like this. You know the rules. So that's why we did what we did. It's your father's fault. Don't blame me, signorina."

"This Englishman has been here for only a few days. What has he got to do with it?"

"No, not him, not this one, not this bastard . . . the old one who's staying at your father's house." Enrico's voice was impatient now, his confidence growing. "He was getting close to what was really happening, asking questions."

"So you cut off her fingers?" Lucia asked. "Did you do that?"

"No." He shook his head at her nervously, willing her to believe him. "Silvano, he did that. He's dead. He was killed by your friend. He was the one with the rifle?"

"But you helped him, didn't you? You helped Silvano? You beat her up and you . . . raped her and you made a tape while you did it. She put those scratches on your chest. Why did you do that to my sister?" Her voice was still calm, still quiet, and her calmness gave him confidence. Maybe she was afraid of him, too, like her sister had been at the end. Enrico Guilini kept his eyes fixed on hers, concentrating on her face.

"Signorina, you don't know this business. It's a good business for the bosses, but we don't get much out of it. Just wages. We didn't want any trouble, but your old man wouldn't pay. This English cop started poking around and made things difficult. All this time we had the girl. She's a brave girl, your sister, but she's not polite. You have to know your place, keep your mouth shut, know who's the boss." A slow, reflective grin spread slowly across his stubbled, sweating face. Before he spoke again he laughed a little. "She's not polite, your sister, so I taught her manners. Then she was nice." He shook his head, smiling reflectively. "She was very nice."

"You're a pig," said Lucia, shaking her head disgustedly. "I am ashamed to even look at a man like you. My friend said you people were scum, but I didn't believe him, not until now. To think you touched my sister! It makes me sick."

"Come on, she loved it," jeered Enrico. "I'd seen her before, at your father's. And you, too, but you never notice me—I'm only a chauffeur, like dirt to you and your sister. Snotty little bitch, riding about in big cars, on her horses, ignoring us. She treated us all like . . . like . . . dirt, like I say. She stopped being snotty when we taught her a thing or two, and we didn't even tell her the best part. That would really have made her cry, eh? Maybe we should have told her the best part."

Enrico began to laugh then, laughter that grew and grew, on and on, filling the cellar with his noise. Lucia got up and stepped away from the bed, one hand pressed to her head as if to shut out the laughter, pointing the pistol at him until at last the laughter died away. He was still grinning at her, still scornful, daring her to fire, confident that she wouldn't pull the trigger.

"You wouldn't shoot me," he said, sniffing hard. "Your friend might, but not you. And he won't if you don't want him to. D'you think he really will give me the money . . . hey?"

"Tell *me* the best part," said Lucia coldly. "Maybe she didn't hear the best part, so tell me. What is the best part?"

He began to laugh again. "Don't you know either, signorina? You still don't know what's going on? With your education and your money you can't even guess? You're another stupid rich bitch, just like your little sister." Enrico paused as a new idea struck him. "Hey! Maybe we'll get away with this. Next time we could take you, and get more money from your father, eh? Why not? When we get you we'll . . . I'll think of something really special for you, signorina. You may get to like it after the first few times, eh? Just like your little Gina, eh?"

"Shut your dirty mouth," cried Lucia, "and tell me the best part."

When he'd told her the best part she killed him.

At the sound of the shots Simon slammed down the phone and rushed from the house, leaping down the front steps three at a time, sprinting across the gravel, bursting through the door and down the steps to the cellar. The sound of firing was still ringing in the air, a fine mist of dust and plaster still settling from the ceiling. He half fell into the room and found Lucia standing quietly by the bed, sliding the empty magazine from the butt of the pistol.

"There," she said calmly, handing it to him with the pistol. "I think it's safe. I learned to do that myself." Her voice shook slightly and she sat down suddenly on the crate beside the bed.

Simon looked at Enrico's body, twisted and bloody on the bedsprings, and shook his head slowly. He took a longer look at Lucia, at her pale face, her dark hair thickly speckled with white dust and plaster. He took her hand and pulled her up, turning to lead her away from the bed, toward the door, away from Enrico Guilini.

"What did you do that for, Lucia?" he asked her quietly. "Did he try to get away?"

"No. It was for my father," she said quietly, gazing at him directly. "He told me about my father," she said. "And what my father did to my sister."

"You already knew about your father," said Simon. "Aldo and Philip have proved he was behind the kidnappings. That's obvious, so why this?"

"I know what they told me, and I knew it was true," she said urgently, "but I still didn't *believe* it, not really. I just couldn't see how or why he could do it to Gina. That . . . pig, over there, told me what he did, and what happened, and why, especially why. He called it the best part. Knowing my father, I should have worked it out for myself."

Simon led her out of the house, to sit on a wall in the sunshine, watching as she shook the plaster from her hair. She found a comb in her bag and began to sweep the dust away, her hair cascading forward over her face, combing it out with long, firm strokes.

"Well," said Simon, "tell me about it. Maybe we can make sense of it all at last."

Lucia looked out across the garden, gathering her thoughts, the comb held firmly in her hand, and when she spoke she didn't look at him. She kept her eyes on the garden, her tone flat and factual, as if she were talking of other people who had nothing to do with them.

"My father and these men have been kidnapping people for years. When Kleiner told my father he had hired Philip, a top English policeman, to find the kidnappers my father was not really worried. What could Philip do that the Italian police couldn't? My father knew all the plans, all the security—he helped arrange it. But Philip was round all the time, learning more, asking questions. He started to investigate the members of the consortium, one by one. My father didn't like that. Philip did not investigate the ones who had already lost children, so . . . my father thought . . ." Her shoulders slumped a little, then she shrugged.

"Your father decided to have Gina lifted, to turn suspicion from himself," put in Simon, "and make a million or so on the side from the insurance? Isn't that right?"

"Yes, that's right. But when the Puccios and Guilinis . . . when they got Gina, they . . . they kept her. Now it was not a fake kidnap but a real one. My father could do nothing. Not only did they know all about him, they also had Gina. Meanwhile, there was Philip, probing about, getting closer. My father did not dare do anything. Antonio knew what they were doing to Gina. He told my father and *still* my father wouldn't pay."

"Philip wouldn't let your father pay. He already suspected

something was wrong with the consortium, but he didn't know what," said Simon slowly. "Christ! I bet your father was going crazy. But why let scum like that get their hands on his own daughter—why on earth did he trust them? Didn't he know what kind of shits he was dealing with?"

"I don't know," said Lucia. "Anyway . . ." She jerked her head in the direction of the cellar. "He, Enrico, he said that was the best part. The part Gina didn't know—that her father had arranged her kidnapping to protect his own hide. That's when I shot him. But I think I was going to kill him anyway. You killed the people who murdered your family. I shot the man who raped my sister. He could not rape and kill my sister and walk away with money—that was too much."

"I half intended to keep him here until we had the boy back," said Simon slowly. "Or we could have given him the money and let him go. He was trash. His friends would have killed him even if you hadn't. He was a dead man, anyway. All the same I wish you hadn't done this, Lucia. A bullet-riddled body is a hard thing to explain away, especially if the police find it in your cellar." He looked down at the pistol. "Did you have to use up the whole magazine?"

"I didn't mean to. I was scared. It was so loud and I didn't know it wouldn't stop. I just kept pulling the trigger and it went on firing. I didn't know it would do that."

"It's an automatic pistol," said Simon patiently. "That's what automatic means. Let me think . . . we have to get him out of here, then clean the place up a bit, and have a talk, I need to think this through, and you still have to go to Gina's funeral."

"I can't," said Lucia. "I can't even look at my father, especially now, knowing all that he did. How can you expect me to face him, standing at Gina's coffin?"

"I don't know how, but you must," said Simon firmly. "Don't even think about it, just *do* it. Now, let's try and get organized. We don't have a great deal of time. Our first move is to get rid of the body."

The air in the cellar still reeked of cordite fumes, and the acrid smell of blood. Simon gathered up the money lying on the blood-drenched floor, packed it back into the suitcase, careful to avoid it spoiling the other notes, and carried it out to the car. It took their combined effort to roll Enrico Guilini's body off the bed springs, thudding it down onto a wide sheet of faded canvas torn from an old garden awning that Simon found stored at the back of the room. Once the body had been wrapped in that, they carried it between them up the stairs, out of the house, and across the slippery gravel to the car, panting and straining under the weight.

"He's so heavy," panted Lucia, heaving the body up into the trunk. "I'm pretty strong, but he's so heavy."

"He wouldn't be quite so heavy without a dozen rounds of nine-mil ammunition in him," Simon pointed out dryly. "You really believe in making sure, I'll say that for you. There! In he goes. Let's clean up the cellar and then you can start to pretend this hasn't really happened."

"Be quiet, Simon," begged Lucia, beginning to shake. "Please, this is not a joke. What are we going to do?"

"It's done now," said Simon, taking her hands in his. "So we must cover our tracks. Lucia, don't think so much. I wasn't joking; in a day or two you'll really begin to wonder if it happened or whether it was just a bad dream."

Leaving Enrico's body locked in the trunk of the car, Simon returned to the cellar, found a tap with a hosepipe attached, and, after clearing leaves and debris from a blocked drain in the corner, turned it on. Then he began to sluice down the cellar, scrubbing the blood from the floor and bedstead, sweeping the crimson water down the drain, and spraying the hose into every corner.

"This won't do any real good," he warned Lucia, who was sitting on an old chair by the door, smoking, watching him. "Not if the police are keen to find something. We could scrub away for a month and still leave traces of what happened. He's also carrying a dozen rounds from my pistol, just to help the police make a match. We only have to make one mistake and we're finished."

Lucia lit another cigarette, her voice calmer. "I don't care.

If you want me to tell Aldo I shot him, then I will. What difference does it make? I'm glad I shot him. The other night, you were right and I was wrong. Some people need to be shot."

Simon stacked the broom and bucket in the corner, took her hand, and led her out of the cellar's gloom up the stairs, into the warm midday sunshine, then rolled down his shirtsleeves and reached for his jacket, which lay on the wall.

"Try telling that to a jury," he said frankly. "At the moment there are other priorities. First, you must go to the funeral. I have to see Aldo about getting the Colombo boy back, then I must see Philip. I gave Aldo all the information we got from Enrico, and his team are working on how to get the boy out even now. I must get over to his office. Meanwhile, I don't want your father alarmed; that could be dangerous. It's hard to say how he'll react, but if I were he I'd try and deal with anyone who could give hard evidence against him. That might include you."

"I won't be able to look at him. How can I?" asked Lucia. "He does it to the others, then to his own daughter, and still he talks and smiles at me. He is disgusting."

There wasn't much Simon could say to that. He took her hand and held it gently in his, sitting beside her in the sunshine, letting it warm them.

"Philip told me you hate your father," said Simon at last. "It was one of the first things he said about you. Do you really hate him? The real, deep-down hate? Or do you really just not like him very much?"

Lucia took her hand from his and fell into her familiar pose, her arms folded, looking at him steadily with those startling green eyes. "You know now that my father is a crook," she said. "I always knew that. When I was small, when we lived in the South, before he married Gina's mother, I remember how he would come home with things he had stolen. When we came up here to Milan, he simply became a bigger crook, and a more successful one. Hard, honest work was much too slow for him, so he used other methods. I didn't know what, or how, and I didn't want to know. I took his money simply to get away and study and make my own life. He got rich, but he was never kind, he never listened, he was never a real father. I became a doctor, so that even his money would do some good, and I'm a good doctor. Just living with him killed my mother. He didn't care, she wasn't good enough for him, he said, not young enough—so he married my stepmother and they had Gina. I liked my stepmother. She was kind to me—and I loved Gina. When she was a baby she was just like a doll, quite wonderful. Then, when he drove my stepmother to leave him, he kept Gina. In Italy, a woman who leaves a man, even a man like him, has no rights. He didn't really care for Gina, he only wanted to hurt her mother. He looks successful now, so important. He knows people like Klaus Kleiner, but he's still a crook. Now I know he's a killer too." She fell silent for a while.

"I think he's killed Antonio," she went on, "or got Fredo to do it. Fredo does all the really dirty work for my father. You must be careful of Fredo, Simon. He's a dangerous man." Then she shrugged and gave Simon a small smile. He said nothing. There was nothing he could say to her, no way to express the pity he felt or change the situation, or repair the damage Fiori had done to her. She was looking past him now, deep in thought, her eyes fixed on the far distant mountaintops.

They sat on in the sunshine for a little, until Simon stirred himself and got up to stand before her, spreading his hands helplessly. "I read somewhere that objects of hate are caused by wounds within us," he said. "I think that's true. But not everyone in this world is like your father. When this is all over, come away with me. You've not been very lucky in your men, Lucia. First your father, then your husband, now someone like me who seems to do something dreadful every day. But we're coming to the end of it. We know what's going on, and we can live through it. That's important, isn't it?"

Lucia looked at him steadily, her fingers playing lightly with the cigarette, then smiled thoughtfully, nodding at him, a little smile growing on her face.

"Yes," she said at last. "I think that's the most important thing there is right now; to live through this. But can we do it?"

"I don't know," said Simon frankly. "I've managed up to

now because I just didn't care one way or the other. That gives me a definite edge." He pulled her toward him, off the wall, held her hands for a moment, then led her firmly to the car. "Let's get rid of Enrico and go and see Aldo, and get all this over and done with. Then we can get on with our lives, and to hell with people like your father."

SEVENTEEN

Lucia handed him a map and Simon spread it out on his knees, studied it for a while, and then gave her directions to drive the car deeper into the country, along ever-narrowing lanes. From time to time he asked her to stop the car, got out, and went away into the woods, returning after a few minutes, shaking his head.

"What exactly are you looking for?" Lucia asked him at last. "I'll have to start back soon or I shall be late for the funeral."

"We need to dump our boy somewhere he won't be found for at least a few days, and that's not as easy as it sounds. Those last two woods looked pretty thick from the road, but they were criss-crossed with footpaths. Drive on and go left at the end of this road."

Eventually they found what he was looking for, a long strip

of woodland beside a country lane, a windbreak for a hillside of vines. Simon got out of the car and disappeared into the undergrowth. It was several minutes before he returned.

"Come on," he said, leaning into the car. "This will do. Reverse up here and help me to get him out. Come on, take the feet."

They dumped Enrico Guilini's body in the woods, a hundred yards from the lane, turning the naked body out of the blood-soaked canvas, and watching it roll stiffly down the dried-mud slope of a ditch and come to a stop at the bottom.

"Exit Enrico Guilini," said Simon thoughtfully. "But I have another idea . . . a little frill."

"What are you going to do now?"

"Nothing much . . . just litter the spot with the notes that have got blood on them, we can't use them in that state. Now I must phone Aldo—he'll be wondering why I rang off so suddenly."

"There's good news and bad news," said Simon, getting back into the car after speaking to Aldo on the telephone.

"I could use some good news," said Lucia, starting the engine, "so let's have that first."

"The good news is that Guilini wasn't lying. Aldo sent his surveillance boys over there and the information checked out. So now we know where the boy is. Aldo is getting his lads together now and wants me to meet him as soon as possible."

"So, what's the bad news?"

"The bad news is that the kidnappers have been in touch with Colombo, and they're not messing about. They want three million within forty-eight hours or they kill the boy. That's a threat we have to take seriously. They can't hang about with your father gunning for them—and he doesn't give a damn what happens to young Colombo. Like young Guilini back there, they need the money to run for their lives."

The offices of the counterterrorist forces in Milan occupy the top floor of a tall building and are reached only after passing through a long series of checks and barriers that guard the elevators and stairs. The Criminalpol building is the nerve center for counterterrorism in northern Italy, a place the extremists of right and left and the *capos* of organized crime would dearly love to destroy. Here, side by side, in loose conjunction, sit representatives of the *questura,* the *carabinieri,* the *polizia,* the Squadra Mobile, the Squadra Volante, the Squadra Antiterrorismo, and SISMI, the Secret Service. It was here that Simon found Aldo, sitting at his desk with three of his men, studying a street map.

The outer offices were busy, crammed with men and women, telephoning or talking in groups, studying files or gathered here and there around scruffy, exhausted figures, most of whom had one wrist handcuffed to a radiator, desk drawer, or chair. The din was tremendous, but counterterrorism is a thriving industry. When Simon's escort went out and closed the door in the glass partition at his back, the decline in the noise was a considerable relief.

Aldo sat on the far side of his desk, facing into the room. Three men sat in front of him in folding chairs, their heads turning, their eyes lifting slowly from the map as Simon entered, their faces carefully blank. They rose together without a word as he came in, picking up their chairs and moving out of the way.

"Simon, meet Sergio, Rico, Eugenio . . . Signor Quarry. You have all seen the file on Signor Quarry? He is in with us on this," he said. "Guilini's information checked out. We have located the flat where the boy is being held. I've already been to look at the area. The flat next door is empty and we have run in a wire to the Puccios' flat, so we can listen to what goes on. The rest of my team are there now, moving in very slowly, staking out the building. It's in the old part of the city, an area with rather poor public housing, mostly tenements filled by immigrants from the South. See here—the top flat is rented to one of the Puccios. What a family! Being in a top-floor flat could make it difficult to get close, but, on the other hand, with the building staked out they can't easily get away. I got a floor plan from the city architect. It's a fairly simple layout, all two-room flats, with a small bathroom and kitchenette. They are up here, on the fifth floor, and the child is held in the bedroom, here. It's secure because there is only a skylight window . . . all these buildings are firetraps. The problem is to get in and stifle them before they can put up much of a fight. According to the wire tap, they are not doing much, just sitting about, chatting, playing cards, but it's certain they are armed and nervous. Any ideas?"

Simon studied the street map and the floor plan for a while, scratching his chin thoughtfully, doodling on a scrap of paper with a pencil. Finally he shrugged his shoulders and looked around at Aldo and his team.

"You know more about this sort of thing than I do, but it looks pretty obvious," he said, tapping the plan with his finger. "There are only two ways in. Through the door here, or through the kitchen window via the fire escape. You might try putting someone in up the fire escape, but they creak and groan and can be noisy. Fire escapes are designed to let people out, not burglars in, so it may be locked up at the bottom. On balance, I would go for the front door. You can either knock and ask them to open up, or blast your way in. If the boy is in the bedroom . . . here . . . and you are quick about it, that should be the safest way."

"The classic way to deal with the situation is to surround the building, let them know we have them penned in and then sweat it out for a few days," said Aldo, looking around at his men, who were nodding in agreement. "But I'm not inclined to do that this time. They might kill the boy or use him as a hostage. I think we'll go in."

"Good," said Simon briefly. "I'm glad to hear it. This kidnapping is just part of the problem. Getting the boy back frees our hands, that's all. There's plenty still to do after that."

"Waiting them out is the best way, because we know it works," Aldo went on, "but they've killed one kid and have nothing much to lose by killing another. It's not a predictable situation. But the big reason for going in now is that we have surprise. They don't know yet we're on to them, but that may not last. Everything suggests we should hit them tonight."

"Good," said Simon again. "Why wait? Look, if you take a big team you'll get in each other's way. You could keep your team here, around the building, or down the stairs, and I'll come in with you."

Aldo shook his head. "Oh no, you won't. This is official business. I'll have one man for backup on the stairs, in case we don't take them on the first rush. We can't clear everyone out of the building while they have the boy, without the risk of tipping them off. So, one man with me, one close behind, one in the courtyard—that's four, and we have four men to deal with inside. That's a bit tight, but there is not a lot of room in there."

"Well, it's your turf, but I'm here if you need me," said Simon.

"No, thank you," said Aldo hurriedly, putting up his hands. "Definitely not. That's out of the question. You can come and watch but you stay out of it. I don't want the boy hurt, and I want them alive, if possible. I'd like a few witnesses for Fiori's trial, if we can get them to talk."

Simon shrugged. "I'd like to come along, and so would Philip. The Colombo lad is his particular concern, but we won't get in the way."

"We'll see," said Aldo, smiling, pushing his chair away from the desk. "I can hardly exclude Philip. Where is he?"

"He'll be here soon. He's at Gina Fiori's funeral, partly out of respect, partly to keep an eye on Fiori. Klaus is there, too, and I would be there as well but for this. You wanted to see me but you don't want my help. What do you want?"

"Wait a minute." Aldo got up and gestured his men over to the door, rapping out instructions in Italian. When they had left, and gone off to gather up their weapons and equipment, he closed the door firmly and came back to sit behind the desk. For a moment they looked at each other, saying nothing, smiling slightly, waiting.

"Well?" asked Simon.

"I wondered what you think of your employer, our mutual friend, Klaus Kleiner?"

Simon looked back at him steadily, reflectively. "Well, personally speaking, he's been all right with me so far. Why do you ask? You must know him better than I do."

"I also know more about him than you do." Aldo was smiling again. "But no doubts about your contract? No second thoughts?"

"Look," said Simon, a touch impatiently, "if you've got something to say why not say it?"

Aldo pushed himself away from the desk and spun around in his chair to face one of the steel filing cabinets ranged at his back, opening a drawer to pluck out two files, one thick, one thin. Then he spun back to face Simon and placed the files on the desk between them.

"You seem to be a reasonable man, Simon—personally speaking. And I'm going to let you a little way into a secret. This," he tapped the thin file, "is the secret life of Simon Quarry—mostly extracts from files held in London, Paris, Athens—but not much. This one"—he tapped the thick file—"is the life and times of Klaus Kleiner, off the record and behind the scenes. Commander Wintle told us to check up on all the consortium members, including Kleiner. This is part of what we found, but we had a file on him already."

"Why would the Squadra run a file on Klaus Kleiner?"

"Because he very nearly started a civil war here after his daughter was kidnapped. Maybe that's excusable—he was crazy about that kid. But we've had problems with the rich here in the past. Did you ever know Giangiacomo Feltrinelli?"

"No, never heard of him."

"I thought you might have. He was a publisher, like you were. He funded most of the terrorist groups here in the late sixties and seventies, until he blew himself up with one of his own bombs; it couldn't have happened to a nicer fellow. Anyway, at Philip's request we opened a file on Kleiner and, since he operates all over the world, we sent out a request for information, and in it came, from Scotland Yard, from the French

DST, the Spanish DGI—from every intelligence unit in the West. Klaus thinks my government has put me with him to help out. That's only half true. I'm also there to keep an eye on him."

"What has all this got to do with me?" asked Simon. "I don't care what Kleiner has got up to. I'll be gone in a day or two and I'll never see him again."

"If Kleiner wants you, you'll see him again. He offered you a deal and a million dollars. Philip says you didn't take the money or care about it, but you took Kleiner's contract away. Maybe that was wise. If you hadn't he would have pressed you some other way. He won't take no for an answer. Don't think he's just another businessman, he can play rough." Aldo flipped open the file and thumbed through the first few pages before looking at Simon again.

"Let me tell you a little about our mutual friend. When Kleiner was in his early twenties he served five years in the French Foreign Legion."

"Really!" Simon was surprised, even startled. "I wonder why Philip didn't mention that?"

"He may not know. I certainly didn't tell him. This is a confidential file, and Kleiner enlisted under a false name; that's not unusual, most Legionnaires do. His father made him join. He was a hard old bastard—he said he could teach his son all about business, but the Legion would make a man of him. He was right about that. Kleiner served in the Algerian War, in the Battle of Algiers, and in the 1st REP, the Régiment Étranger Parachutiste of the Legion. That was the unit that tried to overthrow the French government when the Algerian War ended. They were going to jump on Paris. De Gaulle disbanded them and Kleiner was discharged. Later on, he came to the attention of the DST, the French Secret Service, and they looked at his Legion papers. His father died, but Kleiner had stayed in France. He funded the OAS terrorists there until the movement collapsed. He then moved to Spain, where his factories in San Sebastián and Pamplona pay tribute to ETA, the Basque terrorist group. He has extreme contacts with hard men all over the world. You see where we are going?"

"Well, no . . . but you live and learn," said Simon.

"I hope so," said Aldo. "The point is this. Kleiner got an early training in a very hard school. He doesn't like losing—in Algeria or Milan. He has only the slightest respect for the law or democratic government and he's stinking rich. That's a dangerous combination. You're in with him now, and my advice is don't get in any deeper."

"If he's as tough as you say, I can't see why he needs me—and yet Philip says he was looking for me."

"I know why he needs you," said Cirillo, closing the file. "He needs backup. He's too well known to clout people himself and he hopes you'll do it for him . . . whatever he says otherwise. I know that, because he offered the job to me."

"How did he find out about me—from you?"

"No, nor from Philip. I suspect he got it in London from Alec Yates. Alec Yates is Kleiner's contact in London and if his notes in your file are anything to go by, Yates is no friend of yours."

Simon nodded. "He's not. He tried to get me killed a couple of years ago."

Aldo chuckled. "Did he now? *That* isn't mentioned in your file. I'll put a note in. Anyway, putting you and Kleiner together would amuse Yates and he could provide Kleiner with the means to pressure you if need be. Your file is not closed, just inactive. Also, the British government owes Kleiner a favor."

"For what?" asked Simon.

"He's opening a big factory in Merseyside, and anyone who can provide eight thousand jobs in a depressed area, with a general election coming up, can get just about anything he wants from the government of the day. But, as usual with Kleiner, there's more to it than that. He's using the Merseyside plant to demonstrate to the politicians here that he means business—that he wants their support against the gangs. There are no kidnappings in Liverpool, so they get the jobs, not Milan. There is always an angle with Kleiner, never forget that. He offers you what you want, and threatens something you don't want. As you can imagine, it's no contest. Given the choice, people choose what they want."

"I've noticed that myself," said Simon dryly, "and quite recently. Is he serious about the gangs?"

"Very—and so are we. We support him in that and something has to be done. Fiat has had three managers killed in Turin and nearly twenty kneecapped . . . big company managers are often targets. Last year a terrorist group broke into a management training school, lined up a hundred students, and shot ten of them dead. We need all the help we can get against these people, and the kidnappings fund their activities. Fiori may not be a terrorist, but it's better than even money that he works with them when he has to . . . and so the Squadra gets involved. But watch out for Kleiner. He is quite ruthless, and if you cross him . . . if you don't do what he wants, well, do you see what I'm getting at?"

"I do," said Simon thoughtfully. "And thanks for the tip."

"You're welcome," said Aldo. "Now, one other thing—what have you done with Enrico Guilini? We should take him in and lock him up."

"Ah, well . . . this may be embarrassing. I let him go," said Simon apologetically.

Aldo looked at him hard. "You are, of course, kidding," he said flatly. "Are you trying to tell me you let him get away?" He snapped his fingers sharply. "Come on, what really happened?"

Simon looked back frankly into Aldo's eyes and smiled. "I haven't laid a glove on him. Wheel in your biggest lie detector and wire me to it if you don't believe me. I let him go. That was the deal; I could kill him or I could give him lots of money—Kleiner's money—and let him go. He won't squeal. He's much too scared of his family and Fiori. In fact, we may never hear from him again if they get to him first," he added, dropping his voice.

Aldo looked at him again hard, his face full of doubt. "I see," he said slowly. "And you don't think he might contact his pals and tell them what we know? One telephone call to the flat, and good-bye little boy."

Simon shook his head. "Oh no," he said positively, slapping the desk with his hand. "That won't happen, not a chance. He won't be talking to anybody. Anyway, surely you have a tap on the telephone line. You could intercept him; he won't go there in person, knowing it's staked out. But don't you want to hear what he's said already—about Fiori, and this whole business?"

"Fiori can wait. At the moment I'm more interested in Guilini," said Aldo. He was leaning forward across the desk now, looking at Simon closely. "You swear you never touched him? Not a bit? Yet he told you all we needed to know?"

Simon looked through the partition to the outer office and saw with relief that Philip Wintle, Klaus Kleiner, and Lucia were coming toward them, behind an escort. "On my mother's grave," he said. "He was in perfect condition when I came up to phone you. Here comes Philip and the others. When they're here, let me tell you all about Fiori."

"If I understand what you are saying correctly, Fiori had nothing to do with these kidnappings." Philip's voice expressed his clear disbelief. "But all the evidence we've gathered points the other way."

"No, I'm not saying that," said Simon patiently. "Lucia will bear me out. What I am saying is . . . look, it's complicated. Fiori was and is the original boss of the kidnappers. All the early kidnappings are his doing. To divert suspicion from himself he arranges to get his own daughter snatched. After all, what better cover can there be? He's a victim now, poor old Fiori. Knowing what they were like, he must have seen the risk. At the very least the girl would be terrified. That's called looking after number one."

"But it goes wrong," said Kleiner. "His men turn on him, keep the girl and squeeze him on their own account."

"But why did they kill the girl?" asked Aldo. "What was the point of that?"

"To keep Fiori busy while they also snatched the Colombo boy and squeezed us again," said Simon. "Maybe also to hurt Fiori, who would certainly go after them anyway. Maybe they're just bastards. In any case, they did it. They also intended to kill Philip and maybe take Lucia. That would keep Fiori quiet while they got the Colombo money—assuming he cares anything about her at all."

"Who arranged the present snatch of the Colombo boy?" asked Kleiner curiously.

"The Puccios, using a setup Fiori had already arranged," replied Simon. "They need the money to get away from Fiori. He doesn't give a damn about the Colombo boy. That is why Guilini was quite content to sit in the hospital behind a police guard."

"If we are to crack this gang and put Fiori where he belongs," said Aldo heavily, "we need witnesses. So far we have none. What we have are just stories, hearsay, and a few business papers. Nothing much there a court can use in a criminal case."

"With our unwitting help, Fiori has eliminated anyone he thinks can testify against him," said Philip. "I don't think that driver of his, Antonio Puccio, will be seen again, and at the moment I don't give twopence for our chances of putting him away for Klaus's required twenty years. Right now I simply want the Colombo boy back."

'We'll get the boy back tonight, as soon as the streets are quiet." Aldo pointed through the glass partition to where the three members of his team were waiting outside, dressed in black overalls now, their weapons littering the tops of nearby desks. "After that we'll see what we can do about Fiori."

The little group in Aldo's office sat together silently for a moment, listening to the murmur of voices outside. Klaus Kleiner broke the silence after looking at his watch. "It's nearly seven," he said. "I'll ring Signor Colombo and bring him up to date, but nothing much can happen before, what . . .? Ten? Ten-thirty? Would you all like to join me for dinner?"

"Sorry, we can't," said Aldo and Simon together.

"I have to brief my team out there," explained Aldo, nodding as Simon gave way. "If you want to be in at the finish, meet me at this point here, two streets from the apartment"—he tapped the map—"at ten-thirty. Don't come too close. It might also be an idea if someone, say, you, Klaus, stayed near a telephone to give us a contact point."

"To fill in the time, I'm taking Lucia out to dinner," said Simon, glancing at Lucia intently. "Our last effort didn't get very far so we'll try again. There's nothing to be gained by sitting about here, biting our nails."

Klaus looked across at Philip. "Well, that leaves us," he said. "Will you come back with me to the Principe? I'd like to be somewhere I can be contacted."

"I'll come back to the Principe," said Philip, "and Simon and Lucia can collect me there at around ten?"

"We'll do that," said Simon, "and we'll all meet up there later on—for the celebration."

After Philip and Kleiner had gone, Simon got up and moved restlessly around the office, nodding a greeting through the glass to Aldo's team, putting a hand on Lucia's shoulder as she wandered past. "Shall we go?" he asked her. "It's too early for dinner but we can stop and have a drink somewhere."

"In a minute," she said. "I'd just like to sit here for a minute. It's been an awful day."

Aldo got up from his desk and crossed the room to a filing cabinet, returning with a bottle of Scotch and three glasses, which he placed before them.

"Why don't we all have a drink here?" he said. "Try some single malt."

"Not for me," said Simon.

"Lucia?"

"Yes, please."

"You look tired, Lucia," said Aldo. "Is anything the matter? Anything you want to tell me?"

Tension was building between Aldo and Lucia. *If he asks her about Guilini,* thought Simon, *if he even mentions his name, she'll fall apart.* The strain of the last days was carved on her face.

"What weapons are your boys carrying?" asked Simon, turning to Aldo, tapping his knuckles on the glass partition. "They look ready for anything."

"Standard stuff," replied Aldo briefly, taking his eyes from Lucia. "Stun grenades, some gas, a shotgun, and Heckler and Koch weapons."

Aldo rose and came to stand beside Quarry, pointing out through the glass. "The main piece we use is the 35-KAI assault rifle. We use the retracting-stock model, nice and short, only about fifty centimeters long. For sidearms, we stick with Heckler, or rather my boys do. They have M13 pistols, nine-mil."

"What about tonight?" asked Simon. "What will you use?"

Aldo went out and came back with the shotgun. "This is like yours, a twelve-gauge pump, but it carries solid shot, not buckshot. As the boss, I have the job of blasting the door hinges and the lock in—and solid shot is safer with the boy inside. Have you seen it?"

"Never," said Simon, keeping the conversation going. "I'd like to try it—for hunting, of course."

"I'll give you a box as you leave. The shotgun barrel isn't rifled of course, but the solid rounds are—it increases the accuracy while retaining the impact. And then I have a pistol as backup." Aldo put down the shotgun and reached under his jacket. "This is the Beretta SB, a nice, compact pistol. It goes well under a suit and carries thirteen rounds in the clip. I wouldn't carry anything else. I have an H. and K. in the car, though, and a bodyguard, day and night."

"It's double-action," said Simon doubtfully, turning the pistol over in his hand. "I'm dubious about double-action. What's the caliber?"

"The usual—nine mil."

"Ah, that's good. Have you got any spare ammo? I need to top up."

"Certainly . . . over here."

Aldo walked back to his desk, opened a drawer, and hunted around inside. Eventually he produced a box of cartridges and watched as Simon produced the Browning from his waistband, slid out the empty magazine, and began to ram cartridges into it with swift, sharp movements of his thumb. Then he put the pistol down, produced a second magazine from his pocket, and began to fill that, looking up to meet Aldo's curious gaze.

"I normally keep one mag empty and swap the rounds from one to the other every day, to keep the springs strong. At the moment I feel like having them both full."

"Very sensible," said Aldo smoothly. "Not that you will need to use either tonight." He reached over, picked up the Browning, cocked the action, and sniffed the barrel. Then, holding it up to the light, he peered into the breech. "This has been fired," he said, looking directly at Simon, "and recently. What at?"

"Targets," said Simon flatly. He reached over the desk to take the pistol back and slapped a full magazine back into the butt, cocking the action, and sliding the pistol under his jacket, all in one smooth movement. Then he sat back in his chair and looked across the desk, directly into Aldo's frowning face. "Why don't you relax, Aldo? Everything's been taken care of. There's nothing for you to worry about."

Aldo rubbed his knuckles against his jaw and glanced at Lucia, who sat on the far side of the desk, staring silently into space. Then he looked at his team, chatting quietly beyond the partition, and back at Simon, who met his gaze squarely, a quiet smile playing about his lips.

"I see," said Aldo, slowly nodding, looking between Simon and Lucia. "All right!" He slapped his hands together suddenly. "Let's leave it. It is now"—he looked at his watch—"just after seven. We will move in at midnight. Be where we arranged at ten-thirty or eleven."

Simon looked at Aldo and began to rise. "We'll both join you later. We'll be there before eleven."

"I'll tell my people to watch out for you," said Aldo. "And, as they say in England, don't do anything I wouldn't do. *Ciao*."

EIGHTEEN

Time doesn't really fly. Most of the time it crawls. Look at the hands of the clock once, then look again an hour later, and only two minutes have elapsed. That's how time crawls when you are waiting for something to happen. On that particular night, little groups of people were waiting, all over the city.

In a grubby apartment on the fifth floor of a tenement building on the edge of the city, the kidnappers were waiting. They were waiting for the morning, until they could send someone out to make a second contact, set up a meeting, get the ball rolling. In their much plusher apartment on the other side of the city, the Colombo family waited for news that the nightmare was over. On the top floor of the Criminalpol building, Aldo Cirillo and his team studied the street and floor plans, worried out the problems, decided on their moves. They were used to waiting. Waiting took up most of their time. From their windows they could see the tower of the Principe, even the lights of the room where Kleiner and Wintle were dining, saying little, chatting now and then of this and that, just waiting.

Fiori and Fredo Donati were also waiting, but on a longer time frame. Fredo Donati was restless. He prowled the house, and stood on the steps before the front door, keeping it open to let the soft night air sweep in, gathering up the heavy scent of funeral flowers, sending it down the hall to the study, where the draft sent Fiori's cigar smoke up in little whirls. Fiori sat behind his desk, still dressed in the suit he had worn to the church and the cemetery, the broad black lapels of the jacket speckled white with cigar ash, heavy eyes on Fredo as he came back into the room and went directly to the cabinet to pour out drinks and bring them over to the desk.

Fredo Donati was a slight, compact man, with jet-black eyes set in a pale face, a heavy dark moustache curving down on either side of his mouth. Unlike Fiori, who was never tidy, Donati was always neat. He dressed in well-cut, close-fitting suits, which made him seem smaller and more compact than he actually was. His shirt gleamed white, his tie was carefully knotted, his shoes shone. He looked the competent one, the one in charge here, but his manner toward Fiori was somehow deferential.

"A bad day, *capo,*" he offered.

Fiori grunted, reaching for the glass.

"We'll see worse before this is over."

"Maybe . . ." Fredo thought about this for a moment. "Maybe the worst is over. They may suspect something but there's no proof."

Fiori laughed, a deep rumble that changed into a cough. "Oh, they suspect all right, and they're looking for proof. I can hear it in their voices, in the way they can't look at me directly anymore, but they still have no witnesses. Quarry has seen to that. He should not shoot to kill. Also, they've found where the Colombo boy is being held."

"Are you sure?"

"Oh yes. Lucia told Wintle at the graveside. He said, 'Good, good,' right out loud. Then the two of them went off with Kleiner to meet Cirillo. They're all very thick now."

"So, what will happen, *capo*?"

Fiori shrugged heavily, the glass in one fist, eyes brooding on the desk. "I don't know. We must wait and see. Maybe they'll get the boy back alive. Then it depends on whether they take the Puccios alive. We may be lucky. There can't be many left to rat on us. We must wait till the man arrives from the south. He should be here soon."

"And then?"

"And then we'll deal with Kleiner and Wintle and Quarry. The consortium will crack up and the police will lose interest. Cirillo is only involved in this because of Kleiner. He has many other duties, but those three . . . ? They'll never give up."

"Maybe we should have shut down when Signor Wintle arrived, *capo,* but it is very expensive not to operate. We have people to pay, payoffs to make. We need cash."

"I know that," spat Fiori. "It's my money, remember. They have been lucky, that's all. We tried the bomb and they found it; you sent two beefy boys to deal with a man like Quarry, and he smashed them up. That was your mistake, Fredo." Fiori jabbed a fat finger across the desk. "Those *raggazi* couldn't handle a man like Quarry."

"I am sorry, *capo*."

"Never mind, Fredo. Third time lucky, eh? Our turn will-come . . . maybe tonight."

"So we wait, *capo*?"

"So we wait," said Fiori.

"He knows," said Lucia quietly, tapping her cigarette nervously on the table.

"He suspects," said Simon, his eyes on the menu.

"He thinks you killed him."

"He doesn't know what to think." Simon looked up at her over the top of the menu. "It's a new factor, that's all. Aldo is thinking, 'Well, he's whacked Guilini—why did he do that? Or did she do it? And where's the body? And what happens now?'

His brain was working overtime back there. Just remember that deep down he doesn't care. Unless it gets difficult or obvious who did it he doesn't give a damn about Guilini. It's just another rat out of his way."

"I'll try to remember that," said Lucia bitterly. "I killed a rat—simple!"

"How was the funeral?" asked Simon, putting down the menu and settling back in his chair.

"Great! Terrific! How do you think it was?" There was an edge to her voice now. "We buried my sister. I've spent better days, even in Milan."

"I didn't mean that. I meant . . . with your father?"

"I didn't speak to him. He stayed on one side of the grave with Fredo. I stayed on the other between Philip and Klaus. They both shook his hand before we left, but I just looked at him. I think he knows that we know about him."

"Well . . ." Simon shrugged his shoulders dismissively. "He's not stupid. Anyway, it'll all be over soon, so let's change the subject. I like this place, it's nice—full of normal people."

The restaurant was pleasant, a long wide room with a low, whitewashed ceiling and tables placed at a discreet distance apart. The walls were pastel-colored, covered with paintings and tiles and small pots of flowers, the floor a maze of flagstones. It was starting to fill up with a cheerful, chattering, early evening crowd, and a pleasant smell of cooking, of pasta and cheese and sauces, filled the warm air. Simon realized yet again that he was hungry.

"Signore?" The waiter appeared at their table, standing by with his order pad. He handed Simon the wine list.

"We'll have a bottle of Frascati, and a bottle of San Pellegrino," said Simon, waving the wine list aside. "Well chilled—and we'll order in a minute."

"Yes, signore, at once. One chilled Frascati, one San Pellegrino."

"Doesn't anyone in this town speak Italian?" Simon asked Lucia. "Even the waiters can speak better English than I can. How will I ever learn Italian?"

"It's a business town with lots of fairs, conferences, and exhibitions," explained Lucia, half smiling. "Milano is full of foreigners all the time. If you can speak English, or better still English and German, in Milan, you can get a better job. It's quite simple."

The bottles arrived. Silence fell while Simon and the waiter went through the ritual of inspecting the labels, drawing the cork, and tasting the wine. "That's fine," he said, looking up at the waiter. "Not for me though . . . for the signorina. Nice and cold, but we'll have an ice bucket to keep it that way." He poured out some water, caught Lucia's eye, and raised his glass. *"Salute!"* he said. "And here's to better times. Also to the time when I can have a decent drink. This is fine, but boring—but you must admire my willpower."

"I do," she said, "Well done. Cheers!" Her face darkened and then became worried again. "So Aldo suspects that Enrico Guilini is dead. What happens when they find the body?"

"I don't know," said Simon frankly. "Aldo isn't crazy and it was very stupid of me to show him my pistol. I could have bitten my tongue off, but by then it was too late. I had to go ahead and reload it." He shook his head sadly. "Stupid . . . stupid. I was trying to distract him from thinking about you. He was making too many rapid connections. But he'll find it hard to believe you did it. He likes you."

Lucia smiled slightly and lit another cigarette." Yes, I suppose he does. A little while ago he asked me to marry him."

"Jesus!" exclaimed Simon. "And what did you say?"

"I said I would think about it." She blew a long stream of cigarette smoke into the air and looked across the table at Simon, her eyes tired. "It seemed like a solution. He's very nice, strong . . . he could do all the worrying. I'm tired of looking after myself. But now . . . will you tell him I did it, or shall I?"

Simon looked at her for a moment, brooding over her words. Then he shook his head at her. "Just let him be," he said. "Aldo will think it over and let it lie. Aldo knows that Guilini is no loss to anyone. Drop it. As for the rest—you know how I feel.

But you have had enough pressure. I can say no more."

Lucia put her glass down hard and rested her elbows on the table, cupping her face in her hands. For a moment Simon thought she was going to collapse. The weight of the day's events on top of the weeks before was suddenly proving too much.

"Please don't cry," he said, looking quickly around the room. "Not here, please, Lucia. Just hang on a little longer."

She spread her hands across her face and looked at him through her fingers. "Is it really so easy?" she asked softly. "How can you kill someone and then go out to dinner? The very idea of food makes me choke. I actually feel sick."

Simon waved the approaching waiter away again with a shake of his head, and stared across at her, thinking. "Look," he said finally. "Try and see it as a job, or an accident, or something that just happened. What really upsets you is that there is no legal sanction. If Aldo shot someone, or Philip did, or that team of heavies in Aldo's office did, you'd clap and cheer them on. You'd buy them a drink, because they do it for a job. You think I do it for pleasure and that sticks in your throat. It's worse than ever now, now that you know what it's like. But you have to think about all of it, the background, the cause, not just the act."

"I don't understand you. These last few days, I thought I'd gotten to know you, but you talk about killing as if . . . as if it doesn't matter. Maybe Philip is wrong about your so-called 'edge.' He says you have this power because you don't care about your own life. But maybe it's because you don't worry about killing other people. Well, I can't do that, Simon. I'm a doctor. I'm supposed to save life, not take it."

Simon closed his eyes wearily. "Whatever we start to talk about, it all comes back to the same point, doesn't it? Let me explain about this damned edge that Philip keeps harping on about." He looked over her head for a moment, searching for words. "Look, the world is full of thugs, looking for trouble, right? You find them on buses and trains and in public places. They get their kicks from frightening harmless people. It's what they do for fun . . . yes?"

"Yes . . . so?"

"Well, if people like that try it on with me, I come back at them, hard. *That's* my edge. The sheer surprise of a thug or two finding out that some passerby, some civilian, some mug simply won't put up with them, gives me my edge. That's all. Don't complicate it, Lucia. Don't try and make me into a monster because I defend myself. You see, the thugs expect to win. Most people don't want trouble, so even if they decide to fight back, they lose. I expect trouble, which is not too surprising after all that has happened in the last few years, so I can handle it, but I'm not special. I'm an ordinary person and I like it that way. I led a very ordinary life until the Jihad killed my family. I came here to give Philip some backup, that's all. I have never willingly lifted my hand against anyone who wasn't actually begging for it. I want you to believe that. You know it's true anyway."

"Maybe I do," she said quietly, looking down at the table, "but I still don't like it. Look, if Aldo lets it drop, what will happen to us?"

Simon shook his head, spreading his hands. "You might also ask what happens to Aldo. I can't think that far ahead. Philip can clear up these kidnappings, and then I must go back to Spain. I hope you will come with me—as you know."

"Well, yes. Of course I'm coming with you," said Lucia, as if that much was obvious. "I've already told Philip, and the hospital. I've even arranged for someone else to look after my patients at the clinic. Now I must tell Aldo, though I think he already knows. I think we are stuck with each other now, for better or for worse."

"No married couple could ask for any more," said Simon. He gazed at her across the table, his eyes fixed on hers for a moment, smiling. Then he looked away, raised his hand, and beckoned to the waiter. "Aldo will be all right. He was very nice to me today and now I know why. Look, enough of this for the moment—let's eat and then we can go and pick up Philip."

"We have to leave this part of the affair to Aldo," Philip pointed out as he climbed into the back of the car, "and I'm very happy to do so. His group rescued that American general from the Red Brigades a few years back, and he knows what he's doing. However, since he has agreed that we can go along, I think we should be there. Besides, I'd like the personal pleasure of returning young Carlo to his family—but I don't think you'll need this, Simon." Philip picked up the Winchester shotgun from the backseat and placed it gingerly against the door.

"Maybe not," said Simon glancing over his shoulder, "but I still have to look after you. I've loaded some solid shot that Aldo gave me . . . heavy stuff."

"You two enjoy all this, don't you?" said Lucia, a sharp edge to her voice. "You sound like a couple of lads just out for a bit of fun. It's not fun at all. People may get killed tonight."

"Come on, Lucia," said Philip softly. "We're just anxious to be in at the finish, that's all. When we get there try to park somewhere close to the hiding place. We can wait just around the corner while Aldo's boys earn their pay. We're expected, so there should be no problem."

They drove through the center of the city, through streets filled with the late evening crowds, out into the quieter suburbs, then into a quarter where old decayed buildings lined the streets, interspersed with wide areas of rubble-strewn wastelands overlooked by tall blocks of modern flats. Each block was draped with wash lines, the clothes flapping slowly like flags in the warm night air. They were approaching the street they wanted, going slowly, cruising down the narrow center of the road between lines of closely parked cars.

Suddenly there were more people about, a small crowd, a parked police van, two men unrolling a tape barrier across the road; both looking up angrily as Lucia saw Aldo and swerved past them to brake to a stop. Aldo was deep in conversation with another man; they appeared to be arguing as Simon rolled down the window and leaned out.

"The gang's all here, Aldo," called Simon softly. "What's happening?"

Aldo turned his back abruptly on the other man and came over to peer into the car, smiling at Lucia, nodding at Philip, his face worried, his manner harassed. He was dressed in dark overalls and carrying a heavy-caliber shotgun.

"Problems, problems. A journalist rang Colombo to see if there was any news and he blurted it all out, so the operation is blown. Just one squeak on a radio about this and we're dead. The press have been all over the place in the last half hour and picked us out. The TV cameras have already arrived and more press people are arriving every minute. It will make a hot story for the Telegiornale; you can't keep anything quiet in this damned city." He jerked his thumb at the man behind. "That's what I'm trying to explain to this asshole, they'll wake up the whole area if we're not careful. What a mess! We'll have to go in soon, so we're cordoning off the block now."

"I remember we had this same problem during the Iranian embassy business," said Philip, climbing out from the back of the car. "Well, at least you know the routine, Aldo. Set up a tight cordon, tape off the side streets, and make them keep the cameras in their cases. Most important of all, keep their TV lights out. You'd better act fast before the gang gets tipped off. If one of them comes out for a pack of cigarettes, that's it. Can we help in any way?"

"No," said Aldo shortly. "Just stay by the car. Don't talk to anyone, or let them hear you speaking English. I don't want the press getting interested in you. I have a lot to think about and I don't need any more problems."

"Fair enough," said Philip, nodding. "And the best of luck to you. We'll wait here until you bring out young Carlo. Switch off the lights, Lucia, but stay in the car."

"Can I come and have a closer look?" asked Simon, joining Aldo on the pavement. "If I promise to keep out of your way?"

Aldo studied him for a moment, then nodded abruptly. "If you like," he said. "The building is just around the corner. You can come and see how we are going to do it, while I check the cordon."

As they made their way toward the corner, two more men, both dressed in civilian clothes but carrying submachine guns, came to join them, pushing a small group of television cameramen before them, escorting them back reluctantly under the checked-tape barrier into the crowd already mustering in the street behind, chattering excitedly, straining to see what was happening.

"There they go," said Simon bitterly. "The representatives of the Fourth Estate. They will get the kid killed if they keep on making noise, but a lot they care. They won't admit it in as many words, but if the Colombo boy is killed, they get a better story, more space in the paper, fat expenses on a series that will run. What joy! They can interview his mother and photograph her in tears, and sneak into the morgue to get a photograph they can splash on the front page. The boy's relatives will really enjoy that, and if anyone points out how much this hurts people, they can spout a lot of garbage about the public's right to know. When did private grief become public property, eh? I'll tell you when. When that pack of overpaid scum and their editors decided it sold papers."

Philip and Cirillo were staring while Lucia looked up at Simon, startled, from the car window.

"What on earth brought on that outburst?" asked Philip, surprised. "Or do I simply gather you don't like the press?"

"No, I bloody well don't," said Simon. "I've seen the bastards in action. After my family were killed, they camped outside my house and office for weeks. They weren't interested in the *issues*—they think their readers are too thick to care about issues, just like they are. All they want are gruesome pictures to run above stories of other people's misery. They lie, distort, and trivialize, and as the final straw, they are damned smug about it at the same time. I'd like to go over there right now and rap one or two of them in the mouth. That bastard with the flashgun camera, for a start."

"Steady on," said Philip, soothingly. "I have sometimes found myself unwarmed by that glow of self-esteem with which most journalists seem to surround themselves, but I suppose they are only doing their job."

"Some job," said Simon, turning away, "and they're not making your job any easier, are they, Aldo—eh?"

"No . . . what a shambles," groaned Aldo, and acknowledged his men's presence with more instructions in brief bursts of Italian. "We've cleared the streets and cordoned off the area, but the media are here in force. This was supposed to be a Squadra job—I don't have the manpower for crowd control. I will have to get a dozen more men here to control the mob. Pray to God we don't get spotted, that's all. It's not a bit like the way they do it on TV, is it? No sirens wailing, no loudspeakers. Look, if you intend to prowl about, be sure you are wearing this." He handed Simon a red fluorescent armband and began to slip another up his own arm, tugging it on over the sleeve of his dark overalls. "Anyone with one of these is on our side . . . but you are to stay out of the building—clear?'

"Very clear," said Simon. "Don't worry."

Pulling on the armband, Simon stood back a little, waiting while Aldo conferred briefly with his men. The night air was balmy and, looking up through the gently flapping washing that spanned the sky above the narrow street, Simon could see stars. It was long after dinnertime, and the streets were quiet, with the occasional person hurrying home being quickly intercepted by the police and hustled swiftly back behind the cordon. The sounds of television sets came through the open windows, sudden bursts of chatter and music carried down on the warm, slow-moving air, but one or two heads were already poking out of the windows, calling out loud inquiries to the people below.

"We had better go in now," Aldo said softly. "It's a little early, but it's useless to wait any longer. Listen to me, Simon—you stay right here until it's over." The slight quiver in Aldo's voice showed he was more nervous than he looked, and Simon slapped him gently on the shoulder.

"Good luck," he said briefly. "Hit them hard, before they hit you."

Simon stood back close against the wall as Aldo and his two men slipped across the street, heading toward the main doorway of the apartment block. When they had disappeared inside, Simon turned away and strolled back to the car. The street was suddenly quiet, the crowd holding its collective breath, calm behind the barrier. Even the press and camera crews were quiet, waiting, cameras ready, lights unlit, microphones silent.

"What's happening?" asked Philip softly, looking up at Simon from the side window of the car. "The suspense is killing me."

"Me too. They've just gone in, so it'll probably start at any moment. I'll just get the shotgun and wait up at the corner. There's no real need, but what the hell . . . I'd rather be in the open."

"Aldo won't like it," said Philip warningly.

"I'll just stand by, that's all." Simon opened the back door and took out the shotgun. He was standing by the front door, checking the weapon over, when the front door opened and Philip got out.

"Maybe I'll come up with you." Philip said. "This hanging about is nerveracking. Lucia, you stay in the car. And this time do as you are told."

"You'd better stay here with her," said Simon. "I'll just take a closer look and keep you posted."

Even as he spoke, they heard the shooting. Muffled by the walls, they still heard it, a sudden dull boom, then another, then a tearing burst of automatic fire. Closer now, somewhere out in the open, came sharp reports from a pistol—shouts—the crash and tinkle of glass.

"Jesus!" said Philip. "It's started."

"Wait here," said Simon, pushing Philip back into the car, "and start the engine, Lucia." Carrying the shotgun in the crook of his arm, he began to run back toward the corner.

Once inside the front door of the building, Aldo Cirillo hardly hesitated. He looked at his men, nodded, worked the action of his shotgun, and started for the half-lit stairwell. With Aldo leading, the three of them began to race up the stairs, their rubber-soled boots quiet on the concrete steps. On the third floor the last man fell back, following more slowly, while Aldo and the other man, Sergio, went on, moving even faster now, running up to the fourth floor landing, and then on to the fifth. There, one on either side of the apartment door, they waited, catching their breath.

"Pronto?" Aldo whispered, his chest heaving.

"Sì . . . pronto," replied Sergio.

Aldo fired. He stepped out, pulled the heavy Winchester shotgun hard into his shoulder, and fired at the top hinge of the door. In that confined space the noise was tremendous, the sight impressive. A great shower of splinters leaped from the door and sprayed back across the dark shadows of the hall. Aldo chambered another round and fired again at the lower hinge, and then again at the lock, his blood up. Sergio, his hands over his ears, was yelling, *"Andiamo . . . capo . . . andiamo!* Let's go!"

Aldo fired again, blasting the lock off. Then he threw the shotgun aside, dragged out his pistol, and went like a bull at the door. Shoulders hunched, the full weight of his body hit the door halfway above the shattered lock, knocking it right out of the frame, bursting over it into the room, pistol out, roaring, *"Polizia!"* at the top of his voice. Sergio came in behind him, diving deep into the room, both men fanning out toward the walls on either side. For a split second nothing happened.

Three men were sitting around the table in the center of the room, under the light of a single bulb, forks still frozen in their hands, while another stood transfixed in the kitchen doorway behind, shaken by the sudden noise and blast, staring wide-eyed at Aldo. Then all four leaped into life. One sprang up from the table to knock out the light, smashing the bulb into fragments. As it went out, the table was flung aside and came cartwheeling toward Aldo in the dark. There was a blast of gunfire. Aldo snapped off a shot and flung himself across the room, heading for the bedroom door. Sergio cut loose with his automatic, probing the room with short bursts of gunfire as the men fled in all directions. From the kitchen doorway one of the kidnappers was firing back, raking around the walls and through the outer door with long, tearing bursts from a submachine gun, knocking Aldo's third man out of the way. Aldo fired at a figure silhouetted against the kitchen light, the shot striking home, the weapon flying from the man's hands as the bullet hurled him back. Sergio fired now, giving cover as Aldo dived across the overturned table, stood up, kicked the bedroom door open, and leaped through. Shutting it behind him, he searched about in the dark, dragging the boy off the bed, down to the safety of the floor.

"Lie still!" he shouted. "Stay there!" As he pushed the boy under the bed, the door crashed open and another long, stabbing blast from a machinegun split the darkness, bullets raking the bed. Aldo aimed carefully at the dark mass of the man above the muzzle flashes and fired, hearing the solid thud as his bullet struck, seeing the figure thrown back into the outer darkness, where his team and the kidnappers were still shooting it out. There was a sound of breaking crockery, the smashing of window glass. The kitchen door crashed back against a table loaded with dishes. Aldo leaped over the bed and snapped a shot through the window as a dark shape ran past outside, turning to clatter down the fire escape. Aldo whirled around, the pistol in his fist, and found Sergio behind him, leaning on the doorframe as a light came on suddenly in the room behind. It seemed to be over.

"Va bene?" Aldo's legs suddenly felt weak. "Have we got them?" Sergio gestured back into the room with his pistol. *"Sì—* Rico is hit but not badly, I think. Where is the boy? We have three out here, but one got away."

"He went this way, down the fire escape," said Aldo, indicating the smashed windowpane behind him. "Here's the boy, help him out of here. Send up some more men." He raked the glass from the window frame with the barrel of his pistol and leaned out, peering down into the courtyard. The fugitive was already three floors below, leaping down the stairs six at a time, making the whole fire escape shake under the weight of his pounding feet. Aldo thrust his arm out, leveled the pistol, and fired, hearing the bullet strike metal and careen off into the night. He cursed, pulled his arm free, and ran out of the room, leaping over upturned furniture and bodies into the hallway, running hard for the stairs.

The fugitive was down in the courtyard now, heading for the street, getting away. Those on the floors above heard a brief scuffle, a ripping burst of machinegun fire, then the heavy boom of a service pistol. He shot his way out of the courtyard, cutting down one of Aldo's men, making a break for the main street, running hard, full tilt, into a tall man who came around the corner.

It was the surprise, as much as the impact, that knocked Simon off his feet. The blow threw him back against the wall, the shotgun flying from his hands and clattering to the ground. Above him the man staggered, regained his balance, halted, then leveled the machinegun at Simon and fired. The bullets smashed into the wall close above Simon's head, spraying his face and hands sharply with brick chippings. Then the man was away again, leaping across Simon's legs, sprinting down the street, ducking in and out between the parked cars, yelling as the waiting crowd scattered out of his path, his weapon held in full sight, high above his head.

More shouts came from behind. One man, then another, then a stream of them came running from the side streets, all in black overalls, all wearing red armbands, one group running hard toward Simon, waving their weapons, yelling with alarm.

"Don't shoot!" cried Simon, scrambling to his feet, warning them. "There he goes—down there!" He swept up his shotgun and set off in pursuit, leading the police in a wild charge toward the scattering crowd.

The man was fifty yards ahead now, running hard down the center of the road, in the narrow space left between the cars, heading for the outer darkness. The crowd was moving now, splitting in panic, scrambling for safety, people falling, scuttling on all fours out of the way, scattering like sheep before the wolf.

What happened next happened slowly. Running hard, his

head back, Simon saw Lucia's car pulling out from the curb. Wheels locked hard over, the car moved out slowly into the man's path, completely blocking the road, shielding the crowd. Simon saw Philip climb out, the Cobra pistol in one hand, the other hand raised, palm forward, a clear sign for the fugitive to halt. Suddenly, shockingly, the blazing, blinding television lights came on behind Philip, silhouetting him sharply, a dark, formless shape against the dazzling glare.

"No!" screamed Simon. "Don't do that! Get down!" Straining hard, his legs still refused to move any faster. He saw the gunman ahead swerve and stop, bumping into a car, half blinded by the glare, an arm raised across his face. Then he saw him jerk the machinegun up to his shoulder and rake Philip with fire. Windows shattered on the car behind, one of the television lights snapped out, Philip's body reeled back under the impact of the shots and fell to the ground. Then Simon saw the man heading for the car; Lucia must be in there somewhere, hidden behind that shattered glass. Simon stopped, took a deep breath, leveled the shotgun carefully, and fired a solid round directly into the man's back.

NINETEEN

Simon Quarry sat down to wait on the hard bench outside the Emergency Room. Doctors, nurses, and orderlies passed to and fro, pushing gurneys, wheeling stretchers, hurrying from ward to ward, their faces white in the harsh light of the lamps, but no one spoke to him. Only one or two people paid him any attention at all, giving him curious glances as they hurried past. This was the man they had seen on their television screens, the man with the shotgun.

The press and television people were there in force, pushing cameras and microphones into people's faces, trailing cables about the corridors, shouting, fighting each other, clamoring for statements, for news, for any sort of story. They had come over in ones and twos to pester Simon for information, but he just looked at them with hostile eyes and said nothing. Eventually the police came in and drove them away, leaving him sitting alone, waiting. There was nothing else to do.

They had come to the hospital in an ambulance, driving fast through the empty streets, siren wailing, flanked and followed by a host of outriding motorcycle *paparazzi,* who had appeared as if by magic as soon as the shooting was over. Inside the ambulance Lucia and a paramedic labored over Philip as they lurched along, cutting away his clothes, fixing up a drip, stopping the flow of blood, fighting to keep him alive until they reached the hospital, that same hospital from which Lucia and Simon had extracted Enrico Guilini earlier in the day.

When the ambulance skidded to a halt outside Pronto Soccorso, they had taken Philip away, Lucia running hard beside the stretcher, holding up a drip. Then Aldo had arrived, bringing the young Carlo Colombo, small, white-faced, dirty, hurrying along behind a stretcher bearing a wounded man. Aldo had looked at Simon briefly, saying nothing, then vanished into the depths of the building.

Hours later, sometime in the middle of the night, Lucia came out, her face lined and tired, her white coat spattered with blood. *That's Philip's blood,* thought Simon, getting up slowly as she came toward him.

"Well? How is he?"

She sat down on the bench and groped in her pocket for cigarettes and lighter, lighting up and taking a long, deep pull at the cigarette before she answered.

"It's too early to tell. He was hit three times, in the chest, shoulder, and abdomen. If he were a younger man, maybe . . . he could pull through . . . though it would be difficult. But as it is . . . well, I don't know. We're doing all we can, but don't hope for too much. On the other hand, he's strong and fit. I think he has a chance."

Simon let out a long sigh, sitting down beside her on the bench. "Well, he's a tough old bird," he said at last, "and he'll give it all he's got. May I see him?"

"Perhaps . . . soon," said Lucia. "The doctors are tidying him up after surgery, and he'll be pretty dopey when he comes around, so you won't be able to stay long or talk."

"And what about you?" asked Simon. "When I saw the car windows go in, my heart stopped. There's some blood here," he touched the sleeve of her coat. "Are you hurt?"

"I'm all right. I have some glass in my hair, a few cuts, that's all. Philip pushed me down on the floor before he got out of the car. This time I stayed there."

"Philip must have been crazy, trying to stop an armed man like that. Why didn't he just shoot, or stay out of it?"

"It's not his way," said Lucia, stubbing out her cigarette. She took his hand and rose, pulling him to his feet. "Come on, let's go and see him. But we mustn't stay too long—just for a minute."

Philip Wintle looked old and gray and frail. He seemed to be suspended in the narrow bed by tubes and drips, but at least he was conscious and his eyes were bright. Simon pulled a chair up close to the bed and sat down, forcing himself to smile.

"Well," he said, looking down at Philip and shaking his head, "you've really done it this time, haven't you? Letting yourself in for it like that, after all I've tried to teach you. At your age you ought to know better."

"I know," whispered Philip. "Isn't it a bitch? I'm sorry if I messed it up. I was afraid he'd get away from you, or shoot someone else, so I thought I'd stop him . . . foolish. But then we can't leave all the dirty work to you. Where's Aldo, and Kleiner?"

Simon shook his head. "I don't know. You didn't mess it up. If anything, I mucked it up. Aldo's team nailed the other Puccios in the flat, and between us, you and I fixed the one who got away. I gave him a barrel in the back, and he's out in the morgue with his mates. That's all the witnesses gone again, so Aldo will be furious. Anyway, you got the Colombo boy back, and, apart from a bit of dirt and the shock of it all, he's fine. You can rest content on that score. His family are on their way over here. That must have cracked the core of this kidnapping business, so Kleiner will be delirious with joy." Simon was leaning close to the bed now, talking urgently into Philip's ear.

"There is one snag, though. Our exploits were recorded on television and we're celebrities. Kleiner won't like that at all."

"I was afraid of that," said Philip weakly. "But what could we do?"

"We ought to go," said Lucia firmly, from the foot of the bed. "That's enough for now."

"What about Fiori?" Philip's voice was so soft now that Simon had to lean even closer to hear what he was saying. "Any word from that quarter?"

"Not that I've heard," said Simon again, shaking his head, "but I expect he's sitting tight. If Fiori stays still and keeps quiet I don't see how we can touch him, even though he's responsible for all this. Don't fret about Fiori, though. I think we've pulled his teeth. He won't find it easy to work after this."

"That's enough!" said Lucia sharply. "Let Philip sleep. You can both forget about my father."

"Don't be too sure. Go and see Aldo," whispered Philip. "He's a good man. You may need his help if you're to stay out of trouble here—legal trouble. I can't help you from here. I think you should take Lucia and get away while you can. Go back to Spain and keep your head down until the whole thing blows over."

"We'd rather stay here with you," said Simon firmly, looking up at Lucia. "Don't worry about me. Why don't you just rest now? There's no hurry and you're in good hands."

"I'm sorry I got you into this, that's all," said Philip. "But go and see Aldo, please. Tell me what he says, then we'll think what to do next. It's not over, Simon."

Simon got up, then leaned down to squeeze Philip's hand. "You never give up, do you?" he said, shaking his head. Then he went over to where Lucia was standing and led her toward the door.

"Where can I find Aldo?" he asked quietly. "I think Philip will rest easier if he knows what's going on, and what might happen next."

"He's probably with Carlo in one of the rooms at the end of the corridor. Go down to the end and turn left. You can't miss it. The Colombo family will be there by now, and you'll hear the noise. I'll stay here with Philip, but I won't be too long."

"You'll call me? At once? If . . . well, if anything happens."

"Go on," she said firmly, pushing him toward the door, "and do as Philip says."

Simon could hear the noise as he approached the open door of the private room. The Colombo family, father, mother, uncles, aunts, filled the little room, packed in, watching young Carlo, who sat up in bed, surrounded by his toys. There were so many relatives that they had spilled out into the corridor, talking loudly or weeping with relief, all far too happy and excited to go home. Simon squeezed past them and found Aldo sitting in an empty office farther down the corridor, his feet on the desk, sipping a cup of coffee. Aldo looked tired and grim, his face and overalls streaked with dirt, his hair disheveled. His first look at Simon was unsympathetic, his manner blunt.

"Hello, so there you are at last. What a bloody mess this has all turned into. And I thought I told you both—quite clearly—to keep your noses out of Squadra business. But, hell, how is Philip? I should have asked that first. Is there anything I can do?"

Simon pulled a chair out from the desk and sat down. Suddenly he, too, felt very weary. "Lucia says it's touch and go," he said. "He has too many years to shrug off lightly, so we'll just have to hope for the best." He looked directly at Aldo. "He wants to know what you're going to do. What's happening?"

"All hell has broken loose, that's what's happening. I'm hiding here rather than face the row back in my office. You do realize that you and Philip, two foreign nationals, hired by a famous industrialist, Klaus Kleiner, another foreigner, have fought a gunfight in the center of this city, killing an Italian citizen, and all this was seen by a few million viewers on TV? My bosses expect me to *stop* things like that. How am I supposed to explain it all away? Kidnapping is run-of-the-mill stuff compared with tonight's exhibition. This is front-page stuff, and when the full story leaks out—Christ! Maybe I should take that job Kleiner offered me if it's still open. After all this I won't have one with the Squadra."

Simon smiled wanly. "Well, you did warn us, and I'm sorry, but I don't see what else we could have done. I hope those few million viewers noticed that the local hero had a submachine gun and fired it into the crowd, and had already shot down two of your officers as well as Philip. Anyway, it's too late now, we can't change that. What are you going to do about Fiori?"

"I'm not going to do anything about him. Fiori is the least of my problems. The sooner you and Philip are out of Italy the better I'll like it, and Klaus is fixing that now. I can't do much about Fiori except hand this file over to the criminal police and get back to my proper job with the Squadra. Between us we've killed all the witnesses, so Fiori should be very pleased. We've done his dirty work for him. The bastard is home free, unless the financial or criminal police can find more to go on."

"So he gets away with it. He lies low for a year or so and then starts again. Kleiner won't like that—Kleiner won't like that at all. Fiori is responsible for what happened to Philip, and Gina, and a whole lot of other people."

"Well, as I say, we don't have the evidence." Aldo swung his feet off the desk and went to pour himself another cup of coffee from the percolator in the corner, looking inquiringly at Simon over his shoulder. "Do you want some of this?"

"No, thanks." Simon looked at Aldo closely. "Look, this is what happened to me the last time. A lot of people got hurt and the bad guys got away with it. Surely you can find *something* to stick Fiori with."

"Face facts—and the fact is that he probably will get away with it," said Aldo candidly. "But there is another angle. Fiori knows you have a deal with Kleiner. He must know about your famous contract, so he may decide to have another go at you—you might prefer to move first."

Simon shook his head. "The contract is a joke and you know it. Klaus can have the bulk of his money back anytime," said Simon slowly, "but I can't go after Fiori. Lucia is her father's daughter, and I can't touch him, even if I wanted to."

"Well, I'm glad you finally got around to telling me how it

is between you two," said Aldo slowly, coming back to the table. "You know I asked her to marry me?"

"Yes. She told me yesterday," said Simon. "But what can I say?"

"Not much," said Aldo, "but I think you should get out of here, go back where you came from, and leave Lucia alone."

"Well, I can't do that," said Simon. "And maybe Fiori doesn't want more trouble. Even if we can't prove it in court, we still have juice . . . Kleiner can ruin him one way or another, you can hound him for years, and but for his daughter I might get very cross with him about Philip. As for Lucia and me . . . well, what she does will be her decision."

Aldo laughed. "That passes all the bucks," he said shortly. "And we can't harass Fiori without evidence . . . I told you that."

"So that's it?"

Aldo sat down again, putting his feet back up on the desk, taking a sip from his coffee, and looking at Simon carefully before replying.

"I'm a policeman. A special sort of policeman, maybe, one who can bend the rules here and there, but still a policeman. All we have here is corpses. You've done what you came here to do—now get out. I'll drag my feet as long as possible, but if you are still here when the law lumbers into action tomorrow morning you're on your own. There is also the small matter of Enrico Guilini."

"I haven't touched Guilini. I wouldn't touch him with a twelve-foot pole."

"Don't bullshit me, Simon. You got me to remove the guard and Lucia wheeled him out of the hospital. I've got witnesses to that, and her signature on the release. Two hours later you ring up and tell me all we need to know, and a couple of hours after that you show up with an empty pistol and tell me you let him go. Come on, Simon. I can add up two and two and make four."

"Prove it," said Simon shortly. "Didn't you just say you have to prove it?"

"You killed him—or Lucia did—face it," said Aldo. "What

about your contract with Kleiner? Didn't he offer you a million dollars for one flick of your finger?"

"I don't want his money and I didn't come here for a million dollars. I came here for Philip. I think you should face Fiori and tell him to back off, for his own good. He's no fool—he'll see reason."

Aldo shrugged, smiled, and pointed over Simon's shoulder. "That's up to you, and count me out—but if you do go to see Fiori, you'd better take that stuff with you," he said. "My men found them in the ambulance."

Simon glanced over his shoulder and saw his shotgun lying on a table beside the door, the metal black against the white cloth. Philip's Colt Cobra pistol lay beside it.

"Well, well," he said, surprised. "I'd forgotten all about them." He went across the room, lifted up the pistol, checked it, then put it back on the table. "Still fully loaded," he said. "Philip didn't even get a shot off."

"Listen, Simon," said Aldo. "These last two kidnappings are not due to Fiori, and there is no evidence on the previous ones. Klaus may well decide to cut his losses and abandon the consortium. I don't think he bargained for a lot more bloodshed and for all the publicity. He won't like that at all. You're supposed to be the man with discretion."

"That's his hard luck," said Simon slowly. "With all his experience it's a pity Kleiner didn't realize what he was getting into. Did he really think that a man like Fiori would just cease to function simply because Klaus Kleiner came on the scene? People like Fiori *feed* on people like Kleiner. They always have and they always will."

It was Aldo's turn to look thoughtful. "Kleiner can look after himself and you had better think of your own problems. When we find Enrico Guilini's body the bullets in him might match with that big pistol you carry. That pistol is a loose end, so get rid of it. You have no status here in Italy. Without Wintle or Kleiner to vouch for you, you're just another foreign gunman and we don't need more of those. I think you had better get out of Italy." His eyes looked hard at Simon across the rim of the cup. "And don't come back."

"That's sound advice, Simon," said a voice at their backs, "and I think you should take it. But rule number one in this life is that you can't do a deal with a policeman. They don't have the power to keep it, and they don't often have the intention. Besides, your work here isn't finished."

They both looked around, Aldo swinging his feet down off the desk, Simon rising to his feet. Klaus Kleiner stood in the doorway, as fresh and as immaculate as ever, the shoulders of his raincoat spattered with rain, a briefcase tucked under his arm, smiling at them cheerfully.

"I smell coffee," he said, putting his briefcase on the table and coming into the room. "May I have a cup?"

"Help yourself," said Aldo, pointing at the percolator. "It's over there."

Kleiner poured himself some coffee and sat down. "I've just looked in on Philip but he's asleep. I've also spoken to the surgeon, who seems fairly optimistic about his chances. I'm not so optimistic about you, however. We have to get you both out of here and come up with some story to explain away tonight's events. We also have to deal with Fiori. So, I've phoned London and booked Philip in at one of the best hospitals. There he will have the finest doctors, the most modern facilities, and no questions asked. I am having my Lear stripped out right now and equipped as a flying ambulance. Lucia and the surgeon here say he can be moved, although they are naturally set dead against it, and it must be done carefully, the aircraft kept to a low height and the patient heavily sedated. If all goes well we should be able to move him around ten in the morning, and Lucia is going along to look after him. There will be an ambulance out to the airport and another at the far end—quick clearance—the lot. That gets Philip out of harm's way, and in good hands. Now, Aldo, as for you and the Squadra . . ."

"Just wait a minute," said Aldo, his voice rising. "What's going on? I'm supposed to be in charge here. Who said you could simply take over?"

"Your superiors did," said Kleiner abruptly. "I'm getting my people out. I've called on a few contacts in the government, and spoken to the minister, and he's quite content to leave this in our hands. The official story is that tonight's shooting, indeed this whole business, was a SISMI operation against the Red Brigades. If you stay here and stick to that and there is no one about to say anything different, any fuss should soon die down. Having two Englishmen involved may cause comment, but if that fact should leak out, so what? International cooperation is not unknown. In fact, we need more of it, and you yourself spent a year in London . . . and so on and so on . . . it's quite plausible."

"Well, you certainly move fast," said Simon frankly. "What have you got fixed for me?"

"We have to conclude our contract," said Klaus, spreading his hands. "Then you can go where you will, or come with Philip and Lucia and me to London. It's up to you. I have to stop Fiori, so I intend to explain that he'll not get a cent of credit or a decent deal anywhere, ever again, if he moves against me or my people. That much I can do, and I intend to tell him so, and that's all. If he agrees, we'll leave him alone."

"Leave Fiori alone now and your troubles have just begun," said Simon bluntly. "You've messed about with his business, and he'll probably hit you like a train as soon as he can. He's a gangster, so you have to tread on him completely. That's the only choice you've got, the only one you've ever had. It's too late to stop now."

Kleiner looked at Aldo, his face suddenly grim. "Is he right?" he asked. "What do you think?"

Aldo shook his head. "It's hard to say. If the law can't touch him, it's out of my hands. You can try to ruin him and I can try to dig up more evidence, but so far he's in the clear and probably laughing his head off."

"Not for long," said Klaus. "I once said I would teach the Italians the meaning of the word 'vendetta'. Maybe Signor Fiori needs private lessons. He does it my way or I'll ruin him."

"The best of luck," said Aldo briefly. "I'd like to see his face when you tell him that."

"So would I," said Simon.

"So you shall," said Kleiner. "I want you to come with me."

Simon looked at him for a moment, then nodded thoughtfully. "If you intend to go anyway, I suppose I'd better come along. I owe you that much. But getting into a brawl with Fiori is not the way to handle this, Klaus. He's a street fighter. I know you're a hard man, but why try to fight Fiori with his own weapons? That's exactly what he wants. Stay away, ruin him, cut his money supply, break him financially. You can do all that and never set eyes on him. That's cleaner, and safer. Don't go rolling in the gutter with him. Leave him alone. Anyway, that's my advice."

"I don't want advice," said Kleiner. "I can get that from Philip. I want some backup, and you have a contract with me to provide it. You told me, right at the start, that if you made a deal you stick to it. Or do you only keep your word until it gets difficult?"

"I'll keep to the deal," said Simon quietly. "Though I think you are wrong, It may be very pleasant to throttle someone who has been jerking you around, and I know you hate the fact that it was you who brought Fiori into the consortium. I am simply pointing out that there is more than one way to skin a cat, so don't do it his way—do it yours."

Kleiner heard this out patiently, then nodded. "You're not listening, Mr. Quarry. I only intend to talk to Fiori, nothing more. But he's a dangerous man and he has his personal hit man, Fredo Donati. All I'm asking for is some backup—say, an hour of your time, then our contract will be complete. On the other hand, if you won't help me, why should I help you? I'm helping you avoid trouble for—what . . . four killings? I'm getting Philip out of here—you might consider what might happen to you both if I wash my hands of you."

"Don't say I didn't warn you," said Aldo softly, glancing over at Simon.

"You warned me," said Simon. "That was a good try, Mr. Kleiner, very neat, very typical, but in this case your 'You can do what I want the easy way or the hard way' methods just won't work. You need Philip and me out of here before the shit hits the fan about you. We're hot news and you're involved up to your neck, and you don't like it. That's why you made the arrangements, and that's why you'll stick to them. As for me, how do you think I managed before you came along? If I walk out of here right now, who will stop me? Will you, Aldo?"

"Not me," said Aldo cheerfully. "The sooner you get out of here the better I'll like it."

"So that cat won't jump, Kleiner, I can't stop you rounding up some of your old Legionnaire buddies and trying to give me a hard time . . . and I know you're a bad loser. I can only promise that win, lose, or draw, you'll know that you've been in a fight."

"Well," said Aldo, his voice breaking into the short silence that followed. "That's certainly laying it on the line."

"Yes, I suppose it is," said Kleiner thoughtfully. "I had forgotten how you feel about money . . . about being pressured. Maybe I could make another suggestion, a straight deal for half an hour of your time. You like backup, and so do I. Back me up while I go and see Fiori, and our contract will be complete . . . you have my word on it."

Simon looked at him for a moment, considering.

"I wonder what your word is worth," he said. "But if I come along you'll get Philip out of here, and cause no more trouble . . . no pressure . . . nothing?"

"You have my word," said Kleiner. "But of course I'll have my million dollars back. I'm not as indifferent to money as you are. Do we have a deal?"

"I think we do," said Simon. "We can be done with all this within the hour. The cash is outside in Lucia's car—less what one might term 'reasonable expenses.' "

"And then you'll get the hell out of my country?" asked Aldo.

"We can say good-bye now," said Simon.

TWENTY

Fiori leaned forward in his chair, switched off the desk-top television set, and turned on the lamp again. Sitting behind his desk in that dark, shadowed room, he looked more than ever like a huge, hunched spider, his shadow bulking across the wall at his back. Fredo and another man sat on the far side of the desk, watching him carefully. Fiori took a cigar from the box on his desk and played with it for a moment, deep in thought, before trimming off the end and applying the match. He didn't offer one to either of the others, and only when the cigar was going well did he take it out of his mouth and jerk his head toward the television set.

"Well, Fredo . . . Gino, there it is. Now we've seen it all, right there on *Telegiornale*. I always knew that one would be trouble." He tapped his nose lightly with a forefinger. "I could smell it coming, right here. Now they've settled the Puccios, they'll come for us—for me. That one is like the English bulldog . . . he won't let go."

"Which?" asked Gino. "The old one who was shot, or the other, the one with the shotgun?"

"Both of them, and their paymaster . . . all of them. But it's different now." Fiori nodded toward the screen again. "The old one, Wintle, is shot, and it's the one with the shotgun we must worry about now. You and Fredo were to hit both of them—and Kleiner—but you won't need to look for them . . . they'll blame me for this, and now they'll come here."

"Maybe not, *capo,*" said Fredo. "Maybe Quarry will go away."

"Quarry go away?" exclaimed Fiori. "If you think that, you're more stupid than you look, Fredo. How did Cirillo's men find the boy? We couldn't do it! Who gave them the address, and so quickly, eh? They found the boy within a day. Where is Enrico Guilini since my daughter took him out of the hospital before we could get there, eh? You saw her on the television, coming out of the car. If Quarry has him, he's certainly talked. Did you hear all that guff about the Red Brigades? That was to keep the regular *polizia* and the *carabinieri* out. They'll keep this an affair for the Squadra Antiterrorismo, and they can do what they want, law or no law. It's the big people in government helping Kleiner . . . forced to help Kleiner. With no Puccios to talk, we can get around the law, but not around Quarry and Kleiner." Fiori let his heavy eyes rest on Gino for a moment.

"It's different now . . . a little," he went on, "but we need to hit this Quarry and Kleiner. Fredo and you will do that, but there must be no connection with me—clear? With the Puccios gone, my problems are almost over, except for those two. For tonight you wait here with us—if they come here we play it by ear. If not, you go after them tomorrow. Now take that shotgun and wait over there by the door."

Fredo waited until Gino had taken up his position by the door, then he rose and walked over to the table in the corner, helping himself to a whiskey from the decanter, looking across at Fiori as he did so.

"A whiskey, *capo*?"

Fiori shook his head, brooding, his eyes on the desktop. "No, not now . . . well, perhaps. Yes, why not? But a grappa. You *know* I don't like whiskey."

Neither offered a drink to the man seated by the door. Fredo brought the drinks back, handed the grappa to Fiori, dropped into the chair, and took a sip before looking across the desk at his boss.

"We are ready now, *capo*," he said. "We can do the job if Quarry comes here looking for trouble. He's a stranger in Italy—no one cares about him."

Fiori shook his head. "You're still an optimist, Fredo. I am not—not anymore. I have lost my daughter, my business, my respect, because of these Englishmen and Klaus Kleiner. We tried to play the game their way, but it didn't work. Maybe the old ways were better. We shall see."

"Meanwhile, we wait," said Fredo, picking up his glass again. "Is there anything more I can do?"

Fiori shrugged heavily, leaning forward to sip from his glass of grappa. "No," he said. "We do nothing. We wait, we keep still, we let this storm pass."

Fredo shook his head doubtfully. "Is it wise to kill Kleiner, *capo*? If he's killed, it'll make a big noise. It might be better to leave him alone."

Fiori snorted. "You think we have a choice? Anyway, he's not so big. Aldo Moro was bigger . . . they killed him! The German, Hanns-Martin Schleyer, was as rich . . . they killed him! Besides, I've often talked to Kleiner. Up here," he said, tapping his forehead, "something has snapped. His girl was around for years, drugging, drinking, dying, starving, selling herself. And Kleiner hates to fail, to be made a fool of. He's been wanting to get his hands on a kidnap gang, and now he has he'll tear us apart. That was my first mistake—not to hit him before."

"We didn't take his daughter, or get her on drugs," protested Fredo. "He must know that."

"I know that, you know that," said Fiori, "and Kleiner knows that, but he doesn't care. He wants blood. I didn't know that people like Quarry or Wintle existed—look what they've done to us already. No . . ." He shook his head decisively. "All three of them will have to go. We don't have a choice, it's them or us. Cirillo is a threat, but he'll soon have other cases. The Squadra doesn't lack for problems."

Fredo shook his head ruefully, half-smiling. "You know, *capo,* it's almost funny. We had a sweet business, and it fell in on us, over things we didn't do. *We* didn't take Kleiner's kid, *we* didn't take Colombo's kid. It was not *your* fault the Puccios went bad over Gina—yet this is what finally gets us into trouble."

Fiori grunted. "We ran out of luck. When you've killed Quarry and Kleiner, we'll start up again. We'll keep it small, no big plans, two grabs a year. Now . . . get me another grappa."

As Fredo went across to the bar, Fiori leaned forward and switched on the television set again. There on the screen Simon Quarry was shooting a man in the back.

Kleiner let his car coast into the curb two hundred yards from the Fiori mansion, switched off the lights, and looked across at Simon. The road in front of them was dark and empty. No one was about at this hour of the morning, and no sound broke the silence, apart from some sharp ticks from the cooling engine and the faint rustle of the wind outside. Except for a small hint of dawn in the eastern sky, the night was still intact.

"When we go in," said Kleiner, "I'll do the talking. You keep an eye on Fredo Donati. I have the deal in writing, right here in my briefcase. I just need time to discuss it. Fredo is the man to watch, and he's very devoted to Fiori. They go back a long way together."

"*You* don't have anyone like that, do you?" said Simon. "No friend, no Philip, no Fredo?"

"Not anymore," replied Kleiner. "I had friends in the Legion, but there, during the war, you needed friends. Since then, apart from my wife, I've managed quite well without them. Of course, I still need people. You can't succeed without help, but they are like the fuel in my rocket; they drive me up, but they're expendable."

"You poor bastard," said Simon.

"I manage," said Kleiner. "I get what I want."

"Then let's go and get what you want here," said Simon.

They got out of the car and waited while Simon checked the shotgun, then they went forward together, staying on the inside of the pavement, keeping close to the wall. The driveway gates were wide open, set back hard against the posts. They slipped inside, their shoes crunching gently across the gravel, then stepped onto the grass. At the house the lights were still on, beaming from every window, streaming out across the lawn, putting everything outside the light into deep shadow.

"It looks like a bloody lighthouse," Simon murmured in Klaus's ear. "I wonder if we're expected."

Klaus checked his watch. "It's close to five o'clock . . . we're running out of time. Let's just go in. Maybe I should have phoned to say we were coming, that we need to talk?"

Simon shrugged. "Maybe . . . but it's too late now. I think we shouldn't give him any legal excuse to swat us again, like roaming around his house after dark with weapons in our hands. Or rather my hands."

"Then let's go inside," said Kleiner. "The sooner we say hello to him the better."

"Fiori will be in his study," said Simon, "and the staff will either be in bed or will have gone home. Come on . . . let's get in there."

Side by side they crunched across the gravel and up the steps, pausing while Simon tried the door. It was unlocked. He pushed the door wide open and stepped inside, followed at once by Kleiner. The hall was empty, the stairway behind deeply shadowed. The air reeked of Fiori's cigars, the smell strong after the fresh night air outside. From somewhere deep inside the house they could hear the sound of intermittent talk, backed by a loud crackling. The two men exchanged glances. "Television?" whispered Simon. "At this hour?"

Kleiner shook his head. "Hardly," he said quietly. "Shortwave radio, I think. Some sort of receiver. Where now?"

"Straight ahead . . . come on!"

Simon stepped away from the door and walked swiftly down the hall to Fiori's study, flinging open the door and walking straight in, Klaus Kleiner treading hard on his heels. If Fiori was surprised to see them, he didn't show it.

He was seated behind his desk, his face lit by the dark-shaded lamp, the small crackling radio at his elbow spitting out short bursts of traffic news. Fredo was sitting to one side, a glass of whiskey on the desk before him, a small submachine gun resting in his lap. To the right of the door, another man, a stranger, sat in a chair, rising quickly to his feet as the two men came thrusting into the room and stopped before Fiori's desk.

Fiori looked up at them, saying nothing, then leaned forward to switch off the radio. He continued to stare at them thoughtfully until the silence became overbearing. Finally it was Fiori who broke it, after gesturing the second man to sit down again.

"Ah! Here you are at last, Mr. Quarry, and who is that behind you? Just Herr Kleiner? No one else? I was also expecting Captain Cirillo. Come in, come in, and sit down. I have been watching your exploits on television this evening, Mr. Quarry. I hope the Colombo boy is safely home again. And, tell me, how is Commander Wintle? But I forget myself . . . will you both have a drink? Fredo . . . please?" Fiori was very bland, polite, smiling, the perfect host welcoming long-expected guests.

Kleiner and Simon hesitated for a moment. Then Simon nodded and moved softly toward the desk, collecting a chair as he came, the shotgun held high across his chest, putting the chair down and dropping into it. Kleiner also came forward, taking another chair and placing it by the desk, a few feet in front of Simon, and sitting down.

"Is the shotgun really necessary, Mr. Quarry?" asked Fiori.

"I've no idea," said Simon, "but if Fredo cares to put that piece down, and that man over there"—he waved his thumb over his shoulder—"does likewise, I would be happy to do the same. Mr. Kleiner here just wants to talk."

"Then let's talk," said Fiori. "Put the gun down, Fredo . . .

and you too, Gino. These gentlemen are not looking for trouble."

Simon waited while Fredo put his weapon on the desk, then placed the shotgun on the floor at his feet, nodding gently to Kleiner as he sat up.

"Well, then, what can I do for you both?" said Fiori.

"For God's sake, Fiori, stop being facetious," said Kleiner. "And let's get down to business."

Fiori half smiled, sitting back in his big chair, hairy hands flat on the desk, his face unworried, his eyes watchful, flicking from one to the other.

"I see," he said finally. "So Enrico Guilini talked. Well, what else could I expect from trash like that. What did you do to him, Mr. Quarry? You will have to ask yourself if any jury or *magistrato* will believe a story from a person like that. Maybe that is why Captain Cirillo is not with you. Guilini's story is not enough for him . . . if, of course, Guilini is still alive to repeat it. Is he?" He looked at Kleiner, his eyebrows raised. "Or has Mr. Quarry here dealt with Enrico in his usual forthright fashion?"

"I never touched him," said Simon, "but we knew about you already. Let's not mess about, Fiori. The game's up, and you know it."

Fiori's eyebrows rose a fraction. "Is it? Really? Then why are you here? What have I done? I was not involved in taking Colombo's boy. And you can't think I would help to murder my own daughter? No one would believe that."

Kleiner laughed. "My God! You really are a bastard, Fiori. Why go on with this? We know why you gave Gina to those people."

Fiori drummed his fingers on the desk, glaring at Kleiner. "We can talk now," he said. "Man to man, eh? Frankly? You hired Commander Wintle and started him poking around my business. Naturally I had to do something before he focused on my methods. I let them take Gina but you forced me to do it." He turned his gaze on Simon. "Why do you work with this man?" he asked. "He calls me a bastard because I take money from rich people who have too much anyway, but he can close a factory in Calabria and put thousands of people out on the street to starve. Who is the big bastard here, Quarry, tell me that?"

"You did what you did to save your own skin," cut in Kleiner. "You did it to save your business."

"There is no proof of that," said Fiori. This was a different Fiori now, smoother than before, more plausible, confident of his position, quite unafraid. "It may embarrass me for a while, but that's all." He shrugged. "But people soon forget—the police won't find enough to go on."

"Philip Wintle soon found you," said Simon. "Once he realized these kidnappings were an inside job, it was only a matter of time. But you're a rich man, Fiori, successful, you had nice daughters—why did you do all this?"

"Why do it?" asked Fiori, surprised. "Why? For money, Mr. Quarry, of course, for lots of money. Easy money at that. Why else would anyone get involved in all this? Ask Herr Kleiner here, he knows all about money. Money is like a drug, Mr. Quarry. You get a little, you soon want more."

Fiori sat back in his chair, a big cigar jutting from the fingers of one fist as he looked from one to the other, smiling broadly. For a moment Fiori looked almost pleasant.

"Gentlemen, I don't go to church anymore, but I can remember the pleasure of the confession, how light and carefree you can feel after it. Besides, it has all been so good and it all worked so well, it is a pleasure to explain it to someone. I usually have to mix with idiots—not Fredo here, but most of my people are either peasants like the Puccios, who are little better than animals, or those fat, complacent sheep in the consortium I can easily fleece. Of course, there is you, Herr Kleiner, but you secretly think I am provincial trash. Yet I have managed to use you all."

"Let's hear all about it," said Simon, settling back in his chair. "There's no hurry—is there, Klaus?"

"I can wait," said Kleiner.

Fiori scratched his heavy jowl, drank some grappa from the

small glass before him, and looked up thoughtfully, his eyes following the heavy coils of cigar smoke to the ceiling.

"Where shall I start? Do you know the secret of success, Mr. Quarry? Information. I know you will agree with me there, Herr Kleiner. You need money and a little luck, but success mostly depends on information. When Fredo and I came up here, over twenty years ago, I had nothing. I drove a taxi for eighteen . . . twenty hours a day. It's a living and you can make good money, but there's no future in it. There are simply not enough hours in the day. I worked, I saved, I bought another taxi. Fredo drove it . . . then I got another. Finally I had a little fleet. We ran the taxis, so we heard all the gossip. My drivers were told to tell me anything useful they overheard from the passengers. Taxis are directional, too. You hear of a stock market boom, a company in trouble, or a takeover, then you put the taxis by the stock exchange and soon you get the inside story. You hear of a scandal, you send them to cruise around the press offices and the newspaper quarter. Businessmen will attend the most highly confidential meeting, swear everyone to secrecy, carefully shred all the notes and documents afterward, then climb into a taxi with a colleague and discuss all the details at the tops of their voices. It's all so easy. When our fleet got bigger, I had voice-activated tapes installed in all the limousines, started by the meter arm. I also hired drivers who at least understood some English. So, I got share tips; I heard of good bets on horses; I learned who was doing well or doing badly. I heard all the dirt, all the scandal. I made a lot of money like that. The real snag was that to use the information we collected we had to raise cash. Ready money is a marvelous commodity, but how could I raise it in large sums? The overhead of a taxi business is terrible. But if you have inside information, kidnapping is very easy. The first kidnaps were simple to organize, because we knew how the people we needed lived and moved. I once netted nearly three million dollars for three weeks' work. And they don't notice us. Taxi drivers are like postmen—a part of the scene. Soon I realized that I had to work from the inside, so I bought armored limousines, started a school for drivers, hired out domestic staff. It was all so easy because we were already on the inside. Security? What a joke! I *was* the security."

"So what went wrong?" asked Simon, leaning forward in his chair. "Why did you let the Puccios get control?"

Kleiner kept his eyes on Fiori, saying nothing, the briefcase resting upright on his lap, his long fingers curled over the top, playing with the handle, spinning the small milled wheels of the combination lock.

Fiori was well into his tale now. "Not so quick . . . my business grew. I bought into the companies where we had snatched a member of the owner's family, and we used their own money to do it. If you worry a man, especially a man who loves his family, he can't think straight. I could get the owner to sell out, for maybe half of what it was worth, because he needed the money badly, and quickly. I would raise the cash, buy his company, then two nights later I'd get the money back." Fiori laughed and took another swig of grappa. "I found *that* very interesting. It all tied in quite beautifully. The problem—and there is always a problem—was to conceal our growth and not be too obvious. So I expanded, into legitimate business."

"We all know about Extramilano," said Kleiner, interrupting. "And whatever else you can do, the days of expansion are over. Your credit is going to dry up completely."

Fiori shrugged. "Who needs credit? I knew you were looking for a link, and getting close. That's when we decided to eliminate Signor Wintle and you, Mr. Quarry, with the bomb. That was a mistake, but how was I to know that at the time? Wintle was in the way and you were dangerous. I had to protect myself."

"You still haven't said what went wrong," said Simon.

Fiori smiled blandly and lit another cigar. "When Kleiner put the consortium together, I thought that I might have some difficulties, but he came along and suggested I should join them. Remember that, Klaus? I offered to do more. I agreed to act as the security chief. I already provided the chauffeurs and guards, so I became a key figure. I even suggested improvements. It started to go wrong when they organized group insurance to get access to more cash. That was the start of my bad luck. Kleiner brought Commander Wintle over from KSI, which had to guarantee the security arrangements to the insurance companies. Suddenly someone was checking up on me."

"You should have soldiered on," said Simon. "Until you put the bomb in the car, you were just one of the other victims."

A shadow fell across Fiori's face. "Maybe," he said. "It also began to go wrong when your daughter died, Klaus. You became active against the kidnap gangs . . . you posted rewards. You told Commander Wintle to track down the gangs. I knew all about it, but what could I do? I could hardly argue against it. Is the Commander dead? I hope not . . ."

"He's in Intensive Care," said Simon shortly. "If he dies in the hospital it's another of your problems solved."

Fiori took another sip of grappa from the glass on his desk and shook his head, lips pursed. "I thought there was no risk when I arranged for them to take Gina. Well, that was wrong again. The Puccios went into business on their own account, and once they had Gina they had me . . . what's the phrase? over a barrel? I would have found them eventually and killed them, and that's why they applied so much pressure. They wanted to get the money from me and Colombo and run. But Wintle was always sniffing around, asking questions, hiring you. I couldn't object because that's what we hired him for, but suddenly I had only enemies around me, and my whole operation became unstable. Except for Fredo here, I still don't know which of my people I can trust. But you know all this." He turned his heavy eyes back to Kleiner. "Why are you here?"

"I want to offer you a deal," said Kleiner. "A clear, simple deal, and it's this. Keep off my back. I don't like people to mess with me, and you ought to know that. If you start up again I will ruin you financially, and Aldo Cirillo will take your operation apart, piece by piece, and I'll fund the Squadra while he does it. One way or another, you'll be finished."

"That's not a deal," said Fiori. "That's a threat. Anyway, I don't think you can do it. If you could, you would have done it by now. But you want to try? Go ahead. But don't think it will be easy."

"Wait a minute . . . that's only half the deal," said Kleiner. "What you do to the others I don't care about—everyone has to look after themselves. But you leave me and my consortium alone and maybe we could be useful to each other. What you make now is peanuts to what we could make together—and I can always use a partner who isn't too fussy about the means we have to use."

"Jesus!" exclaimed Simon, glancing at the impassive face of Fredo Donati. "We have two of a kind here."

Fiori's eyes rested on Kleiner's face for a moment, brooding. "No . . . I don't think so," he said at last. "I can't trust you, and I don't need you. Also, I don't understand you. I'll give you another deal, a simple one. You leave me alone, I'll leave you alone. It's a standoff. But that's all you get."

"It's not enough," said Kleiner. "I can't spend the rest of my life waiting for Fredo to turn up in the night, and neither can Quarry."

"That's all you get," repeated Fiori. "And Quarry has a thing going with my daughter." His eyes shifted toward Simon. "Take her back to where you came from, Mr. Quarry, and don't come back. If you do, your luck won't last. Now get out of here, both of you."

Kleiner stood up, resting the briefcase on the edge of Fiori's desk, pulling on his gloves. Simon looked again at Fredo and stood up as well, waiting to go, watching Kleiner reach for the briefcase.

"I'd like you to reconsider," said Kleiner. His voice was almost pleading. "I have it all in here, in writing." He tapped the briefcase with a gloved finger. "A simple letter, setting out a simple deal. I also have a large sum of money outside in my car, a little sweetener. What do you say?"

"No deal," said Fiori, lounging back in his chair. "With you—no deal, no way, no time."

"Kleiner likes to have it in writing," said Simon wearily. "Like my contract. Why don't you take a look at it, make a million bucks, and we can get the hell out of here."

"That's right," said Kleiner, unsnapping the locks on the briefcase. "Why don't you take a look at it?"

"I told you, no," said Fiori. "And I told you to get out of here."

"That's a pity," said Kleiner. "A real pity." He reached into his briefcase, pulled out a pistol and shot Fiori full in the face. There was no time to stop it, no time to think. As the shot boomed, the impact flinging Fiori back in his chair, Simon was moving, the big pistol coming out of his jacket and jumping into his hand. Simon kept turning to face the man by the door, who was bringing up his shotgun as Simon fired, two quick, hard shots, the big pistol bucking in his hand, sending the startled guard reeling back along the wall.

Behind him, Kleiner's pistol boomed again, twice, as Fredo lunged forward out of his chair, reaching for the machinegun. Simon saw one bullet strike splinters from the desktop, but the other slammed into Fredo's side, the impact knocking him clean off his feet, still clutching the weapon as he went down, but, though on the floor, Fredo wasn't finished. Somehow he brought the gun up and got off a burst, hosing fire around the room, sending more splinters flying from the desk. Simon saw the television set explode in a fountain of glass before Fredo's bloody face, and fired through it into Fredo's chest, seeing the strike, then felt a blow as Kleiner slammed back into him, knocking him aside and snapping off another shot down into Fredo's head; hair flew off, a piece of bone. Kleiner was still shooting, firing another round into Fredo's shattered head, a bullet into the dead man by the door, another to send Fiori crashing out of his chair. Then his pistol clicked, empty. Kleiner shook it angrily, then threw it away, reaching toward the desk for Simon's shotgun.

"Don't touch that!" said Simon. He leveled his pistol at Kleiner's face and stepped forward, ramming the muzzle against Kleiner's throat, pushing his chin up with the top of the barrel. "They're all dead . . . it's finished."

"Is it?" asked Kleiner. His eyes were wild, his gaze a challenge—one hand still reached for the shotgun as Simon pushed him back.

"You always intended to kill Fiori," said Simon. "So what the hell did you need me for?"

"I needed backup. Anyway, what do you care about Fiori?" spat Kleiner. "I offered him a deal but he turned me down. My father always said that a man who can't be bought can't be trusted."

Simon shook his head, wondering. "You're crazy," he said. "Where do people like you come from? Do you really believe you can get away with anything?"

"Don't you?" said Kleiner. "Face it, Quarry, we're two of a kind . . ."

"I don't think so," said Simon. "If I were like you I'd pull this trigger . . ." He eased the hammer down under his thumb and slid the pistol back under his jacket. "But I'd need more of a reason than I have right now. I wouldn't push it, though—if I were you."

Kleiner rubbed his neck and looked at Simon thoughtfully. "I won't," he said at last. "But now that we understand each other a little better, why don't we get the hell out of here and talk about another contract?"